Assassination:

The Princess
Book 1 of The Orphan's Tale

D M Wilder

Assassination

The Orphan's Tale, Volume 1

D M Wilder

Published by D M Wilder, 2016.

ASSASSINATION

First edition. March 21, 2016.

Copyright © 2016 D M Wilder.

ISBN: 978-1393422068

Written by D M Wilder.

Also by D M Wilder

The Memphis Cycle
The City of Refuge
Mourningtide
A Killing Among the Dead
Pharaoh's Son

The Orphan's Tale
Assassination

Watch for more at www.dianawilderauthor.com.

Table of Contents

Books by D M Wilder

THE MEMPHIS CYCLE:
The City of Refuge
Mourningtide
Pharaoh's Son
A Killing Among the Dead,
The Thirty Cubit Crocodile
The American Civil War:
The Safeguard, A Novel of Georgia in 1864
Paris, 1834
Assassination: Book I of The Orphan's Tale
Vengeance: Book 2 of The Orphan's Tale

Disclaimer

THE ORPHAN'S TALE SERIES is a work of fiction in its entirety. Perhaps the series is best described as a fantasy without magic, or at least with only the sort of magic you encounter in Paris. While some characters have stepped out of history, their presence in this book is my own invention, as are the names and positions of the other characters. In the same way, the procedures and organization of the French police in this story come from my own imagination.

Paris has always been a city of change, beginning to move toward its current configuration during the rule of Henri IV. As an example, the 'Champs Elysées' came into being in 1709. The great boulevards of Paris were envisioned by Napoleon I, though it was through the imagination of his nephew, Napoleon III, that the great boulevard St. Michel and the boulevard St. Germain, were sent lancing through the City in their present locations. You will not find them in this series.

I have tried to be accurate regarding the layout of Paris and its arrondissements during the time of the story, relying on maps from the period. While I have done my best to be accurate about the major thoroughfares of Paris and the buildings and establishments there at that time, I have at times been forced to invent street names and installations.

The alterations I have made were done with a desire to facilitate the story. I hope they have succeeded.

Image of Notre Dame Cathedral; by Alfred-Alexandre Delauney
D.W

Characters and Terms

Arrondissement - A district of Paris

Beauchamps, Edwin - English Attaché in Paris

Cheat-Death - Master criminal, deceased

d'Anglars, Christien - Minister of Police, France

d'Arthez, Gilles - Senior Inspector

de Clichy, Elise - Proprietress of The Rose d'Or

Dracquet, Constant - Suspected criminal

Fanchon, Jacques - Older Citizen of Paris

Franchotte, Yvette - Co-owner of the Rose d'or

Guerin, Alexandre - Chief Inspector of Police

Guillart, Jacques - Sergeant of Police, Archivist

Lamarque, Valéry - Prefect of Police, Paris

Lanusse, Henri - Elderly lock-picker

Larouche - Orphan street urchin

LeNoir, Jacques - Hired assassin

L'Eveque, Christien - Senior Inspector of Police

Malet, Albertine - Paul Malet's mother, deceased

Malet, Paul - Senior Chief Inspector of Police

Michaud, Joseph - Pawnbroker

Plessis, Rosalie - Opera Singer

Plougastel, Georges - Malet's Second-in-Command

Vaux, Jacques - Fugitive Criminal

Vidocq, François - Founder of the French Sureté

Young, Joseph - American sailor

CHAPTER ONE

The Decoy

LIGHTS WERE DANCING on the river Seine below the old Pont Neuf. It was early autumn; the evening wind brought the scent of wood smoke, touched with a tang of mossy stones from the river itself. The last deep notes of the carillon of Notre Dame de Paris.

A knot of armed Police officers was gathered just at the opening of the place Dauphine, at the northwestern end of the Île du Palais. They were speaking quietly and looking from time to time at a tall, broad-shouldered man in a black coat, standing some ways apart from them and gazing up at the stars.

As they stood there, another man came hurrying up and saluted. "Time!" he panted.

"Best tell him, then," said the lead constable, nodding toward the man.

"What are you to tell me, Severin?" the tall man said without turning. His voice was deep and quiet, overlaid with the hint of an accent.

"Just that the decoy's coming, Chief Inspector."

The man turned at that and directed a keen gaze at the messenger "Ah?" he said. "Already?"

"Yes, Monsieur!"

"And have the assassins been sighted as well?"

"I saw them myself as they emerged from the sewer. Inspector L'Eveque reports that some were hiding along the Quai de la Mégisserie, as well."

"Very good," said Chief Inspector Malet. "You have done your part well." When he saw that the messenger was hovering he said, "What is it?"

"May I be in on the kill, M. l'Inspecteur?" Severin asked.

"If you'd like," said Malet. He cast one last glance skyward up at the stars and then said, "Places, gentlemen—and remember your parts."

He watched them scatter and then positioned himself at the corner of the row of tall, old houses lining the place Dauphine and trained his narrow gaze on the Pont Neuf.

The oldest bridge in Paris was also, for the moment, the most ill-omened, due to the number of throat-slit, weighted bodies dredged from the silt close to it in the past several months. Their number and the uniform manner of their deaths had piqued Paul Malet, the ranking Police Inspector in Paris, and he had approached the Prefect of Police with the suggestion that he be allowed to do something about it. This evening was the culmination of two months' intensive planning on Malet's part with the cooperation of the other Chief Inspectors of the various Parisian arrondissements.

Malet's eyes narrowed as he caught the snatch of a whistled tune. He frowned into the night and after a moment he saw the decoy approaching the northern end of the bridge.

He was a well-set-up young fellow, well dressed, twirling a gold-headed cane with jaunty aplomb. A diamond glinted in the folds of his cravat, and the crimson silk lining his cloak caught the lamplight in brief, ruddy flashes. His step was uneven at the moment, as though he had had several glasses of wine. He was whistling a waltz tune.

He had been treated to a programme enjoyed by the victims over the past months; a splendid performance at the Opera, with Rosalie Plessis herself singing that night, followed by a fine supper at one of the most expensive restaurants in Paris.

The young man had been dressed in the first stare of fashion and instructed to flaunt all his supposed wealth. It was an enviable evening in all respects but one. Unfortunately, the programme finished with the subject walking all alone down one of the loneliest stretches of street in Paris.

The whistle grew suddenly louder.

Malet leaned forward as several shapes seemed to appear from the river. Hmm. They had been hiding in a culvert, as he had suspected. Now they moved softly toward the decoy.

They were getting too close. It was time. Malet raised his hand and lowered it; silent shapes shifted among the trees of the place Dauphine and edged along the quay. Malet drew a deep, silent breath and stepped forward, himself.

The river was chuckling against the bridge supports. The silent, furtive men moved closer; the decoy strolled to the side of the bridge and stood looking down at the reflections of the stars in the rippling water.

The shapes converged on the decoy.

Malet, watching in the shadows, caught the flash of steel and stiffened. The man had been provided with a small but expensive sidearm for his protection, but it was questionable whether he would have an opportunity to use it.

Speech now, somehow muffled. "Good evening, M'sieur."

The decoy tried to turn.

"Ah, no, M'sieur," said the voice. "Just look at the pretty water and the pretty stars and hand over that pretty cane."

Malet leaned forward, one hand raised.

"Please," the decoy said, his voice shaking. "I—I have some money—"

"Ah?" A different voice this time. "Then give it to us, and quickly."

The decoy started to reach into his waistcoat.

"No," Malet said under his breath.

"Hand over your pocketbook, M'sieur," the voice said. "With two fingers only, and very, very slowly."

Malet nodded to the others beside him. "Go after them. He is in too much danger now."

The decoy whipped around just as someone shouted, "Kill him! He's a cop!"

Malet cursed as he heard the sound of knives being drawn. "Now!" he shouted without troubling to lower his voice.

At the same moment the decoy cried, "I arrest you all in the name of—" Bang!!

The little pistol that was supposed to slide smoothly down the man's sleeve and into his hand plummeted past his groping fingers as he spoke, and crashed to the pavement, to go off with a roar and a spurt of flame.

The night was suddenly alive with pounding feet, shouting voices and cloaked figures hurrying forward from the shadowed side streets that rayed out from the place du Châtelet and opened on to the Quai de la Mégisserie.

A cudgel blow to the head sent the decoy flying as his attackers, surrounded, closed with the Police. Gendarmes with swords drawn, police constables with clubs and guns joined battle with the crowd of attackers.

Malet watched for a few seconds and then made his unhurried way through the confusion of the melee, spinning one thief into the arms of a uniformed constable, rapping another on the skull with the head of his walking stick, and pulling a third back by the scruff of his neck.

This one looked up, gasped, and shouted, "Malet! Run for it!"

Malet's teeth showed in a smile. "You're a little late, Picou," he said with ominous cordiality as he thrust the fellow into the arms of two constables and moved into the thickest of the fighting.

Someone jammed a pistol up against his ribs. Malet seized the hand and wrist holding the pistol and wrenched them up and back as the firearm went off with a roar. The sound of the shot froze all motion for a second. The gunman was sprawled on the ground with a fractured jaw the next moment.

Malet sent the weapon sailing over the balustrade of the bridge and into the river with a negligent flick of his hand and then turned back toward the throng. "Anyone else care to try?"

Three attackers broke free and ran.

A squad of constables started after them.

"Let them go," said Malet. "They are in for a surprise in short order." He looked around, located the decoy, and went to him.

The young man had struggled to his hands and knees and was nursing a bleeding forehead.

Malet leaned down, gripped him by the elbow and hauled him to his feet. His hand lingered for a moment until the man was steady.

The decoy gazed blankly up at him. A nearby street lamp illuminated a well-bred, handsome face that warmed as Malet smiled at him and tallied the man's injuries.

"Did we get them all?" the man asked breathlessly as he wiped the blood from his forehead.

"We got them," said Chief Inspector Guerin of the 3rd arrondissement. He was standing behind Malet and eyeing the decoy with profound disfavor. "One of them a little more permanently than we had wanted." He motioned behind him. A group of men, handcuffed and bedraggled, were standing a little apart in the custody of eight heavily armed constables. A crumpled form lay beyond them. "You are bleeding on M. Martel's clothing, Saint-Légère."

Malet swept a glance over the blood and then said reflectively, "I believe the possibility of blood was considered when the garments were loaned, M. Guerin. Not all of us can stay safely behind a tree. Martel is my tailor. He understood the risks." He turned back to the decoy and said, "You, sir, don't appear to be badly injured, but you'd best go to the Prefecture right away and have those hurts tended, just to be safe."

One of the constables was standing at Malet's elbow, waiting to hand him something. He turned away to speak with the man.

"You were a fool to have dropped your gun when you did, Saint-Légère!" Guerin snapped. "You nearly ruined everything!"

Malet speared Guerin with a look and then frowned down at the object that the constable had just handed him, lying across his palm. "'Junior Inspector Charles de Saint-Légère, age 36,'" he read. He handed the decoy the glass-bound card and the billfold. "You may wish to keep this out of your pocketbook from now on," he said.

Saint-Légère took the card and the billfold. "I am sorry, M'sieur," he said.

Malet's smile reappeared. "It's a mistake," he said. "Not a crime." He offered the pistol to Saint-Légère, who took it and pocketed it with a grateful smile.

Malet turned toward the knot of prisoners. "Line them up," he said. "Take off their masks."

He watched as this was done and then, his hands clasped behind him, paced down the line. "Well," he said, "I have never seen a more villainous-looking crowd this side of a gibbet. And there are some old friends here."

Several of the prisoners shifted uneasily.

Malet passed back before them and said, "Hello, Bordelon. Aren't you up past your bedtime? Don't you usually assault women in the parks at noon?"

He halted before one fellow who was standing with his face averted. "And I see you, Favrot," he said. "So it's no use to hunch over. You have graduated from picking pockets to cutting throats. So we promote you from prison to the guillotine." He fixed the fellow with a considering stare and then moved on to the man beside him, who was standing at attention.

He stiffened and carefully scrutinized the man. His gaze, which had been calm, scornful and detached, suddenly had all the narrow, blazing intentness of a tiger. "Look what the tide has washed in!" He threw this last over his shoulder at the man standing a little behind him.

The man moistened his lips but said nothing.

"Does your master know you have got your hands soiled in this business?" Malet asked gently.

The man did not answer.

"Does he?" Malet repeated. "We will speak again." He turned and looked back at the Police officers behind him. Chief Inspector Guerin was standing with his arms folded and his face expressionless.

Malet drew a deep breath and turned back. After a moment he smiled at the next man. "Aren't you getting just a little old for this sort of thing, Lanusse?"

The prisoner, a white-haired, paunchy man, shrugged and grinned. "You got me fair and square, Inspector," he said. "I just have one request."

"And that is—?" said Malet.

"Let me take my cigars in with me. I will die if I can't smoke, and I am sure you'd hate me to cheat the guillotine."

Malet's teeth showed in an honestly amused smile. "Constable Severin, make a note of it, if you please: the prisoner Lanusse will be allowed tobacco while he's confined to prison."

Malet turned back to the others. "Take them to the Conciergerie for holding," he said. "I am certain that several of the Chief Inspectors will wish to speak with them."

"I have a gift for you, Chief Inspector!" cried a merry voice.

"And about time," said Malet with a sudden smile as a younger man of middling height came toward him followed by six constables guarding three handcuffed prisoners. "What do you have for me?"

"Some cockroaches that were trying to re—infest the sewers," the man replied. "It only remained to let them get into the 'bag' and then draw the strings shut upon them!"

"Very good," said Malet. "Put them with the rest and take them to the Conciergerie."

L'Eveque nodded to his men and then went over to the decoy and frowned at the blood.

Malet watched as the prisoners were hustled away toward the prison. "It was a successful operation in every sense," he said. "M. de Saint-Légère, you are to have your injuries tended at once, as I directed. And I will wish to see your report when it is written. It will be incorporated with my own."

He saw that Saint-Légère was bowing to him. He returned the courtesy and then turned to the man beside him. "M. Guerin," he said. I would be grateful if you would accompany me to the Prefecture for a moment. I have something urgent to discuss with you."

"As you please," Guerin said. He favored Saint-Légère with another inimical glare and then turned and followed Malet.

CHAPTER TWO

After the Hunt: Stalemate

THE PREFECTURE OF POLICE for Paris is a tall, square stone building on the Île du Palais, fronting the flower markets on the place Charlemagne, with the bulk of the Conciergerie prison along the boulevard du Palais to one side and the open space of the place du Parvis Note-Dame along the rue du Palais on the other. It is convenient to the vast complex of the Palais de Justice, the high courts of France, as well as the city morgue in the Square de l'Île de France, where all the miscellaneous suspicious corpses found during the night are brought to be scrutinized by the Police. To the northeast, the flower market lends a touch of color and fragrance to an otherwise forbidding area, while the entire island seems to be dominated by the broad-shouldered silhouette of the ramshackle, decaying cathedral of Notre Dame de Paris.

There is nothing ramshackle about the Prefecture. The ordinary visitor entering the building is immediately confronted by the confusion of bureaucracy and a noisy cacophony of a perfection achieved only in government offices.

First he must sign in with the officer of the day and state his business. Someone making a report to a simple constable deals with a plain desk without adornment, with sputtering pens and paper not of the highest quality. A sergeant, reading that report, sits in a more secluded desk, with better supplies. If the report merits the attention of an Inspector, it is brought across a carpet and laid on a desk protected by a sheet of glass.

If that Inspector feels that The Prefect would be well-advised to scan the information contained in the report, then the visitor must speak with the Chamberlain—who is always dressed in full evening attire with a heavy gold chain of office that shames that of a provincial mayor—and, if he is lucky, is admitted to the sanctum sanctorum, a haven of dark, carved paneling, of fine chairs and velvet draperies, of splendid oil paintings and gilded moldings.

Paul Malet, the ranking Chief Inspector in the Seine et Oise Departement, was second only to the Prefect. He was now serving as the Prefect's substitute while the man took a leave of absence. He signed in with the Officer of the Day, offered his identification card, and waited for Chief Inspector Guerin to do the same.

"All right, Malet," said Guerin when he had handed the pen back and straightened. "What's so urgent that we must discuss it tonight?"

"Not here," said Malet. "Come back to the Prefect's offices, where we can be private."

He fell silent as the Chamberlain came up, led them back to the Prefect's offices, and then left after offering to send refreshments in.

"Well, then?" said Guerin. "Say what you have to say and have done with it. I am tired and my bed's awaiting me."

"It must be splendid to have so much leisure time," Malet said. "Did you look at those prisoners?"

"I did. They turned my stomach. They're a collection of rabble. Did you wish my agreement on that score? You have it with all my heart. And I will admit that the trick was neatly turned. You have my compliments."

"It was more valuable to have your cooperation," Malet said.

Guerin bowed, although the sardonic bend of his mouth remained. "Thank you," he said.

Malet disposed himself in a chair. "There were one or two surprises among the prisoners we bagged."

"You didn't seem surprised by any of them," Guerin said. "You knew most of them by name. Interesting that you would be so conversant with the names and histories of such criminals. I suppose you have an advantage over those of us poor mortals not blessed with a bastard birth and a prison upbringing."

Malet ignored the insult. "One of them at least was a surprise," he said. "—or should have been to you."

Guerin raised his eyebrows and smoothed the thick line of his side-whiskers. "And who was that?"

"Must we fence like this?" Malet demanded. "Ensenat. I know you recognized him."

"Well?"

"'Well'?" Malet repeated. "You know as well as I do that he's closely tied with—"

"—Constant Dracquet," Guerin finished with the air of one sorely tried. "I am not a patient man, and I find monomaniacs particularly tiresome." He speared Malet with a level, half-amused look. "Yes," he said. "The man is employed by Dracquet in a menial position. I believe he's some sort of gardener or stable hand. I don't believe his employment includes cutting throats, or at least trying to, and I suspect that when M. Dracquet hears of his involvement in this venture he will cast him off completely."

"Like master, like man," said Malet. "I would like to see Dracquet's reaction to this."

"He will probably find this entire matter an embarrassment and a disgrace," Guerin said. "I would, and so would any honest man."

"The question is whether Dracquet is an honest man," said Malet. His tone was beginning to lose some of its courtesy. This was a matter that had been discussed too often between them. "I am certain that he's the force behind most of the crime in this Departement—"

"'Certainty' and 'proof' are not interchangeable, Malet. There is nothing on Dracquet, and hunches do not equal certainty. You know that as well as I do."

Malet ignored the interruption. "—in this Departement," he said. "His name has come up again and again in every major criminal undertaking that I have investigated or read about. Look at the ones we arrest, and you find him behind them like a shadow."

"I say again: where's the proof?" said Guerin. "Has he done anything provably wrong? No? Then he's innocent." He added bluntly, "One involved in upholding the Law for as long as you have been shouldn't have to be told that."

"And for most of those years I have been trying to get the proof," exclaimed Malet. "And I have been blocked—for what reason I can't begin to guess! —by you! I need your cooperation, as I have told you time and again. I have watched and been helpless against him, but things are different now. We have one of his close lieutenants in the Conciergerie at this moment!"

Guerin started to speak but Malet silenced him with an impatient gesture.

"Don't annoy me with your talk of gardeners and stable hands!" Malet exclaimed. "You know as well as I the sort of position Ensenat holds in Dracquet's household. I think it could be a chink in his armor, and with some swift, decisive action—"

Guerin pushed himself to his feet and headed for the door. "No," he said.

Malet followed him. "You can't be serious after what you have seen tonight! Don't you understand what we are dealing with? The man is tied in with murder! We must act! We can keep hooking the small fish, we can keep raking in the hired assassins, we can find the arsonists, we can arrest the go-betweens, but if we do nothing to stop the man at the very heart of this tangle and pulling the strings, we are wasting our time! I haven't been able to nail him, but with your cooperation—"

Guerin took up his coat and hat. "It is my time that's being wasted," he said with a yawn.

"But I tell you he's known to have—"

Guerin set the hat on his head. "Rumors! Libels! Slanders! You say you haven't been able to 'nail' him—what a term! —has it occurred to you that he can't be 'nailed'? That however much you may lick your chops at the prospect of going after someone you think is the kingpin of crime here, you are aiming the wrong way?" He flashed a scornful look at Malet and then shrugged into his coat and started toward the door.

Malet drew a deep breath and said quietly, "You took an oath to uphold the government and protect the helpless. If the man is the monster I believe he is, then he's far deadlier than a mad dog! You owe it to your charges to make certain that he won't harm any of them!"

When Guerin did not respond, Malet stepped in front of him. "I beg you, Inspector, cooperate with me! I will do all the work. I won't use any of your people. I won't take up any of your time, and when I do get my proof, you will get all credit for catching the man. I will write the report and you can sign it. All I want to do is catch that criminal before he does any more harm. And make no mistake, he will do more harm! Please! Let me—"

Guerin spoke over him with cold incisiveness. "You might be keeping Lamarque's seat warm while he's away, but I am still master in my own arrondissement, and I will thank you to remember it and keep out of it! You don't have my permission to stick your nose in the affairs of the 3rd arrondissement or any of its residents. If M. Dracquet does anything illegal in the 8th, which, you may recall, is your territory, by all means feel free to harass him within the bounds of your own territory!"

"But—"

"Forget it, Malet! You will have to give up your pet project!" Guerin's eyes narrowed, and he added, "And let me suggest that you concentrate someone who has actually done wrong—such as those slash-murderers you have been trying to chase lately—rather than hounding an innocent man!" He paused, as though calculating the effect of his next words. "I have long suspected that, having crawled out of the gutter, you wish to send everyone you can back into it. But you won't succeed here, and so I warn you!"

"I tell you—"

"Stand aside," snapped Guerin. "You are blocking my way!"

Malet moved aside and watched Guerin open the door. He said, "You were once the finest officer in Paris. I heard of you from as far away as Picardy. And now you do this. What changed you?"

"Good night, Malet," Guerin said. He turned on his heel and strode off, leaving Malet looking after him with his brows drawn together in a puzzled frown, heedless of the people in the anteroom.

MALET WALKED SLOWLY to the Prefect's desk and sat. After another moment he drew a deep breath and buried his face in his hands.

Another door slammed! It made no sense—

"Don't pay him any heed," said a voice in the doorway. "As scriptures say, 'As a dog returneth to his vomit, so a fool returneth to his folly.'"

Malet raised his head and saw Inspector L'Eveque smiling at him.

"Are you all right?" asked L'Eveque.

"I am fine," Malet said. "Just stalemated. Again."

"You will find a way around it," L'Eveque said. "You always do, as I've seen." His merry eyes narrowed in a smile and he said, "But I am here to ask leave to introduce someone to you. I am hoping you will take an interest in him."

Malet sat back and smiled back at the man. "Of course, Christien," he said. "Bring him in."

L'Eveque turned and went to the door. "Come on in, Saint-Légère," he said, and stood aside as the young man who had been acting as the decoy entered. He was wearing a bandage tipped over one eye.

"Chief Inspector Paul Malet, acting Prefect of Police for the moment, permit me to present to you Junior Inspector Charles-Maurice de Saint-Légère. We were in the army together: he left as a Major in 1829, and he's just come from England within the past year. Charles, M. Malet was my commanding officer for five years, and I have never ceased regretting leaving his command, though I am certain he's been blessing the day ever since."

Malet rose and returned Saint-Légère's bow. "I am pleased to meet one who distinguished himself this evening," he said.

Saint-Légère lowered his head. "I distinguished myself by dropping my gun," he said. "I must apologize. I am more used to carrying a sword."

Malet made a motion with his hand. "That was hardly a mistake," he said. "Don't refine on it. It took me a lot of practice to master keeping a pistol up my sleeve. I see you have had your hurts tended."

"They were nothing," Saint-Légère said with a shrug. "Just a rap to the skull. Sir, that went off beautifully!"

Malet half-bowed. "Sit down," he said. When they had, he said, "England? Did you live there long?"

"I was born and raised there," Saint-Légère replied. "My parents were émigrés—"

"He's the cousin of the Duc de Fontrevault," L'Eveque said. "He never mentions it. He could be living in the faubourg Saint-Germain and swilling champagne every evening, but he's a cop instead. I don't understand it!"

"I could level the same accusation at you," Saint-Légère said.

Malet said, "Then you must permit me to welcome you back to France, M. de Saint-Légère, and thank you for your dedication."

Saint-Légère looked startled for a moment: Malet had spoken in excellent English. "It was my honor," he replied in the same language with a bow. He rose when L'Eveque stood.

"I don't wish to overstay my welcome," said L'Eveque, "Nor do I wish to keep this poor hero from his bed. I will take my leave of you, sir, with my best wishes, as always."

Saint-Légère bowed. "It was a pleasure, Monsieur."

"And for me as well. I look forward to reading your report after M. Guerin approves it."

Saint-Légère did not comment, but for a moment he seemed almost stricken to Malet's concerned eyes.

L'Eveque was looking from Malet to Saint-Légère. "Just remember, Charles," he said, suddenly intent, "This man is the finest superior I have ever had, and a very fine friend, as well. If you ever need guidance, you should go to him." He turned to Malet. "I am certain M. Malet wouldn't gainsay me."

Malet rose and walked with them to the door of the Prefect's offices, watched them leave, then went back to his desk. He was smiling; Christien L'Eveque had always been able to amuse him, and he valued the man's friendship. If Inspector de Saint-Légère enjoyed L'Eveque's friendship, then he was a man of quality.

Malet turned from thoughts of L'Eveque to considering the man he had captured that night: Ensenat. If Malet was right, he had just gained a formidable weapon to use in a fight that he had begun to consider a private crusade. He would question the man the next day.

CHAPTER THREE

The Plot Thickens

A FINGER OF WIND PUSHED between the lace curtains that shrouded the window and touched the face of the man lying in the large bed. The sudden coolness caused the man's eyes to shift from contemplating the draped canopy ceiling above him to frown at the window. It was bright: what time was it?

He reached for the gold watch on the stand beside the bed. He pressed the stem and gazed at the enameled face when the case opened. He had seen the inscription 'From the Grateful Citizens of Vautreuil, 1814-1826' that had been carved inside the heavy gold case too often to pay it any heed. The hour and minute hands had passed the finely painted name 'Bréguet' that sat just above six o'clock.

Time to rise. Paul Malet set the watch back on its stand and then lost himself in a luxurious stretch. He threw the covers aside, swung a pair of long, well-muscled legs across the mattress to the floor, and stepped from his bed to cross to the window and gaze out over the courtyard of his house to the street below.

The old houses lining his street were cloaked in a fine mist, the last remnants of the marsh that had been drained three hundred years before to form the Marais district of Paris. The sun seemed to be trying to break through the clouds overhead, and the breeze had risen slightly and seemed somehow colder.

The rigors of a childhood spent in a prison had long ago inured Malet to cold, but he valued propriety, and it would be most improper to be caught standing at his bedroom window clad only in his nightshirt. He turned aside to don a dressing gown of brocaded, wine-colored silk, knotted the sash about his waist, and then opened the windows inward and rested his folded arms on the stone balustrade.

"Good morning Inspector!" called the costermonger who was leading his horse and cart along the fog-dimmed street. "You're late rising today!"

"Busy night," said Malet.

"There's busy and then there's busy," said the costermonger with a rueful grin. "Knowing life, your 'busy night' wasn't the enjoyable kind, if you know what I mean."

"No," said Malet with an air of interested innocence, "What can you mean?"

"Go on with you, Inspector!" called the costermonger. "If you aren't half a card—! Anyhow, a splendid day it is, indeed!"

"Your eyes are better than mine if you can see that far through this fog," Malet returned with a smile.

"It will be," said the costermonger, who had this conversation with Malet most mornings and would have been hurt if he missed it. "Just wait and see!"

"I will take your word for it," Malet called down. "And what's the news in the city this morning?"

"Just that you're a hero again!" the costermonger called back with a grin. "They're singing your praises in all the papers!"

Malet dismissed the French press with a contemptuous snort. "I will be a buffoon next month," he said. "Especially if we don't get any further toward catching that pack of thugs who torture their victims before murdering them."

The costermonger looked uneasy for a moment. "I heard they found another," he said, lowering his voice. "Cut up like the others. How many is that? Six?"

"Eight," said Malet. He had been following their activities from a distance for the past several months; the attacks had not occurred in his arrondissement, and he had had no wish to step on the toes of his fellow Chief Inspectors, who had showed no inclination to take advantage of his expertise. But two weeks ago the killers had shifted their territory northeast, within Malet's bailiwick. One of their victims had been left by the

Pont d'Austerlitz: it had made him very angry. He had joined the hunt.

The costermonger's expression cleared a little. "I heard you're working on it, M. Malet!" he said. "It's just a matter of time!"

"We'll see. You be careful, now."

The costermonger replied with a very Parisian shrug and turned his cart away down the twisting old street.

Malet watched him with a smile, then turned back toward his bedroom and made his way to his dressing room. It was a splendid morning, despite the overcast sky, and he had a lot to consider.

Constant Dracquet.

The name was a thought in itself, and Malet let his attention focus on it as he poured water in the porcelain basin, thoroughly wet his shaving brush, and rubbed it against a cake of Castile soap.

He had first heard of the man while he was Police Commissioner in Vautreuil, in Picardy, in 1815. He had watched the man's rise to power. Dracquet was an enigma, a shadow. Malet had immediately detected the stench of corruption about him. Subsequent events following Malet's transfer to Paris in 1826 had served to strengthen his distrust of the man, but he had been unable to mount a campaign against him, for he had had no real reason to do so, and the Law frowned on hunches.

Evidence against Dracquet was faint and inconclusive, and the 8th arrondissement had not been touched by anything pertaining to Dracquet's activities, shady or otherwise, since Malet's arrival in 1826. The inquiries that he had been able to perform, and Malet believed in staying within official guidelines in his investigations, had been maddeningly inconclusive, and he had been effectively blocked by Guerin's refusal to cooperate. He had spent nearly seven years watching Dracquet and waiting for a chance. And now, with one of Dracquet's lieutenants in custody on a serious charge, he had that chance and, almost more important, a powerful hunch.

He had lately caught a sense of urgency. He could feel things stirring, shifting, a sort of increased concentration, almost a sense of exultation that filtered down to the lowest strata from the highest—from Dracquet himself, perhaps? An echo of his own hopes and confidence? And could Ensenat's presence be an indication of Dracquet's personal involvement?

Malet smiled as he wiped a line of foam from the blade of his razor, tested the sharpness of the edge, and bent his attention to the mirror again. He felt almost elated. That had to be it, and this time things were different. This time Dracquet would not be able to dodge him. He could take few people into his confidence, and he would have to devote almost his entire attention to the matter, but it was worth the price to bring down Dracquet and his shadow empire. Who knew what they might find in the wreckage?

Malet toweled the last remnants of soap from his now smooth chin, smiled at his reflection, took up his comb, and set his hair in order. What indeed? The possibilities were countless and delectable.

But first he had a hunt to plan.

THE ARCHED STONE CEILING, blackened by centuries of soot, dipped to pillared supports. The room was always dark; candles had been set atop the capitals, rank upon rank, multiplied into a constellation of pallid corpse-candles floating above a sea of darkness and silence.

This was the great Salle des Gens d'Armes of the Conciergerie, the royal prison on the Île du Palais. It had been a place of dread and darkness for centuries, and it was through here, within a space of time less than a year, that over two thousand people passed on their way to the guillotine.

Chief Inspector Malet stood in the very center of the room, his arms folded, his expression unreadably somber. The flickering candles cast faint shadows of his tall form in every direction. He often paused here on his way to question prisoners to listen to the echoes.

For the huge rooms were full of echoes. Although they had almost been extinguished by the passage of forty years, Malet's ears were sharp enough to catch them. Names shouted above the din of a frightened throng, cries of dismay and terror, the sound of footsteps dying away along the hallway, going toward the tiny room where the victims of the Terror were taken to be relieved of their few possessions, shorn and bound.

De Colberts from Normandy had been numbered among them, his scapegrace father's family. Had they thought of him then, a child of five, far away in that prison in Provence, almost the last of their line, an unwanted bastard?

Malet shrugged at the thought. The past was past, and the echoes were merely echoes. For the moment, he was waiting until the prisoner he wished to question—Jean Ensenat—was ready for him. He had a great deal to ask the man, but other visitors had come before him. Malet could pause and listen to echoes.

But real echoes intruded upon his ears, voices coming down the hallway toward him.

"If there is the slightest sign of it—the slightest sign, mind you! —we must have silence." The voice was clear and calm.

The speaker came into view as Malet watched from behind his pillar. He was beautifully dressed in the discreet height of fashion, his face cold and calm. He said, "We can't afford—"

The man beside him touched his arm and motioned toward Malet's shadow.

The first man broke off and turned slowly toward Malet.

Malet, scorning to hide, stepped into the open. His gaze met and locked upon the gaze of the other man, and they stood silently for a long moment.

"Chief Inspector?" came a respectful voice from the doorway behind the other two.

Malet did not turn his head. "Yes?" he said. The ceiling splintered his voice into a hundred echoes.

"He's ready for you."

Malet nodded, took up his stick, and moved into the bowels of the Conciergerie.

ENSENAT WAS STANDING in the corner of his small cell with his hands tied behind him. The man seemed frightened and defiant.

"Good morning, Ensenat," Malet said as he closed the door behind him and latched it. "I am sure you have been expecting me."

"It never takes long for vultures to gather around a carcass," Ensenat said.

"Not terribly original. Nor even terribly insulting. Sit down. I have some questions for you."

"You're wasting your time," said Ensenat. "I have already given a statement to your paunchy fool of a scribbler."

Malet passed Ensenat's description of the Police Archivist with a half-smile and sat on the hard cot as though it were a carved chair of state. "The statement was given willingly."

Ensenat's eyes flickered. "It's all in that statement."

Malet folded his arms. "But I don't believe the statement," he said gently.

"You haven't even read it yet!" Ensenat objected.

"I refuse to waste my time. Why were you at the Pont Neuf last night?"

Ensenat curled his lip. "I was walking along," he said, "and some cops grabbed me by mistake! Must I be blamed because they're a lot of bumblers?"

"I have little patience with lies, Ensenat," said Malet. "I have even less with clumsy ones. I had the area ringed very securely. You couldn't have broken through. And I saw you myself in the thick of the fighting."

"Well, then, you're wasting your time with me," said Ensenat. "My goose is cooked."

"Your goose is cooked more thoroughly than you suspect," said Malet. "Dracquet left you right before I came."

Ensenat made a convulsive motion.

Malet's smile widened. "I saw his face," he said. "Whatever he said to you wasn't pleasant. I am sure he told you that you are on your own, that you'd get no support from him. Isn't it time to cut your losses?"

"I don't understand you," said Ensenat.

"I think you do," said Malet. He folded his arms and looked Ensenat over. "Let us be blunt. I know who and what you are. I know your connections, and I know how you work. You know me, and you know I have been after you and yours for years. I have been stymied before, but it's your bad luck that I am acting Prefect at the moment. Here I am, and my hands aren't tied now, and your people have cast you off. Can you fight me, all alone as you are?"

"I have nothing to gain," said Ensenat, "Fight or not. I am a dead man."

"Maybe not," said Malet, studying his fingernails.

"What?"

"There was no murder last night. I checked your actions during the previous nights' murders. It's possible you aren't implicated. And it's possible I may—mind you I said may! —not be able to hold you. And you may be able to cooperate with me."

Ensenat closed his eyes and held them so for a long moment. "All right," he said with an effort. "Caught between a tiger and a viper, I choose the tiger. I will talk to you, but I will need something from you. An assurance—"

Malet's brows drew together, but he made no comment.

"My life's worthless if Dracquet thinks I am going to rat on him!" Ensenat burst out. "I have got to get clean out of here!"

"What did you have in mind?" Malet asked.

Ensenat looked up, caught his expression, and exclaimed, "Damn you! This is leading right where you wanted it—"

Malet merely lifted his eyebrows.

Ensenat drew a shaking breath. "America," he said. "I could go there and never be found. I could change my name and start again and never have to worry that he was catching up with me."

"America," Malet said thoughtfully.

"That's right. France is too hot for me, and Dracquet wouldn't want to let things slide, especially now that he's involved—" he broke off.

Malet looked up from contemplating his watch. "'Now that he's involved—' in what?" he said.

Ensenat smiled and shook his head. "Oh no," he said. "No, Inspector, I will hold my peace. It's my safeguard against you reneging."

Malet's gaze fixed and narrowed. "You're very bold. There's nothing to keep me from getting up and leaving you to your fate."

"Oh no, Malet," Ensenat said. "What'll stop you is your own greed. You have wanted Dracquet so long, you're like to choke. And now that you have him close to hand, you won't let him go. I know!"

Malet considered and then nodded. "All right," he said. "What's your price?"

"Come back when you can promise me safe passage to America and thirty thousand francs to see me established. We'll talk then."

Malet rose. "I will see what I can do," he said at the door.

"Tell them to cut me loose when you get outside," said Ensenat.

Malet nodded. "I will have you moved somewhere safer."

"Thank you," said Ensenat. "Get me what I want. Be fast about it."

CHAPTER FOUR

Death of A Rat

"FIFTEEN HUNDRED LOUIS and passage to America? Informers are getting expensive. Will he be worth it?" The Minister of Police, Christien de la Haye, Count d'Anglars, sat back in his chair, steepled his impeccably manicured hands before him and watched Malet as he paced from the window to his chair and back again.

"I think so," said Malet over his shoulder. He gazed unseeingly over the courtyard of the Count's house, turned after a moment, and paced back to his chair.

d'Anglars sighed and sat back. "My dear Malet," he said, "I would find it much less fatiguing if you would finally alight." He smiled at Malet's expression. "No, you don't annoy me, my dear sir. It's only that I find myself sadly reminded that I lack your energy."

Malet sat.

"Thirty thousand francs," Count d'Anglars said again. "On what case can he give us information?"

Malet managed to convey the impression of restlessness even while sitting still with his hands folded. "Not a case," he replied. "A man."

"Indeed?" d'Anglars reached for the glass of sherry that was always poured for Malet's visits. "And who is this man?"

"Constant Dracquet." Malet watched as d'Anglars set his glass down untasted.

"Dracquet, you say?" d'Anglars mused.

"Yes, Excellency." Malet touched the rim of his glass, but his eyes never left the Count's face. Though his expression remained suitably grave, his eyes began to dance as d'Anglars pushed himself to his feet and started to pace in his turn.

"You do have a lead on him?" d'Anglars demanded after a moment. "This isn't a false alarm?" He answered his own question before Malet could speak. "No, you never play that sort of prank." He paused and then repeated, "Dracquet, you say?"

"Yes."

Count d'Anglars' elegant features warmed suddenly in an almost unwilling smile. "You have been watching a long time for this chance," he said.

Malet kept his eyes lowered as he raised his glass and sipped from it. "Yes," he said at last.

d'Anglars saw the twinkle in Malet's eye and sat again. "Hm," he said. "And you have been blocked all these years. Oh, I have noticed. Short of turning things upside down, there was no way I could interfere." He added, almost to himself, "And I won't use the weapons of chaos, no matter what is at stake."

"Nor would I ask you to," said Malet.

d'Anglars' voice lost its smile. "We have seen too much of chaos in our lives, you and I," he said. He went on as though he had not voiced that last thought, "The damnable thing is that he presents so respectable a front. He moves in the best circles of society—in which case, my dear Malet, I find myself wondering why he makes his primary home in Montmartre, of all places! —gives parties and receptions that the crème de la crème all attend."

"Yourself included?" Malet asked.

"I?" d'Anglars raised his head as suddenly as a man who has been unexpectedly struck. "No, Inspector, I have not attended his receptions. I always seem to be ill at those times."

Malet smiled. "Most unfortunate," he said.

"But all that is to the side," said d'Anglars. "Thirty thousand francs to capture the man I am certain was responsible for M. de Grandpré's assassination outside the Chambre des Deputés six years ago? Vidocq could get nothing on him, but I could sense it... And those terrible murders near Reuilly. I know he was involved in them, but there was no proof. Selling weapons to the Spaniards in 1823—! And all other sorts of filth and treason!"

"It's all connected," said Malet. "Like steps on a staircase. The more power the criminal gains, the greater distance he sets between himself and the actual crimes. Go-betweens, hired assassins, spies—it's all part of the hierarchy. Destroy the web, and the spider will merely spin another. You must first kill the spider."

d'Anglars raised his sherry again and took a large swallow. "Ah yes," he said. "If anyone would know, it would be you. Some people are still puzzled by the fact that you, raised in a prison, the protégé of the greatest criminal of modern times, chose to side with the Law"

"They puzzle too much over the obvious."

"I have never had that difficulty, myself," said d'Anglars. "Nor has anyone, honored with your acquaintance." He continued briskly, "Fight Dracquet. Use the informer. The thirty thousand francs are yours. I will order a draft now. That will settle this part of the campaign. You can plan your attack as you wish, and I shall support you to the fullest extent of my power."

"I had him moved to a more secure cell. Do you wish to come with me to speak with him?"

d'Anglars hesitated and then nodded. "I believe I do," he said.

"HE DIDN'T DIE EASILY," said d'Anglars through white lips. He took out his handkerchief after a moment and blotted his suddenly damp forehead.

Malet looked up from the contorted face on the bed before him. "No, he didn't," he said.

"He appears to have died of asphyxiation," said Jules Sonnier, the police surgeon for the 8th arrondissement. "Odd, but there aren't any marks on his neck."

Malet drew the collar of the man's shirt aside and frowned at the throat. He felt along the line of the man's windpipe. "Not strangled," he said. "He choked to death."

Sonnier leaned forward. "On what?" he asked.

"Feel his throat," said Malet.

Sonnier obeyed and then watched as Malet ripped Ensenat's shirt open and stared at the man's abdomen, which was covered with a dark bruise.

"Just as I suspected," said Malet. He drew the torn shirt back and brushed his hands together. "Cut him open and you will find a wad of cloth. Probably a handkerchief. It was shoved down his throat."

"But the bruise?" said d'Anglars, who had recovered a little of his color.

"Someone held him with the handkerchief ready," said Malet, "while another punched him in the stomach, forcing the air out. And then they crammed the handkerchief down his throat. It would be drawn farther down his windpipe with every breath he tried to take."

"Good God!" said Sonnier.

"Sometimes condemned men do that to escape execution," Malet said. "I always thought the rope or the guillotine would be less painful."

"People are fools at best," said Sonnier, "And frightened people more so." He sighed and folded his arms. "Do you need me anymore, Inspector?"

Malet shook his head. "No, M. le Docteur," he said. "You may go. And thank you."

"Shall I perform an autopsy?"

Malet frowned and looked over at d'Anglars. "Monseigneur?" he said.

d'Anglars shook his head. "If M. Malet is certain of the cause of death, there's no need to—to cut the corpse. His family might be grieved."

"He has none," Malet said. "He came from filth, dealt in filth, and died a filthy death at the hands of filthy men."

The bitterness in his voice made d'Anglars raise his eyebrows, but he said nothing.

"Doctor," said Malet as Sonnier reached the door. "Send the guards in, if you please. I want to speak with them." The doctor nodded and left.

"Will it accomplish anything?" asked d'Anglars.

"It will shake them up," Malet said with a grim smile.

"DO YOU REMEMBER SEEING anyone—anyone! —coming along this hallway within the past day?" Malet asked.

The four guards shook their heads.

"Come now," said Malet. "You must have seen something. Think back."

There was no answer. Malet had expected none. His smile thinned. "Nothing, again!" he said. "Your memories are completely clear." He paused the space of time it took to draw a deep breath, then spoke again. "Then let me tell you something that you should keep at the very front of your minds.

"While you played cards—" he nodded toward a white-faced young man, "—or relieved yourself—" this to a paunchy, middle-aged man, "—or drank the wine you weren't supposed to have at your post, and carefully looked anywhere but where you were supposed to be looking, you became accessory to a murder, and that is a crime. And crime is my concern. So: from now on I will be watching you: your every step, your every move. One slip—only one! —and you will be mine." He nodded toward the corpse on the pallet. "I will show as much mercy toward you as you showed this poor piece of offal! You have my word on that. Do you understand me?" He paused for a moment, then jerked his head toward the door. "Now get out of my sight!"

d'Anglars watched them scramble toward the door and then lowered his eyes to the corpse. "We are stalemated again," he said.

"Yes," said Malet.

CHAPTER FIVE

At Notre-Dame: Message and Reply

THE MUSIC THROBBED in the night air, low and tremulous, more felt than heard. It soared to a crescendo and then ceased as though it had been cut off, making sigh of the evening wind suddenly loud.

The thin-faced man hovering at the corner of the cathedral drew a deep breath and took a closer grip of the heavy package cradled in his arms. Vespers was concluded, and the faithful would be leaving the cathedral. Malet would be among them, and the man would be able to deliver the package and the message to him and be finally free of the fear that had gripped him since the moment that afternoon when Constant Dracquet had put the package and the message into his shrinking arms and told him to find Malet and deliver them.

The messenger looked up at the facade of the cathedral. The great stained glass rose, glowing from the torchlight behind it, seemed to float above the triple portals that opened on the west. The Virgin was enthroned in the center with the Child on her knee, crowned and haloed, holding a scepter, surrounded by hues of sapphire and ruby. She seemed to be gazing reproachfully at him. The Child's hand was raised in blessing, but His head was turned away.

The messenger looked down from the window to the center portal. Torches, set in sconces to either side, threw the crowded carvings into stark light and shadow. Christ, enthroned in majesty, raised his hands above the last judgment of mankind. The dead, in the lowest register, stirred and jostled each other in their struggle to emerge from their tombs. Above them, the blessed turned adoring faces up toward Christ as the damned were led away in chains.

The messenger looked away from the procession, his heart pounding, caught by the sudden fear that he might see his own face among those of the damned.

He was afraid of his master, but even more of this task. To do as he was bid was, to his mind, tantamount to putting his head in a lion's mouth. He had heard whispers, and he had read the message enclosed with the package. No one, receiving that message, would fail to perceive the insult, least of all a man like Malet.

The two iron-bound timber doors swung slowly inward; like the opening of the sluices of a dam, the motion released a flood of the faithful that streamed out from the cathedral.

The messenger took a deep, shaking breath and stared fearfully at the faces and forms that passed him. Twenty minutes later the stream of worshipers had dwindled to nothing, and Malet had not come out. The place du Parvis was getting cold; he stepped within the cathedral and looked around.

A stoup of holy water was before him. Memory stirred; he dipped his hand, crossed himself, and started up the nave. The tiers of arches, stretching right and left, soaring upward to the high, vaulted ceiling, frightened him. He turned and ducked left, into the close safety of the ambulatory, and came to a trembling halt.

A tall man in a black coat was pacing toward him down the passageway. His head was lifted, but his eyes were downcast. He held a good black beaver hat in the crook of his left arm. His right was tucked behind him. His step was slow, pensive, deliberate. A sword clanked softly in a scabbard at his side.

The messenger darted behind a pillar and watched the man's approach, wondering if he dared step out and stop him. The speculation was cut off as the man paused before a rack of votive candles and gazed down at them with an almost archangelic detachment.

The messenger heard the clink of coins, then a soft clatter as the man set a coin in the offering box and lifted an unlit candle. He touched the wick to one of the many flames before him, waited until the candle was burning, and then set it on a wrought iron spike in the rack. He gazed at the candle for a moment, then went to his knees upon the prie-dieu before the rack, set his hat on the kneeler beside him, rested his elbows on the railing, and lowered his head to his folded hands.

The messenger hesitated. If he stepped forward now Malet would not be likely to make a grab for him. They were in a church, after all. But the prospect of disturbing him made him uneasy. It would be like nudging a tiger with his elbow.

He finally cleared his throat. "M. l'Inspecteur," he said.

Malet raised his head. "Yes?' he said.

"I—I have a message to deliver to you."

Malet's hands were still clasped before him, and he had not looked at the messenger. "A message?"

"Yes—and this," the messenger replied, offering the package.

Malet looked over at the messenger. His eyes encountered the package. "Open it," he said.

"But it's wrapped," the messenger objected.

"Then open the wrappings."

The messenger obeyed, and uncovered a long, wooden box with the name of a wine merchant on it.

"Open the box," said Malet.

The messenger frowned at the lid, located a small brass hook, and unclasped it. He lifted the lid to show a jeroboam of very fine champagne: Chateau Mallebranche. The messenger offered it to Malet.

Malet's expression did not change. "No," he said. "Put it on the floor."

When this was done he said, "And what was the message?"

The messenger offered the note.

Malet opened the paper and read it aloud. "'To console you for so resounding a defeat.'" His voice was low and soft in the quiet dimness of the cathedral. The man refolded the note and tucked it into the inside breast pocket of his coat. "This is unsigned," he said. "Does your master have a name?"

"Sir, I-I may not say."

Malet considered in silence for a long moment. He finally said, "Tell

Constant Dracquet that my sword is not broken, and victory in one battle doesn't guarantee victory in the war." He paused, still on his knees, and his voice grew a little less remote. "And as for you, my friend, take care that you don't discover one day that the name of your master is a far more dire one than you originally thought. Good night." He lowered his head once more against his folded hands.

The messenger gazed for a moment, his heart pounding, then turned and hurried down the ambulatory to the doorway and stepped out into the cool night. He turned to look back at the portal of the Last Judgment, his eyes raising fearfully to the line of damned souls.

His heartbeat increased; his gaze flickered from the severe serenity of the judging angel to the contorted, mocking grins of the demons guarding the damned. And the faces of the damned themselves, as twisted with fear and despair as he felt his own soul to be.

He stopped, his breath fluttering to a halt in his throat. But why did they despair? The only thing holding them on the path to Hell were their own hands gripping the chain. If they would only release their hold and open their hands, they would be free. It was their choice —

Choice. His hand rose to his throat. They had a choice, and so had he. He looked back within the cathedral, toward the bank of candles and the man kneeling motionless before them.

Take care that you don't one day discover that the name of your master is a far more dire one than you originally thought.

He turned and walked away from the cathedral.

He could choose, and his choice —

His walk became a shaking, shambling run.

MALET MADE HIS WAY past the heavy, iron-bound timber doors and paced slowly out below the portal of the Last Judgment. The doors closed behind him as he passed through them and out onto the place du Parvis. The bulk of the Prefecture lay before him. Beyond it he could see the spire of the Sainte-Chappelle, which had once housed the crown of thorns. To the north, just visible beyond it, lay the Conciergerie and the vast complex that was called the Palais de Justice.

Stalemated! Malet had been the colonel commanding the most prestigious regiment of Napoleon's Horse Artillery during the wars. As an artillerist, he knew when his guns had been spiked, and this time they had been spiked with an almost insolent ease. The bottle of champagne, which now was gracing the table of the priests at Notre Dame, was a final, insulting fillip.

He was stymied, he knew it, and there was nothing he could do about it. Constant Dracquet would continue to spin his webs and Paul Malet could do nothing more than nurse his suspicions and send shadows against him for as long as he served as the Prefect's substitute. And when that time was past, he would be forced to return to his own arrondissement and watch from a distance as Constant Dracquet pursued his aims unchecked. And he had been so close to success!

Malet raised his eyes to the stars and promised that if he had another chance against Dracquet, he would press it to the very limit and be in on the kill himself.

If only he could have another chance!

It was enough to tax the fortitude of a hero.

CHAPTER SIX

Inspector Malet is Given a Weapon

MALET ARRIVED AT THE Prefecture the next morning in a profoundly vicious mood and found Inspector de Saint-Légère's report awaiting him, forwarded by Chief Inspector Guerin. At Guerin's direction, Saint-Légère had taken full responsibility for being clumsy enough to drop his weapon at the crucial moment, thus alerting the thugs and nearly spoiling the trap.

Malet read the report, his brows driving together in a scowl. He opened the drawer of the Prefect's desk, took out a sheet of Police stationery and wrote in a precise, strong hand:

The Prefecture

Paris

10 September, 1834

Alexandre Guerin

Chief Inspector

3rd arrondissement

M. Guerin:

I cannot feel, as you seem to, that Junior Inspector de Saint-Légère's action of dropping his firearm in the heat of an engagement, in

which he was outnumbered five to one and in fear for his life, is a
fault of any magnitude. The success of the operation was due in good
part to M. de Saint-Légère's courage and initiative in volunteering
for his part in the investigation. This report must be re-written and
resubmitted without its offensive tone of blame.

Paul V. Malet

Provisional Prefect of Police, Paris

When the report came back the next day, duly rewritten, Malet enclosed it with his own, forwarded it to Count d'Anglars, and promised himself to invite Christien L'Eveque to bring Junior Inspector de Saint-Légère along with him the next time they dined together. That resolve was relegated to things to do in the near future by the pressure of running the Seine et Oise Prefecture in M. Lamarque's absence.

MALET, ENGAGED THE next day in writing his daily outline for the Prefecture, was mending a quill pen that had just split when the Chamberlain rapped twice, opened the door, and then entered and coughed.

He looked up and frowned. "Yes, Clerel?" he said.

"This gentleman wishes to speak to the Prefect on a matter of some urgency," Clerel said. He motioned to someone standing just beyond the doorway, and Charles de Saint-Légère stepped into the office. His demeanor was deferent, but Malet could sense that the man was very worried about something and, in an odd way, embarrassed to be there.

Malet's eyes sharpened, but his voice was calm and non-committal when he spoke. "The Prefect has been called away, as you know," he said. "I am acting in his place until his return. Is there a problem, M. de Saint-Légère?"

Saint-Légère hesitated as the Chamberlain bowed himself out of the room. "There—there is," he said when Clerel was gone. "I wouldn't ordinarily trouble you, but Christien L'Eveque has spoken so highly of you, and assured me that I could turn to you. I don't know where else to go, and the matter's urgent."

"You flatter me," said Malet. "What is wrong?"

Saint-Légère drew a deep breath and held it for a moment. "I have been offered a bribe," he said.

Malet's eyebrows drove together for a moment and he set down his pen, but he spoke calmly. "A bribe?" he repeated.

"Yes, Chief Inspector."

"A bribe to induce you to do what?" Malet asked. His slight accent was fractionally more pronounced.

"To ensure my friendship toward certain people in my precinct," de Saint-Légère replied.

The notion of anyone thinking it necessary to pay the Law for its friendship had always sparked in Malet a mixture of contempt and amusement. "I see," he said. "Please. Sit down." He indicated an elegant, gilded fauteuil upholstered in crimson damask. "And was there anything specific?" he asked when Saint-Légère was seated.

"Nothing specific, no," Saint-Légère replied. "It was merely the nature of the gifts and the manner in which they were offered that made me uneasy." He paused and added, "I received the impression that a small lie from me from time to time would be expected."

"There is no such thing as a 'small lie,'" Malet said, but he was speaking to himself. He sat back and scowled down at the pile of reports before him. "In what quarter of your arrondissement was this telling of small, friendly lies to be done?"

Saint-Légère told him, and then watched as Malet frowned off into space, consulting a mental map of the city.

"Hm." Malet said at last. "Hardly a den of crime. A very respectable section, in fact. Who offered this bribe?"

"A certain Constant Dracquet," said Saint-Légère.

The name made Malet stiffen. Dracquet! Was it possible? He reached into the breast pocket of his waistcoat and took out a billfold. "This Constant Dracquet," he said quietly, gazing down at a folded piece of yellowed paper that he had taken out.

"Yes, Monsieur?"

"What is his address?"

Saint-Légère told him, slightly puzzled by his tone.

Malet caught the sense of puzzlement; it made him tip the edge of a smile. "I have been interested in the doings of a particular M. Dracquet, at that address, for some time," he said. "And you say he openly offered you a bribe? How very interesting."

"No, M. l'Inspecteur."

Malet looked up from studying his steepled fingertips. "I beg your pardon?" he said.

"M. Dracquet didn't openly offer me a bribe, though he made me several gifts that I felt I had to return. He denied any intent to bribe me when I approached him."

Malet's brows lifted. He said, "Then what is the bribe that you speak of?"

"It's an item of considerable value," Saint-Légère said. "It was brought to me with this note." he handed Malet a fold of cheap, anonymous paper.

Malet was frowning now. He opened the note and read it aloud:

> *You have been afoot too long, Major de Saint-Légère. It is time you were mounted again. But if your sense of honor forbids your accepting this beauty, you need only take him to the place de la Concorde and tie him to the lamp post closest to the church of La Madeleine.*

The note was unsigned, and the handwriting obviously altered. Malet folded it again and then looked up at Saint-Légère. "Nothing in this note ties this to Dracquet," he said.

"Nothing, sir."

"Hm," said Malet. He rose and went to the window, to stand looking out with his arms folded. A crowd was gathering in the street below his window, with a splendid dark bay horse in the very center. Malet loved horses, and this one was worth a second glance. "You refused the bribe, of course," he said after a moment.

It was not a question: Saint-Légère realized that Chief Inspector Malet had not doubted his honor for a moment. He found it a startling, and very flattering, thought.

"Of course," he replied, smiling.

"Then the matter is closed." Malet said. He was disappointed. It had been so close... "You didn't accept the bribe, nothing illegal has been done, and the office of the Prefect has no reason to intervene."

"Perhaps not, M. l'Inspecteur," said Saint-Légère. "But this isn't the first time that I have been offered something like a bribe since I started to work in the 3rd arrondissement."

Malet stiffened. "Oh?" he asked. He had not turned from the window.

"Yes, Chief Inspector. I was given all the duties proper to a Police Inspector—admittedly of a junior grade—before I was assigned my present territory. On four separate occasions I was offered handsome gifts of money by various people."

Malet turned away from the window and scowled at him. "Indeed?" he said.

"Yes, M. l'Inspecteur," Saint-Légère said. "I was offered money by various shopkeepers and property-owners in my territory. I declined them—much to their surprise, I fear—and was called in by Chief Inspector Guerin."

"Did he say or do anything that would merit the Prefect's attention?" Malet asked. This lead might do as well as the other.

Saint-Légère considered. "No, sir," he said at last. "He said that I was to make a note of people who made such offers, note the offers, and bring them to him to handle. I refused to have anything to do with them. I was assigned my current territory four days later."

"I see," said Malet. "And, having refused these gifts, you were sent away to a position of lesser responsibility?"

"Yes, Monsieur." Saint-Légère considered and then added with some difficulty, as though performing a task he found distasteful, "Though in fairness to Chief Inspector Guerin, I must admit that it is closer to my lodgings."

Malet dismissed the excuse with a flick of his fingertips. "And what, pray, are your new duties?" he asked.

"Walking a beat, reporting three times a day, writing a report at the end of the day."

"In essence, then, you were reduced to Junior Constable." Malet turned back toward the window. "And you saw nothing further that would pique your interest?"

"Nothing, sir. Though I did meet M. Dracquet within the past several months. My lodgings aren't far from his house... I don't know, sir. There's something strange about this entire business. Whoever offered the bribe—and I am certain it's Dracquet, even if I can't prove it—he won't let it drop. He's very insistent. I have a feeling... Something important is about to happen."

Malet's shoulders stiffened. Saint-Légère was still speaking, but Malet suddenly heard, in his mind, Ensenat's voice saying, *Now that he's involved—* He thought again, *'Involved—' in what?*

Saint-Légère was still speaking. "-and he wants to be sure of me. The bribe has been brought to my home several times."

"And what is this bribe?" Malet asked at last over his shoulder.

"A horse," de Saint-Légère replied.

"A horse?" Malet repeated.

"A magnificent horse," Saint-Légère said. "A valuable horse, a horse to put Pegasus to shame. A horse," he added, "that would earn me a fortune simply by standing at stud."

Malet turned from the window. "A tall black bay with one white foot. A thoroughbred; probably English."

"Why, yes," de Saint-Légère said. "How did you know?"

"He's tethered right outside. In the care of a guttersnipe. Obstructing traffic and causing quite a snarl."

"What!"

"Outside the Prefecture itself, no less!" Malet said through his teeth, his voice taking on a note of thunder. "Take sanctuary in the Cathedral and they'll stable him in the choir! They certainly are persistent! This touches my honor! What do they think we are? Stupid criminals infuriate me!" He set his hat squarely on his head, took up his walking stick and started toward the door.

"But M. l'Inspecteur—"

Malet turned at the door. "Come along!" he snapped. He waited until Saint-Légère had donned his hat, then stalked across the waiting room. He nodded curtly to the constables in the anteroom and went out the double doors. He cut straight across the congested street, narrowly avoiding being struck by two carriages, and up to the horse, who eyed him mildly and then, recognizing Saint-Légère, nickered at him.

"You, boy," said Inspector Malet to the urchin who was showing a sudden tendency to sidle away.

The child did not stop. Malet's thumb and forefinger caught him by the ear and brought him to a halt, yelling with pain.

"It isn't polite to leave when a grown-up is speaking to you," Malet said with awful gentleness, showing his teeth.

The urchin, a boy all of seven years old, struggled like a wildcat and swore with more force and venom than Malet had heard since his prison days. He subsided after his ear was roughly shaken.

"You see this horse?" asked Malet.

The boy's eyes traveled eloquently up the horse's legs to his ears and back down again. "Yes, Monseigneur," he said with elaborately sarcastic politeness. "I had noticed him."

"Who left him here?" Malet persisted. He released the ear but held his cane like a cudgel.

The boy rubbed his earlobe and grimaced. "Can't say," he replied. "Fellow gave me a sou and asked me to hold him for a minute or two."

Malet held out his hand. "Show me this sou," he said through the edge of an ominous smile.

The boy stared up at him and then thrust his grimy hands into his pockets. He turned one out, then the other, then rooted through the rest of his threadbare clothing, even going so far as to take off his cap. "It must have fallen out, Monseigneur," he said without even pretending to be dismayed.

Malet scowled down at the boy, who returned the scowl with one of his own.

"You are lying," Malet growled. "You know who it was and he's paying you to report what happens to this animal. Very well, you shall earn your pay. Tell the man that he left this beast on municipal property without a permit. Tell him, further, that the creature has fouled that property and obstructed the flow of traffic along a city street and created a public nuisance. Do you understand me so far?"

The child stared up at him and finally nodded.

"Excellent," said Chief Inspector Malet. "Then you shall tell him, further, that I am confiscating this horse and impounding him. If your employer wishes to pay a fine of fifty francs plus the beast's keep for two days, he can get the horse back two days from now. Otherwise he goes to the city stables for auction to the highest bidder in three weeks' time. Now be off with you and don't let me see you here again!"

The boy took off at a run, pausing as he rounded the corner of the rue de Lutèce to thrust out a licorice-stained tongue at Malet and de Saint-Légère.

Malet ignored him and unknotted the lead rope. "Now to the stables," he said. He hesitated a moment, though, and took out a plain metal snuffbox from his coat pocket. He shook out a palm full of—not tobacco, to Saint-Légère 's surprise, but small toffee candies—and offered them to the stallion.

The horse lowered his head and lipped at them. Malet smoothed the arched neck and said quietly, "I can understand the temptation. If you were in the army with Christien L'Eveque, then you were a cuirassier, weren't you? And he certainly is a beauty."

Saint-Légère nodded wistfully and stroked the stallion's soft, black nose with a fingertip. "Best horse I have ever seen," he said.

Malet said nothing, and they walked along in silence to the police stables.

The stallion was turned over to the care of a delighted hostler. Malet fed him another palm full of candy before he was led away.

Malet took his handkerchief and wiped his hand. He was frowning thoughtfully, and he said nothing as they headed back to the Prefecture.

The traffic had resolved itself, and the urchin was nowhere to be seen. Malet nodded and then turned to Saint-Légère. "That leaves you," he said.

"Me?"

"Have you any idea what was going to happen, or even when?"

"No, sir. I had nothing more specific than a vague hunch. But I think something is coming very soon, and I suspect it's something very important."

Malet frowned down at his hands again. "Since this is a question of ethics, I will handle it myself in behalf of the Prefecture. I am taking you out of that quarter for the time being. That little brat saw you go into the

Prefecture, and it might spoil things—

"The boy!" said Saint-Légère.

"I beg your pardon?"

"Forgive me, M. l'Inspecteur," said Saint-Légère. "But he looked familiar, and I just remembered why."

"Indeed?"

"Yes, Monsieur! I have seen that child in Constant Dracquet's household time out of number! I told you I don't live far from there. The lad's always there. I am sure of it, it's the same boy!"

Malet's hand half-raised and then lowered again. "Well, well, well..." he said through a dawning smile. "You are certain of this, then? The boy's a member of the household? You'd know him again if you saw him?"

"I certainly would," Saint-Légère said. "He may not live there, but he's been there every time I have gone by. And it was he who was holding the horse."

Malet's smile was almost blazing, but he spoke quietly. "The Gendarmerie needs a man at the Bois de Boulogne," he said. "They have a mounted patrol and they are short an officer. They wrote the Prefect yesterday requesting the loan of an inspector who can ride. They'll be astonished to find that we have a Major of Cuirassiers here. You will report there for the next few weeks. I will tell them to keep you as long as they need you."

"Thank you, sir!"

"Don't thank me," said Malet. "You're an honorable man. You like horses: well, then, go ride them. I will handle Dracquet and his intrigues, myself. In fact, I think I will take a direct hand in this. I am getting curious: I wonder what bribe he will find to tempt me."

Malet's smile altered after a moment and became kinder. "Come back with me to the Prefecture and tell me all that you can think of regarding this bribe as well as the other incidents while you were patrolling," he said. "Write up everything you can remember, and then relax. Tomorrow you go to the Bois de Boulogne—unless you need a little more time."

Saint-Légère said, "I am at the Chief Inspector's service, of course." His voice dropped slightly, and he said, "But what'll I tell Madame?" He seemed to have been talking to himself.

"'Madame'?" Malet repeated.

Saint-Légère blushed and laughed. "My landlady, M. l'Inspecteur."

The landlady of a bachelor's lodgings. Malet knew all about such women. "I see," he said, dismissing the subject and then pausing. Saint-Légère lived near Dracquet, after all, and his proximity had probably sparked Dracquet's interest in the first place...

"Oh not at all!" said Saint-Légère. "She's the loveliest lady in Paris—and she is a lady!"

"I see," Malet said again, caught by the nudge of a developing idea. "Perhaps I will be meeting her soon..."

CHAPTER SEVEN

The Wrath of Larouche

INSPECTOR MALET MIGHT have laughed at the thought, but he had had between his thumb and forefinger, for a little over a minute, the ear of one of the uncrowned kings of Paris. As he was leading the stallion to the stables, the boy was heading back to his haunts with his emotions in a state of turbulence that was unusual for him, cannonballing into pedestrians and returning their insults with pungent ones of his own. He was completely free of money, debts, obligations, and comforts. He was what is called a gamin. He did not know exactly how old he was, though he guessed he was seven years old, more or less. He had no family, and no memory of ever having had one. He had been left in the streets in the wake of a cholera epidemic, and he had somehow managed to live out his seven years in defiance of all the odds.

He knew all the alleyways, all the convolutions of the sewers, the places where food was left out for cats, and the houses where soft-hearted people might give him a handout. He had also encountered those who preyed on children. He had escaped those pleasure-merchants partly through luck and partly through the fact that the only attractive thing about him were his large, bright gray eyes.

His eyes, black-lashed and very clear, were set in a pinched brown face with a pointed chin, and they sat beneath quirky brows and a thatch of bleached brown hair that stood out in spikes because it was cut, when it was cut at all, with a knife. The eyes missed nothing and understood almost everything, and the wiry little body in which they were set was filled with the restless energy of having nothing to do and nowhere to go.

He could steal anything that could be lifted, from rags to food, and he was a master at swinging up on the backs of hackney coaches and riding all over Paris. His crowning triumph had been the time that he had jumped up behind a colonel of cavalry during a grand review and rode with him under the Arc de Triomphe before the sniggering of the troopers behind him had alerted the colonel to the fact that something was amiss.

He had spent the night in jail for that little escapade, but it had not troubled him: the jail was a roof over his head, and he had had enough to eat, an uncommon occurrence. He had trouble finding places to sleep. He generally preferred stables to anywhere else, but his luck finding accommodations did not match his luck in other matters.

He was always sneaking into the Opera—he liked the tragic operas—to the Ballet, and to various performances throughout the city. He was adept at squirming in through adults' legs and hiding under seats and behind pillars. He watched fireworks on holidays and saw soldiers drilling and dreamed of one day becoming a soldier, himself.

He liked to attend mass at the Cathedral, too. The music and the colors and the lights were magnificent, and they whirled him up and away, beyond the confines of his hungry, cold little life and into a vast place where no one was hungry, where everyone smiled, and where there never was any darkness.

He knew how to read and write, due to the kindness of an old priest in one of the poorer quarters. Père Louis had baptized him, though Larouche hadn't understood what had happened, and then had taught him in the hope of eventually coaxing the wild little boy into his home to live. He had almost succeeded, but he died before that could be done, and the boy, mourning him, had not come back.

The child had a vast capacity for love, but he was very cautious about the people whom he chose to love. He could count them on his fingers. The boy's one ambition was never to be hungry again, and he longed to have someone who would tuck him into a warm, soft bed, say his name, kiss him good night, and tell him a bedtime story.

The name was a very important part of the longing, for he had none. He was called 'Larouche' by those who knew of him, for what reason he couldn't guess. He answered to it for want of something better, but he longed for a real name. Nothing came of this yearning; people went on calling him Larouche, and he went on answering to the name.

Now he made his way back to M. Dracquet's house, simmering with annoyance. The anger faded after reflection: whatever had happened had been the fault of the police, not him. Dracquet had promised him five francs for holding that horse—he'd been a beauty, that one! —and five francs would buy a lot of food and even an almost new pair of shoes.

He came to Dracquet's house and rapped on the door of the servants' entrance. He was admitted and ushered into Dracquet's presence. Ten minutes later he was ushered out and shown through the door without the five francs.

"Don't come back!" said the junior footman and slammed the back door behind him.

Larouche looked up at the house, crooked his fingers in a rancidly obscene gesture that he should not have known, turned, and headed back to the heart of the city, his hands jammed into his ragged pockets and his mind seething with thoughts of revenge.

It wasn't his fault that the horse had been confiscated! He'd followed orders to the letter! It wasn't fair! Well, he'd fix Dracquet somehow! He'd fix him good! He would think of a way!

And as for that cop-! The big bastard! How dared he seize him, Larouche, by the ear? That tall police officer had wounded his pride, and he was really going to smart for it now! He had made it very obvious that he was the master in that situation. Well, Larouche would be the master, and he'd see how Monseigneur Cop liked it!

LAROUCHE MADE HIS WAY back to the Prefecture later that evening. The tall cop had come from there, and Larouche suspected that he was permanently assigned there. His clothing had been of good quality and well-tended, so he probably ranked fairly high. The man's watch chain had been an eye-catcher to one who was familiar with all types of 'turnips' and their chains.

He toyed with the idea of lifting the man's watch and then dismissed it. He had stolen food and rags, certainly, but those were necessities of life. He had never yet picked anyone's pocket, and he didn't really want to. Père Louis would not have approved. Besides, the man had been quick, very quick for a man his size. Larouche had no desire to be hauled off to prison for picking a cop's pocket.

He sat quietly in the shelter of a flower stall in the place des Fleurs and waited as the sky darkened above him, his eyes fixed on the archway that marked the front entrance to the Prefecture.

The lamplighters came along the street. Larouche watched as they unlocked the box that guarded the rope pulley, lowered the lamps from the posts, lit them, and then drew them back up to the cross-pieces. It took all of ten minutes, and they were laughing and chattering about a play being performed at the theater of the Port Saint-Martin that night. Larouche watched them from his shelter and then turned his attention back to the Prefecture.

No motion: Larouche frowned at the doorway. Monseigneur Cop had not come out yet, and it was getting very dark, though the lamps cast a warm glow along the street. The man would not go out the back, if Larouche was right about his probable seniority—

He broke off in the middle of his thoughts as the door opened and the tall cop came out. The man paused at the door, turned to make a smiling comment over his shoulder, and then stepped out into the clear September sunset. He moved straight past Larouche, toward a line of cabs.

Larouche stepped out of the booth and followed the cop at a distance, unhurried, intent, until he stepped up to a fiacre, gave directions, and then opened the door and went inside.

Larouche swore a rare oath, sprinted after the departing cab, and jumped up underneath the seat as the driver whipped up his horse and they went clattering off into the twilight.

Twenty minutes later the cop descended from the cab, paid the driver, took up his walking stick, and headed south.

Larouche looked around. They were near Montmartre; the lights of the city were spread below them to the left. He looked at the cop, who was walking along with a magnificently heedless grace, inclining his head to those who greeted him, ignoring the others.

Someone said, "Good evening, M. l'Inspecteur!"

The man answered, and Larouche whistled soundlessly. *An Inspector, eh?* he thought. *Well, well, well!*

He followed at a distance, watching the way the man walked, noticing where he turned his gaze. An arrogant man, he was convinced of it. It showed in the way he moved, in the way he held himself. Like most tall, strong men, he probably had an acute dislike of appearing ridiculous.

Well, he'd see about that! There were ways to even a score, and this was one that certainly needed to be evened. He had an idea…

The man had stopped walking now. He was quite alone, away from the other strollers, standing under a beech tree and looking toward the eastern horizon. The lights of Paris lay below them like a galaxy. The night sky glittered above them, and the two seemed to merge, until Larouche felt for one dizzy moment as though he had stepped off the earth and was gazing out into an infinity of stars. It was a magnificent view, and the man was leaning back against the tree and surveying the city as though he owned it.

Larouche smiled to himself. *Well, well, well*, he thought again. *We'll see about that!*

The man removed his hat, ran his fingers through his hair and then shook his head in the evening wind. Larouche caught the sense of a burden being set aside for the moment.

Larouche could see that he was tired. As he watched, the man drew a deep breath, held it a moment, and then released it. He relaxed against the tree and looked down at Paris again with a smile. He did not put his hat back on.

Larouche eyed the hat and grinned to himself.

He jammed his cold hands in his pockets, hunched his shoulders against the evening's chill, and descended the heights. He found a cab just departing, swung onto the back, and waved jauntily to a couple of strollers who had seen him and were pointing.

CHAPTER EIGHT

An Old Acquaintance

"WELL, AND IF IT ISN'T the Dauphin himself!" said Henri Lanusse with a gap-toothed grin the next morning. "Come on in!"

Malet smiled grimly and closed the door behind him. He was in the Conciergerie once more, in one of its miserably small cells, gazing upon the prisoner who stood before him with eyes that tallied the years' changes.

Lanusse looked him over with almost proprietary pride. "And how long has it been since anyone called you that?" he asked.

Malet's eyes flickered but he answered evenly as he turned Lanusse and untied the ropes about his wrists. "Since the month of January in the year 1803. Just before I left that accursed prison. There, you're free. Sit down."

"Thirty-two years, then," said Lanusse, rubbing his wrists. "Almost thirty-three. I remember how stunned we all were when Cheat-Death's hand-picked successor marched out of the prison gates, left everything behind—connections, gold, clothing—and went straight to the Prefect of Police for the Bouches-du-Rhone Departement and enrolled as a Constable."

"You were a pack of fools, then, if you were that astonished," said Malet. "I told Cheat-Death to his face just before I left that I would leave for good when I got free."

Lanusse shook his head. "The shock killed him untimely—"

Malet snorted. "The man was in his eighties," he said. "He had a full life of crime behind him."

"Untimely," said Lanusse. "He never recovered from it. I can remember him peering ahead of him like he was staring at a ghost and saying over and over again, 'Gone! Gone!' In that grating old croak of his."

Malet was unmoved. "He led a long, fruitful life of betrayal and murder," he said. "How many times did he tell me never to take anyone for granted? And yet he never thought to look askance at me."

"Maybe he loved you," said Lanusse.

Malet cocked a scornful eye at him. "He loved no one but himself, and nothing but power, and he hated everything else." he said. "He was smart enough to realize that he wouldn't live forever, and he wanted to pass his power on to one who could, he thought, cause society as much havoc and consternation in its use as he did. It pleased him to make use of me—nobly born, as he liked to think—to be his heir. I was a weapon that came readily to his hand, to be used against those he hated. A weapon that needed to be honed and balanced. That's all."

Lanusse was listening to him with his mouth half-open. "You always did talk like one of the poets, and you're doing it again," he said. "I couldn't understand you, but you always were grand to listen to."

Malet expression was suddenly rueful. "No," he said, "You never did understand. But it doesn't matter."

Lanusse looked Malet over again and said, "The Dauphin... Y'know, if he didn't love you, then why didn't he kill you after you left? He could have, you know."

Malet looked thoughtful for a moment, but he spoke over him. "I thought I'd look in on you and see what was happening," he said. "You're getting old now—"

"Not likely to get much older," said Lanusse. "Could it be you like me?"

Malet frowned. "Why should I feel any affection for you? "You're a blasted crook."

"A blasted crook who snuck you sweets," Lanusse said. "How could you forget? You used to like me a little, remember?"

"I remember," said Malet. "There wasn't much harm in you. You always were a gnat rather than a hornet. I read your statement to Sergeant Guillart: what possessed you to get involved in that foul piece of crime? You were almost free and clear of danger, and then to dirty your nose in this piece of folly at your age—!"

"I heard of easy pickings," said Lanusse. "I never knew of murder—" he broke off at Malet's snort.

"There are those," said Malet, "who take care not to hear what upsets them."

"I am one of 'em," said Lanusse. "I admit it. I never had much to recommend me, at any rate, but skill with the locks. I had a good pupil in you, as I recall! Well, let be, let be. I have got my cigars—"

"And a few more," said Malet, raising his hand to his pocket and taking out a packet wrapped in brown paper.

Lanusse took it with a grin. "Much obliged," he said. "It will make the time pass faster." He sat and clasped his hands over his stomach with an attempt at a smile.

Malet watched him in silence.

"I wish—" Lanusse began. "No," he said after a moment. "I won't say it. I know you, Dauphin. I watched you learn from the finest crooks in the world, and I watched you turn your back on them. I guess you did the best thing." He added, "I know you did the best thing."

"I did the only possible thing," said Malet.

"Maybe," said Lanusse. "If you could only—"

"If I could only what?"

Lanusse drew a deep, shaking breath. "See your way clear to giving me another chance," he said in a rush of words. "I don't want to die! I never hurt anyone! I-I thought it was just cutting in for some easy money! That was the only night I got involved in that. D'you think I'd have got involved in murder if I'd a' known? No sir! You know me! You were like one of my kids, a little! You know I'd never do that!" He looked piteously at Malet, who had remained as aloof and stern as a carved sphinx and fell silent.

"Do you think that I can set aside thirty years of duty for the sake of a few sweets given to a skinny little boy thirty-nine years ago?" Malet asked, but his voice had not hardened. "Is that why you gave me those sweets? Because you wished to ingratiate yourself with Cheat-Death's successor?"

Lanusse's moment of terror had passed. "I snuck you the treats because you were a skinny little kid," he said with dignity. "No other reason. Children die, and you might have died, too. How was I to know what I stood to lose or gain? You were all alone, except for that American sailor who took you under his wing."

He paused to think, which was almost a physical activity for him. "You know," he said, "They all beat their brains over why you turned, but I am thinking he was the reason. He became your papa, and he was a good 'un. He taught you the way to go. I remember now, how you were, learning the locks and such from me. Like you were learning how to use a weapon, not like an apprentice crook. When your papa died your heart was broke. I remember now, you standing all alone and looking out over the sea..."

He took out one of the cigars, accepted a match from Malet, lit the cigar, and sat back in a cloud of blue smoke. "Well," he said, "You turned, and here you are. So why're you here?"

"I am springing you," said Malet.

"What?" demanded Lanusse.

"You heard me," said Malet. "But there's a quid pro quo."

"What's the breakteeth words you're throwing at me?" Lanusse demanded. "Squid?"

Malet sat back and regarded the man. "It would be a terrible thing, Lanusse," he said, "if you were to awaken one day and find you'd grown to be as stupid as you are always pretending to be."

Lanusse looked hurt. "D'I deserve that?" he asked.

"You did," said Malet. "But to answer your question, it means it will cost you."

"Oh," said Lanusse. "What's the price?"

"I want you to tell me everything you know about a man I am going after."

"Whatever you say, Dauphin!" Lanusse said, beaming.

"His name is Constant Dracquet," said Malet.

Lanusse's eyes widened. "You're going to tangle with him?" he demanded. When Malet nodded, he said, "Whew! I don't envy anyone nearby when you come to blows!"

Malet smiled grimly and said nothing.

"By God!" said Lanusse after a minute's wide-eyed thought, "Dracquet's finally coming head-to-head with the one who can fettle him, and at a time when he's puffed bigger'n a pouter pigeon with ideas and dreams! Shit!" He drew on his cigar, blew out a cloud of smoke, and sat back. "He's had it coming," he said. "And I will be on the side of the angels at last! Get out your notebook and start writing, Dauphin! I got a lot to tell you! Mind you, it's all what some fancy lawyer called hearsay at a trial I was at, but you're welcome to it!"

LANUSSE SPOKE AT SOME length while Malet wrote in his notebook. When he was finished, Malet set his gold pencil back in the notebook, bestowed both in his breast pocket, and looked Lanusse over with a calm, measuring eye.

"And there's one other thing," he said.

"Anything, Dauphin," said Lanusse.

"That you clear out of Paris. And you go straight."

Go straight. Lanusse shrugged. He had been wanting to do just that for years, but things had always prevented him. Maybe now he would be able to if he didn't let himself get lazy. "Well, Dauphin," he said. "I will try. But I still don't understand why you're doing this for me."

Malet lifted his eyebrows, and Lanusse saw just for a moment, remote and dim, those same eyes, wet with tears, set in a younger face. It had been on the battlements of Toulon prison, overlooking the sea.

Never mind, lad, Lanusse had said then, his arm flung awkwardly around the shoulders of a fourteen-year-old boy who had been gazing out at the ocean. *Never mind. He's beyond hurt now, and God's welcoming him home. You can remember the things he taught you, they're still with you. And you haven't lost him, he will always be there, inside you, when you need him.*

The boy had turned against his shoulder and wept with the racking pain of utter heartbreak. For a moment it had been like comforting a nearly grown tiger cub before the boy had reared back and pushed away.

But Lanusse remembered, and so, he saw, did the man that the heartbroken boy had grown into.

"Just so you try, Lanusse. I will put in the words to make your path smooth. I don't—" he paused, his brows drawn together. He took a long breath and spoke again. "I don't want you to die in prison. I want you to die comfortably in your bed of old age, and I am giving you a chance to do just that."

"Thank you, lad," Lanusse said. "I won't disappoint you. And is there anything else?"

"Just this. I am embarking on a war. Tell your cronies to clear out of my way—"

"A war?"

"A war," Malet repeated. "I want room to fight, and anyone who steps on my toes won't have enough left of him to weep over when I am through with him. Spread the word."

Lanusse was suddenly serious. "I hear you clear as a bell, Inspector," he said.

CHAPTER NINE

The Ambuscade

Larouche spent the night burrowed into the hayloft of a livery stable not far from the Jardin des Plantes. He arose early the next morning, begged a stale roll from a street hawker by the Pont d'Austerlitz, ate it, and then gathered a handful of stones. He went back to the Jardin des Plantes to practice his throwing, to the distress of the park's large population of fat pigeons. When he was satisfied that he was in practice, he hurried to the Prefecture to wait for the man he was now referring to in his mind as 'Monseigneur Inspector'.

The man had still not arrived there after three hours, and Larouche was getting annoyed. Had he been mistaken about the man's rank and assignment? He frowned and looked at the rock in his hand. It was possible. What was he to do? He pondered the question. That cop needed to be taught a lesson by Larouche, but finding him might well be impossible.

Or maybe not. He had several plans that might work. Cops like him did not vanish without a trace. He could be found.

He looked up at the facade of the Prefecture just as the door opened and the man came out of the building.

Larouche swore. What time did he arrive there, then? Six in the morning? Well, it made no difference: there he was, and Larouche and his rocks were waiting. He lifted the one in his hand, took careful aim and stopped. Only a fool assaulted a cop in his own territory!

He tucked the rock in his pocket and set out after the man, who had hailed one of the line of cabs that was always before the building. Larouche jumped on the back and rode along through the city, clutching his shirtful of rocks and thinking vengeful thoughts.

They crossed the Seine at the Pont au Change, followed the rue St.

Denis briefly to the rue des Halles, and then caught the rue Montmartre, which they followed until it reached the church of Notre Dame de Lorette. North of the church they turned right to the rue des Martyrs, which they followed into the 3rd arrondissement. Larouche, peering forward, could see the butte of Montmartre towering ahead of them.

The fiacre came to a halt outside an inn whose sign named it the Rose d'Or. It was close to Dracquet's house; Larouche had been there once or twice to beg a hand-out. The people there were generous. It was a favorite haunt of the teamsters and workmen, and one of the owners, a pretty, dark-eyed woman, always had a treat for him. The younger cop from the day before lived there. That was about all Larouche knew of the place, and he wondered why 'Monseigneur' had decided to go there.

He shrugged, selected a comfortable perch in the nearest tree, and disposed himself to watch. There would be plenty of time to nab Monseigneur Inspector, and this was a good area in which to do it. His pride would be in rags before Larouche was through with him. He selected a nice, hefty stone and waited, smiling...

CHAPTER TEN

The Rose d'Or Receives a Visitor

The Rose d'Or was a neat establishment, built on the site of another inn that had been destroyed by fire in 1693 when Montmartre was still a little village safely outside Paris. It was a rambling stone building, several stories high, with a gabled roof. The inn proper bordered a cloistered, shaded courtyard edged with beds of roses and chrysanthemums. A good-sized stable with a walled, cobblestoned yard opened onto the street.

"Well, he's gone, Brutus," said Elise de Clichy, who owned the inn. She was speaking to the large, black gelding tethered to a ring in the stableyard. The horse was a particular pet. He delicately thrust his muzzle against her chin, begging a kiss. She complied with a faraway smile. "I suppose I will miss him." She shook herself slightly, smoothed Brutus' soft nose, and went back into the inn.

Elise had been surprised when Charles de Saint-Légère had told her the night before that he was being transferred to the mounted gendarmerie at the Bois de Boulogne for an unspecified length of time, and that he would be leaving early the next morning. She suspected that the transfer had something to do with the sudden, unexplainable interest that a man named Constant Dracquet had taken in Saint-Légère, and the appearance of that magnificent bay stallion over a week before.

Saint-Légère had mentioned, as well, that another Police officer would be coming to lodge at the Rose d'Or in his place. Elise had found that interesting. Something odd was afoot: the Paris Police had had nothing to do with Charles de Saint-Légère's arrangement with the Rose d'Or.

She had not troubled Saint-Légère with her speculations, but refused an urgent offer of marriage, the tenth Saint-Légère had made in the year since he had come to live there. She had Claude, the older of the two men who helped at the inn, escort him to a coach. She had pressed a packed lunch on him, containing several of her sugar cakes, made him promise to write, and then went back into the inn.

He would be coming back, so it was useless to mope. She had an inn to run, and the morning rush was coming.

Still... She paused to gaze out the door one last time. She was fond of Saint-Légère, and she was honest enough with herself to admit that her feeling for him was a little deeper than mere fondness. It was best to wait and see. He would be back.

Elise had known suffering in her life, even though she had not yet reached her twenty-ninth year. She had known love and disappointment and grief. They had almost driven her mad, and in the end she, born a lady, had turned her back on the glittering world of the faubourg St. Germain and become an innkeeper. She did not have time to brood over the past, and she could indulge her passion for sheltering strays and lost souls.

Charles de Saint-Légère was neither of these. He had originally come to the Rose d'Or upon his return to France in 1832 when Christien L'Eveque, Elise's close cousin and dear friend, had told him that the landlady brewed the finest English style ale in Paris. She did: it had been the best he had ever tasted, and he had told her so. Their conversation had been an interesting one, and when it was finished, he was one of the inn's employees, rooming there at a reduced rate in exchange for his services as a sort of watchman.

Elise knew she would miss him, but she could sort out her emotions while he was gone. She smiled, closed the door, and went back into the inn.

Later, as she was preparing a batch of gingerbread, Yvette, her co-owner, came to her with the news that a gentleman had called at the inn and was asking to speak with her personally. He was in the small salon. 'Lise had best watch her step: he didn't seem one to trifle with.

Elise laughed at Yvette as she untied her apron, and said, "When have I ever tried to 'trifle' with our customers, Yvette? You should know better. Did you invite him to sit down?"

"I drew a chair forward for him, but he only nodded to me and went to the window," Yvette said, shivering a little. "Be careful, Elise! He's armed!"

"Haven't you looked at some of our customers? They're all armed!" She set her apron aside and went to the small salon.

She paused outside the room. A medium-crowned hat, a pair of gloves and a fine, silver-topped walking stick were lying neatly on the table outside the room. They were of excellent quality, to her mind hardly the sort of items that a terribly dangerous man might purchase and wear.

She opened the door and stepped into the salon.

A tall, broad-shouldered man was standing by the fireplace, one foot propped on the forepaw of the dog-shaped andiron, his hands loosely clasped behind him. He was looking thoughtfully out the window, but he turned as she opened the door, and directed a slightly frowning gaze at her.

His hair was thick, dark, and graying, and his eyes were a very light brown, almost green, set under straight, dark brows. They seemed to see everything about her, from her overall appearance to the smudge of ginger-bread batter on her wrist.

The scrutiny did not unsettle Elise. She had encountered his kind be-fore. This man wore a light, straight sword: he was probably the Police Officer Saint-Légère had mentioned, though differing from the ones to which Elise was accustomed as an eagle differs from a kestrel.

She met his gaze without embarrassment and started to greet him, but before she could speak he unclasped his hands, inclined his head, and bowed to her. She had been judged a lady; the unexpected courtliness of the gesture disarmed her.

She smiled at him and held out her hand. "I am Elise de Clichy, Monsieur," she said. "I was told you wished to speak with me."

He bowed over her hand and returned her smile with some warmth. His smile was pleasant: it softened the clear lines of a face that had the calm aloofness of a statue without it.

"Yes, Madame de Clichy," he said. "I do. My name is Paul Malet. I spoke yesterday with Charles de Saint-Légère, who lives here. I will be handling a matter that he brought to my attention. I can't go into it in any great detail, but I believe he has discussed it with you." His gaze was very direct.

"He has, indeed. He hasn't confided in anyone else." She added, "I assure you that you can trust my discretion in this and other matters."

"So I have been told by several people including your cousin, Christien L'Eveque," Malet said. "For various reasons, all of them urgent, it will be necessary for me to live here while I pursue this matter. In view of all that he has told me, I thought to hire a room here for, say, three weeks at the least. Will that be possible?"

Elise had heard of Chief Inspector Malet over the years, but she had expected a man quite different from the one who faced her, someone a little more coarse, with more swagger. This man was undeniably a gentleman. His accent interested her as well: he was not a native Parisian. The final 'E', usually silent, was lightly voiced. It was a regional trait from the south of France. She found it charming.

He was waiting for an answer. She tallied her guests and consulted a mental map of the inn.

He misunderstood her hesitation. "I can provide references if you need them, Madame," he said. "Inspector L'Eveque has been acquainted with me these seven years."

She did not have to consider. "Christien has spoken of you with admiration and affection, M. Malet," she said. "And so I don't think that will be necessary in your case. I might start requesting them in future, however."

"It's no trouble," he said with a touch of insistence that she found amusing.

"But not necessary," she repeated, favoring him with her best smile and reflecting on the relative stubbornness of the Police as a group.

They traded looks for half a minute, and then he shrugged. "As you wish," he said, "But you can never tell who might be a murderer or a thief."

She began to chuckle. "Pardon my speaking so, M'sieur," she said, "But while I thank you for the lecture, it is unnecessary. And as for any danger from you: it's obvious to me at least that murdering me or robbing me is the farthest thing from your mind. Yes, I know you're armed, but so am I." She took out her pocket pistol and showed it to him.

Inspector Malet watched her with amused approval. "Ah," he said. "A 'ladies' special'. I see you keep it primed. May I see it?" He held out his hand. It was well tended, with strong, shapely fingers.

She handed the gun over to him.

He examined it closely and finished by looking down the barrel. "Rifled?" he said. "Hm. And I can tell it's seen some use. Here—" he gave it back to her and added, "You are wise to carry another as a back-up, but I'd suggest a better hiding place than your pocket: how about under your apron, or up your sleeve?"

"How did you know?" she demanded as she replaced the pistol in her pocket.

Malet shrugged. "You notice these things after a while," he said. "Now: if you have no objection to letting the rooms to me, we can discuss payment."

"If it's official Police business, I can be reimbursed by the Departement," Elise said.

Inspector Malet shook his head. "The Departement takes its own sweet time in matters of reimbursement, as I know to my cost," he said. "I will pay you myself, obtain a receipt, and submit it with my report when it's finished. They'll move a little more swiftly for me than for you, I think."

"You are most thoughtful, Monsieur," Elise said as she went to the door and then stood aside as he opened it for her. "Would you like to look over the available rooms?" she asked.

"If I may. If they overlook the street, so much the better."

Elise paused and considered. "M. de Saint-Légère's rooms do," she said. "The guest rooms face out over the courtyard: they are quieter that way. The people who actually live here—myself, M. de Saint-Légère, Mlle. Franchotte, who is also an owner—you met her, sir—Claude and Alcide, our two men, and the other servants—have rooms overlooking the street. The courtyard is pretty at this time of year. You would enjoy the view."

Chief Inspector Malet was frowning thoughtfully. "The view is not a prime consideration at the moment," he said.

"You could take M. de Saint-Légère's rooms while he's away at the Bois de Boulogne," she said. "I am sure he wouldn't mind."

Malet's eyes suddenly narrowed. He said, "Let me see them." He paused, remembered his manners, and added, "Please." For a moment he sounded a little like a contrite schoolboy, an odd effect for a man of his height.

Elise chuckled again and said, "This way, then, M'sieur," and started down the hall. He moved very quietly; she had to look behind her to see if he was following.

CHAPTER ELEVEN

Malet Engages a Room

"Good God! Is there something wrong with putting all one's books and papers in the same place?" Malet demanded, scowling around at the room. They were in the small parlor adjoining Saint-Légère's bedroom. "And shoes, too! How many pairs does he have?"

"He's an unmarried man. You must make allowances."

Inspector Malet snorted. "By that token, then, I should start flinging my shoes and papers about!" he said. He stepped over a pile of outdated newspapers as he went to the window. He paused to stare at the pile. "How fortunate that he doesn't smoke!" he commented. "This place is a firetrap! Is he saving these for some reason?"

Elise did not think an answer was required. It was just as well, since she was having trouble restraining her laughter. She busied herself with gathering Saint-Légère's papers and setting them to one side.

He snorted again and turned his attention to the street. "Excellent," he said. "I will take this room. Can you have your men move Saint-Légère's belongings into another? The clothespress shouldn't be hard to manage. I will pay for the hire of two rooms."

Elise caught sight of Saint-Légère's pipe across the room and started toward it, hoping to hide it before Malet's eyes lit on it. "That won't be necessary," she said.

Malet was still looking out the window. "Yes, it will," he said. His tone admitted no argument.

"Very well," she said. "When will you move in?"

Inspector Malet turned back from the window. "Tonight, I think," he said after some thought. "That is, if it's quite convenient."

Elise's way to the pipe was blocked by a pile of books. She tried to step around them and bit off a cry as they began to teeter.

Malet saw this and went toward them with the obvious intent of moving them aside for her. "That'll give me time to settle matters with my housekeeper," he said, adroitly managing to avoid knocking anything over with his sword. "If you need me before then, you can send to the Prefecture. I will be there for the next several weeks."

He skirted the pile of newspapers and was brought up short by the sight of the pipe and matches.

His brows drove together as he lifted the pipe between his thumb and forefinger. "Good God!" he said. "He does smoke! Why hasn't this inn gone up in flames?"

"Well, M'sieur," Elise said, "he may not be the neatest man who ever lived, but he's careful. I have had no complaints about him in the year he's lived here. I wish my other guests were as considerate. But I promise that this will all be cleaned up before you arrive tonight."

She gently took the pipe from Malet's fingers and smothered another chuckle at his expression. He was obviously not used to having things whisked out of his hands.

He submitted with fairly good grace, however, merely lifting an eyebrow and watching as she set the pipe in her pocket. "Is it quite cold?" he asked. "I'd hate to have that set off your pistol."

Elise succumbed to her laughter at last. "It's fine," she said. "I will write up a receipt for the two rooms now—by the way, we have a small room that's barely more than a closet, and I will move M. de Saint-Légère's belongings there. It's not as expensive as a regular bedroom—five sous a day—and that should save the city some money."

"Very good," Malet said. He took two folded, sealed documents from the inner pocket of his coat and handed them to her. "Here are two items for you," he said. "The first—" he tapped it, "—is a directive from the acting Prefect of Police commanding that Junior Inspector Paul de Colbert be stationed at the Rose d'Or pending further notice—"

"De Colbert?" Elise repeated.

"At your service," Malet said with the hint of a bow. "The presence of a Chief Inspector at your inn is almost certain to cause comment, especially since the one in question is filling in for the Prefect at the moment. De

Colbert is a family name of sorts—" his mouth tilted oddly for a moment, "—and I have used it before on assignments requiring some measure of secrecy. It's possible that someone might interest himself in my presence here and try to read the orders. I will sign in as Paul de Colbert when I arrive." He added, "The second is an authorization for me to lodge here and be reimbursed for my expenses."

Elise opened the two documents and scanned them. "Don't you think the person who might try to read these will be piqued by the fact that the handwriting of the acting Prefect matches that of this Junior Inspector de Colbert?" she asked.

"He might," Malet agreed with sudden, almost startled, respect. "That's why the order was written out and signed by the chief archivist of the Police, and not by me. Do you find them in order?"

"Of course I do," Elise replied. "I am happy to be of service. And I do believe you will enjoy your stay here. I know M. de Saint-Légère did, at least until recently." She hesitated, then said, "I am certain that M. de Saint-Légère mentioned Constant Dracquet—"

Malet grew very still.

Elise continued without looking up. "I do know something of the—the matter that brings you here," she said. "And I am familiar with the man's reputation. Christien has confided in me from time to time. M. Dracquet doesn't live far from here, and his men have recently made it their practice to come here for drinks or food. Do you wish for me to keep track of their names and activities while they are here?"

Malet considered for a moment. "Yes," he said at last. "But don't be obvious. In fact, if it becomes too difficult, I would prefer that you do not."

"Very well," she said, and turned the talk to his projected stay. When arrangements had been made to their mutual satisfaction they descended to the public rooms and drank a glass of lemonade, which Elise insisted on providing 'on the house'.

Chief Inspector Malet departed after about a half hour, most likely heading back toward the Prefecture. Elise saw him to the door, wished him a pleasant afternoon, and softly closed the door behind him.

She turned to find Yvette watching her, round-eyed and nervous.

"Well?" said Yvette.

"Well?" Elise repeated.

"Was he unpleasant?" Yvette asked.

Elise considered. "Not at all," she said. "He's a gentleman. A charming one, in fact, and quite harmless, at least toward us."

"I don't know..." Yvette said. "He had a sword."

"He's an officer of the Police," Elise said, pouring herself another glass of lemonade and motioning Yvette to sit down. "Of course he wears a sword. And he will be staying with us on the orders of the Prefect, so you may as well learn to enjoy his company."

INSPECTOR MALET PAUSED in the stableyard and looked around at the Rose d'Or as he pulled on his gloves. He nodded to himself after a moment. The inn would do very well, indeed, and far better than he had hoped. It was a fine establishment, and the two owners certainly appeared to be ladies of character and quality, though the tall blonde one who had squeaked and stared at his sword was a little too skittish for his taste.

He had not expected squalor, certainly, but the size and quality of the inn had been a pleasant surprise, as well as the perception and intelligence of its senior proprietress. He would enjoy his stay there.

He looked around at the neat, well-tended houses with flowerboxes at the windows. Very nice, indeed! His eyes moved from the faces of the passers-by to the beds of late roses along the street and the window-boxes of the inn. He loved flowers—the garden in his house in the Marais was celebrated for its beauty—and he liked roses, especially the deep, almost wine-colored ones. If he had been at his own house, he would have picked one for the bud vase on his desk. Since these were not his, he left them alone.

He donned his hat, stepped out onto the street, and set off at a brisk walk, intending to head northwest, back toward the Prefecture.

He considered twirling his walking stick. It was a magnificent fall day, he was in his usual splendid health, they were closing in on that group of vicious slash-killers and, best of all, he had miraculously been given another chance to nail Constant Dracquet.

He decided against it. Cane-twirling was appropriate for the Champs

Elysees, but not a street in middle-class Paris. Besides, it was not dignified–

On the heels of that thought, like a defiant jeer, came a dark blur from the left, a blow, the sudden feel of wind in his hair, and the clatter of his hat against the pavement.

Someone had thrown a stone and knocked his hat off.

It took him a moment to understand what had happened. He stared at the hat, bent and picked it up, and stared at it again.

Someone had thrown a stone and knocked his hat off!

No one had ever done anything like that to him before! People had stopped and were laughing at him. It was worse than being shot at!

"Damnation!" he hissed, looking intently toward the left as he set the hat back on his head.

It was on the pavement again a moment later. This time the stone had come from the right.

He waited some minutes before replacing it. Nothing happened. He took a deep breath, released it, and started walking again. A second later the hat was on the ground again.

"Best give it up, Captain!" someone called as Malet retrieved the hat for the third time.

"You're right," Malet growled, and set off toward the Prefecture, feeling an unaccustomed itch between his shoulder-blades at the thought that the next stone might hit him on the back of the head. It was almost infuriating when no more came.

After another block he hailed a cab and gave directions to the Prefecture. Once inside, he replaced his hat.

LAROUCHE WATCHED HIM, grinning, and then turned away toward the Rose d'Or. They gave generous hand-outs there, as he recalled. He was not disappointed.

CHAPTER TWELVE

The Provisional Prefect of Paris

The bluish lips were drawn convulsively back over protruding teeth in a grotesque rictus as the clouded eyes glared upward into nothingness. The past evening's rain had drenched the hair and over the night it had frozen to a cap of ice. The room was very cold, although it was past noon. The hair was only now beginning to thaw and relax into ringlets.

Chief Inspector Malet frowned thoughtfully down into the staring eyes and then lower still to the arms, lying stiffly alongside the torso. Something in their position made his frown deepen, and he bent to look at the elbows. He nodded and straightened after a moment. The man would be delivering no more bottles of champagne.

"The rigor is still well established," he said. "There's no sign of it passing. This one was probably breathing his last about the time I was eating yesterday's supper. Not a good supper, unfortunately, but I don't doubt he'd have been glad to trade places with me." He spoke thoughtfully, with no hint of a smile.

It was hard to tell if the Chief Inspector was joking, so the man beside him, Inspector Layard of the rue du Bac precinct, temporized by making a noise that lay between clearing his throat and laughing.

Malet flashed him a glance.

Layard straightened. "Suicide, do you think, Chief Inspector?" he asked. "He definitely died from hanging. There's the rope, you can see the marks on his neck from hanging—and you can see that his hands are free."

"You say he was found at the Pont Royal?"

"That's right, monsieur."

Malet nodded. He looked down at the livid face and then eyed the coarse hemp rope around the neck. "There are no splinters in his fingertips," he said. "And yet this is a very rough rope."

"But he's a suicide!" Layard objected. "He wanted to die."

"Most of them change their minds halfway through and start clawing," said Malet. "Of course—" he shot a sudden, uncomfortably keen look at Layard, "—he could have gotten the splinters while knotting the rope."

"Well?" said Layard.

Malet raised his eyes to the man's face. "Oh I have no objection to a verdict of suicide," he said. "Provided, of course, that you can explain to my satisfaction the fact that his arms were tied."

Layard had been on the force ten years, but this was the first time he had had to report at the morgue in the Île de France square, east of the cathedral, to review a corpse found in his bailiwick. He had heard that Chief Inspector Malet was a stickler, and now he believed it.

"What?" he demanded. "I saw no marks on his wrists!"

"Here," said Malet as he lifted the corpse's arm. The body was still in the grip of rigor mortis; the arm moved stiffly. "If you look carefully," he said, "you will see a line of bruising on the inside of his elbow. His arms were looped together behind him with a thin cord, from what I can tell. Very effective, and it doesn't mark the wrists."

"But who—"

"That, my lad, is for you to find out," said Malet with a smile. "It may be easier than you thought: this fellow has the look of a tough about him, and if you ask among the dockworkers, or whores, or other such, you may find what you need to know."

Malet glanced at the young man's expression and continued, "Also, this particular hanging has the look of an execution about it. I have seen this man before, and he was very nervous then..." He remembered the man's behavior in the cathedral, and his own last words to him. Perhaps the man had decided to seek a better master, after all. He had lost his life for it—and gained his soul. *I would have advised it even so,* he thought.

Malet looked up at Inspector Layard and continued, "Keep the office of the Prefect advised on the progress of the case."

He pulled on his gloves and swept a glance round at the rows of corpses laid on their tables, and said almost off-handedly, "We have had quite a haul today, especially that slashing victim. That's the eighth, and the newspapers have gotten wind of them. Let's hope we are not so lucky tomorrow. Gentlemen— "He nodded to the others in the room and went to the door.

Layard watched as the Chief Inspector moved away. He reflected glumly on the meaning of the word 'stickler'—and then forgot his reflections as Malet turned and smiled warmly at him.

"And by the way, M. Layard," said Malet, "You did an excellent job noting all the details when the body was found, and then following up by taking measurements. Not enough people do that. You will find it invaluable in your investigation. Good day."

Layard, suddenly aware of the respectful gazes of the constables around him, was filled with the warm feeling that he had just been publicly honored. He watched Malet pass between the silent rows of corpses and out of the cold room; as the man turned he smiled and raised his hand in a half-salute.

MALET LEFT THE ICY rooms of the morgue and stepped out into sun-drenched. Corpses had long ago ceased to bother him, but he was always glad to leave the morgue. He paused just outside the doorway to don his hat and gaze westward at the apse of the cathedral. The worn, shabby stones seemed to glow in the golden mid-afternoon sun.

"And was there anything noteworthy, M. l'Inspecteur?" asked a voice to his right.

Malet frowned slightly and looked over at a man who had come up beside him. "Nothing out of the ordinary, M. Franck," he said with thinly veiled distaste. Franck was a lead writer for *Le Moniteur*, a press organ that Malet considered only slightly above a scandal sheet. "A collection of corpses in varying stages of decay."

"And—?"

"And nothing else," Malet said briskly as he headed toward the rue du Cloître Notre-Dame. He accorded a cold nod to the man and started to push his way through the crowd of beggars and thrill-seekers who jammed the square outside the morgue.

Franck stepped directly in front of Malet.

"You're blocking my path," said Malet.

"Come now, Inspector," said Franck. "I hear there's another slash victim in there. Is it true?"

Malet tried to step around the man, but Franck followed him.

"Another slash victim," said Franck. "That makes how many in the past two months? Eight? Nine? Was this one tortured to death like the others?"

Malet stopped, looked Franck up and down and said, "I believe I have been courteous with you up to now, and it has given me no results. Will you stand aside, or must I resort to stronger methods?"

Franck moved out of Malet's way with a half-smile, then fell in beside him. "You have never given the press any cooperation," he said. "I don't understand why. We keep the public informed, that's all. We can be a very dangerous enemy—"

Malet halted and turned to face him. "So can I. Are you threatening me, M. Franck?"

"Not at all," said Franck with a smile. "I only seek to discover why you despise us."

"I don't despise the press," said Malet with frosty cordiality. "I simply have a distaste for those who, sitting in a sewer, feel the need to add to it."

"Indeed!" said Franck, who appeared to be torn between his personal indignation at the insult and his professional appreciation of a well-turned phrase.

"Indeed," said Malet.

"In return for that gratuitous insult, M. Malet," said Franck, "I should think you would at least grant me leave to view the corpses."

Malet considered for a moment and then reached into the breast of his coat and took out a notebook. He opened it, took out a gold pencil from his pocket, wrote swiftly, and then tore out the page and handed it to the man.

"Give this to the guard at the door," he said. "Tell him to show you number eight first."

Franck took the note in astonished silence and watched as Malet turned and continued on toward the Prefecture.

Malet was smiling to himself as he strolled down the boulevard du Palais. Number eight was a 'floater' that had been pulled from the Seine the evening before. It had been dead for so long that the fatty tissues had turned to dark brown corpse-wax, and the features were distorted to a nightmare's rendition of a human face. There was no stench, but the river scavengers had eaten away great chunks of flesh. M. Franck was in for an unforgettable afternoon if Malet was any judge of people.

There might be some repercussions from his sojourn in the morgue. Malet considered for a moment and then shrugged. Or maybe not. If all went according to plan, there would be no more slash-victims after another day or so. The trap was nearly read to be sprung; it only required the right day.

He dismissed Franck after a moment and turned his thoughts to the afternoon's activities. He had a campaign to plan, one he had been wanting to pursue for years, and he was looking forward to it. And it would be nice to be able to give a figurative black eye to Chief Inspector Guerin of the 3rd arrondissement.

Guerin had been the ranking Chief Inspector in Paris up until Malet's arrival from Picardy. Malet had been placed in a position senior to Guerin, and the man had taken that fact, coupled with Malet's illegitimate birth and prison upbringing, as an insuperable insult. Their dealings had always been cold.

Guerin had rebuffed all Malet's attempts to secure his collaboration in pursuing Constant Dracquet. He had done it in such a way that Malet had begun to wonder if Guerin's refusal might perhaps be triggered by more than mere personal dislike.

But things were just a little different now. A strong lead against Dracquet had come at a time when he had all the power and latitude of the position of Prefect at his disposal. And—only conceive of it! —the matter in question, an ethics problem, was one that could properly be handled only by the Prefect of Police or his stand-in.

For Malet, filling in for The Prefect, although technically a great honor, was normally tedious. He theoretically enjoyed without reservation all the Prefect's rights, privileges and powers throughout the Île de France during such times, but, mindful of the folly of abusing such power, he usually carried out his duties with diplomacy and restraint.

It would be different this time. He had a criminal to catch, he knew just how to go about it, and no one was going to stop him.

CHAPTER THIRTEEN

Warping the Loom

Malet presented his card and signed in at the Prefecture. Once passed, he strode down the main aisle of the anteroom toward the offices of the Prefect, pausing along the way to speak to Jacques Guillart, the Chief Archivist of the Prefecture.

"Will you be able to obtain what I requested this morning?" Malet asked.

Sergeant Guillart transferred his smile from the paper he was filling with a neat, elegant script to Malet's face. "I was able to obtain part of it, sir," he said. "I placed the collection of Inspector de Saint-Légère's reports on your desk. I did weed out some that were completely banal, the report of the mysterious disappearance of a shoe, for example, but I gave you a fair sample of his work. I think you will find it interesting. I always enjoy reading his reports."

"Very good," said Malet. "And what of the rest?"

Guillart lowered his voice. "As far as Dracquet goes," he said, "That'll take a little time. I have flagged some information that I think will come readily to hand, but it will take a while to dig through the archives and pull out everything that refers to him. Do you have any parameters for me to work in?"

Malet considered and finally nodded. "Yes," he said. "I don't want ancient history. Go back no further than five years. And I want to see only the most believable connections."

Guillart nodded. "Just as I thought," he said. "I will get on it right away."

"Thank you," said Malet. He doffed his hat and, pausing, said, "And Guillart?"

"Yes, Chief Inspector?"

"Please handle this by yourself. It's extremely important."

"That goes without saying," said Sergeant Guillart.

Malet's thoughtful frown suddenly gave way to a smile. "You're an excellent fellow, my dear Guillart!" he said. "We would be lost without you!"

Guillart laughed and shook his head as Malet went on back toward the Prefect's offices.

The Chamberlain, Geraud Clerel, intercepted him halfway back, as was his habit, and escorted him to the doors of his office, giving him along the way a summation of the visitors who had come by while Malet was busy at the morgue. He was a portly man of portentous demeanor, proud of his gentlemanly appearance and prouder of the prestige attending the office of Prefect of Police.

Malet heard him out, returned his bow with an inclination of his head, and allowed the man to help him doff his coat. He listened courteously as Clerel said, his fingers smoothing the fine cashmere cloth of the coat, "Monsieur should be aware that there is a gang of footpads presently abroad in the city who make it their business to wrest the overcoats from solitary gentlemen."

"Do you feel my coat is in danger, then, sir?"

Since Malet had said this without smiling, Clerel took the question seriously. "Any fine garments are in jeopardy, M. l'Inspecteur," he said.

"Ah!" said Malet. "Then, my dear Clerel perhaps I would do well to dress from the gleanings of the ragpickers. And it might be wise for you to do so as well."

Clerel settled the overcoat across his arm. You need not take so drastic a step, I assure you, M. l'Inspecteur en Chef! And I can't conceive that such creatures would have the temerity to attack Me. I pursue a path governed by prudence, and never venture out when it is inadvisable."

"Very wise. I am persuaded that there is much you could teach us all, were we only willing to pay proper attention."

Clerel, who would have found it hard to believe that he could be an object of satire, nodded and replied, "I would be willing to impart any knowledge that might benefit the Force, as Monsieur is well aware."

"You're an ornament to your calling," Malet said as he drew out the chair behind the Prefect's desk, flipped his coattails aside, and sat.

He took out his notebook, opened it to his latest notations, and then froze as Clerel said, "And I must advise the Chief Inspector that His Excellency, the Minister of Police, called today to—"

"What?"

Clerel looked reproachfully at Malet, who had never interrupted him before. "—to offer the invitation to partake of a nuncheon tomorrow," he finished with a bow. "Does the Chief Inspector wish me to bear a reply to His Excellency?"

Malet's lips twitched, but he inclined his head regally and said, "Your kindness in so doing, M. Clerel, would be greatly appreciated." He paused for effect and then added, as he took up a pen, "And M. le Comte will doubtless recognize the compliment implicit in sending yourself as a messenger."

"Then I shall depart at once," Clerel said with another bow.

"But avoid the coat-snatchers," Malet said gravely.

"Indeed, I shall summon a hackney," said Clerel.

"Very prudent of you," said Malet. "How shocking it would be for Madame la Comtesse to be confronted with a naked man not of her acquaintance! And how uncomfortable for you!" He lifted a demure countenance to Clerel's suddenly suspicious regard and then watched as the man bowed once more and made his majestic way out of the office.

Malet waited until the door was firmly closed before indulging in a quiet spell of laughter. Filling in for the Prefect had its compensations, and one of them was Geraud Clerel.

Another, and more dangerous, compensation was the power of the position itself. Malet, a thoroughgoing autocrat, had no illusions concerning the seductive nature of power. He kept a strict accounting of himself. In this case, however, he thought, scanning his notebook, he would be justified in using it.

He went down his list of items to consider in pursuing Constant Dracquet. He had already requested the search of the Police archives. Guillart had that well in hand—and he would have the man's house shadowed around the clock. He had decided it would be unwise to use men from the 3rd arrondissement, especially in view of his suspicions concerning Chief Inspector Guerin.

Charles de Saint-Légère had said a few things that had confirmed Malet's suspicions regarding the relationship between Chief Inspector Guerin and Constant Dracquet. It would be interesting to see how Dracquet would handle another Police officer living within eight blocks of his house.

Should he consider contacting the Criminal Investigations division, known as the Sureté, for assistance?

Malet sat back to think. It was not a question that he wanted to consider. He and the Sureté, and its director, Vidocq, got along with all the cordiality of two cats meeting in a gutter.

Francois Eugene Vidocq had been the first to formulate the idea that it takes a thief to catch a thief, and he put it into successful practice. The Sureté of that time was peopled by ex-criminals of dubious present honesty. Shortly after Malet's arrival in Paris from Picardy, his skill at fighting criminals with their own weapons had drawn Vidocq's attention.

Malet's successes over the next two years had intrigued Vidocq. He made inquiries into Malet's background and then approached Count d'Anglars with the request that Chief Inspector Malet be transferred to the Sureté, where his unprecedented talents could be more successfully used in undercover work.

The Parisian Prefect of Police, Valery Lamarque, had been a little bitter, since Vidocq had tapped several of his most promising officers, but he was genuinely fond of Malet and wanted him to be successful. He had endorsed the proposed transfer and promotion and accompanied Malet to M. d'Anglars' elegant house fronting the place Vendôme, where he was to be informed of the promotion.

No one had been prepared for what had happened next.

Malet had flown into a rage, and the scene that he had thrown in the house of M. d'Anglars was one that was still discussed more than four years later.

He had crumpled the transfer papers, hurled them to the floor and ground them into the carpet with his heel. He demanded to know what he had done to deserve such an insult, and, fuming, offered his immediate resignation. He begged to inform everyone present that he had left the prison at the age of fifteen and felt no urge whatever to consort with criminals aside from protecting society against them, and he certainly had no desire to associate with criminals masquerading as honest citizens.

He told them all that if he ever were to lose his wits enough to wish to return to prison, he would murder someone who deserved it and be honestly thrown into jail.

At a nod from d'Anglars, The Prefect had taken Malet's arm and hustled him, still seething, away from there while d'Anglars did his best to soothe Vidocq, who wanted to challenge Malet to a duel. It had taken all of Lamarque's tact and charm over the course of a week to calm Malet down.

Things finally returned to normal. Chief Inspector Malet remained with the regular Police, and the 8th arrondissement's subsequent dealings with the Sureté were handled exclusively by Malet's second in command, Senior Inspector Georges Plougastel.

Vidocq, and the Sureté, had a long memory for insults. Malet suspected that if he did involve them, they would find some way to take this juicy case away from him. Dracquet was his meat and he did not want anyone else in on the kill. As The Prefect's stand-in, Malet had access to the roster of officers and the power to recruit them for special assignments. Malet knew some men he considered incorruptible. He would use them.

Saint-Légère had suspected that something big was about to happen, and Ensenat had hinted at it before he was murdered. Dracquet's connections extended across Europe: it might be serious indeed. Malet had some informers he could tap, though he suspected that the informers would be afraid to go up against someone of Dracquet's stature.

On the other hand, Malet thought with an ominous smile, Dracquet had never had to come up against him before. He had been praying for a chance to cross swords with the man, and it looked as though the chance had come at last.

Malet's faults did not extend to underestimating himself. As Cheat-Death's chosen successor, he had mastered all the tools in the criminals' arsenal, and he was more adept at their use than the criminals were.

He smiled and closed the notebook. Well. He had begun to spin his webs, and he would be watching them carefully. He bestowed the notebook in the breast pocket of his coat and shuffled through the papers on his desk. Saint-Légère's reports, tied with string, were at the top. He would take them to that inn in Montmartre and review them that night.

He smiled as he set them to one side. It would be pleasant to see Madame de Clichy again. She appeared to be an intelligent, charming and capable lady, and he had enjoyed talking with her. He would take care to remove his sword before going into the inn, though, since he did not want to upset the blonde lady who was a co-owner. What was her name? Mlle. Franchotte, that was it.

But that would be in the evening. He had the more routine concerns of the Prefecture at the moment.

He lifted the first document. It was the weekly report on the status of prostitution in the city, a matter of considerable exasperation and tedium to him. He sighed and began to read.

CHAPTER FOURTEEN

The Guest

All the scattered shoes and piles of newspapers were cleared out of Charles de Saint-Légère's rooms within two hours. The papers were consigned to the kindling pile in the kitchen while the shoes were bundled into Saint-Légère' wardrobe. The wardrobe was manhandled into the small storage room by Claude Kerouac, who had been coachman for the de Clichys when Elise's father was alive, and his nephew, Alcide. The chambermaids then descended on the room under Elise's direction and cleaned it from top to bottom.

The mattress was turned and aired, the linens and curtains were stripped and replaced by clean, freshly ironed ones, and the carpet was taken outside and beaten clean of dust. The wooden floor was scrubbed, the furniture was waxed until it glowed, and Yvette placed a vase of her best roses on the table in the sitting room.

Inspector Malet sent two valises and some trunks over to the Rose d'Or later that afternoon. He arrived that evening just at supper time and signed in under the name 'Paul de Colbert'. Elise noticed that he wasn't wearing his sword.

He greeted Elise and Yvette, and then followed Alcide to his rooms. Alcide reported that he looked around the rooms, missing none of the changes that had been made, paused to sniff Yvette's roses, and then thanked him in a really pleasant way.

He declined a supper in his private parlor, and instead went downstairs shortly afterward to the common room with a pile of papers and pen and ink. He ate a surprisingly light meal of bread and cold meat and drank a small glass of wine.

The crowd began to swell around nine o'clock, and Elise called in two of the younger maidservants to wait tables. Malet moved his seat farther into the corner, away from the customers. He did not appear to have any trouble working in the noise and bustle.

Elise brought over another glass of wine, and sat to chat with him. Word had gotten out that a new Police officer was posted to the Rose d'Or, and Elise caught several speculative glances from their regular customers.

Malet intercepted one of those stares, returned it with slightly lifted eyebrows, and then turned back to Elise.

"Pay them no mind, M. l'Inspecteur," Elise said with a smile. "They have heard that you are replacing M. de Saint-Légère, who was very well-liked. They are wondering what sort of man you are."

"They'll find out soon enough."

As it happened, they found out that very evening.

A customer, new to the inn, tried to force his attentions on one of the maidservants, a pretty little redhead named Marie. He tried to steal a kiss, and, failing that, had seized her and tried to take matters further by force. The girl, frightened, was reduced to tears.

Malet had stepped in at that moment. He identified himself as an officer of the Police and called the customer to order. When the man tried to fight, Malet easily bested him and then ordered that Marie be brought over.

"This man assaulted you, I believe?" he asked.

"Y-yes, M'sieur," she said.

"So. Did you put your hands on her, my good man?"

"That's right! She enjoyed it! Do you have anything to say about it?"

"That remains to be seen," Malet said. His eyes rested meditatively on the man's face for a moment, then flicked to Marie. "He claims you enjoyed it: did you?"

Marie, still a little shaken, mutely shook her head.

Malet looked back at the man. "She doesn't appear to agree with you," he said. "I find myself wondering how you would like it if your situations were reversed." His expression grew remote. "In fact, when woman-molesters and rapists are sent to prison, they often end up experiencing firsthand what their victims suffered, only tenfold, at the hands of the other prisoners. Not pretty for them." He looked over at Marie. "I saw what happened," he said gently. "If you wish to make a complaint, I will be happy to write it up for you."

The silence grew long. Elise touched Marie on the shoulder. "Marie," she said.

Marie drew a long breath. "N-no," she said. "Thank you, M. de Colbert. I don't want to-to think of it."

Malet inclined his head and then looked at Elise with lifted eyebrows.

"I must ask you to leave, Monsieur," she said with dignity to the man. "I do not wish to see you here again."

The man looked from her to Malet, his face growing red.

"You heard the lady. Leave at once." He watched the man leave, and then looked at Marie. "Will you be all right?" he asked.

She had regained her composure enough to hurry to the bar and pour a glass of very good cognac, which she gave to Malet with a flash of a glance at Elise.

THE STAFF AT THE INN decided that they liked him after his championing of Marie, and he fit in well with them. The next few days were peaceful, although they were interrupted by inquiries by some of Constant Dracquet's lower-ranking people regarding the presence of another Police officer at the inn. Elise answered their queries civilly and relayed them to Malet, who nodded in an unsurprised way, but made no comment.

Malet was always one of the first ones up. Elise had been astonished to find him sitting in the kitchen the first morning, impeccably groomed and dressed, quietly reading the past day's Globe and pouring a cup of coffee from a pot that he had brewed himself. Judging from the plate before him and three broken eggshells on the table, he had also cooked his own breakfast.

She had apologized for her lateness, but he had merely smiled, consulted a beautiful pocket-watch, and told her that he hardly expected anyone to be up before five o'clock, and he was accustomed to preparing his own breakfast.

Elise had shaken her head. "Very well, Inspector," she had said. "This time you may make your own breakfast, but do me the honor, in future, of allowing me to prepare it for you!"

He had inclined his head and returned his attention to the Globe.

"And next time, wait for your hot shaving-water!" Elise had added.

Malet had chuckled. "Don't trouble yourself, Madame de Clichy," he had said. "The cold water is fine."

"I insist!" said Elise, determined to be up before him if it killed her.

It became apparent that he had resolved to allow her to arise before him, for she never heard him stir until she had descended the stairs, after which time she could hear him moving about. It was a piece of consideration that touched and amused her more than anything else could have, and she always greeted him warmly when he came downstairs for breakfast.

His defense of Marie had served to disarm Yvette completely. She was still shy of him, but he no longer made her nervous, and she treated him, to Elise's amusement, much like one of the inn's favored guests, bestowing smiles and silence with equal generosity.

Malet reviewed most of Charles de Saint-Légère's reports during that time, and he grew to admire the man's character and ability. He had reread Saint-Légère's outline of the bribery attempts, filled in with information obtained unobtrusively from the inn employees, and conferred with four other men from the Police whom he had hand-picked for their sterling records and their ability to handle extremely sensitive matters. They had been given their instructions concerning Dracquet. As for Malet, his inkling was that the plot was of international importance. He paid special attention to news from London and Spain. It was a busy time, but full of thought. It only remained to sit back and wait.

And enjoy his time at the Rose d'Or...

TWO EVENINGS AFTER his arrival at the Rose d'Or, at suppertime, Malet was sitting in the common room and reading a closely written, stamped report that had just been delivered to him at the inn. He had been too engrossed in it to notice when Elise brought his supper, a roast pheasant from Alcide's father's farm, over to him, and set it before him along with a glass of her English ale.

"M. l'Inspecteur," Elise said for the third time.

Malet started and looked up at her, and then saw Alcide with the tray containing his supper. He colored faintly and apologized for being preoccupied.

Elise chuckled and said, "Not at all. You are always the soul of courtesy, M'sieur. It must be quite important. If you wish, I can have this taken back and kept warm until you're ready for it."

The report was an outline of Dracquet's known activities within the past twelve months. Malet set it aside and rose. "I wouldn't dream of being so rude," he said with a nod to Alcide. "I have read enough, and I find that I am famished: this smells delicious! But have you dined yet, Madame de Clichy?" he asked, eyeing the pheasant.

Elise hid a smile. This part of their conversation had followed the same lines since his first evening at the inn three days before. Now it was becoming a ceremony between them. "Not yet," she said.

"Then would you honor me with your company at supper?" he asked. "There's plenty here for two, as you can see, and I'd be delighted to share it with you."

"Thank you, M'sieur," she said. "I believe I shall." She sat in the chair that he had drawn aside for her and busied herself with arranging her skirts while he carved the pheasant.

He nodded toward his glass. "And what is this?" he asked.

She smoothed the napkin over her lap. "My English ale, M'sieur," she replied. "You haven't tried it yet. I am known for it, and my customers generally like it. I thought you might, as well."

He set a choice portion of breast meat on her plate and selected a drumstick for her as well. "English ale?" he said, his eyes widening a little. "I see..." He gave it an odd look and added, "I fought the English in Spain. Are you sure it won't poison me?"

Elise smothered a chuckle and said severely, "It's good for you. Try it."

She watched him take a sip, reflecting happily on the fact that she had come to like him so well in such a short time. They could converse comfortably on any subject, and she had come to recognize his subtle flashes of humor

"If it poisons me," he mused at last. "At least it will be a pleasant death."

Elise reached for the glass. "I don't want you to die!" she said. "I will take it away at once."

"No, no," he said as he whisked the glass beyond her reach. "Suffering's good for the sou, and this is a very satisfactory mortification. I wish all pain could be like this."

"Well!" she said, raising a forkful of pheasant to her lips. She firmly suppressed a smile.

Malet looked suddenly contrite. "I was only joking," he said.

"I know."

"Then may I please have some more?" he asked.

CHAPTER FIFTEEN

The Sojourner in a Strange Land

Inspector Malet seemed exhausted and withdrawn the next evening when Elise brought his supper over to him, though he observed their little ceremony regarding supper and, as usual, gave her the choicest bits. The meal was a simple dish of escalloped veal in pastry with potatoes and onions, something at once elegant and simple, but he did not seem to be hungry. He picked at it while she relayed a query from one of Dracquet's men regarding what hour might find their Police officer at the inn.

Malet said, "Tell him my hours are very irregular, and then don't elaborate, if you please."

Elise chuckled. "Those are almost my exact words," she said.

He nodded and turned his attention back to his supper while she sat there talking of this and that and trying to make him smile.

He requested a second glass of ale and drank it quietly, then cut through her chatter with an incisive question on the political situation in Paris at the moment that made her pause and then answer.

"Tell me, M. l'Inspecteur," she said after giving her reply, "Why do you credit me with the wit to answer a difficult question like that?"

He cut off a piece of veal with the edge of his fork and then, having speared it, paused and looked up at her. "Do you think you don't have the wit to answer it?" he asked with a slightly quizzical lift of his eyebrows.

"Oh no," she said. "I don't mean that at all. It's unusual to find a man, especially-forgive me-one of your age and rank, willing to credit any woman with sense enough to run her own life, much less think intelligently. You puzzle me."

He frowned and raised the fork to his mouth. After chewing and then taking a swallow of ale, he said, "But why? Surely all men aren't such idiots as that!"

"You'd be surprised," she said.

"Maybe I would," he admitted with a sigh. He frowned down at his plate. "I seem fated to be surprised by people."

"We all are. People are never predictable. It's foolish to expect them to be."

"No," agreed Malet. "That's quite true." He frowned thoughtfully into space and lifted his glass of ale. "But I don't know enough about people," he said with a touch of sadness coloring his voice. "I don't understand them. I can deal with criminals. I have been successful at it, but then it's the way I was raised. I know all about them!

"But the others, the decent, helpless folk: they elude me. They always have. I wonder if it's too late to learn. I wonder sometimes if I should even try..." He sounded very wistful and even a little forlorn.

Elise did not move, and she hardly breathed.

Malet was still frowning, and his voice had become very quiet. "Sometimes I feel as though I am walking among a foreign people," he said. "As though, while I know their language and their customs, I am not really one of them."

Elise's smile faded. She knew that he was telling her something he had never before admitted to anyone. The thought filled her with sudden warmth. She felt like one who has coaxed a shy, half-wild creature to eat from her hand. She schooled her face to calmness and looked down at the table. "Why do you think that?" she asked.

Looking up, she saw that he had suddenly realized what he had just said. He looked for a moment like a fencer who has discovered that his guard is disastrously lowered. He pushed his supper aside. His eyes were shuttered when he looked up at her, his expression carefully neutral.

"Why?" she repeated gently, touched and worried by his obvious distress. "Why do you feel that way?"

He took up the papers lying on the corner of his table and shuffled them. His cheeks had more color than usual.

"It doesn't matter," he said at last with a fairly convincing show of indifference, except for the catch in his voice. "It was a foolish thing to say. I beg your pardon for wasting your time."

"Why, if it's how you truly feel?" she asked. "I can understand."

"Some truth is best not spoken," he said. "It can annoy."

"But I promise you didn't annoy me," she said.

When he would not look up, she decided to let the subject drop. She motioned to Marie, who took his plate and cup. "Bring Monsieur some more ale, child," she said, and then, turning to Malet as Marie moved away, "And, M'sieur, I apologize for troubling you with my questions. You are obviously tired from a long day, and you spoke at random. I assure you, it is forgotten."

"I am a bastard, Madame de Clichy," he said, not looking at her. His voice was subtly altered, as though he were forcing the words out, afraid of her reaction. "My mother was an opera dancer. They tell me she was beautiful. My father was a ... a nobleman who liked to collect beautiful things. de Colbert was his name. He saw my mother and wanted her. He promised to marry her, and she, loving him, trusted him. I was conceived, and then she discovered that he was already married, with a family in Normandy. She killed him, was sentenced to die, and bore me in prison. She was executed immediately after. She was twenty-one."

When Elise did not comment, he continued in a lower voice. "My father's family—the de Colberts—didn't want a murderess' bastard brat. They said so in a letter. I was raised in the prison."

If Malet had looked up, he might have been surprised by Elise's expression, but he kept his eyes lowered. His voice was carefully expressionless. "It was an unsurpassed education for a Police officer," he said with an attempt at a smile. "You learn so many things in those places: you learn all about crime, filth and the ways to kill or—or cause pain. If you listen to the lies, you start to think that you can only rely on yourself. You learn everything but how to become a friend, and how to be an ordinary mortal, no matter how desperately you want it. If you're wise, you stop wanting it after a while."

He frowned down at his hands and said, "The prison permeates everything, unless you learn to look up at something else. But then, having looked up, it's difficult to look down again. And there's always the fear that you might fall back into the filth." He fell silent.

Elise dropped all pretense of casualness and looked straight at him. "My dear M'sieur!" she said. "Did you believe I'd think less of you?"

"It's happened," he said after a moment. "The sins of the parents, they say... My past is a matter of public record, anyhow— Everyone knows about it. I." He broke off with an almost pathetically helpless gesture of his hands.

"But you left the prison and became 'an ordinary mortal', as you call them," Elise pointed out.

Malet raised his eyes to her face. "Do you think so? Look again, Madame de Clichy. I am not one of them! I protect them. It's what I set out to do years ago, and I don't regret it. But I know as well as you that I am not of the same stamp as them, and I never will be. They know it, too."

"You know, Inspector," Elise said quietly, "Just then you sounded like an eagle trying to apologize for the fact that his wings make it impossible for him to be a mole. Your 'past', such as it is, makes no difference at all to me. I count myself fortunate to have made your acquaintance, and I would like to keep that acquaintance if you will permit me."

He looked down again and kept his eyes lowered as Marie brought another cup of ale. He raised the cup to his lips with a hand that shook slightly. "The good fortune is mine," he said.

He adroitly changed the subject the next moment by presenting a new letter from Saint-Légère, which had come in with the morning's dispatches. Malet always delivered them to her at suppertime.

This letter was a lively and affectionate one, as had been the others. Saint-Légère had the ability to write as he spoke. It was as though he were sitting at the table with them, describing the activities in the Bois de Boulogne. He wrote of the people who shared his patrols and recounted some incidents that had both Elise and Malet laughing. Yvette came over to hear the letter, too, and then Claude, Marie and Alcide as well.

After they had all read the letter and exclaimed over it, he watching her with an expression that made her pause, the subject they had first discussed was long passed, and Elise did not know how to reopen it without giving offense.

And yet she wished to speak of it again, for that glimpse of hurt and vulnerability had touched and softened Elise more than anything he could have said to her. She had suddenly realized that she was beginning to love him.

THE MOON WAS CIRCLED by a faint ring of dark rainbow and half hidden behind a veil of fine clouds. Elise slid from her bed and went to her escritoire. She had set Saint-Légère's letter there. It might help to banish this mood. He was skilled in the art of flirtation: most well-bred men of his age were, but his letters and sallies had the added spice of sincerity.

He had finished by writing of his thoughts concerning the distance between them. She had not shown it to the rest of them. Now she reread the paragraph and smiled.

> *I think of the miles that separate us, my dearest Madame, and wish that I could somehow take the wings of the swallow that nests beneath my window and fly to you. Were there some way to send a message by him, some way to give you but a part of the happiness I feel when I fill my thoughts with your loveliness and wit, then I would be happy indeed. As it is this letter, poorly phrased though it may be, conveys all my heartfelt regard. Could it but assure me that all is well with you, then I would indeed rest content.*

She chuckled and folded the letter away. Poorly phrased, indeed! His birth and upbringing were obvious in every line. It was a pity, she thought, that she could not love him. And almost exhilarating to think that she had somehow found a way to love again, even though, the prospect of a new love brought back to her, all unwanted, the memory of terrible unhappiness.

The wind was chilly when she opened her windows and looked out over the street. It was as though something were calling to her, awakening all the old longing and grief.

But it had been over seven years! Not all men were like Raoul! Surely she could lay the past aside now and reach again for happiness.

She was too restless to sleep. She had been a fool even to try. Perhaps a cup of tea with warm milk in it. She opened her armoire and took out her pink brocaded wrapper, donning it with the ease of many years of acquaintance, not seeing the fine lace at the neck. She opened her door and stepped out into the hallway.

The inn was silent, except for loud snores from one of the guest rooms. She went softly down the stairs and into the kitchen. It only took a moment to get the stove hot again, and to prepare a cup of tea.

She had just sat at the wide, scarred table to sip her tea when the sound of quiet footsteps, moving down the stairs, made her look up.

Malet stood in the doorway, watching her with a slight frown.

"Inspector?" she whispered.

He bowed.

"What are you doing up at this time of the night?" she demanded.

His smile flashed for a moment. "I am going hunting," he said, coming into the kitchen. She saw that he was carrying a sword and a pistol. "Why are you awake, Madame de Clichy?"

She lifted her eyebrows at him. "This is my inn and I have the right to be here," she said.

Malet's smile grew slightly dry. "So you do," he said with another bow. "But—this is a sincere request—lock the doors after me and don't let anyone else go outside tonight." He saw the puzzlement in her expression. "The hunt is going to be a wide-ranging one," he said. "And the prey can be dangerous. Lock the doors."

She hesitated on the brink of a half-jest but stopped. "Yes, M. l'Inspecteur," she said. She watched him rise, take up his sword and pistol. "Inspector?"

"Madame?"

She spoke through a throat that was suddenly tight with foreboding. "Please. If the prey is dangerous, then take care for yourself. You have value for many people."

He smiled again and was out the door.

CHAPTER SIXTEEN

Dracquet Requests an Audience

Elise awoke late the next morning and watched the wind chase skeins of clouds across the blue morning sky. She drowsily tried to remember what had happened the night before to worry her. Remembering with a sudden chill of fear, she arose, dressed, and went downstairs.

Yvette and Claude were in the kitchen, talking urgently together. She froze and then went to them. "Is all well?" she asked.

Claude was beaming. "Most well!" he said. "Would you believe it? Those monsters—the killers who— Well, never mind. They were all caught! All of them! The Police set an ambush, led by Chief Inspector Malet, and got them all!"

"Was—was anyone hurt?" Elise asked.

"Some of those murdering scoundrels were," Yvette said. "But the newspapers report no one else hurt."

"Malet," said Claude. He raised his eyebrows at Elise's expression. "A scratch only," he said.

"That is a scratch too many!" Elise said.

"He was smiling when they spoke with him," Yvette said. "He said he was fine."

Elise considered and then smiled and asked for breakfast. The inn hummed into its ordinary routine.

Yvette came to her later that morning while she was spicing the chickens for that night's supper with the news that Constant Dracquet had sent some of his men by.

"It was that fellow René Benoit, and he was as offensive as usual," she said. "He's the sort of cad who tries to kiss chambermaids."

"I'd rather deal with him than with his employer. M. Dracquet makes me very nervous. Did Benoit try to kiss you?"

"Not this time," Yvette said. "He just said that I was to tell the 'Police Officer' that M. Dracquet wishes to speak with him at eleven o'clock to-morrow morning at his house."

"A summons!" said Elise. "He's trying the same tactics he tried with Charles."

"It will be interesting to see how successful he will be," said Yvette. "I suspect that anyone who tries to annoy our Inspector ends up regretting the effort."

Elise smiled at that. "I suspect you're right, Yvette," she said. "I know he will be interested in hearing that Benoit came by. We'd best go tell him right away."

Yvette's eyes widened. "To—to the Prefecture?" she asked.

"But of course. We'll make a day of it!"

"But who will take care of the place?" Yvette asked.

"Alcide and Claude," answered Elise. "As well as the rest of the staff. Come on, Yvette. You don't get out often enough!"

Elise bundled her into a pelisse and bonnet and, by main bullying, got her out the door and into a cab.

SERGEANT JACQUES GUILLART was a plump man of about forty-three whose career in the Parisian Police was due to his ability to write a round, clear hand and turn a good phrase. He reviewed the reports submitted, rewrote those with glaring errors in syntax or punctuation, and filed the rest. He supervised a staff of thirty and coordinated all communications between the Prefecture and the various Police and army posts throughout Paris. He also maintained the Police archives for France.

He judged people by their reports. The Prefect, M. Lamarque, for example, wrote a fair hand and had a sober turn of phrase that was quite impressive. Chief Inspector Malet wrote a strong, elegant hand and had a poetic turn of phrase that made Guillart think at once of ballads and the tales told by huntsmen after a successful chase. Inspector Christien L'Eveque, a merry soul, wrote an entertaining report, but was inclined to go into overmuch detail concerning who was standing where and at what time.

He smiled at everyone, arrived punctually every morning and left punctually every night to return to his plump, charming wife and his family that had grown steadily over the past years. He courted no danger, bowed and scraped to no one, and served as one of those who are indispensable to the smooth running of a great piece of machinery.

Everyone liked Sergeant Guillart, and he liked everyone, himself. But he did have one or two very dear friends, aside from his family, and one of them was Chief Inspector Paul V. Malet. At this moment he was standing before the Prefect's desk, smiling down at Malet and offering him a neatly folded napkin.

The Chief Inspector took the napkin, warmly returning the smile, and opened it to reveal a particularly plump, golden pastry bursting with raisins and walnuts.

"Guillart, this is too generous of your good lady," Malet objected. "Every day I am here she sends in some treat by you, and I have done nothing whatever to deserve it! Surely The Prefect isn't treated to this kindness every day!"

Guillart only shook his head. "I will tell Justine what you say, but she will smile and disagree and keep sending these in for you with her best greetings. You may as well resign yourself to your good fortune."

"One can but try," Malet said. "And Guillart: do try to get those reports on Dracquet's supposed family ties with Burgundy."

"Of course," said Guillart. He bowed and withdrew, wiping his fingers and chuckling. The Chief Inspector could never seem to understand what he had done to merit the friendship of the large and clamorous Guillart clan.

Malet had saved Guillart's life in 1830, during the July revolution, but the friendship of the Guillart family predated even that action. It stemmed from something that had happened during Malet's first year in Paris, six years before.

He had come bursting into the Prefecture one day dragging a sobbing child along by the wrist. Due to a sudden emergency, Guillart had been filling in as Officer of the Day, and it was to him that Malet had come.

"She solicited me!" he said through his teeth. "On the rue de Rivoli, by the Hotel de Ville, no less! Look at her! No more than ten years old if she's a day and painted like a whore!"

He had released the child, who had collapsed into a chair, sobbing, tears spilling over her garishly rouged cheeks as she rubbed her wrist.

"Do you want to press charges?" Guillart had asked. He had heard that Malet was a terror to criminals, but the thought of charging a child was abhorrent to him.

"Against her?" Malet had demanded. "Of course not! Look at her! What crime did she commit? No, the crime is against her!"

Guillart looked at her wrist, which was beginning to bruise. "I think you hurt her," he said.

Malet had been pacing up and down the aisle. He whirled round, looking stricken, and hurried back to her.

"Did I?" he asked. He dropped to one knee beside the chair and examined the wrist. "Dear God! I didn't mean to! I am sorry, child! But—but her damned pimp came up to her and tried to hustle her away, muttering something about 'taking a hit' later on! The snake!"

He got to his feet, almost sputtering with anger. "Pimping for a child! You should hear the filth he taught her to spout to a prospective customer! Those who prey on children—!" He was pacing again.

"What did you do?" asked Sergeant Guillart.

"Do?" Malet repeated through his teeth. "I decked him and got her away. He won't be breathing very well for the next few months!"

"Did they know who you were?" Guillart asked.

"They do now!" Malet answered. "I told them. They seemed impressed, though it may have been my sword at their leader's throat. I suggested that they leave."

He frowned down at the girl, who was staring up at him as though he were a cross between Prince Charming and Michael the Archangel. "How old are you?" he asked after a moment. His voice was gentler.

"N–nine this week," the girl had answered. Her voice was high and clear.

"See?" Malet said. He took out his handkerchief and held it before her. "Here: spit on this!" he commanded, and then scrubbed at her face with it after she had.

"There!" he said, handing her the handkerchief, which she furtively tucked away in the ragged bosom of her dress. "She's pretty under all this paint! What sort of foul scum would even think— How long have you been doing this, child?"

She began to cry again. "One week, M'sieur."

"One week?" Guillart had repeated. "Well. What is your name, poppet?"

"J-Julie."

"Do you have any family, Julie?" Guillart had persisted.

"No, M'sieur."

"Do you want to go back to the streets?" Malet had asked.

She threw herself into his arms, sobbing.

Malet's blank expression made Guillart chuckle.

"What a question, Inspector!" he said over the girl's head. Of course she doesn't. Poor sweetheart, it must have been terrible for you. You don't ever have to go back. I know a home for you. Take my handkerchief and don't cry. You can hold my hand."

He looked up at Malet, who had set her in a chair and was frowning thoughtfully down at the girl's lowered head. "Sir? Did you have any plans for placing her? If not, I know where she can go."

Malet had shaken his head. "Thank you, Sergeant," he had said, bestowed a brief and, in all, very gentle, smile on the girl, and left.

And that is how Julie had come to be adopted by the Guillart family.

Madame Guillart, a country woman from Provence, where Guillart had been posted as a foot soldier, had never forgotten. The Chief Inspector had been stunned eight months later when Madame Guillart asked him to be her newest baby's godfather, and he had been rendered speechless by the news that little Valentin Guillart was to be his namesake.

Julie, now a pretty girl of fifteen, regarded him as a sort of angel. It was she who had baked the pastries this week, and she had personally selected the best, plumpest one for 'M'sieur' this day.

SERGEANT GUILLART MADE his unhurried way back to his desk,

smiling, but wondering nevertheless why Inspector Malet was so subdued this day. The fact that he had spent the night chasing murderers did not explain it, since the man seemed to thrive on very little sleep. But he wasn't worried: Malet seemed puzzled rather than disturbed.

He returned to his desk with a smile. When he got there he found the Officer of the Day chatting with two women, a brunette with dark, lively eyes, and a taller, chastely bonneted one with a demurely downcast face but very curious, bright blue eyes.

"M. le Sergeant, these two ladies are asking to speak with the Chief Inspector," said the Officer of the Day. "They say it's an important matter regarding one of his cases."

Guillart stepped forward, smiling. "Welcome, ladies," he said. "M. Malet is here: may I announce you?"

The dark woman said, "I am Elise de Clichy, and this is Yvette Franchotte. M. Malet is presently staying at our inn."

"The Rose d'Or!" said Guillart as he bowed over their hands. "Of course! He spoke very highly of the place, especially your English ale and your veal. I am very happy to meet you! Jacques Guillart at your service. Please follow me! M. Malet will be delighted to receive you!"

"I KNOW DRACQUET WAS hounding Saint-Légère," Elise said some minutes later, "And I suspect that is why he wishes to speak with you. Here's the message."

She gave the slip of paper to Malet and watched as he read it. Her smile wavered as she remembered the past night. He showed no sign of fatigue, and there was nothing to indicate a wound. She smiled again.

He looked up after a moment and noticed that Yvette was standing by the window and gazing out over the place du Parvis toward the facade of the cathedral. "There's a charming walk along the river there, Mlle. Yvette," he said, "And the flower market is still open."

Yvette turned and nodded. "I seldom come this way anymore, M'sieur," she said shyly, and sat.

Malet checked his watch and then closed it. "It's close to noon," he said.

"If you ladies would permit me, I know an establishment near here that serves the best salmon I have ever had. We could lunch there."

Yvette's eyes were wide with delight. "On the Île du Palais itself?" she asked.

"Close by. At the place du Châtelet. I will send someone to reserve a table." He rang a bell on the desk, gave instructions to the office boy who came in, and then returned his attention to the message.

He finally set it aside with an ominous smile. "If Dracquet wants to speak with me," he said, "He will have to catch me before I leave. I suspect that his hours aren't so early as all that!"

He paused, thinking. "Saint-Légère's told me that he walks a beat now."

"Yes," said Elise. "I have the route mapped out. I asked for it in case an emergency should arise."

Malet frowned into space. "Hm," he said. "I think I will take over his duties for the next two days. We'll see if Dracquet catches up with me."

CHAPTER SEVENTEEN

Spindrift on The Eddies

Gut-shot and screeching, I tell you! Holding his innards in with both hands, lying in the muck and shrieking for help, and all we did was laugh at him!" The speaker raised a bottle of gin and took a long pull.

"Beautiful, I tell you! Beautiful! And I expecting it all along!"

"Serves him right, the mad wolf!" cried a woman in a prostitute's brightly colored silk dress. "It's the best news I ever heard! They'll never prey on us again!"

Larouche stood quietly behind the pillar and watched the celebration that had been going on since just past 4:00 a.m., when the news had hit the streets. The monsters were dead, and one of Larouche's particular nightmares had been laid to rest.

The uproar filled the huge market of Les Halles. High-class courtesans mingled with street-walkers and pimps of the lowest type. Crippled old soldiers and beggars laughed and slapped each other on the back, and children ran here and there, shrieking with joy and filling their faces with the free food that the shopkeepers were handing out.

Larouche was feeling a little ill, since he had eaten four large cooked sausages, half a loaf of bread, and a great fistful of sweets, but he was still smiling. Sitting still by his pillar helped, and he only needed to remember that the monsters were dead to feel very well, indeed.

"Who killed them?" someone demanded.

"It was Malet!" shouted the man with the gin bottle. "Their gig was up the minute they set foot on his territory! Didn't I say all along they were goners from that moment? And now see where they are!"

Malet's name brought a moment of silence. It was a name to conjure with. All the people gathered there knew of Malet, even if they had never encountered him. He loomed large in their imaginations, a being as inscrutable as a sphinx and as terrible as an avenging angel. They feared him if they strayed on the side of crime and blessed him if they were one of the helpless ones who sought refuge in the safety of his arrondissement. But not even his name could keep down the noise for long.

"Did anyone see them?" demanded a beaming pimp with a dripping nose.

"Aye, Constable Grual said he did! He was there when Malet brought them in, he and his troop of Sergeants de Ville! Three of them dead and two others well on the way, and two more gone off the devil knew where—but Malet found out! They're gone, all of them, and good riddance to them! We're safe!"

Larouche hiccupped and tasted sausage. He should have saved two for later, but he had thought that if he ate them now, he wouldn't stand a chance of losing them later and going without. He shivered and folded his arms about himself. His clothing was threadbare, and the weather was getting cold, but he would rather be cold than tortured and then slashed to ribbons, like the victims of the monsters.

Someone shouted, "Here's to Malet! I say long life to him!"

"Amen," said a woman's voice beside him.

Larouche looked up and saw a courtesan named Letitia, or TiTi, Descaux, the mistress of the Duc d'Aillard, the Minister of Finance. She was elegantly dressed and had obviously only strolled to Les Halles to purchase some delicacies and greet other strollers. She often gave treats to Larouche and she was smiling down at him now.

"Hi," said Larouche.

"Hi," she said. "Why are you here, you little scamp?"

"It's warm," said Larouche. "Besides, everyone's happy."

"And well they might be," said TiTi. "Those demons are dead, and we can all breathe easier."

"They say Malet did it," said Larouche.

"He did," said TiTi. "He's good at fighting monsters..." She was smiling at a memory, but she turned to Larouche after a moment. "I knew him years before he came here," she said. "He was Chief of Police in a city in Picardy. That was long before you were born. He wasn't too high and mighty to keep a whore from being attacked by a solid citizen, and I will never forget it."

Larouche hiccupped again.

TiTi eyed his ragged clothing and suddenly smiled. "Here, child," she said, opening her reticule. "I am giving you twenty francs. Get yourself a warm coat and some shoes. Run along and do it now. You are safe now, and you may as well be warm—and you don't need to hear these ghouls go on about those monsters."

AN HOUR LATER LAROUCHE was wearing warmer clothing and had enough money left in his pocket to buy food for a week. Meat and bread and maybe even a sweet, if he hoarded his money.

He skipped happily along despite the remains of a severe stomach ache and the unaccustomed weight of a heavy pair of shoes. Life was good, the monsters would never trouble anyone again, and it was time to go seek out Monseigneur and inquire into the state of his hat.

CHAPTER EIGHTEEN

Malet at Point Non Plus

Malet walked along almost reluctantly with his head down and his hands tucked behind him. His slowness was not due to the latest attack of the stone-thrower, who had been dogging him for the past week, though he was bare-headed and holding his hat in his right hand. He had decided that the stone-thrower meant him no physical hurt. He had had ample opportunity to prove otherwise. The attacks had been limited to his hat, and Malet had to admit that the stonethrower was certainly skillful.

He had considered staking out the Prefecture and the Rose d'Or in order to catch the culprit, but he had decided against it. This was a private matter and Malet preferred to fight his own battles

Nor was the hesitation due to fatigue, although Malet had slept all of three hours during the past night. He had single-handedly killed three criminals in the cemetery, wounded two more, and been slightly wounded himself. It had been a stroke of good fortune that he had personally made the kill, though it had not been in his territory. He had spent the afternoon writing up his report and conferring with Chief Inspector Picot of the 2nd arrondissement, where the attack had taken place. Picot had been very complimentary. He had received an excited account from his people, and when Malet had arrived to give his testimony and view the corpses, he had greeted him with a warm smile and the dry comment that if Malet wished to clean out the 2nd single-handedly, Picot l would certainly not stand in his way.

The identities of the corpses had come as the final triumphant touch, and the afternoon had been the wrap-up of a successful hunt. Now he was returning to the Rose d'Or.

"Good afternoon, Chief Inspector!" called a passerby.

Malet jumped, looked up, recognized his banker, and returned the greeting with apparent suavity while silently cursing himself for being abstracted.

He noticed his surroundings for the first time. He had only reached the western end of the Île St. Louis. He strolled to the bridge connecting the western part of the island with the shore and went to its middle, stopping there to rest his folded arms on the balustrade and gaze back toward the Île du Palais and the soaring spire that marked the cathedral.

Dusk was falling. The sky had deepened to a blue that was almost purple, touched here and there with scattered stars. The western sky was still light, and the river, calm in the late afternoon stillness, mirrored the sky and the lights along the quays. Strollers walked arm in arm, exchanging quiet greetings while children ran ahead, laughing and chattering in the last flare of light. It was a soothing sight, and he relaxed a little as he gazed. He drew a deep breath, released it, and turned from the contemplation of Paris to the contemplation of the past evening.

How could he have let his guard down so disastrously? To voice the pain that he had barely been able to put into words in the stillness of his own heart, and to voice it, moreover, to Elise de Clichy!

He should have been more careful, but the supper had been good, the room had been warm, and he had been worn out from a long and exhausting day. There had been that city-wide sweep of the sewers that he had ordered, which had turned up eight corpses in varying stages of decay. Seven of them appeared to be the result of foul play, and all of them had had to be viewed and identified. Then there had been the knifing victim left by the river near the Pont d'Iena. That corpse had turned even Malet's stomach! Poor little child, lying in the icy chill of the Police morgue!

And there had been a host of other distractions, as well. The spies that he had assigned to watch Dracquet from a distance were sending in confusing reports, and he was considering sending in one of his very best operatives as well as questioning a witness he had hoped to avoid using. He had been too tired and preoccupied to think properly.

He growled silently at himself. Excuses! He had been thinking aloud, a careless and stupid trait that he deplored. Appalled at his slip, he had badly bungled his attempt to shrug the comment off. Madame de Clichy had been willing to drop the matter, but what did he do but crown his blunder by confiding further, and in such a way as to make it sound as though he were confessing to a crime and not admitting something that was common knowledge on the force.

But was respect what he wanted from her? He rested his chin on his hands and, gazing at the spire of Notre Dame de Paris, admitted to himself that it was not.

He turned and looked up into the sky. His gaze fastened upon a large square of stars just above the eastern horizon: Pegasus was rising. He remembered the story that the old sailor in the prison had told him of Pegasus, one bright evening when they had been watching the stars.

DID YOU EVER HEAR OF THE MAN WHO SADDLED UP THE WIND, PIPPIN?

NO, PAPA, he had said, in English, his eyes wide with delight. He had loved the old sailor's stories. *Can* you saddle the wind?

ONE MAN DID, the sailor had said. *I WILL TELL YOU THE STORY...*

Malet smiled, remembering. He sometimes had dreams even now of riding Pegasus, soaring and swooping among the clouds, laughing in the wind...

Thinking of the old sailor eased some of the perplexity. The man had always said, when young Paul had been hurt or unhappy. *Well, then, Pippin, what can you do to mend matters? Can you go back? No? Then what is there to do but go forward?*

Malet lifted his face into the wind and looked back over his shoulder at Notre Dame Cathedral. There was no unsaying what had been said. And what, after all, had been so terrible about it? He had confessed to loneliness and bewilderment, that was all. And Madame de Clichy had heard and understood.

He realized that he was only trying to fool himself. How could he pretend nothing had changed? For something had happened that night, and it was useless to deny it. He had been betrayed by his own clumsiness, and yet she had accepted him as an equal and a friend without the slightest hesitation. And he had fallen in love with her in that moment of understanding. It was no more complicated than that.

He had seen her quality at their first meeting. Where he had expected a coarse, stolid woman of the town, capable of running an inn, he had instead found a lady. She shone among the many women he had known in the course of an eventful lifetime like a golden coin in a pile of coppers. Their friendship had touched a responsive chord in him. She was a delightful companion in every possible way, and completely safe. And then in one mad moment he had fallen in love with her.

The hope that she might love him in return was almost too painful for one of his birth and breeding to consider. As a suitor he thought he was beyond the pale of acceptability. He had been aware of this from the first, and, since it was unchangeable, he had accepted it as a part of his condition. And yet he could not help feeling a little like one standing guard outside a great feast, hearing the music and seeing the light pool like warm gold along the cracks in the door while he kept watch in the black, bitter night, hoping that someone might open the door and let him come in. And, for a wonder, it had happened after years of waiting.

Elise had listened to him instead of turning her back. It was as though he had seen the door swing open, just a little, to find her standing on the threshold, holding out her hands to him and smiling.

But had she really meant it? Or was it simply the gratitude and emotion of the moment, soon and easily forgotten? He had encountered it often enough in his years in the Police. Gratitude was easily forgotten, and heroes faded fast. The years had armored him against that truth.

But not against her. Hearing the appalling echo of his own words and seeing himself reflected in her eyes, he had known that she had managed to disarm him. He had unwittingly given her the power to hurt him.

He pushed away from the balustrade and crossed back to the Quai des Celestins, his walk brisk once again. He couldn't go back; he would have to go forward.

CHAPTER NINETEEN

Potatoes, Philosophy and Friendship

Elise eyed the pile of potatoes and sighed. She hated peeling potatoes, but if she planned to get the evening's meal done in any time, they would have to be done quickly, and done by her alone since Yvette was out milking the inn's two cows, and she had given the maidservants and cook the afternoon off. She frowned at her paring knife and picked up another potato.

She was coming late to this task. The luncheon near the Île du Palais had been very pleasant, although their host had been rather withdrawn, and she had lingered over her wine. She and Yvette had strolled along the river afterward, and then gone to a draper's shop to purchase fabric and some ribbons. The time had passed almost too quickly, and now, she thought ruefully, she was paying for it.

She smiled to herself, though. It had been a perfectly lovely day. She was singing as she set the peeled potato aside and took up another one.

The door opened and closed, and a light breeze stirred her hair for a moment. She looked up and saw Inspector Malet standing in the doorway and staring at the pile of potatoes.

She had discovered that he preferred not to enter through the taproom and was used to seeing him going quietly through the kitchen. He had even swiped a small sugar-cake that Yvette had just finished icing—and then looked amusingly like a guilty schoolboy when he was caught at it. He seemed to be hesitating now, his hand still on the latch as though he were just about to turn and leave.

His eyes met hers. His slightly wary expression eased as she stretched out her hand to him. "Come on in, M'sieur, and welcome!" she said. "Have you ever seen so many potatoes? I certainly haven't, not since I came home from Spain!"

"You do seem to have an eternity of them. Are they all for tonight's supper?"

"Of course," Elise said as a strip of brown peel came away beneath her knife. "And if I don't get them peeled quickly, they'll never be done in time. But you, M. l'Inspecteur: did you require something?"

"A glass of water," said Malet. "I am thirsty..."

"There's wine in the taproom, as you well know," said Elise. "Have Alcide pour you some, or, better still, some ale. It will be my treat."

Malet relaxed a little. "No," he said. "Water will serve just as well. I see a pitcher there. Is that for drinking?"

"It is," said Elise. She watched him go to the pitcher and fill a glass. Her smile was unsteady; she remembered all that had happened the night before. It had been like watching a granite statue melt into flesh and blood, and then take up a sword to defend her and her kind.

Elise was not given to making hasty judgments about people, but she knew quickly when she liked someone. It had been that way with Yvette, with Saint-Légère, with Yves and Georges and the others she counted as friends. Inspector Malet was no exception. She had liked him from the moment she had met him in the parlor the morning Saint-Légère had left for the Bois de Boulogne.

He still seemed just a little hesitant. The granite statue was gone forever, and the man in its place was vulnerable and very dear to her. She gave him her warmest smile and returned her attention to her knife and the potato she was holding.

He set down his glass and took a sealed packet from his breast pocket. "This came for you today among the messages for the Prefecture," he said. "I had planned to give it to you at supper, but I think you would probably be happier to get it now."

"What is it?" she asked as she wiped her hand.

He handed it to her with a smile. "Look and see," he said.

It was another letter from Saint-Légère, as chatty as the others. She was smiling as she looked up. The smile vanished almost immediately.

Malet was sitting on one of the kitchen chairs. He had taken off his coat and rolled up his shirt sleeves. She could see a bandage on his upper arm through the fine cambric cloth of the shirt. He was attacking the pile of potatoes. He had peeled ten of them in the space of time it took Elise to read the letter.

"M. l'Inspecteur!" she protested, torn between laughter and astonishment.

He looked up from digging out a diseased spot from one of the potatoes. "Yes, Madame?" he said.

"You shouldn't be doing that!"

"Why not? I assume we'll be eating them."

"But it—it isn't seemly for one of your rank to be peeling potatoes!"

He finished the potato and took up another. "Oh?" he said. "For what rank would it be seemly? I remember hearing that Marshal Gerard would peel potatoes when he wished to think. I have reviewed his campaigns, and it's obvious that he didn't peel many potatoes"

Elise was laughing in spite of herself. "Stop it!" she said. "You know very well what I meant!"

"Do I? I am not so sure. I suppose it wouldn't be seemly for me to peel potatoes, say, in the middle of my headquarters. Although," he added, after a moment's thought, his head slightly tilted as he considered, "I suppose I might be excused for peeling potatoes if we were in the middle of a siege! Even St. Louis did menial things like that, and he was a little more exalted than a Police Inspector, I think."

Elise gave up. "Well, I can do it, you know," she said.

Malet tossed a coil of peel to the side. "Don't let me stop you," he said. "The more who peel, the sooner these get done." He finished the potato, took another and set to work on it.

"You will soil your clothing!"

He shook his head. "I think not," he said. "You appear to have scrubbed these quite thoroughly."

She began to laugh. "Oh very well!" she said. "Peel them, since you insist—and thank you!"

He was smiling as he set the potato aside. The animation and warmth suddenly vanished from his face as she watched, and he became very quiet. She turned and saw one of her customers standing in the doorway.

"Madame, is Claude here?" the man asked. He ignored Malet, who was sitting with his eyes cast down, working with a silent economy of movement.

"I think he went to the farrier," Elise answered. "He left a little under an hour ago, so he should be back soon."

"Thank you, Madame!" the man said and withdrew.

Elise turned back to Malet. The light mood was spoiled, and she was sorry, for she had enjoyed seeing him laughing.

She set a coil of peel to one side. "You went into danger last night," she said. "I wanted speak to you about that."

She spoke very directly. She knew he could be elusive if he chose, but she was willing to chance it

The silence stretched out, broken only by the rasp of a knife against a crisp potato. Malet raised his eyes to hers. He seemed slightly puzzled. "Did that trouble you?" he asked.

"No!" she exclaimed. "What a foolish thing to say! Claude showed me the articles in the *Moniteur*: you saved many people from a hideous death!"

He looked up at her and shrugged. "I am an officer of the Police. I was only doing my duty."

"Is duty, then, the only important part of your life?" Elise asked. "Do affection, inclination or ambition have no place?"

Malet frowned and raised his eyes to hers. "Is that a fair or kind question to ask me?" he said, speaking as directly as she had.

"It's an honest one," she replied.

Malet looked down. He was distressed. Elise watched his expression for a moment and then relented a little. She laid a gentle hand on his shoulder, just above the bandage. She could feel that he had tensed. "This conversation is between you and me only," she said. "If you think the question is unfair, don't answer it. I will understand."

He looked down again and selected another potato from the dwindling pile. Elise had the impression that he was engaged in a silent struggle within his own heart. It was like his reaction the previous evening just before he had admitted, ashamed, that he had been raised in a prison.

Elise watched him with sudden concern. "I am sorry, M'sieur," she said. "I had no right to ask such a question. I never meant to presume."

She started to withdraw her hand. Malet set the knife aside and raised his hand to cover hers. His eyes held no anger or shame; she realized that she was looking into the eyes of a friend, and that he was answering willingly.

"I do care for you," he said. "Your friendship is-is good to have. As to whether duty is the only truly important part of my life, I don't really know any more. I am beginning to wonder just what it really is and to whom it is owed. Now I see that I-I just don't know."

He released her hand and took up his knife again.

"Everything was so clear once," he said. "I resolved sincerely to defend and protect those within my care. I chose that path the day I left that prison. I saw my life before me and I wished to use that life for something—" he paused to seek the proper words. "—something worthy of a life's work. It was a gift: I had so little to give, but what I had I gave freely"

He looked down at his hands: his voice had become very quiet. "I thought it would be so simple," he said. "To offer that life and one day have it taken. I was ready. But the day has never come..." His voice trailed off into silence.

"And now what?" asked Elise.

"I don't know," Malet said as he set the peeled potato into a bowl of water and selected another. "I wonder if I chose the easy way out all those years ago."

"But you had decided that you were willing to die for others," Elise pointed out. "What greater resolve could there be?"

"I was a melodramatic young fool. I decided that I was willing to die for them, true, but I had never given any real thought to living for them.

"Now that I am a grown man and not a child of fifteen, I know that is the greater service, not standing back and thinking myself somehow set apart because I was ready to give my life! How foolish! We all owe a duty one way or another. We can't live for ourselves alone. There's always something for which we give our lives. And isn't the measure of a man in part the cause for which he is willing to give his life?"

Elise's lips had parted, and she gazed at him. "You really believe that!" she said on a note of wonder. "But you were raised in a prison, among criminals!"

"Of course I believe it. Nothing ever happens by accident. We can choose to make of ourselves and our lives a blessing or a curse. I chose the first way. It was the only choice I could make, really... How could I take the weapons put in my hand and turn them against those who needed protection? So I chose as I did, and I don't regret the choice."

"No," said Elise, more to herself than to him. "No, you wouldn't regret it, ever. No matter what the cost to yourself."

Malet had not looked up. He paused and searched for words. "As for me, the years are passing, and I wonder what will become of me. What happens to a guard dog grown old in service? You can't teach that sort to fawn."

Elise recovered herself with an effort, though she still seemed to see him with new eyes. "They don't need to fawn," she said. "One takes the dog into the house, pets it and loves it the rest of its days. That's all. But there is a difference between men and dogs, M'sieur.

"Let me ask you this: what if I were to tell of one who sojourned in a strange land for many years. Let us say that while he knew the language and the customs, he felt himself apart from the others, and yet he sincerely tried to serve them for many years. Unbeknown to him, those people had come to love him: what if one of them came up to him and said, 'You are one of us now: come and dwell with us and be our friend as well as our guardian'? What would the sojourner do?"

Malet had finished peeling the last potato. He carefully wiped the blade of his knife and set it aside. "There, all finished," he said as he wiped his hands on a towel and then rolled his sleeves back down and buttoned the cuffs.

"M. l'Inspecteur," she said, exasperated with his elusiveness, especially in view of all that had just been said. "I asked a question!"

He looked up and smiled warmly at her. "I don't know the answer," he said more lightly than before. "It might depend on who said it to the sojourner, and who he himself might be. It might...make him very happy."

She gave it up, annoyed with him because she suspected that he was laughing at her. "You said it was dangerous last night. I wish to thank you again. In—in behalf of all whose lives you saved."

Malet rose and turned away to retrieve his coat. The color in his cheeks was heightened when he turned back. "It was nothing," he said formally, bowing. "I was truly happy to be of service."

"Perhaps I can return the favor one day," she said.

His eyes were dancing as they traveled from the top of her head to the floor, and he seemed to be estimating her weight. Suddenly he was smiling again. "Be sure you have your pistols," he said with the hint of a grin. "You are no bigger than my housekeeper's spaniel!"

She sniffed and shook her head.

He was still smiling, and he said in a gentle voice she hadn't heard him use before, "I must go out again, and I will be very late getting in. I must question a witness tonight, and I don't know how long it will take. If it's very late, I will stay elsewhere. Don't have anyone wait up for me."

CHAPTER TWENTY

Inspector Malet at The Opera

The last notes throbbed in the hushed air of the Opera House and faded into a silence that lingered for the space of time it took to draw a deep breath. The burst into thunderous applause. Rosalie Plessis remained on her knees with her hands clasped before her as the curtains swept together to hide the stage from view.

The audience rose to their feet in wave upon wave of cheering as the curtains opened again to show La Plessis on her feet now and smiling. She sank into a low curtsey, her dark head bent, and then rose again as the rest of the company came in behind her and bowed.

The cheering did not abate as the company took its bows, as Rosalie accepted bouquet after bouquet from the audience and finally sang three encores, one with the leading tenor. It was another half-hour before she could finally turn away from the curtain and smile at the rest of the troop. "A splendid performance, Rosa!" cried Adele Clout, the contralto. "You will take England by storm!"

Rosalie made a graceful reply, ignored the hissed "Bitch!" of the castrato, Francesco Venuti, and gave her largest bouquet of roses to the lead chorus-girl.

"Here, Lillie," she said. "Give these to the girls. They outdid themselves this evening."

"After a night like this, how can you think of leaving Paris?" demanded the tenor.

Rosalie shrugged. "I would like to see London," she said. "And now, if you will excuse me, I am very tired."

It took another ten minutes for her to reach her dressing salon, the largest in the theater, and she paused at the door to chat with the wardrobe mistress before opening the door with a sigh.

She had not lied: she was exhausted. Singing was a more athletic occupation than many people realized. The presence in Paris of the phenomenal singer, Maria Felicia Garcia, known as La Milacron, was a signal to her to move on. She could not hope to compete with that voice.

Her dresser had promised to heat a bath for her. She could already feel the warmth of the water soaking away the aches. And yet, she could not suppress the exultation. She had sung well that night.

She closed the door behind her and shed the light cloak that had been set over her shoulders. Her anteroom was filled with roses of every conceivable color and size. Their sweet, heavy scent was overpowering, and it was with a sense of relief that she noticed a large bouquet of purple asters.

That bouquet, stirring the memory of a past love, made her hesitate in the doorway of her dressing room. She lifted it and buried her face in it as she stepped over the threshold.

She stopped just inside the door with an exclamation of surprise.
"You!"

The cause of her astonishment was reclining at his elegant ease on the silk-upholstered Recamier by the screen and scanning a volume of English poetry. He raised smiling eyes and rose as she came into the room. "I see you found my flowers," he said.

Rosalie laid the asters aside and gazed up at him. "Hello, Paul," she said through an answering smile.

He inserted one long finger between the pages of the book, and said, "Hello, Rose. I was just reading of you." He opened the book again and read in English,

> "'She walks in beauty, like the night of cloudless climes and starry skies, and all that's best of dark and bright
>
> Meet in her aspect and her eyes...'"

He was smiling as he laid the book aside and took her hands in his.
"How did you get in here?" she asked.
"I said I wanted to see you," he replied.

"And no one tried to stop you?" she demanded, torn between annoyance and amusement.

"Some puffing, lard-bellied bag-pudding who seemed to fancy himself a Police officer tried to be obstructive," Malet admitted. "I took care of him."

"Poor René!" she gasped, trying to suppress a giggle at the description. "You didn't hurt him, did you?

He opened his eyes at her and raised her hand to his lips. "I didn't lay a finger on him," he said as he bent to kiss her wrist, an old caress between them. "I flashed my card and told him to stand aside, and when he wanted to argue, I told him to stop. That's all. Is he your latest flame, then?" His face was completely serious.

"Wretch!" she exclaimed through her laughter. "He is not! Let me look at you! Three years!" Her hand disengaged from his, brushed up his arm to his shoulder, and drew him to her as she raised her face for his kiss.

They had met in 1827, his second year in Paris, when her career was just beginning to blossom. She had been beset by a mob of admirers outside the Opera house. Although she had been a performer for many years and used to the vagaries of crowds, their admiration this time exceeded the limits of what she considered safe or proper. Her footmen had been beaten, and she had been pulled from her carriage. She had cried for help, and he had appeared, tall, calm, and capable.

He had somehow managed to disperse the crowd all alone, rendered assistance to her servants, and then took her back to her home. When she tried to hail him as her savior, he shrugged off her gratitude and told her that he was a Police Inspector, and her rescue was merely his duty.

The reply had been robbed of its coolness when he added with a disarming twinkle that for once he had found his duty a sheer delight. That had emboldened her to invite him inside for some refreshment, and he had accepted.

They laughed at the same things, and by the time he had left her, she had warmed to him enough to ask him to sup with her the next night. The liking had grown, and some time later Paris whispered that La Plessis had taken a new lover.

Paris was correct. Like many women of her station, she had no difficulty expressing her affection physically, but she found him something of a puzzle. There was always a sense of detachment about him, though he was as passionate and appreciative as any woman could want.

They had had a slight quarrel and Rosalie had meant to speak with him the next day, but the cataclysm of the July revolution of 1830 burst upon them before she could do so. She fled the city for some months and stayed under the protection of a man named Constant Dracquet.

It was a long time before Malet could leave his bed, but when he was finally recovered, he never came back.

Her life was busy and full, her career was blossoming, and there had always been other men to keep her occupied, but she had always remembered him with fondness, and she was not surprised to see that he still had the power to make her heart beat faster. She realized there would be many things to regret when she left Paris forever.

But she had other concerns at the moment. She set a hand against his chest and pushed him away, though reluctantly. "Wait," she said. "I am tired and filthy at the moment!"

He smiled then and said, "You're as filthy as a rose."

She smiled at the compliment. "You know better. Performing is hard work. Amelia drew me a hot bath."

"So that's who that little giglet was," said Malet. "She blushes enchantingly."

Rosalie sniffed and went behind the screen. "The child drew me a bath and I will be damned if I forego it!" she said as she unlaced her costume. "Sit down! I don't want you pacing about while I am bathing."

"What's the harm in it? You have a screen there."

"You are tall enough to peer over the screen. You have done it several times over the years if you recall. Sit down!"

He obeyed with a chuckle. "And who was that giggling exquisite in yellow satin with the face that would curdle milk? He made a point of bumping into me backstage."

"Francesco Venuti," she replied. "You must have heard of him. He's a fairly well known castrato."

Malet went over to her pitcher and basin and washed his hands and then dried them on a length of linen. "A castrato! That explains why he had a pair of rolled stockings down the front of his trousers!"

She gurgled with delight and stepped into the tub. "He is a nuisance," she said. "Wretch! Where have you been? I did miss you, you know!"

"Nursing a broken heart, of course," he replied with a smooth promptness that she deplored as he sat again. "Just as you did," he added with a touch of acid.

"Chasing criminals, more likely," she retorted. "I have read the papers! You have been very busy. Which reminds me, Paul: why are you here? You aren't one to pine when your heart really isn't broken, and we did part on terms that weren't exactly cordial."

"It wasn't a bad squabble. And there are reasons and reasons for coming back."

Rosalie paused in the act of soaping her throat and shoulders to say with sudden suspicion, "This isn't official, is it?"

"As a matter of fact, it is," Malet replied. He was back on the Recamier with the book in his hands.

"What?"

He looked up from one of Shakespeare's sonnets. "I am taking an interest in something," he said, "And I am pretty sure you know something about one of the major players."

She immersed the sponge, squeezed it out, rubbed it against the bar of violet-scented soap, and said, "I can't afford to get tangled up in criminal matters, Paul. I am leaving Paris within the month. Forever. I want no part of this if it's going to delay me."

His smile was rather dark as he replied, "You needn't worry, all I want from you is some direction. Point me the right way, and I will do the rest."

She was silent for a moment, thinking of the future and remembering the past. "Come home with me," she said at last. "We can dine, as we used to. It will only take me a minute to get dressed." She chuckled again at his politely phrased offer of assistance and decided to dispense with her stays.

CHAPTER TWENTY-ONE

A Policeman's Work Is Never Done

This is as beautiful as I remember," Malet said, looking around at the green and gold splendor of Rosalie's drawing room.

"Yes," she agreed. "It has happy memories."

"I am amazed that you can bear to leave it," Malet said.

She shrugged. "One does what one must," she said. "I am going on to something better, I believe..." Her face was thoughtful for a moment, but she smiled up at him and tucked her hand in his arm. "Come, my dear," she said. "My servants have probably laid out a cold supper in the dining salon, as usual."

As she had said, a chicken in mayonnaise was sitting on a platter surrounded by cheeses, fruits and a bottle of wine. A loaf of bread sat to the side, along with a lemon tart. The table had been laid for two, with snowy tablecloth and napkins.

"Carve the chicken," she said. "I will tend to the fruit."

He nodded and took up the carving knife and fork. "Where are your servants?" he asked as he sliced the breast.

"They always retire early when I have a performance," she replied. "They never know what time I will be returning, or with whom."

Malet set the sliced chicken on a plate and said calmly, "Do you want me to open the wine?"

She looked up from quartering an apple. "Do you know," she said, "I always liked the way you never judge anyone."

"It isn't my job to judge. That's why we have magistrates."

"I am serious."

He raised his eyes to hers over the wine bottle and said, "So am I."

"Are we sparring again?" she asked.

119

He set the cork aside and poured a glass of wine for her. "Not at all, Rosette," he said with a smile. "I am not such a hypocrite as to forget that I was one of those who accompanied you home from your performances." He poured a glass of wine for himself and then carried the plate of chicken to the table.

"You sang magnificently," he said after they had seated themselves and started on the chicken.

She raised her glass of wine to her lips. "Did you really think so?" she asked.

"Your voice was always splendid. But this time it was sublime. La Malibran couldn't hope to surpass you tonight."

She blushed and looked down. "And yet she is a genius," she said. When he didn't comment, she said, "And what of you? Do you ever sing?"

"I often sing under my breath when I walk home at night," he said. "And when I am shaving, too." His eyes lightened with amusement at her expression. "I sing lullabies to my godchildren, too," he said. "But I don't think they really pay attention. When are you going to London?"

She set her wine down and gazed across at him with frank understanding. "In a little under a month, Chief Inspector," she replied. "Do you wish to know why I am going?"

"I can guess," he said.

"Can you?"

"Of course. You haven't been to London yet, and the British royal family are great opera aficionados, by all reports. A voice of your quality will be an immediate succès-fou. I only wonder that you didn't go to London sooner."

"You side-stepped that very well, Inspector," she said.

"I said what I believed, Mlle. Plessis," he returned. He eyed her plate and set several more slices of chicken on it.

"You always had a good heart," she said. "Very well, then. You came on official business: what do you wish to know?"

Malet speared a piece of chicken with his fork, dipped it in the mayonnaise, and raised it to his lips. "Constant Dracquet," he said. "You were on friendly terms with him once."

"I was his mistress," she said. "I dismissed him."

"I beg your pardon?"

"I gave him his congé," she said. "I didn't like his style."

"He's very wealthy," Malet pointed out.

"He raised his hand to me," she returned with a glittering smile.

Malet's eyes narrowed. "Did he indeed?"

"Indeed," she said. "I gave him a cut across the face with my riding whip and told him to get out of my sight. I told him he was a classless crook without taste or style. He still has the mark of the blow on his face." She met his gaze and read the question in his eyes. "He hasn't tried to molest me since," she said. "I have powerful friends. Sometimes it's safer to be a singer than a queen."

"You fascinate me," said Malet, offering the plate of cut fruit. "But tell me more about him."

Rosalie looked over the fruit and finally selected a sectioned orange. "Is that why you wished to speak with me? To learn about Constant Dracquet?"

"It is," Malet replied.

"You're taking him on, then?"

"That's right."

She chuckled. "I am surprised you haven't gone after him long before now."

"He had some powerful friends, too. I was stalemated. But this is a new game."

Her eyes flashed. "Bravo, Paul!" she said. "Tell me what you need from me."

THEY SPOKE TOGETHER for some time, until Malet finally pushed his plate aside, drained his glass, and rose. "That's excellent," he said. "It's more than I hoped, and I believe it may be just what I need to get matters started. You are certain of his connections with the British royal family?"

"Quite certain," she said. "I was the hostess for His Grace of Rochester in Paris two years ago, and I recall that he and Dracquet talked long and earnestly before Dracquet came up to bed."

Malet lifted his eyebrows. "Did you hear any of it?" he asked.

She touched her lips with her napkin, frowned slightly at the faint mark of lip rouge on the damask fabric, and looked up at him. "I did," she said. "I was wakeful that night, and I had thought to take a book from the library. This was at the rue de Grenelle house that Dracquet also owns. Had we been at the Montmartre house, I would have had books of my own in my own rooms... I went softly to the library, and I heard their voices as I stood outside the door. They had been discussing theoretic happenings, I think. At any rate, I heard Rochester's voice saying, 'Now if only I were king...' And then Dracquet's voice replied, 'All things are possible, Your Grace, as I have said before...' " She fell silent.

"And that was all?" Malet asked.

"No," she said. "I heard a chime of crystal, as though they had touched glasses to the idea. It made me nervous, so I hurried back to my own rooms. Dracquet came up to me later, and he was...very exuberant."

Malet looked thoughtful. "I see," he said as he stood and offered his hand to Rosalie.

She took his hand but hesitated for a moment, her eyes focused on nothing.

"What is it?" asked Malet.

She looked up at him. "I just remembered," she said. "When I was singing Rosina in The Barber of Seville, early in September, I happened to look up into the boxes and I thought I saw the duke, just for a moment.

I had to turn away and sing, and he was gone when I looked next."

"But it was Rochester?" Malet asked.

"I couldn't be certain," she replied. "The man was sitting at a distance, but he was in Dracquet's customary box."

Malet did not say anything.

Her hand was still in his. She rose and said, "Will I be required to testify?"

"Not at all. Your name won't even come into this inquiry. You gave me background, nothing more. It's up to me to turn this to my advantage." His smile grew more ominous. "As I shall," he added.

"As you shall..." she repeated. She saw that he was suddenly restless.

"Must you leave now?" she asked.

"It's late," he said. "I have things to do tomorrow."

"But we have had so little time to talk," she said. "It's been so long... Surely, for old time's sake-since I am leaving France..."

His expression was still withdrawn and slightly ominous, but it softened at the wistful note of her voice, and he took her hand.

She tried to smile at him. "The years do pass," she said. "I missed you when we parted. Was it because of that quarrel that you never came back?"

His gaze seemed to be directed inward, but he replied, "No, not really. France had changed, King Charles had been ousted and Louis Philippe was king, the Police needed me, and suddenly you were the pride of the Opera and busier than you had ever been. I realized that we weren't suited as a couple. I have always had a warm spot in my heart for you. You have never lost my friendship. You know that."

"I do know it," she said. "It means more to me than you realize." She walked slowly with him to the green salon. "You have found your love at last," she said without rancor or bitterness.

He did not deny it. "Unfortunately," he said, "she hasn't found me." He paused and then said wryly, "And I am not in a position to say the words to make her love me... And even if I were, I wouldn't know what to say. "

"Then say nothing, and kiss her lips," Rosalie said. "You're very persuasive that way."

His eyes were lowered, and he shook his head. "No," he said, "I can't do that at the moment. She's a lady to her fingertips, and what I feel for her runs deeper even than that."

Watching him, Rosalie felt her heart turn over with sympathy. She had felt that sort of ache in her own heart. But she could help the pain. She touched his sleeve lightly with her fingertips. "Do you remember the night I taught you to waltz?" she asked. "It was after *I Puritani*, and I had sung only for you. Do you remember?"

The pain faded a little from his eyes and he smiled down at her. "How could I forget?" he said. "It was our first night together. You were so beautiful, and I was all left feet that night."

"You were as nimble as a cat," she said. "I remember, if you don't. It was a splendid night. Do you still waltz?"

"Only with the right partner," he said.

"Who better than your teacher?" she asked and went to the inlaid music box on the pier table. She wound it until it was tight, set it down, and went to him as the brisk, tinkling notes unwound into the quiet room.

He was smiling again. She stepped into his arms, paused to catch the beat, and then moved into the dance with him.

The scent of roses filled the air, and the beeswax candles, adding the light scent of honey, glowed in his eyes as they whirled about the room.

He smiled down at her; his eyes warmed as she moved closer to him, caught in a web of memory. Her right hand came to rest against his heart, quivering with the race of its beat. His arms circled her waist and she felt a light kiss against her cheek. She opened her eyes to gaze into his and smile again.

"Oh Rose, how could I forget?" he murmured. The music was slowing now, and they were barely moving as he bent to touch his lips to her eyes and then, gently, her mouth. The kiss lingered, deepened into passion, and they stood motionless as the music sighed into silence.

The shadow of pain was gone from his eyes and the hand that stroked a tendril of hair back from her cheek was quivering. She felt her heart melt within her. She had loved him so dearly, once...

She moved slightly away from him and held out her hands. "Paul," she said, her voice a thread of sound. "Come to my bed once again."

Her gown slid to her feet in a whisper of silk.

She gazed down at the billows of rose-colored fabric about her ankles, then looked up into his suddenly mischievous smile. "You haven't lost your touch, scoundrel!" she said on the ghost of a chuckle.

"Only with you, Rosette," he said with an echo of her laughter. "You inspire me." His hands moved among the knots of ribbon that fastened the silk shift at her shoulders. It joined the gown a moment later, leaving her naked before him.

He drew her to him and stroked the long, smooth line of her back. His eyes, still fastened on hers, grew hot with remembered passion. "No stays tonight?" he asked as his hands moved slowly upward to pluck at the pins that held the gleaming black coils of her hair in place.

Her smile broadened almost to a grin. "Only with you," she echoed. "You inspire me..."

He was taking too long with her hairpins; she sighed and raised her arms to remove the remaining pins and scatter them on the floor. She shook her hair loose about her shoulders and waist as she stepped deliberately out of the mass of silk at her feet and kicked off her pink morocco slippers.

He caught her to him and traced a tingling path of kisses from her throat to her breast. His right hand twined in the thick, heavy mass of her hair and drew her head back; he paused to smile at her before his mouth came down upon hers.

She abandoned herself wholeheartedly to the embrace, her hands moving eagerly over him, lingering, remembering. "You have me at a disadvantage," she breathed against his lips after a moment.

His eyes flickered, but he drew back and said on the breath of a chuckle, "That can be easily remedied, you know."

"I know," she said as he started to unknot his cravat. She pushed his hands aside. "No, let me," she said. She was smiling as she drew out the emerald pin from the folds of silk and set it aside on a nearby table. The cravat and his coat joined the pin a moment later.

His eyes were fastened on hers. He raised his hand to smooth the hair from her forehead and stroke her cheek. "I have always cared for you, Rose," he said.

"Hush," she said on a quiver of laughter as her fingers plucked at the buttons of his waistcoat. "I know. I have always known." She pushed the waistcoat aside and smiled as she unfastened the buttons of his shirt and slid her hands inside, to savor the smooth, warm swell of his chest and glory in the swift beat of his heart beneath her fingers.

No regrets, she thought. Not on the eve of her departure for England and marriage. No regrets ever, only happy memories...

"You're so beautiful, Rose..." he breathed. He caught her hand to his lips and then swung her up into his arms. She wrapped her arms about his neck and drew him down to her, to kiss him again and again until the room seemed to spin about them.

"Rosette...?" his voice, alive with suppressed perplexity and amusement, eased the spell for a moment.

"Mmm?" She traced the line of his lips.

"You have changed things here. Where the devil is your bedroom?"

She lay back in his arms and broke into peals of delighted laughter.

THE FIRELIGHT HAD SUNK to a soft glow upon the hearth, bathing the room in warm, rosy light. Rosalie paused in the act of brushing her hair to gaze back toward her bed and smile.

Malet was asleep, his lips softened in a half-smile, his cheek resting against his hand. Asleep, with his hair in his eyes and the austere lines of his face warmed and relaxed, he looked mischievous rather than heroic.

She turned and drew the brush through her hair once more, and then set the brush aside and braided the mass. That done, she rose and went softly back to the bed and stood gazing down at him again.

Her lips moved in an answering smile. She carefully eased herself into his arms and drew the covers up over her shoulder.

He seemed to feel the movement. His arms tightened slightly; he drew a breath and expelled it in a sigh.

'Love must lie down with laughter', she thought, *'or it will make its bed in hell.'* Now her heart was filled with laughter and warmth. She settled herself against him, kissed the bandage on his left arm, and then raised her fingertips to trace a scar that cut deep across his ribs. He had been wounded after they parted, and he still bore the marks.

She snuggled more closely against him, yawned and laid her cheek against his heart, and so drifted at last into sleep...

Five minutes passed. The firelight glimmered beneath Malet's lashes. His eyes opened cautiously, and he raised his head.

Rosalie sighed and murmured, then was still again.

He smiled down at her sleek, dark head before he looked toward the right, where his waistcoat lay half-draped across the corner of the bed. He cautiously raised his right arm and reached for it, delicately searching for the breast pocket. After a moment he extracted his leather notebook and gold pencil. He brought the notebook to his left hand, lifted the pencil, and carefully advanced the lead.

He hadn't meant for this to happen, but he had loved her once, and the memories had come flooding back now that she was going away forever.

Rosalie sighed his name and curled closer to him.

"I was telling you the truth," he whispered as he dropped a kiss on her forehead and carefully brushed a stray curl from her cheek when he saw that it threatened to fall into her eyes. "I did love you..."

Then he lifted the notebook and pencil and began to write. He would send some urgent inquiries to Burgundy and then speak with Inspector Gilles d'Arthez, one of his chief lieutenants, about going undercover the next day...

CHAPTER TWENTY-TWO

The Police Precinct at the rue des Trois Frères Receives a Visitor

"Good morning. Your card, please." The Officer of the Day took the round, glass-bound card, glanced at it perfunctorily, noted the name in his log, and gave the card back. It was morning, it took him a while to wake up, and no one important would be coming around to this sleepy little precinct before noon, anyhow.

He yawned and reached for the cup of coffee that sat at his elbow—and jumped as a well-gloved hand whisked it away from him.

"Wait a minute! What—" He looked up and stopped, the angry words dying in his throat as he encountered a glacial stare from the tall, well-dressed man standing before him.

The man smiled grimly, set the coffee down, and covered the last journal entry with his hand.

"What is my name, what is my age, and what is my rank?" he asked. The inflection was the same one the Officer of the Day used with his children when they were naughty.

He stared at the man.

"Come now, Constable," the man said. "You just wrote them down. I watched you do it."

"I–I—" The constable was flabbergasted. No one had ever done this to him before.

"I see," said the man. "You never looked at me, you gave the card back without checking my signature, and you didn't have me sign the book in the first place. How do you know I am not an assassin?"

"I am sorry!"

"You'd be a good deal sorrier if I tried to kill you," the man said, pulling off his right glove. "Your sword's far away, you have no stick, and you carry no pistol."

He twitched the logbook toward him and scanned it. "I see that no one signs in half the time," he said. "Very interesting." He took out a gold pencil from his breast pocket, signed the logbook, and said, "Where do you hold muster in the morning?"

"The—the third room, there on the right."

The man returned the logbook. "Thank you," he said. He removed his hat, pulled off his left glove, took up his silver-headed walking stick, and moved away.

The O.O.D. reached for his cup with a shaking hand. He almost spilled the coffee when he looked down at the log. He had written, *P. V. Malet, Ch. Insp. Age 47.*

"BASTIAN!"

"Here!"

"Bignon!"

"Here!"

The names continued one after another in the morning ritual of roll call, the owner of each name responding as his was called.

"Richard!"

"Here!"

"de Saint-Légère!"

"Here." The voice answered before anyone could remind the head of the Precinct, Inspector Auguste Rameau, that Junior Inspector de Saint-Légère was on special assignment at the Bois de Boulogne. Now everyone turned to see who had spoken.

Inspector Rameau himself was not amused. He looked up with a thin smile. "All right, then," he said, "What joker—" he stopped and swallowed. "Chief Inspector!" he said in a completely different voice.

He stopped and collected himself. Malet might be the acting Prefect of Police, but this was his, Rameau's territory! "Gentlemen," he said, "permit me to present to you M. Malet, Chief Inspector of the 8th arrondissement and Provisional Prefect of Police in the absence of M. Lamarque."

Malet's eyes lightened with amused respect even as he noted the uneasy expressions on some of the faces. He inclined his head to Rameau and said, "Good morning, Inspector Rameau. Gentlemen."

"And to what do we owe the honor of this visit?" asked Rameau.

"I am taking an interest in a matter that M. de Saint-Légère brought to the Prefect's attention," Malet replied. "I thought to come by here and review his duties, if it is permitted."

"There's no question of it being permitted," said Rameau. "Allow me to finish here, and I am completely at your service."

INSPECTOR RAMEAU TOOK Malet on an inspection tour of the Precinct and then gave him a write-up of Saint-Légère's beat. At the last moment he said, "And M. Malet—?"

"Yes?" Malet looked up from the itinerary and surprised a wistful expression on Rameau's face. A nervous-looking young constable was standing beside him and kneading the brim of his bicorne between his fingers.

"Pelletan here just started this week," said Rameau.

The young man attempted a smile.

"Could he walk with you today? Until, say, two o'clock?" Rameau asked.

Malet looked Pelletan over, frowning slightly, and then checked his watch. He put the watch back in his waistcoat pocket and noticed that Pelletan was directing a longing look at the watch and chain. Malet smiled and saw the young man's face light up in response. "It would be a pleasure," he said.

Two hours later Malet was frowning at the houses along the rue Lepic, his eyes caught by one in particular, a tall, tan stone building with wide windows and a courtyard beside it. This house belonged to Constant Dracquet, and it was part of Charles de Saint-Légère's beat.

The area was pleasant enough, but the beat was one that a rank beginner could handle and still be bored. The only reason that the rank beginner who walked beside him was not bored was his very painful awareness of the identity of the man he was accompanying, as well as the fact that Malet had decided to make his visit a sort of training session.

They had strolled down steep, winding streets bounded by tall houses, returning the greetings of the residents. They halted traffic once or twice to allow children to cross. Malet, who enjoyed teaching, had Pelletan do the honors while he offered suggestions.

Malet was patient and gentle, and by the end of an hour, though he was not aware of it, he had a wholehearted admirer who would cheerfully have died for him, and who raised no objection when he said, "That place interests me: let's look closer."

They lunched at a tiny café along the boulevard de Rochechouart, in the shadow of the butte, or summit, of Montmartre. Malet listened to Pelletan's life story as he drank a glass of vin ordinaire and downed a fair-sized portion of roast chicken. It was 1:30 by the time they finished, and Malet was considering going back toward the Precinct.

"M. l'Inspecteur...?" Pelletan was still a little shy.

"Yes, Constable?" Malet said.

"May I ask a question?"

Malet smiled as he drained his glass. "By all means," he said.

"Are you glad you became a Police officer?" Pelletan asked. "I mean, d-did you ever wonder if there was something else you could have done?" Seeing Malet's quizzical frown, he added, "It's so different from what I thought it would be..."

Malet smiled at the boy—really, he wasn't much more than that. "What did you think it would be?" he asked. "Chasing murderers all the time? Cornering spies?"

"I don't know," Pelletan said, shoving his hands in his pockets and stretching his feet out before him.

"Listen to me, lad. What we are sworn to do is to protect those who aren't strong enough to protect themselves. That's all. It is enough for me. Whether it is enough for you is something you have to decide for yourself. It's no shame to you if you decide that it is not."

Pelletan's eyes were bright with something Malet was touched to recognize as hero-worship. "If it's enough for you," he said, "then it's certainly enough for me!"

Malet did not laugh, though he found the young man's admiration a little amusing. Instead, he poured him another small glass of wine, cautioned him about the dangers of drinking while on duty, and wondered if he might be able to entice him to leave Guerin's arrondissement and come to the 8th.

CHAPTER TWENTY-THREE

Master and Apprentice

Malet sat back in the Prefect's chair and smiled down at the inlaid music box that had been brought to the Prefecture while he was away. It had been wrapped in silver paper, and a note enclosed with it:

Welcome back.
Rosette

He wound the box and listened to the brisk waltz, his face warmed by a smile. She had always known how to heal an ache.

He heard a tapping on the door. "Come in," he said, and smiled again as Clerel entered, his arms full of roses. "You found them," he said. "I didn't dare hope they'd be there."

"I went to the Marché aux Fleurs, Chief Inspector, and searched for the roses with the red and white petals," Clerel said. "I bought all they had—three dozen—and the one purple aster, as well. Here's the receipt, and your change."

Malet rose and went over to look at the roses. They were the most beautiful he had seen, pure white on the outside, with the inner part of each petal a deep, cherry-red. "Yes," he said. "Those were the ones."

"Do you wish to have them delivered somewhere?" Clerel asked with elaborate casualness.

Malet's eyes lightened in a smile. "Why, yes, my dear Clerel," he said. "This is the address." he took a fold of paper with an address on it, copied it quickly, and then, after a moment's thought, wrote:

For you, always. You will be sorely missed.

"There," he said. "That's the address and the message. Will you be dispatching one of the office boys?"

"Those chatterboxes?" asked Clerel, his voice for once devoid of its pomposity. "No. I will take them myself. It will be a pleasure."

"Thank you," said Malet. "You are a prince among men."

Clerel bowed and left.

Malet looked down at the music box, closed it, and then took up paper and pen and began to write:

My dear Christien: '

I am providing you with an opportunity to indulge your passion for free meals. Meet me at the prefecture at 5:00 p.m., and we shall dine together, on me. I need hardly ask that you bring a sharp appetite, since I have never known you not to be hungry. My pockets will be to let, I do not doubt, but I am confident that the amusement attendant upon an evening's conversation with you will make up for it.

Yours, etc.

Malet

That done, he folded the note, sealed it, and went out in search of Sergeant Guillart. Once the note was delivered, he could sit back and ponder the British succession.

"YOU SEEM TO HAVE THIS odd notion that you need only crook your finger and your friends will come running!" L'Eveque said some hours later as he raised a glass of champagne to his lips.

"Crooking my finger has nothing to do with it," Malet said with a smile. "I don't deceive myself: it is the prospect of free food that draws them. And you were certainly moving briskly when you came into my offices."

L'Eveque grinned. "Let's say that the food isn't a deterrent," he said.

"I thought not." Malet set his glass down as the waiter arrived with the first course of oysters on the half-shell. He watched L'Eveque down the four before him and then passed his plate over.

"Why aren't you eating them?" L'Eveque demanded.

"I hate oysters," Malet replied.

"Then why on earth did you order them?" L'Eveque asked, exasperated.

"To let you eat mine," Malet replied. "Go ahead: you like them, though God alone knows why!" He lifted his glass of champagne again and sipped. "I understand that you're doing well with your precinct," he said. "His Excellency is very happy with your performance."

L'Eveque sat back to allow the waiter to remove the two empty plates, and then frowned down at the soup that was set in their place. "M. d'Anglars is very kind," he said. "I am happy where I am, and I like my people." He paused and added, "I must thank you again for recommending me and insisting on the promotion. I hated to leave you."

Malet tasted the soup and shook his head. "No," he said, "You were wasted where you were. I was sorry to lose you, but the force was the gainer in the end." He added with a sigh, "I do seem fated to lose my best people, though..."

L'Eveque impulsively stretched out his hand to Malet. "My dear sir!" he exclaimed, "Never their friendship! I shouldn't have to tell you that!" He fell silent as the waiter removed the empty soup cups, set a course of creamed salmon in pastry before them, filled their glasses with a light Sauterne, and then withdrew.

Malet snorted and cut into the salmon.

"So tell me," said L'Eveque after a few minutes of silence. "Why did you invite me to dine with you?"

"Can't I give myself the pleasure of your chatter one evening out of three hundred?" Malet asked. "Must there be a reason for everything I do?"

"No, there mustn't," L'Eveque said with precision, "But I have noticed that there usually is. What is it, Paul?"

Malet cut off a particularly golden piece of pastry with the edge of his fork, speared it, and ate it in a leisurely manner.

L'Eveque waited.

Malet finally said, "I spoke with His Excellency today."

"I trust he was in good health," L'Eveque said.

Malet threw him an impatient look but replied, "He's quite well, and he had some interesting things to tell me about you."

"Oh?"

"Yes. He told me, for example, that you have been gathering information for him in a matter that closely concerns the 3rd arrondissement and its Chief Inspector. Such a matter interests me very much at the moment, for it ties in closely with a matter I am investigating."

"I see," said L'Eveque.

"No, you don't," said Malet, who had finished the fish course. "But you will shortly. I asked Count d'Anglars' permission to discuss it with you, and he granted it." He took a folded and sealed slip of paper from his pocket and handed it to L'Eveque. "Here's a note from him to that effect," he said, "And I suggest you burn it after you read it."

L'Eveque frowned at the note and then transferred his frown to Malet's face. "I don't need an order from headquarters to confide in you, Paul," he said.

Malet shrugged. "Don't be so prickly, Christien," he said. "Maybe you'd confide in me: but it would be most improper, and you know it. You can speak without hesitation now, and never fear that my regard for M. Guerin will prompt me to use that information improperly."

"As though you ever would!"

"I might be tempted. So: read the note and stop delaying. And finish your fish."

L'Eveque opened the note, read it, and then held it in the flame of one of the candles that sat on the table, and watched it burn for a moment before dropping it on his bread plate. "All right," he said. "Ask what you want."

Malet nodded to the waiter, who was hovering at a distance, and waited until the next course had been set before them and their glasses filled with an aged Beaujolais. "I am handling a matter that Inspector de Saint-Légère brought to my attention," he said. "I became interested in the man while investigating this matter, and I have read most of his reports."

"He's a fine man," said L'Eveque. "I have known him since before Waterloo. We were in the 1st Cuirassiers together, and we kept in touch after I was invalided from the army."

"You recommended him for the force," Malet said.

"Yes, I did. He wanted to return to France, and I had a job for him if he wanted it."

"Which he did," Malet said, taking up the fork and the carving knife that had been brought with the roast. "As I said, I read his reports after speaking with him about the matter he brought to my attention. Something he said gave me pause, and I decided to look into it. I waved a red flag today: I spent this morning walking his beat under my real name. Did you know he's not far from Constant Dracquet's house? And then, this afternoon, I sent some of the Prefecture's special agents to Saint-Légère's old assignment and had them ask a few questions of the shopkeepers around there. What I learned is very disturbing, and I understand, from His Excellency, that you are looking into a similar matter for him.'

He cut a slice of meat, laid it almost gently down on the platter, and said, "It appears that there's quite a protection racket going on in the 3rd arrondissement."

"That's right," L'Eveque answered. "I discovered it not long after I was promoted to my precinct. It was quite a shock, coming from your command to Guerin's and encountering it. I have been assembling names, dates, amounts of money—cooperating with Guerin, outwardly. I have been making my reports regularly to the Count. So far, I don't think anyone suspects anything. They think my hands are as filthy as everyone else's."

Malet frowned and lowered the fork and carving knife for a moment. "You're playing a very dangerous game, Christien," he said. "The stakes could be your life."

"You're a fine one to talk," said L'Eveque.

When Malet did not respond, he added, "M. le Comte is the soul of courtesy. I certainly don't object to making my reports available to you."

Malet had been carving the roast as they were speaking. He handed L'Eveque a plate full of sliced beef, set several small boiled potatoes beside them, and then set to work assembling a plate for himself. "Thank you," he said. "That's what I wanted. And now, since I am investigating the matter myself, I want you to stop your work on it."

"We'll see what His Excellency says."

"That's fair. And it's all I wanted to hear."

"And for this you bought me a supper!" L'Eveque said, smiling again.

Malet dipped the salt spoon in the saltcellar and scattered salt across his meat, then spooned some of the juices over it. "I don't see you often enough." He cut a bite of meat and chewed it.

"We do keep busy, don't we?" L'Eveque said.

Malet smiled and sipped his wine. "There's another matter," he said.

L'Eveque set his fork down. "Do you know," he said, "Somehow I rather thought there'd be."

"No, it has to do with Saint-Légère. He's very good. Whether or not our investigations into our respective matters get any results, I think it's wrong that the man should be stuck where he is. It's obvious to me that Guerin wants to force him out of the Police. I don't know how he managed to last as long as he has: I can be patient, but only a week of that beat would have me ready to resign. At any rate, I am thinking of setting things in motion to have him brought to my arrondissement. The proposal would be a promotion, so we'd be following proper procedure. Do you think he will refuse if I approach him?"

"Charles?" L'Eveque demanded. "Certainly not! He will go if I have to drag him to you by the hair! I have been worried about him, and if he were under your command—it would be beyond anything wonderful!" He paused and then said more briskly, "I can gather some recommendations for Saint-Légère' promotion if you wish. He's wasted where he is, but I wasn't sure how to step in."

"Never mind, Christien. I will handle matters," said Malet. "Keep out of it for your own sake. As it is, he will be angry that I am raiding his flock, and I think there's a battle-royal coming at any rate. No matter: I don't fight unless I am sure I can win."

L'Eveque said, "If I can do anything else..."

"You can."

L'Eveque had not quite been voicing an insincere social formula, but he was a little surprised to have his offer accepted so promptly. He smiled, though, and said, "I am at your service, of course."

"Of course," Malet said. His tone was dry, but he broke into a warm smile. "Relax, Christien," he said. "It isn't as bad as you fear. I want you and some others to go to the auction that the remount service is having in two weeks' time. See what price that bay stallion fetches: for that matter, you can bid on him, yourself, but I suspect that he will sell high. Watch who bids on him and see who buys him. Detail your best trackers to follow the horse back to his purchaser's stable and shadow the buyers."

"Is there a reason for all this?" L'Eveque asked.

Malet's frown became a scowl, and it seemed for a moment as though he might deal L'Eveque one of the snubs for which he was famous, but he replied gently enough, "How long did you work with me, Christien? Use your mind: the horse is a bribe. He's also very valuable, and the one attempting the bribery would want to buy the horse back. I want to see who it is. Besides, my dear Christien, other horses will be offered for bidding. Perhaps you can purchase a horse for your friend, Saint-Légère, who seems to be fretting for one. If you do, I will be happy to contribute something toward it." L'Eveque sat back. "That's an excellent idea!" he said.

"I thought it was."

"I will do it!"

"Good," said Malet. He took his billfold from his breast pocket, took out several notes, and handed them to L'Eveque. "These can be my contribution," he said.

L'Eveque looked at the notes and nearly dropped them. The top one was a twenty-franc note. He looked up and saw that Malet was motioning to the waiter. "Thank you," he said. "You are very generous."

Malet turned back and smiled at him. "It's nothing," he said with an air of finality. As L'Eveque watched, his smile softened and warmed. "Christien?" he said.

"Yes, Paul?"

"Madame de Clichy is your cousin?"

L'Eveque lifted his eyebrows slightly, but he answered without showing any surprise. "Yes, she is."

"Is she spoken for?"

CHAPTER TWENTY-FOUR

Inspector Malet at Scoundrel Square

The place Gredin was the name given to a huddle of dingy gray buildings and shadowed doorways set in a small square at the edge of the 8th arrondissement. The name means 'Scoundrel Square', and it had once been apt. The square had once teemed with thieves' hovels and dim little pawnshops and the sort of filthy, dark places that swallowed runaway children. It had been a busy, profitable place for the right sort of people, a splendid listening post, and a haven where one could dispose of goods obtained in ways that the Law might not like.

It was just beginning to show some signs of respectability, thanks to the actions of Chief Inspector Malet. Two years after his arrival, the place Gredin witnessed the biggest arrest of criminals of all sorts and the largest recovery of stolen property in the history of Paris.

The arrests were the culmination of an elaborate undercover scheme that had taken two years to bring to fruition. It had brought in quite a haul. The place Gredin had been ringed by armed soldiers under the direction of the Chief Inspector. It had taken twelve police wagons to transport the prisoners to the Conciergerie.

The members of the underworld of the 8th arrondissement never recovered from the shock. Many of them shifted their territories to the neighboring arrondissements, to the dismay of Chief Inspectors Fauquier of the 12th, and Rabateau of the 7th.

Only one pawnshop remained at the place Gredin, a dingy establishment made singular by the beautifully carved sign above the door that announced to the world that Joseph Michaud, pawnbroker and antiquarian, traded there.

Michaud had been able to remain open due to some shady connections with the Police in the 8th. He had been too smart to engage in anything openly or provably wrong, and when Inspector Malet had come to his door, Michaud had greeted him effusively, offered him wine and butter cakes, and directed that his assistant escort the Chief Inspector about the shop. He even assured the Inspector that the books were available for his perusal, if he wished.

Malet's eyes had narrowed as Michaud's smile had widened: the man had been tipped off, and not recently, by the look of things. Malet knew when he was stymied: he had declined the refreshments, strolled perfunctorily through the shop, and finally left.

Some months later, two of Malet's subordinates were dismissed. Four more were transferred to distant prefectures, their dossiers containing devastatingly frank letters from the Chief Inspector, who did not tolerate double-dealing.

Michaud had remained in business, but it had been a precarious triumph, for he was a thorn in the Chief Inspector's side, and he had the uncomfortable feeling that a vast shadow was looming over his operation. It was beginning to wear him down. He felt like one of the sinners carved on the facade of the cathedral, pursuing his tawdry little crimes on the path to Hell under the majestically contemptuous gaze of a mailed and armored St. Michael.

He began to dream of withdrawing from his very lucrative line of business and returning to the village of his birth, far from that ominous gaze. The longing came to him from time to time as he made his way to his home, glancing fearfully at shadows in the streets, flinching when someone spoke unexpectedly to him.

It was not that the Chief Inspector persecuted Michaud. Even the underworld admitted that the man was fair; if there was nothing to prove wrongdoing, then he always treated his quarry as one who had done nothing wrong. But this fairness did not make him any less formidable an adversary. He had a retentive memory and a long attention span. His patience was legendary: he set his traps and waited for the wrongdoer to slip.

Withering under that patient scrutiny, Michaud was beginning to fear that he would slip soon. He suspected that Malet only suffered his presence because he had from time to time been useful to the police as an informer, a role that Malet viewed with scorn but whose value was undeniable. Nevertheless, Michaud feared that Malet would one day decide that he could dispense with informers and that would be the end.

This day, however, such fears were far from him. Malet was away from the 8th, which was being administered by Inspector Plougastel, a capable man but as far from Malet as an ocelot is from a tiger. He was engaged in negotiating with the seller of a particularly fine piece of jewelry, his gout was not troubling him at the moment, he had eaten an excellent meal and was planning to partake of another as soon as the present piece of business was finished.

Things were going well until Michaud heard a muffled exclamation and saw several of the store's occupants scatter and lose themselves in the shadows.

The ragged, furtive man before him turned, looked over his shoulder, and quickly pocketed the diamond and sapphire ring he had brought in to sell. "Shit!" he hissed as he edged along the counter toward the back door. "What's he doing here?"

Michaud leaned forward to peer down toward the front of the shop and froze. He had a confused impression of a towering being bearing down on him, the peculiar silence of its progress underlined by the faint jingle of a sheathed sword. His heart faltered and lurched sickeningly as he shrank back against the wall. And—were those wings that he saw?

Joseph Michaud was a pragmatic man. He might believe in angelic visitations but not until all other explanations had been exhausted. He took a second to catch his breath, and by the end of that pause he was cursing himself for having such an active imagination that saw winged, warrior archangels instead of tall men in black coats.

His alarm returned after another moment, when he realized who was coming toward him.

The ragged man had reached the door and opened it.

"I will be speaking to you soon, Jacquillat," said Michaud's visitor. His voice echoed appallingly in the silence of the shop.

The ragged man, Jacquillat, cast a horrified stare over his shoulder, yanked the door open, and bolted.

Michaud had faced danger before. He stepped forward with a smile even as he fought down his dismay. "M. l'Inspecteur en Chef! A charming surprise, indeed! To what do I owe this honor?"

"Let us dispense with the pleasantries, Michaud. I wish to speak with you."

"I am at the Inspector's service," said Michaud.

Malet flashed a glance around the shop. "Alone," he said.

"As you wish," said Michaud. He raised his voice. "My friends...?"

The people in the shop filed out. The door closed softly behind the last one.

Malet watched them go from beneath frowning brows.

"Well, Monsieur?" said Michaud.

Malet looked over at him, shook his head with an ominous smile, and drew his sword. He strolled down the main aisle of the store. "I said I wish to speak with you alone," he said over his shoulder. "I meant it."

"We're quite alone," said Michaud.

"Are you certain?" Malet asked. "What would happen if I were to take my sword and run it through this curtain, for example?"

Two men erupted from behind the curtain and ran for the door.

Malet watched them, then lifted an eyebrow at Michaud. "Why M. Michaud," he said. "I thought we were alone!"

"We are now," Michaud said.

Malet flashed him a scornful look and went quietly through the pawn-shop one last time. He paused to open a chest and peer behind a dusty counter before returning, satisfied, to Michaud.

"I am told that you hear a great many things which can be useful," he said. "There's a person about whom I'd like to hear something."

"I have been privileged to be of service to the Police from time to time," Michaud said. "And if I can be of service to the Chief Inspector, I will be honored."

"Really?" said Malet with a dark smile. "Suppose I tell you that I want information on a man calling himself Constant Dracquet."

Michaud had been engaged in inspecting a lady's tiny ivory-leafed silver notebook and pencil. He frowned and set it down. "Dracquet?" he repeated. "He's a very big fish."

"So am I," said Malet. "I can give you some particulars."

Michaud looked up at Malet. "I don't need them," he said. "I am acquainted with the man."

"Do you know?" Malet asked gently, "Somehow I am not surprised."

He lifted the notebook. The leaves were smaller than a man's calling card. He touched the repoussé cover. Receiving no answer from Michaud, he frowned and looked across the counter at him.

Michaud had folded his hands and was staring down at them as though he did not expect to see them again. He seemed tired and a little fearful, but he raised his eyes to Malet's and said, "Permit me to understand things, Monsieur. Are you hiring me to find some information for you?"

"Perhaps you could say that I am questioning you," said Malet.

Michaud felt panic rising within him. "I see," he said. His hands were shaking as he busied himself with putting several small items away. He was agonizingly aware that this Nemesis of a Chief Inspector was watching him silently.

The piercing hiss of metal upon metal made him start and drop a comb. He looked up and saw that Malet had sheathed his sword and unfastened the top three buttons of his coat.

"Let us say that I am requesting information," Malet said. His voice was somehow kinder, with a touch of sympathy.

Kindness! Sympathy! Michaud was off balance. He tried to right himself by blustering a little. "And what'll you do for me in return?" he asked. "Your people should have told you that my services are never free."

Malet seemed amused. "Let us discuss what I will not do in return," he said. "That makes matters easier."

Michaud relaxed. He enjoyed cat and mouse games: he played them, himself. The threat was gone for the moment: why not play? "All right," he said. "What won't you do?"

"I won't close you down," Malet replied with a smile.

"Not close me—!" Michaud repeated, astonished. Hadn't that been what Malet had wanted all along? He spread his hands, palms up, his eyebrows raised halfway to his hairline. "Come now, M. l'Inspecteur, that won't wash! My operation is legal!"

"Barely legal," Malet corrected.

"Barely legal is still legal!" Michaud exclaimed.

"Is it?" Malet asked, strolling down the aisle and casting a contempla-tive eye over the merchandise there. He lifted a lady's spangled fan with sticks of mother-of-pearl and opened it, frowning down at the embroidery on it. "You know, Michaud, I am very surprised to see that you are operat-ing without a license."

"I have a license! Paid up through the end of the year!"

Malet's voice was still gentle. "But it's not displayed," he said. "Grounds for closing this place down, Michaud, as you well know. And I am certain I could find a few more just by looking around. For example—"

"Now wait a min—!"

"Yes?" said Malet.

Michaud's shoulders slumped. "Oh very well," he said. "You have won. I thought you had come to purchase my knowledge. If this is merely black-mail... I'd heard you were an honest, honorable man. What do you have on me?"

Malet turned, the fan still in his hands. "Now why do the shady ones always bandy the words 'honest' and 'honorable' around?" he asked of the air. "It puzzles me. You have been recommended as an informer: very well, I need information."

Michaud stared at him with a sort of fearful hope.

That expression brought Malet up short. He had encountered it before, one terrible night when he had been forced to arrest his dearest friend. The heartbreak of that case had sent him to Paris from Picardy, and the memory still hurt.

He set down the fan and said quietly, "Listen to me, Michaud: I have nothing to justify arresting you. That doesn't mean that I believe you inno-cent. I think, in fact, that you're a criminal, but I can't prove it. As far as the rest of society is concerned, that's as good as being innocent. You are too old for this. One day you will be caught, and I think you know it and are terrified of it. Why don't you step out of it now and go away, somewhere safe, where no one will throw you into prison? It's clear now, and you can go. I can't stop you. Yet."

Michaud lowered his eyes and was silent. After a moment he said, "What information did you want on Constant Dracquet?"

"Anything you can find," said Malet. "He's got something in the works and I want to know what it is." He leveled a very cold look at Michaud and added, "But if you leak a word, if you double-cross me, there won't be enough left of you left to bury."

"I wouldn't think of it," Michaud said with perfect sincerity. "I am not a fool."

"Just so we're agreed," Malet said. They talked a little longer, and then he left.

After the Inspector was gone, Michaud sat with a sigh and wiped his forehead. The Chief Inspector was right, he thought. He should go. He was too old for this. Maybe he would do as Malet suggested...

He straightened. He would do as Malet suggested, but first he would get the information, or the man would pursue him to his grave!

CHAPTER TWENTY-FIVE

Strange News from a Far Shore

"Have you considered viewing the card upside-down, Archet?" Malet asked pleasantly two days later. "Those who suffer eyestrain, as you seem to, say that it sometimes relieves the problem."

Constable Archet, who was serving as Officer of the Day, jumped and dropped Malet's card.

"Be careful," said Malet. "You might break the glass. Are you through with it? You have been squinting at it for four minutes by my watch." He took the card back from Archet, signed the book, and then said kindly, "Try distillation of witch-hazel. My housekeeper swears by it as a remedy for sore eyes. Otherwise, the Prefect—or his deputy—might think that you were unfit for duty and discharge you." He directed a steely smile at Archet and added, "Permanently." He went in toward the Prefect's offices without another glance.

He had a lot to think about. He wanted to review the information that he had received thus far from the operatives he had placed near Dracquet and reconcile that with the background information and the fascinating clue that Rosalie had given him. He also needed to sit down and devote some urgent thought to the nature of the important event that Saint-Légère had thought was coming up. All the signs pointed to it, Malet could sense it, but what could it be? Dracquet was doing very well, and all that Malet had learned of him through the years had served to confirm the impression that he was an intelligent man who did not take needless risks. This made the fact of his current personal involvement all the more ominous. He kept returning to the Duke of Rochester's comment. 'Now if only I were king...'

The Chamberlain intercepted him halfway back to his offices. His expression was more than usually portentous, and his side-whiskers showed signs of having been recently pomaded. The sight was enough to shake Malet from his thoughts.

"News, Clerel?" Malet asked.

"Permit me to take the Chief Inspector's coat and hat," said Clerel with repressive dignity. "And then if Monsieur would be so good as to follow me back—"

"Wryfoot Fanny," Malet said.

"I beg Monsieur's pardon?" Clerel said.

"Wryfoot Fanny," Malet repeated. "She's probably heard that I am here filling in for The Prefect for a time. She usually makes her weekly report to my headquarters, God knows why, since she tends to cruise the Boul' Mich' in search of students—a motherly instinct, if you ask me—but she likes me for whatever reason." His smile gentled. "Actually, she saved my life in 1830. She is more skilled than many physicians I have known, but she persists in being a prostitute. With some success, I might add."

Clerel had been listening with an affronted expression. He said repressively, "I have no interest in the Latin Quarter or its denizens."

"Pity. She offers a flattering discount to the Police."

Clerel's astonished stare suddenly warmed to something resembling a grin. He said with dignity, "His Excellency the Minister of Police has called. I took the liberty of escorting him back to The Prefect's offices. I did not think the Chief Inspector would object—if he's through with his funning."

Malet abandoned Wryfoot Fanny with regret. "Of course I don't object," he said. "Did you offer M. d'Anglars any refreshment?"

"I shall bring something suitable at once," said Clerel, but his voice was wistful.

"After you escort me to the office and announce me to His Excellency, of course," Malet said.

Clerel's face brightened.

"I KNOW IT IS SHORT notice," said Count d'Anglars, stretching his elegantly shod and trousered legs out before him. "I only just received the news, myself, but this is an event of international importance and must take precedence—alas! —over all other considerations."

Malet was feverishly casting his mind over various of his lieutenants and wondering which of them should be given charge of pursuing Dracquet while he was busy.

"I understand," he said. "Have we any idea how long Sir Robert Peel's visit will be?"

Count d'Anglars steepled his fingers before him and gazed over their tips at the sun that streamed in through the window. "His Majesty said that it would be the better part of a week, though I suspect it may be an overstatement. A great deal depends on what you and I can show him."

"But why should he take an interest in the Police system of France at this time?" Malet asked.

d'Anglars folded his hands and considered for a moment before speaking. "You may as well know," he said. "France—and especially Paris—will be receiving a visitor in the person of Princess Victoria, the Heiress Presumptive of England, in two weeks' time. Their Majesties have invited her to travel to Paris aboard their personal yacht, and King William has accepted on her behalf. She will be traveling with her mother, the Duchess of Kent. This will be the first time she has ventured outside England, and His Majesty wishes her to be well guarded."

"And so King William is sending Sir Robert Peel to cast an eye over the police to see what sort of yokels we are," Malet said. He considered, frowning, and then added with ominous cordiality, "And does the King of England plan to send the Duke of Wellington over to review our armies, as well?"

Count d'Anglars sat back and laughed for far longer than Malet thought the comment really deserved. He finally said, "That's why I wish you to accompany me. You are a refreshing change from the host of sycophants and boors that I am forced to deal with each day. Make what alternate arrangements you need for the next several days."

AFTER COUNT D'ANGLARS had departed, Malet seated himself at the Prefect's desk, propped his elbows before him, and sat back to think. So Princess Victoria was coming to France in two weeks' time, and sailing on the King's private yacht, no less!

How tragic it could be for all concerned if something should happen to make the visit a disaster! How truly terrible if the heiress of England should be killed, for example! The succession would have to realign itself, for better or for worse. Such an event could lead to a declaration of war between France and England. And war is a very lucrative business for one who knows how to exploit it...

Malet's eyes narrowed. Dracquet had a sizeable interest in several munitions manufactories. He recalled, as well, hearing that Dracquet had been all but implicated in an unsavory business that had come to light in 1824, after the French invasion of Spain. French manufacturers had been caught selling arms and ammunition to the Spaniards at the moment they were fighting the French. Dracquet had profited from war before—but was he bold enough to precipitate it?

Add to that the fact that Rosalie had told him that Dracquet had connections in England reaching as high as a member of the British Royal Family, and he didn't hesitate at murder. Malet set the piece of the puzzle in its place and scanned the results. Yes, things did fit, though he was not perfectly certain where Rochester stood in the succession.

If he was correct, the stakes were high and so was the chance of failure. It explained Dracquet's personal involvement and tipped Malet off to the fact that he'd best be ready to act on a moment's notice.

It also explained something else: Saint-Légère's transfer to that elementary beat had certainly not been cleared through Dracquet. The last thing that that man, busy with something very important, was likely to want would be an honest Police officer camped on his doorstep. And that indicated to Malet's mind that Guerin was probably not involved in anything worse than a protection racket.

Malet's emotions were complex. He had always disliked Guerin, but uppermost in his mind was relief that the man was not the utter villain that he had feared.

Interesting, but he still had to accompany Count d'Anglars and Sir

Robert Peel through Paris. Malet swore, took out his notebook and pencil, thought feverishly, and began to write.

CHAPTER TWENTY-SIX

A September Afternoon

Y ou are a beauty, aren't you?" Malet said an hour later as the bay lowered his muzzle and nibbled delicately at the handful of sweet hay
Malet offered.

"That he is, Inspector!" said the Police hostler, leaning on the stall partition. "Sweet-tempered to match. Not an ounce of vice in him!"

"Not even gluttony?" Malet asked as he hoisted the filled hay net to the
upper corner of the stall and watched the stallion stretch up his head to nib-
ble at it.

"Well, maybe that," the hostler admitted. "He does like his dinner."

The stallion pulled some hay loose and munched contentedly, the wisp
trailing jauntily from the side of his mouth. The mouthful finished, the
horse lowered his muzzle to nudge Malet in the chest.

"He knows you," said the hostler. "He's started looking for you each
morning."

Malet laughed and stroked the stallion's glossy neck. "He's a good one!"
he said. "I wish I could buy him."

"Maybe you can," the hostler said. "He's for sale, you know. Coming up
for auction. Nobody ever came to claim him. What do you think it'd take
to buy him?"

"More than I can afford. But I'd settle for a foal by him, at any rate. Has
anyone thought to put their mares to him?"

The hostler grinned. "A few have," he said. "There'll be some good foals
this time next year!"

Malet patted the stallion's shoulder and stepped out of the stall.
"Maybe one of them will be mine," he said. He brushed his hands off and
said, "Is my mount ready?"

"Of course, Inspector," said the hostler. "Ready and waiting these past five minutes. He's out in the yard—though if you want me to throw a saddle on that bay fellow's back, instead..."

Malet shook his head. "It's too tempting," he said. "Maybe before he goes to the auction. Which did you pick for me today?"

"Your favorite," said the hostler, opening the door and motioning Malet through. "Lutin."

Malet nodded to the stable hands who were holding the tall, gray gelding. "Good choice," he said. "I have quite a spell of riding to do today."

"Carry you all day and not tire," said the hostler. "Where do you go?"

Malet opened the saddlebags and put in a folded shirt, a purse full of coins, miscellaneous toilet articles and a sheet of paper covered with his writing. He gathered the reins in his hands, set his foot in the stirrup and sprang into the saddle. "Here and there," he said. "I have some people to see. I will bring this fellow back tomorrow."

"Then have a pleasant day, M. l'Inspecteur," the hostler replied with a smile, and motioned to the stable hands to open the double gates to the street.

MALET SAT BACK COMFORTABLY in the saddle and arranged the reins in his left hand. He had once commanded a regiment of Horse Artillery, and he had always enjoyed riding. He usually borrowed horses from the Police stables. It was one of the perquisites of a Chief Inspector, and this time he had some errands to run that would be easier done from a saddle.

And it would be a good way to shake Dracquet's spies, who had been tailing him since the day he had gone to Charles de Saint-Légère's district. René Benoit had had the temerity to deliver a note to the desk of the Officer of the Day at the Prefecture at midmorning:

> *Come to my house for luncheon today.*
> *Dracquet*

Alain Archet had been O.O.D. when René Benoit had delivered the message, and while Malet did not like Archet, he admitted privately that the man had his good points, chief among them being an inability to tolerate poor manners among those he perceived to be criminals and a total lack of fear of such people.

He had looked Benoit up and down, made him sign in, and then refused to admit him. Benoit had departed mouthing threats.

The fact that René Benoit was the messenger interested Malet, for Benoit was a force to be reckoned with in his own right. He had risen from being a strong man in Dracquet's pay to the position of chief lieutenant and confidant.

Malet had made it his business to listen to whispers and had heard that Benoit had an eye to Dracquet's empire. The man had been one of the chief suspects in a grisly series of murders near Reuilly, involving a clique of Ultra-Royalists. Malet had solved the puzzle of the murders, but he had never quite been able to prove Benoit's complicity in them and, through him, Dracquet's involvement. But it had been a close thing.

Malet smiled to himself. If he succeeded in bringing Dracquet down, Benoit could possibly step in as a web-spinner. But Malet intended to nail Benoit before that could happen.

He straightened in the saddle. He had been riding at his ease, proceeding west along the Quai de la Mégisserie at an easy amble, well aware that his followers were keeping up with him. They were drawing abreast of the stone battlements of the Pont Neuf. He could see the tall old houses flanking the triangular, tree-shaded Place Dauphine at the westernmost tip of the Île du Palais.

Time to shake them. He set his heels into the gray's sides as he reined back and to the right. Lutin had been trained as a cavalry charger. He reared, spun round and, the reins suddenly released, broke into a flat-out gallop straight toward the spies.

Malet, leaning forward, caught a glimpse of two white, startled faces as the men threw themselves aside. He laughed and urged the horse even faster as he clattered between the two spies, crossed the northern end of the place du Châtelet, passed beneath the tall shadow of the Tour St. Jacques, and continued east along the rue de Rivoli.

Time to pay a call at the place Gredin.

AN HOUR LATER, MALET, once again in the saddle, had a great deal to consider. Michaud had reported some gossip about Jean Ensenat that Malet had found useful. One of the prostitutes who came to his shop was regularly patronized by the man who had accompanied Dracquet to the Conciergerie the day before Ensenat's murder. He had told her several interesting things about Dracquet's conversation with Ensenat that day, and she had been willing to pass the word on in exchange for the price of a bottle of brandy.

"She wrote it out in her own hand and signed it when I mentioned your name," Michaud had said, offering a sheet of good writing paper covered with a fine, spidery script that bespoke a convent education. "Said she'd do anything for 'The Inspector.'"

Malet had taken the paper and scanned it, then smiled and put it in his pocket. "Give Nanette my thanks when next she comes in," he said. "This will be very useful. If nothing else, it will tie Dracquet in to one murder. Tell the girl to be very careful, though. By all she says, things are happening very quickly."

Michaud had nodded. He fiddled with some silver-topped crystal bottles and then said, "Th-the deal still holds, doesn't it?"

Malet had lifted his eyebrows.

"You will let me run when this is finished?"

"Of course. I gave my word."

Michaud had nodded. "So you did," he said, almost in a whisper. The next words came out in a rush. "I don't understand it. You're letting me run, but you are going all out to bury Dracquet."

"Well?"

"I don't understand it. Why?"

Malet had pulled on his gloves and turned toward the window. His eyes had sharpened for a moment; a shifting shadow had resolved itself to the form of a ragged, wild-haired little boy scurrying away across the square. He watched for a moment. The boy had looked familiar... He turned back to Michaud.

"You're a crook, Michaud," he said. "Dracquet is a murderer. I tolerate crooks if I can't prove anything against them. I never tolerate murderers. Help me catch this murderer and you can leave with my blessing." He had set his hat on his head at an angle and swept out the door.

Now Malet rode northwest along the rue de Bretagne, which took him close to his house in the Marais. He nodded to those who greeted him and, when he reached the rue du faubourg Saint-Denis, turned north and spurred to a trot.

The streets were redolent with the smell of cooking food, and dogs darted here and there and snarled over bits of bone and meat flung down by passing vendors. He was approaching the old stone triumphal arch, called the Porte Saint-Denis, that straddled the street, channeling the clamorous traffic beneath it.

A cocoa-seller, burdened with a square wooden cask strapped to his back, scurried across the street almost beneath the gray's hooves. He turned and grinned up at Malet and offered cocoa in a none-too-clean cup, then shrugged when Malet shook his head.

The Porte Saint-Denis rose above them, its white stone disfigured by the grime of a hundred and sixty years of smoke and soot. Malet could see the words *LIBERTÉ EGALITÉ INDIVISIBILITÉ* carved at the top.

A tangle of beggars shouted for alms beneath it and blocked the way of the passers-by. One of them caught sight of him and elbowed his companions in the ribs with a grin.

Malet ignored the man. He drew rein, checked his watch and then looked around. A confectioner's shop was just before the arch. He took out his snuffbox, opened it, surveyed the toffees inside, and then smiled wryly and dismounted.

"Hold your horse for a sou, Milor'!" cried the beggar who had first seen him, a seedy fellow of middling height with a crooked smile.

Malet surveyed the man from head to foot, his nostrils wrinkling fastidiously, before he handed the reins over. "See you take care of him," he said, "Or I will have your hide for a doormat."

"Mon Dieu, Milor'!" said the man, whose grin was more pronounced. "Keep your trousers on! I will guard 'im with my life!"

Malet favored the man with a frosty nod and went inside, pausing at the door when the man said, "My sou!"

"You will get it when I come out," he snapped.

He bought a handful of toffees, paid the shopkeeper, and went outside again to find the beggar holding his horse with every appearance of innocence, except for the knowing smirks of the others.

"All square?" he said.

"All square, Cap'n!" the man said, handing the reins back and slapping Lutin on the shoulder.

"Then stand aside," Malet said. He flipped the man a coin, mounted Lutin, and rode east again along the boulevard Saint-Martin past the smaller, darker twin of the Porte Saint-Denis, the Porte Saint-Martin.

When he was well along, he reined the horse to a walk and turned to open the saddlebag. As he had expected, the coin purse was gone along with the folded shirt. As he had also expected, two closely-written sheets of paper had been set in their place.

Inspector Gilles d'Arthez of the 8th arrondissement had quite a lot to report, by the look of it.

Malet smiled grimly, opened the sheets, and began to read. He folded them away after a moment and drew a deep breath.

Arrivals and departures, all very discreet, and at all hours of the day and night. Curtained coaches, cloaked visitors-all very interesting. And d'Arthez had kept careful count of those of Dracquet's household that he saw coming and going, and it appeared that the household had swelled by about three people. d'Arthez had caught voices speaking English.—*Hm*, thought Malet—and curtains were always drawn in the house by day and by night. d'Arthez had been good enough to keep careful track of René Benoit's activities as well as those of Dracquet. It would come in very handy. The next report was due in two days.

English voices, Malet thought again.

He drew a deep breath and consulted his watch. Two o'clock. The day was still young. He turned his head to look northwest. The Rose d'Or was not far away, and he recalled seeing a very nice little sorrel mare in the stable. She was obviously a lady's mount: Elise de Clichy's, perhaps? Did she ride?

He looked up at the sky, which was the sort of clear, exuberant blue only achieved in early autumn. The air was crisp, spiced by a breeze from the west that smelled of mown hayfields and late roses. The streets were filled with brightly clad people enjoying the beautiful day, and flower-sellers at every corner offered roses and carnations. He knew cafes where you could buy ices, or enjoy tea and coffee along with thin, crisp, buttery almond tuiles.

He loved to talk with Elise and watch her bustle about the Rose d'Or. How much better it would be to venture out in this beautiful weather and enjoy the beauties of Paris with her beside him! It would be splendid to take her to one of those cafes. Not even the strictest-minded person would find anything to make him raise his eyebrows at such an outing.

But did she ride?

Malet drew the reins between his fingers and thought for a moment and then smiled. There was one way to find out.

CHAPTER TWENTY-SEVEN

A Ride Through Paris

Take three cloves, Georgine. You will have two extra in case the toothache persists." Elise unlocked the small wooden box and shook the cloves into her palm, then gave them to the girl standing beside her. "Tell your mother I have never known them to fail."

Georgine smiled at her, sketched a curtsey, and went skipping off.

Elise watched her go, conscious of a sudden ache in her heart. If her daughter, Marie-Françoise had lived, she would have been just Georgine's age.

But the moment passed. Elise bent over the spice box and savored the rich, heady scent of the cloves and cinnamon, then locked the box and put it back on its shelf in the pantry.

She drew a deep breath and looked around. Supper was well underway, and the cook had matters well in hand.

She untied her apron, carefully folded it and set it aside, and crossed the warm splash of sunlight that spilled across the tiled kitchen floor. It was such a splendid day, she hated the thought of remaining inside. She had to go outside, if only for a moment.

She opened the kitchen door and stepped into the courtyard in time to see Inspector Malet come riding into the stableyard astride a tall, dappled gray gelding.

He hadn't seen her; she could observe him to her heart's content, and what she saw pleased her. He sat the horse with an elegant ease, and she found herself enjoying the set of his shoulders and the unexpectedly green tint of his eyes. He was as impeccably turned out as ever, but she could catch the sense of peril that seemed to cling to him.

He saw her and drew rein, and the sense of peril dissolved as his face warmed in a sudden, almost shy smile. The horse sidled a little and tossed his head, but he stood quietly after a moment and stretched an inquisitive nose toward Elise.

She came forward to stroke the horse's soft muzzle. "He's beautiful," she said to Malet. "Is he yours?"

"He belongs to the Police," Malet answered "I ride him sometimes when I have things to do, as I did today. I'd had some errands to run, and I found I wasn't far from here. It's such a beautiful day. I thought, if you cared to come riding with me..."

Elise smiled breathlessly up at him. "Of course I would!" she said. "That would be wonderful! Wait for me! I won't be long! Tell Claude or Alcide to saddle la Duchesse. I will go inside and change to my riding clothes!"

"La Duchesse," Malet repeated. "The sorrel mare?"

"Yes! She's a delightful ride, and I have been neglecting her shamefully!" Elise said. "Wait for me, now!"

"Of course," said Malet.

Elise hurried into the inn. She turned at the door in time to see him loop his horse's reins in the brass ring at the courtyard and then go into the stable.

She ran up the stairs to the second story, where she found Yvette frowning over an armful of clean linens and towels. She took Yvette by the arm and turned her around toward her room. "Help me into my habit, Yvette!" she said. "I am going riding, and I have got to change quickly!"

"Riding?" Yvette repeated. "It's been years!" Her eyes narrowed. "With whom, 'Lise?"

"With M. l'Inspecteur, of course!" Elise replied. "Come on now, he's waiting! I hope I didn't pack the habit away!"

"Elise-Marie de Clichy, have you run mad?" Yvette scolded as Elise feverishly plucked at the laces fronting her bodice. "Here, let me." She unfastened the laces. "Where's your habit? In the armoire here? Or upstairs?"

"Here, I think—or did I put it in the storage room?" Elise replied. She had stepped out of her dress and was carefully combing her side-curls.

"The storage room," Yvette replied. "You'd know if it were here." She was out the door before Elise could say anything, and back with the habit over her arm before Elise could count to twenty. "There," she said. "Not wrinkled, more's the wonder. Here, protect your hair while I slide this over your head."

"Does it fit?" Elise asked as she emerged from the folds of the dress. "I know I have put on weight." She fumbled with the buttons and then twitched the cuffs down to her wrists. "Oh Yvette! It's tight!"

Yvette settled the skirt and twitched the tiny peplum that sat at the small of the back into place. "It fits beautifully," she said.

"It fits too beautifully!" Elise lamented. "I feel as though I have been poured into it! It's been eight years, and I have grown plump!" She smoothed the maroon wool cloth of the sleeves and touched the loops of braid that edged the wide puff of the sleeve at the shoulder. "Well... Maybe it's not that bad..." She sighed and added, "I never thought it could ever be so out of style..."

"But smart, still," said Yvette. She handed Elise her gray silk hat with its flowing veil and watched her set it on her head. "Be careful, 'Lise," she said. "I don't want you to be hurt."

"Hurt?" Elise repeated. "By whom? Him? Yvette!"

Yvette had been busy adjusting the bodice. "There are ways and ways of being hurt," she said, surveying Elise with her head cocked. "Oh 'Lise!" she said, "You look like a girl again."

Elise flung the trailing skirt over her arm and twirled before her. "I feel like a girl again!" she said. "It's been so long since I went riding with a beau!"

Yvette chuckled and picked up Elise's discarded dress. "Go on with you," she said. "Enjoy yourself! Where are you going?"

"I don't know!" Elise said. "I will be with him, so it won't matter. He said he had some errands to run. It's too pretty a day to stay inside!" She gave Yvette a peck on the cheek and whisked out the door.

Yvette shook her head, but she was smiling.

ELISE HAD NOT BEEN so happy in a long time. Truly at leisure for the first time in years, she felt pretty again. Her habit might be snug and out-moded, but her escort didn't appear to be aware of the fact. His gaze had been frankly admiring when she descended the stairs to the salon, and his continuing admiration had provided a heady undercurrent to their conversation as they rode along the river.

"I never dreamed there could be this much open space on land, until I left Toulon," said Malet, motioning southeast along the Champs-Elysees.

They were directly under the Arc de Triomphe, which towered above them like a great white elephant. They could see the crowded axis that was the Rond Point des Champs-Elysees and, beyond it, the square outline of the Tuileries palace. The day was brisk but beautiful, and the length of the boulevard was crowded with strollers.

Elise looked back from the Tuileries to Malet's face. Surprising a warmly appreciative smile, she returned it and drew her reins through her fingers. "Did you see land so seldom, then?" she asked.

"Let us say that I saw mostly ocean," Malet replied. "Toulon is on the coast. It is a naval port, bounded by hills. The prison overlooks the ocean, and I almost never got out of there except to row on one of their galleys."

"They treated you like one of the prisoners?"

Malet smiled at the anger in Elise's voice. "I was one, to all intents," he said. "Born there, raised there, the son of a prisoner, a protégé of prisoners—how else could they judge me?"

"They could judge you for what you are!" Elise said hotly.

"For what I was. And, my dear, I regret to say that at that time I was a horrible brat."

"Not all the time," she returned. "You grew up and became what you are. And I suspect that what you were even then was something very fine. When did you leave that prison?"

"When I turned fifteen," Malet replied. "I'd been judged an adult." He added, "They were glad to see the last of me, I am sure. It was getting expensive to feed me."

"And was it then you decided to spend your life protecting others?"

Malet turned back to frown at her. His frown eased after a moment. "No, not then," he said. "I'd made my choice long before then."

"Oh?" Elise said. "When?"

Malet smoothed his horse's neck with an elegantly gloved hand. "I'd made the decision years before that," he said, gathering his reins. "But such ancient history must bore you, and it's too beautiful a day to be bored. If we ride south, to the Pont d'Iena, and cross the river..."

"I will ride anywhere you want," said Elise. "But I want to know. I won't be bored. How did you get from that prison to where you are now? I'd heard about you over the years through the papers and through Christien. I never expected you to be as you are—such a gentleman. Then, when we spoke together in the kitchen, I was so caught by what you said. I thought—I don't know. It moved me somehow. And yet you could have been a wealthy man by now if you had chosen otherwise, but you did not. Why not?"

"The fact that a course of action is lucrative doesn't make it right," Malet said. "Whatever else seems doubtful, I know that it is better to be generous than selfish, better to be true than false, better to be brave than a coward. If such a course is doomed to failure in this world, what of it? Society can view me as a fool who's booked passage on a sinking ship because I feel that way. No matter: I choose to go down with the ship."

"You will hear no mockery from me," said Elise. "I had never thought it out before, but I agree with you. But what brought you to that conclusion? Something must have pushed you that way."

She was not prepared for his answer.

"The stars," he said.

"The stars?" she repeated.

He smiled "Yes," he said. "When I was five years old. I told you I was born in prison. My mother died there, and since they were unable to find her family, and my father's disinherited me, I became a Ward of France. I grew up among criminals from all over the world, and I was something of a pet with the more seasoned ones in the prison, and especially a fellow named Jacques Grimault, who was better known as 'Cheat-Death.' "

"Cheat-Death!" Elise said. "I have heard of him. And you were his pet!"

"Most people have heard of him. He was a legend, though he was growing old. He had landed in prison, and there was no way out for him this time, though his luck held in one respect: they couldn't sentence him to death. He decided to train me to be his successor. He assigned various prisoners to teach me their skills: safecracking, lock-picking, pocket-picking, how to fight with knives or fists or feet, how to hide. I learned it all. He even had me given lessons in deportment, dancing and swordplay. The guards were afraid of me, I think. They gave me more than my share of kicks and cuffs when they could. And for all his power, Cheat-Death couldn't or wouldn't protect me from them."

Malet's smile had not faded. "One afternoon I was lashed up against a grating and flogged by the prison hangman for something the warden's son had done. They cut me loose at sundown.

"I had a room up in one of the towers. I crawled back there and collapsed with my sore back against the cold stone wall and stared out the dark window."

Malet was smiling down the Champs Elysees toward the Tuileries. "I was a mass of self-pity," he said. "The prison was my world, and I was smart enough then to know that it wasn't the only thing in the world, but I also knew that I couldn't escape it. I remember how despairing I was. And then, out of the corner of my eye, I saw a streak of light pass the window. I looked up and saw another, and another. It was beautiful! I watched until dawn. I wondered what they could have been, and whether I'd see them again the next night." His voice was full of remembered wonder. "And I did," he said. "Every night for two weeks, I watched and saw them."

He slanted a smiling glance at Elise. "It was the Perseid meteor shower that comes in July and August," he said. "Have you seen it?"

"No," said Elise. "Never. I wish I had. Poor little boy!"

"Not so poor, after all, as it happened," said Malet. "It was the beginning of a new life. I felt as though I'd managed somehow to crawl out of the squalor of the prison into a high place where everything was fresh and cool and unhurried.

"I met a new prisoner at this time. His name was Joseph Young. He was an American sailor who had been impressed into the British Navy against his will. He had somehow fallen afoul of the laws of France and been sent to prison. He always dreamed of returning to the sea and his home in America, in Massachusetts.

"He saw how I watched them. He'd had children of his own years ago, back in America. He became a father to me. Whenever the night was clear, we'd look up at the skies and name the stars. I learned how to navigate by them, and Papa Joseph told me all the old legends of gods and heroes in English, which is why I speak it fluently.

"Prison life was so trivial now: I could judge the actions of man against those of the gods. Who can fear or revere a pack of criminals when he walks with Orion, and who, contemplating Leo, can fear an earthbound rat?"

"But what of Cheat-Death?" Elise asked. "Did he allow you to turn away from him?"

Malet's smile became vaguely vicious. "Oh, I didn't turn away," he said. "I went along through the years, his acknowledged apprentice and successor, learning all his skills to use against him and his when I was finally free of that hell. He never suspected."

"What happened to your papa?" asked Elise. "Did he have to stay in the prison?"

"No," Malet replied. "He died two months before I left. We thought I could secure his release once I had left the prison. I had something I could offer in exchange for his freedom, and he was old and harmless and had been of use in the years he was imprisoned. He was going to live with me. He said I was his last, and best, child. I didn't tell him I had saved enough money to pay his passage back to America. I wanted to surprise him, but he died. I did tell him... He never saw Massachusetts again. I would have given my right arm if he could have..." He fell silent for a long time.

Finally, he turned back to Elise. "Well," he said. "They buried him at sea. After that I watched the stars and waited for my fifteenth birthday."

"And you left the prison and went into the Police."

"Yes," said Malet. "I walked all the way from Toulon to Marseilles. I don't think the Prefect of the Bouches du Rhone Departement was ever so shocked as he was at the moment Cheat-Death's acknowledged heir came before him carrying a ragged pack and asked to join the Police as a constable. I thought he'd soil his trousers."

"Inspector!!"

"I am serious. The police had been waiting to see where I would turn up. They did not expect to find me this way." He smiled and added, "I was the Chief Constable of Marseilles five years later."

Elise nodded and looked around at the park. "Lift me down, M. l'Inspecteur," she said. "I'd like to walk with you a little..."

She smiled at him as he dismounted and reached up to set his hands around her waist. She steadied herself with her hands on his shoulders as he lifted her to the ground. She knew she was no featherweight, but he settled her easily. His hands lingered at her waist, and she did not release his shoulders for a moment.

"Thank you Monsieur," she said softly.

"It was my pleasure," he replied, his voice equally quiet.

She leaned down to gather her skirts and arrange the trailing hem over one arm while he took the reins of both horses in his right hand. He offered his left arm when her skirts were arranged to her satisfaction.

"There's a pavilion here where we can enjoy tea," he said. "Or they have coffee and ices if you prefer."

"Tea," she said. "It sounds lovely... It's been so long since I have done this."

"Then I am glad I talked you into coming out this afternoon," Malet said as they went slowly down the shaded path

Elise stopped and turned to face him. Her voice lowered. "You know, Inspector," she said, "I'd go anywhere with you. I know I'd be safe with you—and you with me."

His expression did not change, but his eyes warmed as he looked down at her, and silently raised her hand to his lips.

She smiled at him and turned her hand to touch his cheek lightly for a moment. "Do you think I am foolish?" she asked.

"I think you are perfectly delightful," he returned.

"That wasn't the question," she said.

"But that is my answer," he replied.

CHAPTER TWENTY-EIGHT

Chief Inspector Malet Enters the Fray

Autumn was Yvette's favorite time of year. She loved the crisp bite of the wind, the leaves that fell like gold and scarlet snowflakes and danced like troupes of gypsies before the capricious winds. It reminded her that the worst heat of the summer was past, and the pageantry of Christmas was coming. It was autumn that brought the sweet-scented late roses that she prized and planted in profusion all around the Rose d'Or.

This autumn had been especially beautiful, and of all the magnificent mornings that she had seen, this specific morning was the finest. She awoke in time to watch the sunrise from her window and went out to milk the inn's four cows. She kindled the fires in the kitchen and got preparations underway for breakfast, including making a pot of cinnamon coffee especially for herself and Inspector de Colbert.

He was late to rise this morning. But that was probably because he had been very busy over the past several days entertaining a visitor from England, a man named Sir Robert Peel. The man was involved in some way with the British constabulary and was in France at the invitation of the Minister of Police to review the French Police system.

M. l'Inspecteur had spent the last four days in the company of the Count and Sir Robert. He had seemed rather grim the first day, and the rosette of a Commander of the Legion of Honor had been conspicuous in his buttonhole. He had brought the two to the Rose d'Or to try the ale and the food. He and Peel had spent over an hour there drinking ale and talking in English.

M. Peel was gone now, and no doubt the Inspector felt that he'd earned a morning lying abed rather later than usual. That suited Yvette perfectly: it gave her time to prepare a proper breakfast.

She filled her watering-pot and carried it out to the street. The roses were in full bloom, and although people teased her about her extravagance, she carefully watered and trimmed the plants every second day. It was time to do it again.

She was famous for her rosebushes, and they were responsible for the presence in the inn of two guests, Aloysius Stanley from Portsmouth, and his wife, Abigail. The Stanleys loved flowers, especially roses, and they had seen them the night before and resolved there and then to stay in a place that had such magnificent blooms. They had spoken of gardening all the previous night, he in terrible French, and when they finally retired, Mr. Stanley kissed Yvette's hand and promised to send her some cuttings from his gardens.

She took her pruning scissors and carefully cut away some flowers that had gone by, and then bent to savor their heady scent. A party of four men passed her as she straightened. She recognized René Benoit and three of Constant Dracquet's people, bruisers who made her very nervous. They usually behaved themselves at the inn, thanks to the presence of Yves' farmhands, but Yvette always tried to keep out of their way.

Dracquet's men! At this hour! Well, well!

Yvette rubbed her lower lip thoughtfully and turned to watch them go along the street toward the courtyard.

Dracquet had sent his men by six times, and each time they had missed their 'police officer'. They hadn't been happy, and yesterday they had been unpleasant to Claude, giving good cause to a man who already disliked them enough.

"What do you want, messieurs?" Claude had asked finally as he wiped his hands on a towel. "The man rises early and leaves early. What are we to do? Detain him forcibly? He is a guest: I would never be so rude, and Madame de Clichy would certainly forbid it!"

"Tell him that M. Dracquet is growing impatient," the leader had said.

Claude had merely shrugged. "You will terrify him, messieurs," he had said, politely opening the door.

Now a motion at one of the upstairs windows, a hand drawing a curtain aside, caught Yvette's attention. She looked up and saw Inspector de Colbert gazing down at her. He saw that Yvette had caught sight of him: he pointed at the men and lifted his eyebrows.

She nodded.

He put his fingers to his lips and lowered the curtain again.

"Trouble ahead," said Yvette with a smile.

"GOOD MORNING, MADAME de Clichy," said René Benoit with labored politeness. "Is your Police officer in today?"

"He's not 'my' police officer," Elise replied. "And yes, he is in. In fact, he hasn't come down to breakfast yet."

"Splendid. Then maybe we can finally speak with this elusive fellow," Benoit said, sitting down. "You did give him my messages, I hope."

"I mentioned that you had called at the inn, yes. Have you breakfasted yet?"

"Not yet," Benoit replied. He motioned to the others to sit down. "We'll have some of your cooking, if you don't object."

"Not at all, monsieur. Your money is as good here as anywhere else. Alcide can take your order when you are ready." She inclined her head to the man and went over to the tap.

Elise looked up and smiled at Yvette when she came in with her watering-can and a large bunch of roses. "Use Raoul's vase, Yvette," she suggested. "We can put them on the mantel in the salon, and the vase will set them off very well."

Yvette agreed, got the vase, and sat before the tap to arrange the flowers.

Alcide went over to the table, spoke quietly with Dracquet's men, and then went back into the kitchen.

"He's annoyed," said Yvette in an undertone. "And M. de Colbert—" She stopped as the boards over their heads creaked.

Benoit looked up, directed a frown at them, and then sat up straighter as heavy footsteps sounded overhead, proceeded deliberately down the hallway toward the stairs and then down the steps.

Elise turned and watched as Mr. Stanley entered the room, puffing a little, bowed to them, and sat at a table. Other customers had come into the common-room as well. Yvette and Marie got up and went over to them.

Benoit nodded to one of the others, a tall, heavyset fellow with reddish hair.

The man returned the nod. "It's taken you long enough!" he said through his teeth as he pushed himself to his feet and stalked over to Mr. Stanley. "I have tolerated your rudeness longer than I thought possible! Now I must insist!"

Mr. Aloysius Stanley might be stout, but he was dignified. He pulled out his spectacles, polished them on a pocket handkerchief, perched them on his nose, and subjected the henchman to a comprehensive scrutiny. Muttering something in English about 'damned silly Frogs', he finally turned to Elise and Yvette with a truly charming smile and asked for tea, cakes and cold beef in atrociously accented French. "And if I may have one of Mademoiselle's blooms for a boutonniere, so much the better!" he said.

Benoit's face was a brief study in astonishment. He masked the expression and motioned his man to sit down again.

"Certainly, Mr. Stanley," Elise said in English. "Please be seated. Will Madame be down shortly?"

"Shortly," Stanley said. "I left her and her maid performing a task of—ah—some delicacy." He turned back in time to see Yvette returning with the choicest of her flowers. "Ah, my boutonniere!" he said. "Thank you, my dear Mam'selle!"

"I would be happy to have one, too," said a quiet voice from the doorway.

Malet was standing there, framed by the heavy, carved lintel. He was smiling on the people in the common-room. His gloves were in his hand, his hat was tucked in the crook of his arm, and his coat sat negligently on his shoulders like a mantle.

He bowed to Elise and Yvette, inclined his head to Mr. Stanley and the rest of the customers, and came into the room, walking with the negligent grace of a tiger. The gold hilt of his sword caught the light and scattered it. He passed Dracquet's men without a glance, his coat brushing past Benoit's knee. He stopped at a table just beyond Elise and Yvette, swung the coat from his shoulders and set it over the back of one of the chairs. He placed his gloves, walking stick and hat on the table beside him, and disposed himself with an elegant ease that made the sturdy, utilitarian chair seem like a carved throne.

Elise hid a smile. It had been a magnificent entrance, a credit, had she known it, to Albertine Malet of the Opera, who had bequeathed to her son that predatory walk.

Yvette finished setting the flower in Mr. Stanley's buttonhole. She selected another and went over to Malet to put it in place and favor him with a graceful curtsey afterward: she, too, could act.

"Thank you," said Malet with a warm smile. "And now, Mlle. Franchotte, if you'd oblige me with some coffee and a bite of one of your excellent breakfasts, I will be quite content."

"Right away, M'sieur Inspector!" Yvette said with another curtsey.

Benoit's eyes narrowed, and he looked Malet up and down, taking in the cut and quality of his clothing as well as his bearing. He hesitated a moment before he finally leaned forward to tap one of the other men on the sleeve and nod toward Malet.

The man, a heavyset fellow with pomaded hair and a bright, brocaded waistcoat, started and set down his cup of coffee. He went over to stand before Malet's table and frown down at him.

Malet, engaged in polishing the crystal of his watch with a silk handkerchief, looked up and nodded to the man, then returned his attention to his watch.

"You're the officer staying here, aren't you?" the man demanded. "The wench called you 'Inspector.' "

Malet lifted an eyebrow and subjected the man to a thoughtful scrutiny. His gaze lingered on the waistcoat while he closed the watch and returned it to his waistcoat pocket.

"I am employed by the Ministry of Police: yes," he said at last, folding the handkerchief and putting it away as well. "I suppose that might make me a 'cop.' And I am currently staying at the Rose d'Or, but that is only a temporary arrangement."

The man's face darkened. "Then, monsieur," he rasped, "you will kindly explain your rudeness in ignoring the messages that were left for you!"

"And what is your name, pray?"

"The messages were left by Constant Dracquet!"

"Are you Dracquet?" Malet asked.

"N-no, I am not, but—"

Benoit, sitting at his table, closed his eyes for a moment.

Malet regarded the man with a sort of distasteful patience. He accepted a cup of cinnamon coffee from Yvette with a word of thanks, took the small pitcher of milk and added some, put his customary three spoonful's of sugar in the cup, stirred, and then set it down.

When the man started to speak again he raised a finger and then, when the man was silent, reached into the breast pocket of his waistcoat and took out his notebook. He opened the notebook, thumbed through it, frowning slightly, then looked up. "Your name, please."

The man stammered out a name. Malet repeated it, then wrote it in the notebook and bestowed it again in his waistcoat.

"Let us set aside for a moment the question of my rudeness," he said. "These messages: where were they left?"

"They were left here!"

"And were they addressed to me, personally?"

"They certainly were!"

"I beg to differ. I received no messages addressed to me by name. I doubt that these ladies—" he nodded toward Yvette and Elise, "—or anyone else here would ignore messages left for me. Did you use my name?"

"I don't know your name, sir!" the man said through his teeth.

Malet stirred his coffee again, set the spoon aside, and sipped the coffee, frowning again. "I see," he said at last. "You are angry because a message addressed to no one didn't reach me. Really, monsieur, you're being unreasonable, and you were asking for any rudeness you and yours may have encountered from me."

He turned away with an air of finality to smile at Yvette, who was waiting with a plate of brioches and a pot of jam. "Ah, thank you, Mlle. Yvette."

He broke the brioche, spread jam on it, took a bite, took another sip of coffee, chewed, and swallowed, ignoring the man, who was still standing before him, breathing heavily through his nose.

"The message," said the man with an effort, speaking slowly and distinctly, "was directed to Inspector de Saint-Légère's replacement."

Malet took another bite of brioche. "Which I am not," he said. "No wonder it never reached me. It doesn't concern me. And now, monsieur, if you have nothing further to say to me, I have yesterday's *Globe*, which I haven't read yet. Good morning."

He unfolded the paper, scanned the front page, and then opened it to the Police section. After a moment he took out a gold pencil and made a notation beside one of the articles.

Benoit shifted in his chair, trying to get his man's attention.

The man did not see him. "I am not finished with you yet, Monsieur!" he said through his teeth.

"But I am finished with you, sir," Malet said. "You have been a boor. I don't suffer fools gladly, but I am even less inclined to put up with the bad manners of self-important oafs like you. Good morning, sir!"

Benoit was shaking his head. His men were muttering among themselves.

"I am certain your commander will be interested in your rudeness!" the man said through his teeth. "I don't think that he will take it kindly when a complaint for disrespect is lodged against you! I will certainly inform M. Rameau—"

"What has Inspector Rameau to say to anything?" Malet demanded. "He's certainly not my superior!"

"Then tell me who is!"

"The man's name is Valéry Lamarque," said Malet. "That is, he is my immediate superior. If you like, I can write down his name for you. You will have trouble reaching him for some time: he's taking the waters at Plombières. I suggest you approach Christien de la Haye, Count d'Anglars, who is his superior." He leaned forward, his eyes fixed on the other's face, and added with calm deliberation, "And you may wish to use my name: Malet. That is M-A-L-E-T. Paul V. Malet, to be exact. My rank is Chief Inspector. If you think you need help remembering it, I will be happy to write it on your forehead for you."

Benoit had sat forward as Malet said his name. He looked to Elise like a man who has drawn a terrible hand of cards after having wagered everything he owned on it. As Elise watched, he whispered something to the man sitting closest to him, which sent the man scurrying from the room.

Malet was still speaking. "Now if that is all you have to say, then I suggest you leave. You are annoying me, I am certain that you are annoying the ladies, and you have annoyed this gentleman here, from what I heard while I was coming down the stairs."

He looked up, motioned to the other men, and said, "And that goes for your friends, as well. Out! Or I will have you thrown out!"

The man glared down at him, his eyes flashing. He looked up as Benoit came up beside him and moved back.

"Maybe the messages were misdirected," said Benoit. "But I am delivering the message now: M. Constant Dracquet wants you to call upon him tomorrow at noon."

Malet appeared supremely unimpressed by this announcement. "And what is your name?" he asked, taking out his notebook again.

"René Benoit," the man answered.

"Ah," said Malet, raising his pencil. "The pimp." He poured himself more coffee and busied himself with creaming and sweetening it to his satisfaction.

"'Pimp'?" Benoit repeated.

"Among other things," Malet said, setting the sugar aside. "You had a hand in that series of murders near Reuilly, where the victims were found without their heads. Interesting piece of work, that: how fortunate for you that that one whore enjoyed your company so much—and that she died when she did. But was it wise? Your master is looking for respectability now that he's made his millions, and you nearly made yourself a liability."

Benoit stared at him, shaken. "What do you mean?" he demanded. His voice had risen a little.

"I am reciting facts. You and I have nothing to say to each other, and I have nothing to say to your M. Dracquet, either. I suggest you leave now before I forget my manners and have you all thrown out!"

He and Benoit traded glares. "You will regret this, monsieur!" Benoit snapped at last and strode from the room.

"You terrify me!" Malet called after him.

The tallest of Dracquet's men rose and glared down at Malet, who gazed imperturbably back at him. "You *will* regret it, you bastard!" he snarled through his teeth, and followed the rest out.

The patrons in the common room looked at one another in shocked silence.

Malet seemed thoughtful, but he finished his coffee and raised his eyes as Elise came over with his breakfast. Claude was with her, looking a little white about the mouth. Alcide was standing behind them.

"Whew!" said Claude. "You made him mad!"

"I meant to."

"Why?" demanded Claude.

"Are you really Chief Inspector Malet?" Alcide demanded, wide-eyed.

"Yes, I am," Malet said, and sipped his coffee.

"Why didn't you say so at once?" Alcide asked.

"Will you shut up?" snapped Claude. "He has better things to do than listen to your impertinence!" He turned back to Malet. "That one fellow meant murder," he said. "Maybe we should tell the Police!"

Malet smiled, speared a piece of beef with his fork and raised it to his mouth. "You forget that I am the police for the moment," he said after he had finished chewing. "And as for why I made Benoit mad, why, 'Haste makes waste', and I want to make them rather hasty. I think I succeeded."

He added more kindly, "Don't worry. I can take care of myself."

"Was it wise?" asked Elise.

"It was politic," said Malet.

"But it was also dangerous. I saw their faces as they left, and especially Benoit's."

"I am not afraid of him. I am beyond his weight, and he knows it."

"You shouldn't frighten small men," said Elise. "They'll kill you."

Malet shrugged. "They're welcome to try," he said.

Elise was silent for a moment. Finally, she laid an urgent hand on his sleeve and said, "Please be careful, Inspector. You could be hurt if you get involved with someone like Constant Dracquet."

Malet took her hand in his for a moment. "I am a Police officer," he said. "I have to get involved with people like him. Should I resign from the Force and let him continue unchecked? I can't do that. You would think worse of me if I did." He smiled and released her hand

CHAPTER TWENTY-NINE

Hunter and Quarry

Constant Dracquet himself arrived the next morning as Elise was sipping a cup of tea with Yvette at breakfast. He entered the dining room quietly, smiled around at the patrons, and then directed a look at Malet that made Elise feel suddenly cold.

Malet seemed to sense the look, for he raised his head. His eyes narrowed fractionally, and he set down his cup as he saw Dracquet.

Dracquet turned to Elise and bowed.

Elise had only seen Constant Dracquet once, but she recognized him immediately. He seemed to radiate elegance and danger. His garments were cut of the finest cloth available, with a discreet artistry that must have commanded a top price. His hair was impeccably trimmed, his hands well-manicured, and his jewelry just what a gentleman should wear. His voice was quiet and cultured when he spoke.

"Madame de Clichy?" he asked.

She inclined her head.

"My name is Constant Dracquet," he said with a smile. "You must permit me to apologize for some unpleasantness that occurred yesterday morning. I assure you that I was almost as disturbed by it as you must have been, and perhaps more so because it distressed a lady. That aside, I hope you will permit me to compliment you on the fine reputation enjoyed by your establishment."

"The first matter is forgotten, monsieur," said Elise. "And I must thank you for the second even as I disclaim."

"Madame is too modest," Dracquet said. "And now, if I am truly forgiven, might I trouble one of your servants to provide me with some coffee?"

"It is no trouble, monsieur," said Elise.

Dracquet bowed again and then turned toward Malet, who was engaged in spreading jam on a piece of toasted bread. Malet looked up as he watched, and their gazes met. The scrutiny was a sober, measuring, unsmiling one.

The silence lengthened until Dracquet suddenly smiled and sat at Malet's table. "Please permit me to apologize for my assistants and introduce myself," he said. "I am Constant Dracquet."

"How do you do?" said Malet. "I am Paul Malet."

"I do very well," Dracquet said with undiminished suavity. "And all the better for seeing you at last, though I believe we have encountered each other before. I left those messages for you."

"I believe it was established yesterday that the messages were left for no one in particular," Malet said.

Dracquet's smile broadened. "Come now, Chief Inspector," he said. "Running rings around a pack of quarter-wits is nothing for a man of your talent. Where's the merit in it? Whatever they thought, I know who you are now."

"Am I to congratulate you for that?" Malet asked with equal suavity. "Knowing my identity isn't difficult. All anyone has to do is come up to me and ask my name."

Dracquet laughed and sat back in his chair. "My men are fools, as I said. They mistook your rank and your purpose here and overstepped their authority. But really, what were they to think?"

"I wasn't aware that you considered capacity for thought a prime qualification in your minions."

Dracquet shrugged off the comment. "I concede the point," he said. "But they had learned that another Police officer was staying at this inn and assumed that his duties were the same as M. de Saint-Légère's. For that matter, I hadn't realized that you were the same man as M. de Saint-Légère's replacement. The realization was something of a surprise, but not an unpleasant one, and it saves me from duplicating my efforts."

"How fortunate for you," said Malet.

"But it does appear that you and I may be having some dealings," Dracquet said, easily ignoring Malet's less than cordial interjections. "The prospect could be a pleasant one, and I am certain that we could work well together."

Malet sipped his coffee, set it down, and said in a meditative voice, "Do you think so? then listen to this: 'Constant Dracquet, sometimes known as Conrad Dracquard, Conrad Dragonard or Guy Matherne. The last is believed to be his true name. In appearance he is of medium height with brown hair and eyes and a scar on the left cheek that appears to be from the cut of a whip. Born, in the province of Burgundy, of bourgeois parents. He currently calls himself a Bonapartist, though he claimed Royalist leanings during the Empire. He didn't serve in the armies and is known to have been in close contact with parties in England. A thick scar on his left thumb is surmised to be an attempt to disguise a brand in the shape of a 'v'. First appeared in Paris in the latter part of 1815 with a considerable amount of money.' "

"Fascinating," said Dracquet as he took out a gold toothpick and used it. "Do continue."

Malet shrugged. "Why belabor the point?" he asked.

"Ah? And where do you get your information?" Dracquet asked, amused.

"My usual sources. I can be thorough when something piques my interest." He smiled at Dracquet and added, "I knew a man from Paris named Dracquet. He was the last of his family; there were no cadet branches. Interestingly enough, he lived in the quarter of town that you occupy, at the same address. Also interestingly, he's been dead for twenty-one years. He was shot by a sniper during Bonaparte's Russian campaign."

"And so?" Dracquet said. "What does all of that prove?"

"Nothing, unless you dislike the thought of soiling the name of an otherwise honorable family."

"That is an interesting comment," Dracquet said, "Considering that you are at this moment using the name 'de Colbert', which your father denied you."

"Did you pay for this information?" Malet asked. "I suggest you request a refund. The name was not denied. I was disinherited, not disowned."

"I see," Dracquet said, turning to Alcide. "Coffee, if you please." He waited while a cup was poured for him, added milk and some sugar, sipped, and set the cup down, then raised smiling eyes to Malet.

"Paul V. Malet," he said. "The 'V' stands for 'Valentine'. Born in the prison of Toulon on February 14, 1787, the product of a liaison between Paul de Colbert, Vicomte de Beaumesnil, in Normandy, and an opera dancer who had taken the stage name 'Albertine Malet'. Exhaustive inquiries have revealed that she was probably Antoinette, the only daughter of the noble Mallebranche family of Chalons, which was exterminated during the Terror of 1793.

"Raised in the prison of Toulon, which he left at the age of fifteen to join the Police, in which he has served continuously except for the years 1811 through 1814, during which time he was in the Horse Artillery, where he rose to the rank of full Colonel. Known to use a pseudonym when it suited him.

"In appearance he is tall in stature and graying, with hazel eyes. He's currently clean-shaven, though he has worn a mustache in the past." He broke off as Malet yawned politely behind his hand. "Do I bore you, Chief Inspector?" he asked.

Malet raised his cup of coffee. "Your sources forgot to mention the scar on my chin. I'd think it rather obvious."

Dracquet shrugged. "I was about to mention it along with the scar from that saber wound that slants across your upper left thigh," he said.

"Touché," said Malet. "Your information is impressively accurate."

"I paid an impressive price for the accuracy," said Dracquet.

"It must be expensive to hire people to peek through windows while I bathe," Malet observed. "I wonder if it's worth it."

Dracquet ignored the jibe. "I have admired you for years," he said. "I admit it willingly. I have long wanted to make your acquaintance. I see that it was worth the wait."

"And I confess to a certain curiosity regarding yourself," Malet said with the hint of a bow.

"I trust your curiosity has been satisfied," Dracquet said. "It has been a source of—entertainment is, perhaps, the word—for me."

"It's been satisfied in part," Malet said. "There is still much to discover, though. And, as I said, I can be thorough when something piques my interest."

Dracquet smiled and sipped his coffee. "But, Inspector, we must inevitably resign ourselves to the fact that each of us is a mystery to the others, mustn't we?" he asked softly.

"Must we?" Malet asked with equal gentleness.

Their eyes met again.

Elise felt suddenly frightened. It was like watching two fencers circling, their swords ready. She turned away. Her full sleeve caught the handle of her spoon and knocked it to the floor. The clatter made both men turn toward her.

Malet's expression was unreadable, but Dracquet swept a glance up from her toes to her face and down that sent the blood scorching her cheeks. The knowing quality of his sudden smile as he sat back and scanned her again, then turned to eye Malet, betrayed his conclusions; Elise felt her cheeks flame. She rose and left the room with her chin lifted. She could feel the eyes of both men on her as she went through the door.

Dracquet flicked one last glance at her and turned back to Malet. "You have a cozy arrangement here," he said.

"You mistake the arrangement," Malet said with a direct look.

"Do I, now?" Dracquet asked.

"Indeed you do."

Dracquet dropped all pretense of courtesy. "I must speak with you," he said,

"Here I am," said Malet with a slightly glinting smile. "Speak."

"In private," said Dracquet.

"I am a busy man just now."

"Don't be foolish. Come to my house at noon and dine with me. My cook is superb."

"I have eaten too much over the past several days. My appetite is rather jaded."

"Come at noon, nevertheless," said Dracquet. "I won't take no for an answer."

"Then I won't say no," said Malet.

"Excellent," said Dracquet. He set a gold Louis beneath his saucer, rose, and left.

Alcide came over to take the cup, and he stared at the coin.

"Keep it," said Malet. He was frowning out the door in the direction that Dracquet had taken. His frown eased, and he rose and set his napkin aside. He added, "The coin will be worth something when he's dead." His sword-belt lay atop his coat on the chair beside him. He took them both and went out.

MALET FOUND ELISE STANDING before the fireplace in the large salon. She had wrapped a cashmere shawl around her, as though to fight a chill. She looked up as he came into the room, and her mouth tightened. She turned away toward the window.

"I am sorry, Madame de Clichy," said Malet. His voice was very gentle.

"I feel smirched," she said.

"You shouldn't," said Malet. "It's no worse than if someone splashed mud on the hem of your gown. It's more shame to him than to you or to me."

Her shoulders stiffened.

He set his coat and sword-belt aside and said quietly, "You have to understand: there is no such thing as honor or honesty. Everything has a price. Virtue is a commodity that can be purchased, and a woman's virtue is the cheapest. Love is nonsense easily seen through by those who have learned to leave myths to the children and the dreamers."

He gazed unseeingly out the window and continued, "The more coldbloodedly you calculate, the farther you will go. You must use others like post-horses and change them without pity when you have worn them out."

Elise had been watching his expression as he spoke. She seized him by the lapels and shook him. "My dear M'sieur!" she gasped. "Surely you don't believe that!"

Malet, looking down into her troubled eyes, wanted to kiss her and tell her to stop fretting. Instead, he covered her hands with his own and smiled down at her.

"No," he said. "But he does. He chose to believe it. It's second nature to him now, but he made a choice once. I wonder if he remembers when it was." His voice had lowered, and he seemed to be talking to himself, though he was still holding her hands against his heart. He released them after a moment.

"I told you of the filth that I encountered in the prison," he said. "And I told you that I left it behind me. He took the opposite way. He sought it out and chose to wallow in it. You can find all sorts of valuable things if you don't mind fishing in a sewer. Shrug him off, he's not worth anything more."

He put on his coat and then settled his sword-belt about his waist and buckled it.

Elise watched him. Her eyes were wide and considering, but her expression was reserved.

Malet took his gloves from his pocket and pulled them on. "You made a dish of veal in a pastry recently," he said. "You may recall that I didn't do it justice."

"I remember the evening very well," she said.

He nodded. "If I could try it again...?"

"I will make it tonight," she said. "And I will fix my own brandied apricot tart for you."

He smiled at her and said, "That would be good."

She watched him go to the door. "Inspector" she said. When he turned she said, "You aren't eating with him at noon."

"No," he said. "I don't break bread with his sort."

She nodded. As he went out the door she said, "Please be careful." She did not hear his reply. She turned back to the window and smoothed her shawl about her shoulders as she watched him pass through the courtyard to the street.

MALET LEFT THE ROSE d'Or and, after some thought, cut over to the rue de Rochechouart in the hope of finding a cab. His encounter with Dracquet had made him late, and he thought it might be faster to ride to the morgue on the Île du Palais than to walk. For once there were no fiacres in sight, but he did see an omnibus lurching along toward him, hauled by two lathered, dispirited horses. He watched the overgrown carriage with annoyance, taking special note of the passengers all but hanging out the windows and draped over the railing at the top of the second level, to their peril.

Malet swore viciously, cast a quick, despairing look up and down the street, surrendered to the inevitable, hailed the ungainly vehicle and climbed aboard after handing the driver five centimes.

It was the only the second time he had taken such a conveyance since they had made their debut in force on the streets of Paris five years before. He decided, as he squeezed into a seat that had been made available to him by his fellow-passengers who, seeing his sword and his expression, had compressed themselves, that it was a wearying and inconvenient method of transportation, and one to be avoided at all costs in future.

And slow, too, he thought disgustedly as they made their way down the crowded rue de Montmartre toward the Pont Neuf. He turned to catch a glimpse of the bustling market of Les Halles, to his left, and turned squarely into a sneeze from a fellow passenger.

He froze the fellow with a glare as he reached for his handkerchief. For this slow, uncomfortable, unsanitary ride he had paid five centimes! He could go faster than this on foot! He drew a deep, annoyed breath that further compressed his fellows, expelled it, and scowled out the window as he thought of Dracquet.

The man now knew who he was and why he was at the Rose d'Or. The gauntlet that he had thrown down at the precinct at the rue des Trois Frères had been picked up. Battle had been joined.

He suspected that Dracquet wanted to persuade him to join whatever he was planning: the invitations to lunch had been too open to be attempts to ambush and murder him. Whatever Dracquet was planning—and Malet had not forgotten the Princess' projected visit, Dracquet's association with the Duke of Rochester and the people Inspector d'Arthez had heard speaking English—he obviously thought he had a good shot at winning him over.

He toyed with the thought of joining Dracquet for lunch but dismissed it. He had been serious when he told Elise that he did not break bread with Dracquet's type. He had left them behind thirty years before.

He looked out the window again. They were crossing the Pont Neuf and approaching the Quai de l'Horloge. Malet could look east along the river and see the cathedral.

The omnibus tipped alarmingly as they reached the quay. The woman beside him screamed and clutched at the basket on her lap, which opened and spilled kittens everywhere. Malet rubbed his ear, nodded politely as the woman apologized, retrieved three squalling kittens for her and then rapped on the ceiling of the omnibus with his walking stick.

"Stop here!" he commanded and pushed his way through the passengers and out the door. Once on the pavement, he cast one last contemptuous glance at the omnibus with its dispirited, plodding horses, and then turned west and walked briskly toward the Quai aux Fleurs. He had the night's haul of corpses to review.

CHAPTER THIRTY

Evening in Paris

The afternoon had melted into a light rainstorm that lasted into the evening before it finally cleared, but the wet pavement shone like silver in the lamplight that turned the mist into shrouds of silk. The mist softened the sounds of passing carriages and the clatter of hooves upon the cobblestones dwindled to a murmur. Haloes circled the street lamps, and Paris seemed to be blanketed in a soft glow.

The man moved quietly down the rue d'Orsel toward the inn, his eyes drawn by the lights that streamed out into the mist from its wide windows. He seemed to think himself one with the shadows, for he limited his presence to the darker side of the street and lingered in shadowed doorways.

A group of people passed him, and he flattened himself against a wall fronted by smoothly cut stone. The people disappeared around the corner. He relaxed, and his right hand slipped lovingly down to the cold, smooth barrel of the pistol he wore tucked into his belt.

He started on toward the inn just as a grip like a vice clamped down on his shoulder and a voice said, by his left ear, "If you are going to attempt surveillance, my lad, then you'd best wait until your head-cold clears. You snort and sniffle so loudly, I could shoot you with my eyes closed." The voice paused, and he could sense amusement when it said again, "Now turn around and let me look at you."

He was forced round unwillingly to stand with his face full in the glare of a street lamp.

"Hm," said the voice, which came from a tall, black shape against the light. "Just as I thought. Tell your master that I am still at the Rose d'Or, and I won't leave until it suits me. And tell him, further, that he's ill-served if all the sneaks he employs are as clumsy as you!"

"I don't know what you're talking about, Chief Inspector!"

"Then how do you know my rank?" the man demanded. "Be off! Or I will remember that Chief Inspector Guerin has declared loitering illegal in this arrondissement. The grip was released; the man took to his heels.

Malet watched him go, laughing quietly to himself. What an oaf! One would think that Chief Inspector Guerin, fearing an investigation into his doings, would employ better spies than that!

He sobered after a moment. It was almost frightening to contrast the maladroitness of that one with the very capable spies that had been set on him by Dracquet. He had been followed from the moment he left the Rose d'Or that morning, and his tailers had been very, very good. It was fortunate, he thought, that they had not been set on him before he went to Michaud.

Michaud. He shouldered his walking stick and went on toward the inn. He had been wise to contact the man. He might be getting old, but his presence in Paris predated Dracquet's, and while he was a considerably smaller fish, his influence was, in its way, more far-reaching. He was in touch with the back-alleys, with the beggars and sneak-thieves. The prostitutes who came to him to exchange the jewels given them by their lovers for ready cash always had their ears wide open, and they didn't mind earning an extra sou or two by chatting with the man. No one feared Michaud as they feared Dracquet, and that made him a valuable tool for Malet.

Michaud had sent several messages to Malet by convoluted means known only to himself, and the information he had sent had been useful, but limited. His sources reported comings and goings, and he gathered snips of speculation, packaged them, and sent them on to Malet.

He reported that he had been baffled by the very tight control that Dracquet maintained in his own household; he had no way of learning what was going on in Dracquet's house. The man's control even extended to having the contents of the waste-baskets thrown in the fire under his own supervision. Malet reflected that the very impenetrability of the man's establishment only served to confirm his suspicions about the time frame in which he was working. If only there were some way to get a 'mole' into the man's house...

"If wishes were horses, Pippin," he said in English, "then beggars would ride." He would have to do some intense thinking.

He had narrowed his focus. He had originally thrown a wide net to catch Dracquet's target. Now, examining his haul, Malet decided that the most promising fish was Princess Victoria, the heiress of England. She was the target. He could feel it. This was the venture on which Dracquet was willing to stake his empire. It was up to Malet to ensure that the gamble failed.

In the meantime, he thought, looking up, the Rose d'Or was ahead of him, and he had to try to mend matters with Elise.

He entered through the kitchen, as usual. Marie was there before the fire, busy basting a roast. She looked up and smiled at him as he came in.

"Good evening, M. l'Inspecteur!" she chirped happily. "We have been looking for you! Dinner is ready for you any time you please, and if you wish to go freshen up, I will tell Madame you have come in."

He thanked her and went through to the hallway. Alcide was standing by the stairs, his face warmed by a wide smile. "Good evening, Inspector!" he said. "Welcome home! Let me take your coat and hat!"

Malet nodded and unbuckled his sword-belt and set it on the console table by the door. "Thank you, Alcide," he said as the boy helped him out of his coat and took his hat, as well. "Have you had a good day?" he asked, and then caught sight of the boy's tie. "Very good!" he said. "You have almost got it. Come to me after supper and I will show you an easy way to tie that."

"Oh, thank you!" said Alcide, who had been eyeing Malet's cravats with envy since he had come to the Rose d'Or. "I will! If—if it isn't any trouble?"

"None at all," Malet said, thinking that the lad reminded him of his housekeeper's eldest grandson, who was going through a titanic struggle with the difficulties of cravat-tying and looked to Malet for help and advice. "I'd enjoy it."

Alcide was beaming, but he schooled his features to propriety and said, "Dinner will be awaiting you in the private dining salon. I will escort you there after you have a chance to go to your rooms and refresh yourself."

Alcide was waiting at the foot of the stairs when he came back down. He bowed and said, "If you will follow me, sir..."

Just like François, thought Malet, eyeing the young man's expression. *He's play-acting.* The thought made him smile as he followed Alcide down the hallway to the dining room and preceded him through the doorway.

Elise was waiting just inside the door. She smiled warmly when she saw him and took his arm to be led to the table. He thought she was looking very pretty. The dress of heavy, golden beige silk in a flowered jacquard weave, with a wide lace collar and cuffs and cameo belt-clasp, was one that he did not recall seeing before. She had styled her hair in a new coiffure, as well, in a cascade of curls to either side that reminded Malet forcibly of his housekeeper's spaniel, Ninon.

The thought made his eyes dance as he smiled at her, but he led her to the table in silence, drew her chair out for her, and waited for her to arrange her skirts before he sat.

"You seem to be in good spirits tonight, dear M'sieur," she said as she smoothed the napkin over her lap. Her voice was as warm and private as a caress.

"You could say that," Malet said, thinking of Ninon once more. "And you are in great beauty tonight."

"Thank you," she said. She nodded to Marie, who had come in with the veal in pastry, and then turned to Malet again. "I have chilled some champagne," she said. "Remembering the last time I served you this dish—you were unable to finish it, if you recall—and all that happened afterward, I decided that you certainly merit a bottle of champagne. Alcide is opening it in the kitchen."

They heard a POP! just as she finished speaking, and Alcide emerged through the kitchen doors with a bottle and two glasses.

Elise raised her glass when Alcide had finished pouring. "A toast," she said. There was nothing in her manner to indicate that she remembered the insult of the morning. Her smile was as cordial as ever, her manner lively and affectionate with no hint of constraint. She sipped her champagne and set the glass down. "Now tell me, Inspector" she said, "How was your day?"

"Madame de Clichy—"

She opened her eyes at him. "Such a tone!" she said. "Are you annoyed with me?"

"Not at all, Madame," he said.

"That is good to know," she said. She looked thoughtfully at the platter of veal and said, "But aren't you going to serve?"

He took up the knife, cut into the pastry, and set a portion on her plate. Alcide came to the table with a *timbale aux epinards*, topped with a cream sauce. He grinned at Malet's expression, set the dish down, and left.

"I will have some of that, as well," Elise said, and watched as he cut into the hot, molded spinach and cheese, and set the serving on her plate as well. "Thank you, M'sieur. Now what were you going to say to me?"

Malet frowned down at his own plate. "What I wished to say, Madame, is that in view of what M. Dracquet seemed to think this morning—"

He stopped as Elise laid down her fork and took his hand warmly between hers.

"Let us forget M. Dracquet," she said. "He's no fit subject of conversation for a lady or for a man whom I view as one of the most complete gentleman I have ever had the good fortune to meet. As far as I am concerned, I have never met him. We shall forget that he exists and go on as we have."

She smiled across at him and added gently, "Now do stop looking surprised, sir, and drink your champagne before it gets warm."

Malet sipped his champagne and then, when Elise raised her glass and said, "To friendship!" drank again.

He said without looking up, "It might be best if I left the Rose d'Or rather than compromise you."

"How on earth could the friendship of a gentleman of your caliber ever compromise any woman?" she demanded. "Inspector? Look at me!"

Malet cut a piece of veal and speared it with his fork. "I don't want to compromise you," he said again.

She stared at him, touched. Now she understood. "You think it would ruin my reputation for you to remain under my roof!" she said. The thought was touching but amusing. "You are quite gothic Chief Inspector! There is no need to worry!"

"But perhaps..."

"I tell you that I will be offended if you leave!" she said.

His eyes flew upwards to meet hers.

"I am serious, and you are ridiculous," she said. "Let us have no more of this sort of talk! It's an insult to yourself!"

"Are you sure?" he asked. "I don't want to hurt anyone I care for."

"You can't hurt me," she said. "Ever."

CHAPTER THIRTY-ONE

A Shadow Comes into The Light

Marie set the broom against the wall and frowned down at the pile of dust and vegetable peels that she had gathered. She should sweep it up and put it in the dustbin, she knew, but she couldn't find the gride, and she didn't want to go searching for it. It was late, and she had an engagement at the theater du Porte Saint-Martin. The evening's production was an adaptation of Hugo's Notre Dame de Paris, and it promised to be an enjoyable evening.

She looked over her shoulder; no one about. She went to the door, pushing the dust before her, opened the door, and swept the dust out into the stable courtyard in a billowing cloud. Let Alcide worry about it the next morning when he cleaned the stables. He was getting too possessive: it would serve him right.

"*Merde alors!*"

The voice made her squeak and jump back, and she caught sight of a shadowy figure hovering just outside the circle of light thrown across the cobblestoned courtyard by the open door.

"Go away!" she gasped, raising the broom like a weapon as the man came into the light.

"Take it easy," the speaker advised. "I am not dangerous; I am just hungry. And one of the fellows around here said you give out soup to poor duffers like me."

"We usually dish it out during the day," said Marie, who was still a little shaken.

"Oh," said the man. He was standing before the door with a battered hat in his hands. "I could sweep the floor for you, or scrub pots." He added wistfully, "I haven't had much to eat for the past few days, and some nice, hot soup would sure taste good."

Marie looked him over. He was undeniably seedy, with a five days' growth of beard, but unalarming. He smiled at her as she scrutinized him.

"Who are you talking to, Marie?" demanded Elise, who had just come into the kitchen. She was still wearing her silk dress, and her eyes were shining with happiness.

The man surveyed her with approval. "Just a bum trying to mooch a handout," he said with a grin.

"He wants some soup," Marie said.

Elise looked the man over and made a decision. "Well, bring him inside and give him some," she said. "There's some bread on the sideboard as well- bring that and some cheese." She looked over at the man. "And you, M'sieur, come inside. The night is chilly."

The man entered the kitchen with a dawning smile. "I will work for it," he said. "I am good at scrubbing pots."

"They're all scrubbed," Elise told him. "We don't leave them sitting around to get crusty."

The man pulled out a chair and sat with a rueful sigh. "You sound like my wife."

Elise took a closer look at his tired face and suddenly stiffened. "Monsieur," she began in a tone of voice that made the man look up sharply, "I believe I know—"

She halted as Marie came back bearing a tray containing a bowl brimming with thick, meaty soup, the generous end of a long loaf of bread, a slab of cheese, and a glass of wine.

"There," said Marie as she set it on the table before the man.

"Thank you, child," said Elise. "Now go and get ready for your evening out." She eyed the man, who was tucking into the soup and added, "And please tap on the Inspector's door and tell him I need him in the kitchen at once."

"This is good soup," said the man as Marie went out the door.

"You are welcome to as much of it as you want, M. l'Inspecteur," said Elise with quiet emphasis. "And there's enough of this evening's dessert left to give you a healthy portion of *gateau aux amands*, too, if you wish."

The man dipped a piece of bread in the broth, popped it in his mouth and chewed it with a smile.

"Marie said I was needed here," said Malet, coming silently into the room. He saw the man sitting at the table and stopped with a muffled exclamation, then hurried forward. "What on earth are you doing here, Gilles?" he demanded.

"This one's sharp as a tack, chief," said Senior Inspector Gilles d'Arthez, gesturing toward Elise with the end of the loaf of bread. "She spotted me right away."

"You haven't answered my question. It's dangerous here for you."

"I have some news for you," said d'Arthez. "Along the lines you set out in your last note. It's urgent, so I thought I'd best chance it."

"You know the proper channels to take. They are designed to protect my operatives and I want them to be followed!"

"The risk is worth it," d'Arthez said.

"I am not so sure," Malet said.

"Come now," said Inspector d'Arthez. He ate another spoonful of soup and then said, "And to convince you I am not a crank or a fool, let me give you a name: Pierre le Noir." He eyed Malet's suddenly white face and nodded. "In the flesh, powder-burnt chin and all," he said. "And there's this as well." He reached into the pocket of his shabby breeches with a grimy hand, took out a coin, and sent it arcing through the air in a flicker of gold.

"Now do you think it worth the risk?" he asked as Malet raised suddenly blazing eyes.

"INSPECTOR D'ARTHEZ is certain it was him?" Count d'Anglars asked half an hour later. "He has no doubts?"

"None at all," Malet replied. "He says it was Pierre le Noir, no mistake, right down to the powder burn on his chin from my pistol."

"My God!" d'Anglars leaned forward and propped his elbows on his knees in an uncharacteristically tense posture. "I thought he fled Paris and was killed in the service of the Bey of Tunis."

"Wishful thinking, it would seem," Malet commented. He was standing beside the mantel, heedlessly toying with an ornate Dresden clock.

d'Anglars watched him set the clock back on the mantel. "Or a deliberate smokescreen to put us off his track," he said. "How did d'Arthez get so close a view of him?"

"He was in the stables currying one of the horses. He saw the carriage come in—it was a big berline, by the way—and caught a look at the man as he stepped out of it. He was half-hidden by a stall partition, but he got a good look. It gave him quite a turn."

"I can imagine," said d'Anglars. "I thought we'd seen the last of him after the Reuilly murders."

Malet nodded. "Dracquet's pulling in some heavyweights with Pierre le Noir in his train now," he said. "He's taking a very great risk in having that man staying with him."

d'Anglars said nothing. His expression was that of a pupil listening to his teacher.

Malet was still thinking. "If Pierre le Noir's involved in this, Dracquet wants a specific result with no margin for error and is willing to pay heavily to be certain. The man's no spendthrift. I have noticed that every sou he pays out is calculated to get results, and Pierre le Noir is the most expensive assassin on the market. And the best."

"But what could he be using the man for?"

Malet touched a carefully articulated porcelain rose and said thoughtfully, "What do you know of the British royal family?"

"I know they're a pack of German prigs," d'Anglars said with uncharacteristic flatness.

Malet shot him an amused look. "I recall that you spent a long time living on the charity of the English—which wasn't very gracefully given, as I understand," he said. "What, for example, do you know about the king and his heirs?"

"The king and queen are childless," d'Anglars said. "As William succeeded his brother, George IV, so William would be succeeded by his brothers and their heirs, starting with the oldest and descending through the youngest."

"How does Princess Victoria fit in?" asked Malet. "Can women inherit the English throne?"

"They can," d'Anglars replied. "The Duke of Kent was the next in line after the Duke of Clarence—the present King. His daughter Victoria became the immediate heiress to the throne after he died."

"And she is a child," Malet said.

"Thirteen or fourteen, I believe," d'Anglars said.

"Hm," said Malet. "And who succeeds her if she dies?"

d'Anglars sat back with a frown. "The next in line is the Duke of Cumberland," he said after a moment's thought. "He is not well liked or trusted by the English people. When King William dies Cumberland will inherit the kingdom of Hanover, even if Victoria survives, since Hanover does not recognize the right of women to inherit the throne."

"And who inherits after Cumberland?" Malet asked.

"Edmund, the Duke of Rochester," d'Anglars replied.

"Something of a black sheep, perhaps?" Malet suggested. "Cards, women, fast horses?"

"You could say that," d'Anglars admitted.

"Just as I thought," Malet said. He gazed off into space with his eyes narrowed. "I wonder..." he said.

"Yes?"

"Can a man inherit the English throne if he is clearly implicated in a murder?"

"I don't know," d'Anglars said. "He might forfeit his right to inherit."

Malet turned away from the mantel and went silently back to his chair. d'Anglars watched him. "What are you implying?" he asked.

Malet smiled and sat back. "I dined recently with the woman who was Dracquet's mistress for a time. She gave me some valuable information on the man, and one of the items I found very interesting was the fact that Dracquet has close ties in England with the Duke of Rochester and his household. When Rochester visited France incognito in 1831, he stayed at a house Constant Dracquet owns in the faubourg Saint-Germain. Dracquet's mistress acted as hostess on that occasion."

"But even if Rochester were to arrange the assassination of his niece through that villain Dracquet, how would it benefit him?" demanded d'Anglars. "He doesn't stand to inherit."

"He could gain two thrones," Malet replied, "providing matters were set up in such a way as to implicate the Duke of Cumberland. Dracquet's an excellent conniver, and they'd reach an arrangement between them that would enable them to achieve both their aims. Or so Rochester would think. But I believe Dracquet would double-cross him."

d'Anglars sat forward. "How?" he asked.

Malet frowned down at his folded arms. "Dracquet has connections to munitions manufacturers. Things would be arranged in such a way as to cause a war. I am not sure Rochester would want to agree to that. If Cumberland were barred from the succession, and if Rochester became king, Dracquet would be able to blackmail a king for the rest of his life. If Rochester tried to free himself by having Cumberland killed, it would only be fuel for the fire. And however powerful the King of England is, I don't think he would be able to beat Dracquet at the assassination game."

"Impressive," d'Anglars admitted. "And that would certainly explain the presence of this assassin, Pierre le Noir, in Dracquet's household for the moment."

"There's no question of it. That is the plot that Saint-Légère sensed. That is what Dracquet's after. Everything fits in. Even this." He handed d'Anglars the coin that d'Arthez had put into his hand. "Do you know what it is?" he asked.

d'Anglars turned it over. "An English guinea," he said. "Minted this year."

"That is correct. Gilles d'Arthez was given it as a tip by a man who spoke with a pronounced English accent and bore a strong resemblance to the face on the coin. Yes," he said at d'Anglars' expression. "Rochester himself is in Paris and staying with Dracquet in Montmartre. If there's anything that would clinch the argument, this is it. And Dracquet's mistress heard an interesting snatch of conversation two years ago... Now we know what Dracquet's after, and why Le Noir is returned from the dead. He is hunting royalty."

"You have convinced me as to Dracquet's purpose," d'Anglars said thoughtfully, "But I am not so sure about Le Noir."

"What do you mean?" Malet asked.

"You forget one last variable," d'Anglars said. "You forget that there can be a multiplicity of reasons for the presence of a particular player in a game."

Malet was frankly skeptical. "And what is the second reason?" he asked.

"You have been watching Constant Dracquet for a long time and now you are after him," said d'Anglars. "You have made no secret of your purpose, and he's afraid of you. He has sent messages inviting your attendance at various meals, and he has taken care to be courteous about it. If you are unaware of your own menace, I promise you that he is not."

d'Anglars looked straight at Malet and added, "You may have renounced the title thirty years ago, M. le Dauphin, but if this plot concerns royalty, then I recommend that you look carefully to your own safety."

CHAPTER THIRTY-TWO

Walking in The Rain

Elise frowned up at the rain and gathered her skirts more closely about her. It had come on to rain very suddenly, and she was caught without an umbrella, far from home, with her arms full of packages. She had been fortunate to find this doorway in which to take shelter, but if the rain did not ease shortly, she would be forced to acknowledge defeat and head home in the downpour.

She sighed and leaned back against the wall. She was just off the rue Drouot, too far from the Rose d'Or to hope to be able to run there. And she had no money. Her supper the night before with Inspector Malet, coming on the heels of her ride in the park with him, had confirmed her suspicion that her wardrobe was in sad need of refurbishing. She wanted to be pretty for him, and she had been embarrassed to appear before him on both occasions in dresses that predated his none-too-recent arrival in Paris. She had set some money aside for herself, and she had decided to use it to purchase cloth for four new gowns. She had gone toward the heart of Paris to buy the finest silks she could afford, had overspent her budget, and had started to walk home.

And now she was trapped in the rain.

People passed before her. Some turned curious eyes on her, but she hugged her packages closer to herself and ignored them. She fixed her eyes on the dark sky and wondered when the rain would stop.

"Madame de Clichy?"

The voice had come from right beside her. She started and looked up to see Chief Inspector Malet standing before her, gazing at her with surprised disbelief. He was carrying a large umbrella of oiled black silk.

"Chief Inspector!" she said.

"What on earth are you doing here?" he demanded.

"Waiting for the rain to end, of course, M'sieur," she replied. "And how did you come by an umbrella?"

"I generally look at the sky," Malet said. "If it looks as though it might be coming on to rain, I carry one with me. And that is why I am not at this moment huddling beneath a none-too-clean lintel and wondering when it will clear." He shook some water from the umbrella and added kindly, "Would you care to share this with me?"

She laughed up at him from the shelter of the doorway and said, "I will ignore the rebuke—though it was kindly phrased! —and accept the pleasure of your escort."

Malet stepped away from the doorway and held the umbrella over her. "If you will carry my stick," he said, "I will take your packages. Good heavens! What are in these? Next time you might consider taking along a wheelbarrow, since I think these might weigh as much as I do."

"Stop it!" she said. "They're just some lengths of fabric—"

"Chain mail, perhaps?"

She chuckled and tucked her hand in the crook of his elbow. "Hardly," she said. "Just some silk." Her fingertips smoothed the fabric of Malet's sleeve and she added, "I also ordered some good wool for coats. I wish I could find some cashmere like this. I looked, but there was none to be found, and Alcide needs a coat badly. Poor boy! He'd like to be a dandy, but he hasn't the money."

"You might tell him that it's no shame to buy from the used clothing merchants at the Carreau du Temple. Quite a few impeccable people do so, with no disgrace to them."

"Yourself among them?" Elise asked, quizzing him.

He replied seriously. "I did at one time, when I was first on my own. I had nothing when I left Toulon prison. Cheat-Death and his creatures had given me a great deal of money, expecting me to set myself up as the new Cheat-Death, but I left it sitting just inside the gate. I didn't want anything of theirs. My salary wasn't very generous, though it was more than I was accustomed to receiving. The Police provided me with two uniforms, but I was responsible for everything else. I had no choice but to dress from the ragpickers for a while."

"Did it embarrass you?" Elise asked.

Malet smiled a little. "Maybe it did," he said. "Just a little. But you must remember that I was just fifteen, fresh from a prison, and looking at middle-class respectability as though it were as unreachable as the evening star. I was shy of them—the used clothing merchants—at first. I went to them alone and ashamed, not knowing what to buy or what to pay. All I had was my uniform. I didn't even know what the proper undergarments were to wear. One of the standholders took me in hand and fitted me out in some decent clothing and led me to a mirror to look at myself."

Malet's eyes shone with the memory, even after thirty years. "My clothes in the prison had been little better than rags," he said. "These were far grander than I'd ever dreamed. It was the first time I'd seen myself in a mirror. I thought, looking at myself, that I'd done right to leave Cheat-Death behind, that maybe I really could become like a gentleman, and my birth might one day be invisible to everyone but me..."

He looked down at Elise with a reminiscent smile that faded as he saw the shine of tears in her eyes. "My dear!" he exclaimed. "What is this?"

She dabbed at her eyes. "Poor little boy!" she said.

"I was a grown man at that point. At least in the eyes of the law. I could take care of myself."

"But it's such a shame that you had to. That there was no one for you to come home to, to spoil you a little, to worry about whether you had new clothing to wear instead of someone else's castoffs."

Malet's brows drew together slightly, but he smiled at Elise and merely said, "That was long ago and far away. Will you buy Alcide a cashmere coat?"

"If I can," said Elise. "He's a good boy, and I have come to think highly of him. Claude was my father's groom, and he recommended Alcide to me. But the cloth isn't available, so that ends that."

"I will give you the name of my tailor," said Malet. "He can find the fabric for you, if you have your heart set on it." He ignored her thanks and said, "Let us return to an earlier subject: why weren't you sitting snug and dry in a cab instead of walking in this rain?"

Elise hid a smile and looked down. "I had no money," she said. She saw his expression and chuckled. "I am sinking myself below reproach in your eyes, I know," she said. "But you must understand, there was a bolt of silk of the most ravishing shade of green, almost emerald, with tiny flowers woven into the fabric. I had to have it, so I bought it."

"And used up all your money," said Malet.

"That is correct, M'sieur."

Malet smiled and adjusted the umbrella.

"And are you not going to give me a thundering scold?" Elise demanded when he did not comment. "Christien says you are very good at them."

"I am doing enough just keeping you from becoming drenched. You certainly don't need a scold. Although I believe I might just hail the next cab—"

"Oh don't!" she said, tightening her hold on his arm for a moment. "I have been enjoying it so, walking along with you and looking into the windows. You're a very comfortable man to be with, you know."

Her hand was snugly tucked into the crook of his arm; he pressed it against his side for a moment, but he spoke lightly. "Am I?" he asked. "How odd of you to say so! Most of the people I am constrained to speak with at any really great length seem anxious to leave my presence as quickly as possible."

They stopped before a shop that sold toys.

"You're speaking of criminals," Elise said after taking a good look at his expression. "M'sieur Mischief! Well, of course they want to get away! But your friends—that is a different matter. Oh Inspector! Just look at the shoulder of your coat! You're getting wet! Hold the umbrella more over yourself, for heaven's sake!"

"I am fine," said Malet. "And I am not wearing a bonnet that probably cost a pretty penny."

"No, you are wearing a very good black beaver hat that cost every bit as much!" Elise retorted.

"Resign yourself, Madame," said Malet. "I am not moving this umbrella."

THEY FOUND A CONSTABLE from the 6th arrondissement awaiting

Malet upon their return to the Rose d'Or. He had an urgent inquiry from Chief Inspector Gaston Rabateau that required an immediate response.

"I can wait in the kitchen, Chief Inspector," said the constable. "I will be comfortable there."

Malet's mouth twitched for a moment. Marie, the pretty red-haired chambermaid, was basting a roast there and the constable was a handsome young fellow in a spruce new uniform.

"There's no need," said Malet as he scanned the message from Rabateau. It concerned a procedural question that was easily answered, though Malet made the reply provisional to the Prefect's final approval. "I will respond now, and you can go to the kitchen and bespeak a glass of wine with my compliments and Madame de Clichy's approval."

He took a sheet of paper from the escritoire and then, glancing at Elise for her permission, sat to compose a reply. He was smiling as he wrote, and the smile remained as he looked up at the constable and handed him the note. "There, my lad," he said. "That should answer M. Rabateau's question. Do, pray, convey my regards to him and the rest of his staff. And here's for your wine." He handed the man a coin.

The constable grinned, saluted, and then followed Alcide to the door.

Malet sighed and sat back, his eyes still on the door as it closed behind Alcide, whose stiff back was eloquent of jealous disapproval. After a moment he looked up at Elise.

"I have been here for the better part of three weeks," he said. "I'd better write you a draft on my bank to pay for my lodging so far. If you have no objection, I will pen a request to my banker, to draw out the funds for you."

"I have no objection at all," said Elise. "Though you may remember that I was willing to wait until the city reimbursed me."

"No," said Malet. "This is better." He dipped his pen in the ink and wrote swiftly.

Elise went to stand at his elbow and watched as his pen moved across the paper, unfolding writing that was precise and clear. Looking from the draft to his face, she saw that his lashes were thick and dark, and she saw for the first time the faint mark of a scar on his chin.

Her eyes moved to the paper and then back to him. The damp had made his hair curl slightly along his collar, and the lamplight caught unexpectedly blue highlights. The collar of his shirt was very white against the brown column of his neck, and the hazel-green silk of his cravat seemed to mirror the color of his eyes. The damp had heightened the faint scent of leather, sandalwood and steel that clung to him.

He dipped the pen once again and tapped off the excess ink against the side of the inkwell; the slight motion drew his sleeve taut, just for a moment, drawing Elise's eyes away from his face to the strong spread of his shoulders.

"There," said Malet, taking up the blotter and applying it to the paper.

Elise's heart quickened its beat as she raised her eyes to Malet's face again. She had known that she loved him, but now long-dormant urges and emotions were awakening. She wanted to touch him.

Elise had left her maidenhood behind upon her marriage over ten years before. Although the marriage had ended tragically, she had nevertheless enjoyed her husband's embraces. *How much more wonderful it must be,* she thought, *to lie in love's arms!* She was an upright, honorable woman: such actions outside the bounds of matrimony were out of the question, but some things were permissible within the limits of propriety.

The draft was finished. Malet blew gently on the ink to dry it, then raised his head and looked up at her with a warm, unguarded smile.

Her hand moved almost of its own accord, coming to rest gently against his face. The light touch warmed, strengthened as she curved her hand against his cheek.

The smile faded from his lips. His eyes met hers and asked a startled question.

Marveling at her own daring, she traced the faint line of the scar on his chin. Her fingers slanted softly up along his cheekbone and then feathered through the hair at his temple. It felt like warm, thick silk.

His sudden smile removed all awkwardness; she was able to speak without a quiver to her voice. "I didn't thank you, my dear sir, for all you do to keep this city safe.

His hand was beneath her chin, drawing her to him. "There is no need to thank me for doing my job."

Their lips met, touched lightly, clung and then parted, and she looked down at him with the breath fluttering in her throat. Her hand trembled as it curved to the line of his jaw.

She could feel him tense for a moment, as though he were fighting against something. And then he drew her closer to him and gently, almost shyly, tilted her face to his and kissed her again.

She never knew afterwards how she came to be on his knee, in the circle of his embrace, but it seemed so right to her that she settled into his arms with a half-laugh of pure happiness. Even in the midst of a delightful whirl of emotion, she was oddly aware of the fact that she had never felt so safe before. She drew away a little to smile at him, her arm lingering about his shoulders while her other hand stroked through his hair and traced the softened curve of his mouth with gentle fingers.

He caught her hand to his lips. "Madame..."

"Hush," she whispered, and claimed his lips with all the passion that was reawakening within her.

A loud knock sounded at the door. It stopped, then began again, more insistently.

"Chief Inspector!"

The mood was broken. Malet's eyes flickered and he turned toward the door. "What is it?" he demanded.

Elise slid from his arms and stepped back, shaken.

The door burst open to admit two breathless and disheveled troopers of the city patrol, along with Claude, who was protesting volubly and uttering alternating threats and pleas.

"These mannerless boobies insisted in charging in here, Madame!" he said to Elise. "I tried—"

"M. l'Inspecteur, there is—" said the head trooper.

Elise's heart lurched with sudden panic; her hand flew to her breast.

"Wait a moment, you specimen of an ape!" cried Claude. "You're upsetting the lady!"

"Hold your tongues!" snapped Malet. He skewered the three men with a glare, then rose, drew a chair forward for Elise, and waited until she was seated. "Now tell me the meaning of this uproar." The second trooper offered a folded piece of paper without comment.

Malet took it, opened it, and read. He raised his head after a moment. "Rioting in this rain?" he said. He shook his head. "You—" he nodded to the first man. "Go back to your commander and tell him to hold the line. You—" this to the second, as he took out his pencil and wrote swiftly on the message, "Take this note to the Prefecture. I have given instructions there. I will follow you directly. Now go. As for you, M. Kerouac, if you'd be kind enough to bring the dry coat and hat from my rooms, I'd be grateful."

Claude bowed and left, followed by the troopers.

Elise watched them leave and then looked up at Malet. "What is it?" she asked.

"Some looting in the 12th arrondissement," said Malet. "By the river, in one of the poorer sections. It started half an hour ago and has gotten out of hand. The Chief Inspector for that arrondissement reports two men are shot and has appealed for assistance to the Prefecture. I will bring reinforcements."

"B-but you aren't going yourself, are you?" she asked faintly, caught by the thought of him in danger.

"I have no choice," said Malet as he cast an eye over his pistols.

Claude returned with his coat and hat and held them as Malet shrugged himself into the coat with a word of thanks.

Elise watched him turn toward the door. "Wait!" she said. "Your umbrella!"

He turned back, eyed the umbrella with the hint of a grin, and said, "I think I will leave it here. Don't have anyone wait up for me. God alone knows how long I will be."

He was out the door the next moment.

CHAPTER THIRTY-THREE

If at First You Don't Succeed
Abandon the Effort

The next day was sunny, clear and warm. The sky was a mild vibrant blue, and the west wind was soft and somehow playful. It tugged at the hems of the ladies' dresses, whisked at the edges of shawls and pushed leaves before it. The Jardin du Luxembourg was crowded with people enjoying the sunshine.

He had found himself with the morning's work finished by 11:30 a.m. He was expected to meet with Count d'Anglars at 3:00 p.m. to discuss the presence of Pierre le Noir and the Duke of Rochester in Paris and what steps to take, but there was nothing else to do until then, and he was too restless with happiness to be able to face the thought of sitting idly in the Prefect's elegant office.

He had decided to enjoy the gardens at the Luxembourg Palace and then return for a leisurely lunch at his favorite restaurant at the place du Châtelet. Now he strolled down the main walkway of the gardens and past the octagonal reflecting pool. There were, as usual, crowds of children laughing and squabbling, sailing their little boats on the flashing, rippling waters.

He paused and watched for a moment, smiling. He had seen a little sailboat once when he was a child. To that day he could remember how desperately he had yearned for one like it, not knowing that such a toy was as far out of the reach of a prison brat as the moon.

Children have a capacity for hope that, though often betrayed, is never quite discouraged, and Paul had hoped that somehow, someday he too would have a little sailboat. The fulfillment of that hope still ranked as one of the shining moments of Malet's life, and in his mind he could still see the rakish lines of the sailboat's hull and touch the sails with fingertips that lost none of their awe in the thirty-six years since he had received the boat.

Malet's smile deepened; now he knew how Joseph Young had sat up during the long nights smoothing a piece of firewood with a homemade knife that he had carefully hidden from the guards. It must have been painfully slow work, but he had done it, for his Pippin, the adopted son of his old age, had to have his toy.

Malet saw a little boy hovering at the edge of the basin, wistfully watching the sailboats; he went to the pavilion set up to one side, paid several sous for the rental of a boat, and then went over to the lone child.

"Here, son," he said, giving the boat to the boy, "Go ahead and sail it. Return it to those fellows there—" he pointed, "—when you're through."

He nodded to the child and turned down one of the subordinate paths of the park that led to the southwest corner of the gardens, where the walkways wound through unexpected stands of trees and secluded nooks. He followed the path to a cul-de-sac and sat on a bench overlooking a bed of chrysanthemums. He folded his hands in his lap and raised his face into the wind to watch the trees swaying before him.

He felt as light-hearted as a boy. The memory of the past evening lingered on, filling him with warmth that effaced even his increasing concentration as he closed in on Constant Dracquet. Everything around him, the trees and flowers, the strollers, even the warm old stones of the Luxembourg palace, seemed to glow with a reflection of his happiness.

He loved Elise de Clichy. That was no surprise, certainly, but he knew now that she loved him. How could he doubt it after a night like last night, with his heart still quivering with the memory of her embraces?

But all was well. The rioting had been a minor affair after all, over within two hours, at the same time the rain had ceased. There had been two casualties among the Police called in, but Malet was confident that they would recover. He had snatched a quick, light meal of coffee and bread at the Prefecture and then returned to the Rose d'Or to find Elise waiting anxiously for him.

She had not spoken of what had passed between them before he left. Instead, she had assured herself that he wasn't hurt and then said, "The rain is over, and I saw some stars through the clouds. Can we go for a walk together?"

Although Malet had not forgotten Count d'Anglars' caution about the presence of Pierre le Noir in Paris, the prospect of an hour or two alone with Elise under the stars had outweighed caution. He had made one concession by engaging a cab to take them to the Tuileries gardens, where he judged that the crowds would afford them some measure of safety. He had taken his pistols with him and resolved to be careful—and then forgot everything in the pleasure of her company.

They had walked arm in arm through the rain-silvered streets for what had seemed like hours, talking of everything and anything while the warming air sent streamers of mist upward from the pavement.

Elise had spoken of her girlhood in the faubourg Saint-Germain, and then she had wanted to hear about his life in Toulon prison and, later, in the Police. He had told her what he thought was fitting, and she had heard what he left unsaid and took his hand in hers, just for a moment.

They had strolled through the evening while the lamplighters came and turned the twilight city into a galaxy of soft lights that mirrored the stars above them. She had wanted him to show her the stars, to point out Orion and Pegasus and maybe even see a falling star. And, wonder of wonders, they had seen one arching down over the place de la Concorde as they passed along the rue de Rivoli.

They had driven back to the Rose d'Or and shared one of Yvette's sugar cakes and two tiny glasses of brandy before he rose to take his leave and go up to his rooms. She had held out her hand with a warm smile, and he had bent to kiss it.

He had held her hand a moment longer, released it, and went out of the salon to the stairs.

He had mounted the stairs and turned at the landing to look down. She had been smiling quietly up at him from the foot of the stairs, and he had known in that moment that he did not want to live without her.

Had he not been a paying guest under her roof, he would have gone back down to her there and then, taken her in his arms, and asked for her hand. Instead, he had bowed to her and continued to his room. But he had been smiling, and the smile had lingered through the night and into the next day. It warmed his lips now as he opened his eyes and gazed up at the blue sky.

He heard a step on the gravel path beside him; he did not look that way, but every sense was suddenly alert. The steps came closer, paused, and then the bench shifted and settled as another man sat.

"Good day, Chief Inspector," said a voice beside him.

Malet's mouth moved in a faint, ironic smile as he said, "Good day, M. Dracquet." He twitched the hem of his coat aside.

Dracquet was silent for a moment as he looked Malet up and down. "You didn't come to dine with me yesterday," he said at last. "Or the day before. It was discourteous of you. I had two perfectly delicious meals awaiting you, and they went to waste."

"I told you that I wouldn't come," Malet said.

"You said you wouldn't say no," said Dracquet.

"That was after you told me you wouldn't take no for an answer."

"You are oddly squeamish for a man of your reputation," said Dracquet. "Did you fear an assassination attempt?"

Malet caught an undertone of anger, but Dracquet's face was bland when he looked up. "I simply don't care to dine with you," he said.

Dracquet made a distasteful motion with his hands. "Squeamish," he said. "Cowardly. There is still a matter that must be handled between us."

"I wasn't aware that we needed to have any further direct dealings," said Malet.

"You are too modest," said Dracquet. "There's much that we can discuss. Our association could be quite lucrative."

Malet said, "Really? What bribe do you offer me?"

Dracquet smiled and shook his head. "You are a valuable and dangerous man, Inspector. I am aware of your quality. A bribe won't answer with you."

"Plain speaking!"

"Hear plainer speaking, then," said Dracquet. "Bribes are offered all the time. It's merely a question of degree. But I have something more compelling."

"Oh?" said Malet.

"Precisely," said Dracquet. He reached into his breast pocket and took out a notebook, which he opened. "I told you that I have assembled a dossier on you. You might be surprised at what is in it...and perhaps even a little chagrined."

"Chagrined?"

"Yes."

"I see. You are going to try to blackmail me."

"The term is too crude," said Dracquet.

"Crudeness is a measure of truth at times. But let's continue: you say that I will be chagrined."

"In a manner of speaking. Colonel Malet." The voice was very intent.

"This won't answer," Malet said. "I have never been ashamed of my Army service."

"Is that so?" asked Dracquet. "Then perhaps you can explain your reticence on that head. The Emperor himself gave you a promotion on the battlefield of Smolensk for 'conspicuous gallantry', as he phrased it, and made you an officer in the Légion d'Honneur. Surely that is justifiable cause for pride, and yet no one seems to know of it, Colonel. Is it possible that I am speaking with a secret supporter of the Emperor?"

"All things are possible," Malet said, "But I would think it unlikely if I were you. Leaving aside the fact that Bonaparte is dead, my military career is a matter of public record, even if I don't choose to sound my own trumpet. And I am openly drawing a rather large pension from the Légion d'Honneur."

Dracquet shrugged. "I am unconvinced," he said. "You left the Police to enter the armies when your career was approaching its zenith. You served as Colonel of France's finest regiment of Horse Artillery from the Russian campaign until you left the army in the fall of 1814. Your prosperity coincides with the Emperor's career, and I find myself wondering if your loyalty might not lie in that direction."

"My career, army or otherwise, is public record, as we have already discussed," Malet said calmly, folding his hands on the head of his walking stick. "None of it has ever caused me the least bit of shame."

Dracquet rose and paced a ways down the path. His expression was very thoughtful. He paused to pick a chrysanthemum and set it in his buttonhole before he turned and came back to the bench. "Very well, Monsieur," he said. "Let me be blunt: you have shown your loyalty to France—no, don't bow! You abandoned a promising career to serve four years in the armies-"

"I was able to resume that 'promising career', as you put it," Malet pointed out, "after I left the armies, and I have risen further in it since then."

"You didn't know that you could when you joined to fight for the Emperor."

"I joined to fight for France."

Dracquet shrugged. "If you insist!" he said. "The point is that you did join, you did fight, and you did well-"

"A colonel isn't precisely a commander of armies. There are more colonels in France at the moment than I can shake this walking stick at, and two out of every three legless beggars you see before a church were heroes of France at one point. If your 'dossier' has somehow given you reason to hope that I will wink at any deviltry you're brewing, let me assure you that you are mistaken!"

"'Deviltry', my dear Colonel?" Dracquet asked in a hurt voice. "You wrong me! And you wrong yourself! Come, sir, I do understand you! You fought at Paris in 1814, at the heights near Montmartre. You must have looked down through the smoke at the city and known that the end had come. You were with the army when it withdrew from Paris. Can you honestly say that you haven't desired a return of the glory of France, even as I do? A departure from the France of today, the doormat of Europe, the laughing-stock of England!"

"I would find that speech less nauseating if it were sincere," Malet said. "I have seen the sort of pies you have had your fingers in, and I don't choose to soil my own hands in them. Let us understand each other: I am a Police officer. What's more, I am an honest Police officer, and if you were to offer me a marshal's baton at this moment to close my eyes to anything that you are planning, I would refuse."

Dracquet sat back against the bench looking wounded. "M. Malet, you wrong me! You are known to be a man of honor and rectitude, and I am merely reminding you where your loyalties lie and offering you a chance to return to them."

"My loyalties lie with France, as I have told you. If you act against the interests of France, as I believe you do, then I am against you."

"You haven't given me a chance to present my proposal," Dracquet said.

"Nor shall I ever," said Malet. "We can have no dealings now or ever."

"You won't even consider listening to me?" asked Dracquet.

"Not for a moment!"

"Old loyalties don't move you?"

"My loyalty is a very old one," said Malet. "It is to France. Your loyalty is only to Constant Dracquet's power and prosperity."

Dracquet smoothed his gloves with hands that shook faintly, but his voice was very calm. "You can't mean that," he said.

"I do," said Malet. "I am the only person in Paris whom you can't fool. I know all about you. You plot your own rise to power. Causes mean nothing to you, and you have turned your back on truth and honor. I say it again: we can have no dealings!"

Dracquet sat back and frowned at Malet. "Very well, then," he said. "I am for myself. But who's not? Show me someone who is truly altruistic, and I will show you a colossal fool! What's the point of self-sacrifice? And yet, Malet, we could deal well together. You serve France now, you say: think how you could serve her with the power I could give you!"

"Come now!" said Malet through his teeth. "You paid a high price for my dossier: didn't you read it? I was Cheat-Death's chosen successor! Power! I could have been far more powerful than you, but I chose another way. I could destroy you with your own weapons if I chose to pick them up and use them!"

Dracquet sat back, looking puzzled.

"To be blunt," Malet continued, his voice raised. "I am not for sale! There's nothing you can say to induce me to go along with you in any venture, though I die for it tomorrow! If you think that I am flattered to have been approached by you, let me assure you that I am not!"

Dracquet pushed himself to his feet and turned to face Malet. "Every man has a price," he rasped.

Malet's expression became sardonic. "Your mask is slipping," he said.

Dracquet's face hardened, but he paused and collected himself. His voice dropped, became almost caressing. He had one last card to play.

"Your past, as you have said, is public record," he said. "You will forgive me if I speak bluntly, I hope, but I can discern what can only be a heartache for a man of your breeding. Illegitimacy is a bar to many things, including a lady's hand. Women, odd creatures that they are, are often averse to wedding what they have no hesitation in bedding. I could change that. The bastard son of an opera dancer may be barred from social intercourse with the upper crust, but what of the son of a nobly born lady and Dominique de Colbert? That is an entirely different matter! My dear Malet, you are better bred than two-thirds of the people in the faubourg Saint-Germain—"

"This discussion is obscene," said Malet, making a motion to rise.

Dracquet set an ungentle hand on his shoulder. "Oh come now," he said. "You're being foolish. Only bear in mind that you would be considered an acceptable suitor to a certain well-bred lady."

For a moment Dracquet had an odd notion that Malet was about to strike him, though he had not changed his position. But then Malet smiled and said, "Really, M. Dracquet. My housekeeper may be of impeccable birth, but she could almost be my mother, and I have done nothing to compromise her virtue or that of any other woman, well-bred or not!"

"And if that well-bred lady were to learn that a man staying under her roof, to whom she has shown a partiality that is, I admit, well within the bounds of propriety... If that lady were to learn somehow that the...gentleman we have been discussing spent a night in the arms of another woman...?"

The moment drew itself out, Dracquet's thin smile, the breeze sifting through the trees overhead, the sound of children at the fountain...

Dracquet's voice edged through the other sounds. "Would you have her learn of this assignation, Inspector?"

"I will not hide the truth," Malet said.

"Would you risk losing her?"

Malet raised his head and smiled at Dracquet. "I have not 'won' the lady," he said. "And I would speak and think and live the truth, as I have always done."

"You cannot be serious."

Malet folded his arms. "Why don't you tell her and find out?" he asked.

Dracquet frowned thoughtfully at him, but he did not speak for a moment. He finally collected himself with an effort and said, "You have said that I am engaged in 'deviltry'—what a term! I say that I am not! Listen: I am leaving Paris tonight and I will be away for several weeks. I have made several valid points. Think over what I have said. I will speak with you again when I return. And accept this as a token of my regard—" he held out a small box, opened it, and showed a gold charm in the shape of the medal of the Legion of Honor, enameled, with the center circle formed of diamonds. "It would look very good on your watch chain, M. le Colonel," he said.

Malet shook his head and would not touch the jewel. "No," he said. "I have the real decoration at home, and it would be pointless to wear this one."

"I insist!"

"And I refuse. Good day. We will speak again when you return."

Dracquet pocketed the box, paused as though he wished to say something else, and then, when Malet lifted his copy of the *Globe* and opened ostentatiously to the agony columns, turned and left without another word.

Malet closed the paper and set it aside after he was gone. "Several weeks, my hat!" he said through his teeth. "You will be moving in one week at the most, or I am greatly mistaken!"

So saying, he stood, folded the paper, tucked it into the pocket of his overcoat, set his hat on his head—and swore as the hat was promptly knocked to the ground by a stone. He lost himself in a luxuriant and heartfelt curse. The stone-thrower was very persistent!

He bent and retrieved the hat and frowned at it. The stones weren't doing it any good. He turned in the direction from which the stone had come and said clearly, but quietly, "Why don't you go and knock his hat off?" and, motioned in the direction that Dracquet had gone.

Larouche, hidden behind a tree, heard him and chuckled silently. "I think I will!" he said.

CHAPTER THIRTY-FOUR

It Is Pointless to Mourn
When the Departed Is Not Dead

Malet walked slowly along the paths of the park, his eyes lowered, his mind busy with thoughts of strategy. For Dracquet to approach him as he had indicated that the matter was close to fruition and he was certain of the outcome. He would not have taken such a risk otherwise. Malet would confer with his people and pull in several more shadows and send another messenger to Michaud. He thought, as well, that he would be wise to pay some attention to his own safety now that battle had been openly joined.

He was approaching the walkway that led to the rue d'Assas, where a line of cabs waited. He raised his head and looked quickly around. It was a habit he had developed when he had first joined the Police in Marseilles: size up the people around you and the area. Obtain an overall picture of the situation and assess the threat. If there is none, relax. It was reflexive after thirty years. He was no longer aware that he did it.

But now he stiffened. Something about a man to the left, walking along with a lady, was at once familiar and out of place. He started to turn just as the man made a convulsive motion. He faced the man fully and came to a complete halt with the odd feeling that the breath had just been knocked out of him and he had been whirled back eight years, to a time when he had been Commissioner of Police in the city of Vautreuil, in Picardy.

Jacques Lambert, the chief magistrate of the town, had been remarkable for his charity and kindness. He had personally endowed a hospital in the city, and his voice had often been raised in defense of all those suffering from the hardships that had followed the fall of Napoleon. He had even succeeded in enlisting Malet's support, despite the fact that Malet was more concerned with keeping people on the right side of the Law than assuaging their sorrows.

And then, some years later, Malet had received an anonymous tip concerning the man. The tipper had hinted very strongly that the man was a convict by the name of Jacques Vaux, who had broken his parole almost twenty years before and was still being sought by the Police.

Virtue, however considerable it might be, holds no weight against official suspicion. Lambert had been Malet's dearest friend, but affection had to take second place to duty. Malet had conducted an investigation, hoping to clear Lambert's name. He had failed, and on the basis of his findings, Sieur Lambert had been arrested and taken to Amiens to stand trial.

Malet had testified at the trial, which caused a sensation. His friend was sentenced to death, the sentence was commuted to imprisonment at hard labor for life, and Malet was ordered to escort him to prison.

It had been a strange journey. Lambert, who had reverted to the name Vaux, was pale with exhaustion and Malet, equally pale, silent and thoughtful, looked out the carriage window into the darkness of the clouded night.

Vaux had finally spoken. "You conducted that investigation personally, didn't you?"

"Yes," Malet answered. "I did."

"On your own initiative?" Vaux asked.

Malet thought of all the excuses he could offer, and silently despaired.

Vaux looked down at his manacled hands. He finally sighed. "Do you know, M. le Commissaire, some day one of those little ones that you pursue without pity may have you in his power. He will show you none of the mercy that you might have shown him."

Malet closed his eyes. "I begged for clemency," he said, almost to himself. "They would not listen." He did not look again at Vaux.

The sky had split with a crash of thunder as the carriage drew up before the prison. Sheets of rain, driven by a screaming wind, poured down the sides of the carriage, and the wind tore Malet's hat from his head and sent it spinning away into the darkness as he stepped down to the cobbled courtyard. He had not tried to go after it; the rain streaked his cheeks like tears as he handed Vaux over to the prison authorities.

Within the month, Malet, heartbroken over the tragedy, had declined promotion to Prefect of Police for his Departement and had requested a transfer to Paris, in the Seine et Oise Departement, to assume command the Police of the 8th arrondissement of Paris, which had recently been annexed to the city. He had learned some months later that Vaux had escaped, been recaptured, and then, reportedly, been killed when a portion of the prison walls suddenly collapsed. They had been unable to locate his corpse, so he was presumed dead.

NOW, LOOKING AT THE man before him, Malet knew that they had presumed wrong. This man was Jacques Vaux! There could be no mistake! Those broad shoulders, that barrel of a chest! Those bright blue eyes! Malet's eyes narrowed as they met the other man's. So he was alive after all! Alive and in Paris, of all places!

He felt a confused moment of joy: this man had been his dearest friend, and his arrest and supposed death had almost broken his heart all those years ago. After a moment the happiness faded, to be replaced by a faint, weary vexation. Vaux was alive and in Paris. A convict! Malet's affection toward the man had no bearing on anything. He would have to be returned to the Law.

Vaux turned to the lady beside him, spoke quietly to her and watched as she hurried away, and then turned without looking again at Malet and cut across the grass toward the small pine wood that surrounded the classical fountain.

Malet hesitated as he took a good grip on his walking stick. He considered summoning a squad of the Guard to back him up, but he decided that it would not be necessary. He carried a pistol, if worse came to worst, though he hated the thought of pulling a gun on this man. But Vaux was older than him and appeared to have put on weight in the eight years since Malet had seen him, while Malet knew himself to be as fit at forty-seven as he had been at twenty-five. It shouldn't be difficult to take him into custody. If only it weren't necessary!

He passed through the woods and into a small clearing. Vaux was waiting there, standing quietly. He even was smiling as Malet approached him.

The warmth of the smile made Malet halt. The man did not seem at all nervous. Malet wasn't used to being discounted. All the old, deep affection that he had felt for this man was welling up within him again.

He was struggling to set it aside, and the effort made him speak more harshly than he wanted.

"You!" he said.

"Me," Vaux agreed.

"You were reported to be dead."

"The report was wrong," Vaux said, folding his arms. "I knew nothing of it. I only knew that I was free." The warmth of his smile had increased, and he was surveying Malet with an almost fatherly air. "The years have been kind to you," he said.

Malet pushed the comment aside. "You were supposed to turn yourself in—"

"That would have been disastrous," Vaux said. "Would you do the same if our circumstances were reversed?"

Malet frowned. "Don't fence with me," he said. "I have seen you and as an officer of the law I must turn you in. You are under arrest."

"No," said Vaux.

"What?"

"I said no. I won't be arrested."

"Must I haul you in bodily?" Malet demanded, feeling vaguely foolish. "You are under arrest!"

Vaux took a step back toward the trees. "You can tell me I am under arrest as often as you wish," he said with the gentle insistence of one reasoning with a stubborn child. "I don't recognize your authority to arrest me. I am not a criminal."

The calm way in which he pronounced this took Malet's breath away. He stepped forward, following Vaux back among the trees. "You're older than me," he said. "I don't want to hurt you, but you will come with me!"

Vaux had his back against a sapling. His eyes were wide and fixed on Malet. "I won't," he said. He smiled again. "My very dear Malet, why must we go on like this? We were the best of friends once! Don't you remember? You are a fine man, a good man! I don't deny it: I have always liked you even when you erred on the side of harshness, for you were always harshest toward yourself.

"Can't you admit that I am not a bad man? How have I ever knowingly harmed anyone after that one time I committed robbery as a boy of fifteen? I repented it! I served my prison term! Haven't I paid for it? Must I go on paying all my life? You are the Law: can't you relent?"

Malet felt oddly breathless. It was as though the years had rolled away, and he had the chance to change his mind and undo what he had so unwillingly done all those years ago and heal the lingering ache in his own heart.

This flashed through his mind in the time it took for him to lower his walking stick and take a step forward. A comparison between Vaux and Dracquet sprang unbidden to his mind, but Vaux had said it: Malet was sworn to uphold the letter of the Law, and under the Law Vaux, as a convicted criminal, was forfeit.

His conclusion showed clearly in his expression. Vaux, watching him attentively, reached slowly into his pocket and took out his handkerchief. He shook it open and held it loosely in his hand as Malet approached.

"I am sorry," said Malet. "My hands are tied. You must come with me." He repeated quietly, "If only it were someone else— I am very sorry..."

Vaux smiled at him and shook his head. "My poor Malet," he sighed. "I do believe you truly are," He paused and looked down. "I guess it's no use pleading with you," he said.

"No," said Malet. "Come along with me." He added awkwardly. "I-I will beg for leniency for you. I think they'll listen to me now..."

Vaux shook his head and tucked the handkerchief, still loosely bunched, back in his pocket. "No," he said. "I won't ask that of you."

No further word was said. Malet lifted his walking stick and advanced, moving toward the trees as Vaux stepped backward and pivoted. Malet followed the motion, circling, until Vaux' back was toward the clearing.

Vaux' eyes had remained fixed on Malet's. Now they lowered, and his shoulders slumped as he sighed and turned half away. He seemed to have abandoned all thought of resistance.

Malet took a step forward, intending to set his hand on Vaux' shoulder and lead him back to the clearing. He decided that a plea for clemency might be successful. Vaux had done no harm to anyone and much good since leaving the prison, after all —

That line of thought was brought to a violent halt as Vaux whipped back toward him, his hand coming round in a back-handed swing that had all the force of his chest and shoulder behind it. The blow connected with the side of Malet's head and knocked him off balance, sending his hat rolling away.

Vaux sprang forward, his fists swinging.

Malet recovered himself with an effort and leapt back. He blocked another blow and thrust with the stick, holding the cane like a sword. His head was buzzing a little from Vaux' first blow. He realized that the trees were hampering his movements; he tried to go sideways into the clearing, but Vaux blocked him and countered with a charge that Malet tried to side-step.

He partially succeeded, but he dropped his walking stick. Vaux saw this and closed in as Malet tried to stoop and retrieve it.

The stick was abandoned. Malet drew back, circled, and joined battle, both fists clenched and ready.

The trees hampered movements on both sides. Vaux, who was shorter and heavier, kept trying to close with Malet and grapple, but Malet avoided him, knowing that the other's more compact mass would be difficult to wrestle. He got in several telling blows and received one or two, himself, though he could not escape the feeling that Vaux was not hitting as hard as he could—but in all he was winning until, sidestepping Vaux' charge and ducking a roundhouse swing that would have felled him like an oak, he caught his foot on his lost cane and went down against a tree. His head struck hard against the trunk.

The next moment his right arm was twisted painfully behind his back as a hand holding a handkerchief clamped tightly over his nose and mouth, stopping both breath and sound. It stayed there even though he tried to wrench sideways and clawed at the hand over his face. His chest was on fire and the world was full of roaring and darkness, when the handkerchief was suddenly withdrawn, and he was pushed face-first against the ground, sobbing for breath.

He felt a hand at his throat, ripping loose the knot in his cravat and pulling it away, then he was half-raised and set against something solid. His arms were pulled behind him and pinned there. He tried to struggle, but the movement made his head spin as the blackness engulfed him...

"MALET..." SOMETHING was steadying his head and lightly patting his cheek. "My dear Malet..."

He struggled toward light and air, his vision slowly clearing, until he could look up and see Sieur Lambert kneeling before him and frowning down at him.

What on earth was Lambert doing on his knees before him? Had the world turned upside down? Malet tried to sit up and found that he could not move. He shook his head, puzzled and yet warmed by the affection in M. Lambert's sudden smile. He returned the smile in spite of the ache in his head–

He stiffened and swore as memory returned. He was in Paris, in a clearing in the Jardin du Luxembourg with his hands lashed behind him around a sapling with his cravat, and his feet tied with a handkerchief. And now the man had the effrontery to be steadying his, Malet's, head, patting his cheek, calling him 'my dear lad' and telling him to wake up!

Malet tried to pull away. "You!" he said through his teeth.

"Yes," said Vaux, keeping his hold. "Look straight at me and stop squirming."

"Squirming!" Malet spat. He drew a deep breath, intending to shout for help.

Vaux clapped an ungentle hand over his mouth. "None of that!" he said. "I mean you no harm. I want to make certain you don't have a concussion." He removed his hand. "You came up hard against that tree, and you have been unconscious for a while. Now do open your eyes wide. Do you feel at all nauseated?"

"Putain de bordel!" Malet hissed through his teeth, trying to twist out of Vaux' grip, *"Espèce de sale, bitte-suçant-!"*

"Behave yourself!" said Vaux. "Now hold still and look at me. Good God, you're strong! Fighting you is like trying to wrestle Cerberus!" He looked down into Malet's glare and suddenly grinned and released him, pausing only to swat him on the shoulder and ruffle his hair.

Malet cursed and tried to free himself. He subsided, panting.

Vaux nodded and got to his feet. "Good," he said. "You aren't hurt. You had me worried for a moment. I might have saved my concern: skulls like yours aren't easily dented, though I think you will have a bruise tomorrow. Since it's apparent that you're unhurt and as full of fight as ever," he said, "I will be taking my leave now." He reached into his fob pocket, took out his billfold, and withdrew several banknotes.

"I am afraid your cravat is ruined," he said. "I apologize for the necessity. It's a very fine one: this should cover the purchase of another." He folded the notes and carefully tucked them in the pocket of Malet's waistcoat. "There," he said. "Take care of yourself, my lad."

Malet stared up at him with a mixture of fury and bafflement. "Wait a minute!" he cried. "You were under arres—" He didn't even finish the word. He was the one who was arrested, at least for the moment. He tried to wrench out of the knots with a muffled exclamation of pure temper, and only succeeded in bringing down a shower of yellow leaves.

Vaux smiled and bent to pick the leaves out of Malet's hair and then check the firmness of the knots about his ankles. "Precisely," he said. "You will pardon me if I don't linger. A lady is awaiting me."

He retrieved the walking stick, laid it beside Malet, and put the hat there, as well. He cast a considering look at Malet, and then knelt beside him again. "I hate to do a thing like this to a man like you," he said as he checked Malet's pockets. "Be fair and concede the necessity." He found the pistol, took it out and looked it over.

Malet's eyes dilated. He made a sudden, convulsive motion, suppressed it, and lifted his chin with an attempt at a smile.

Vaux turned the pistol over in his hand, saw that it was loaded and primed, and then looked up at Malet. "You had this on you and you didn't use it?" he said. "I don't understand: why not?"

Malet's smile deepened as he squared his shoulders and leaned deliberately back against the tree. "Go on," he said through his teeth. "Do your part: I have done mine. I may have regrets, but I did the best I could. Now finish it."

His tone of voice made Vaux look up sharply. "Good God!" he exclaimed. "You think I am going to kill you! You fool! How could you believe such a thing of me? We're friends! Didn't you listen to me? I said I meant you no harm! Did you think I was lying?"

He put the pistol back, located Malet's handkerchief, smoothed it, and folded it into a gag. "This is what I meant," he said. "—though, knowing you as I do, I imagine you'd prefer the pistol."

Malet shrank back against the tree and fought the knots as Vaux leaned toward him. "You can't run forever," he said. "I am warning you! You're forfeit under the law!"

Vaux smiled and shrugged as he set the gag in place and made certain it was effective but not too tight. "Leopards don't change their spots," he said at the edge of the wood, "And I don't expect you to change your soul. But first you have to catch me."

CHAPTER THIRTY-FIVE

Malet Discovers That Death Is
Preferable to Notoriety

Malet hated the idea of anyone coming along and finding him. To be overpowered by a man twenty years older than him, thirty pounds fatter and three inches shorter, to be tied with his own cravat, gagged, and tethered to a sapling like a dog, was bad enough. To have someone else witness it was unthinkable!

He relaxed after a moment with as close to a wry smile as he could manage. He had lost this exchange and his pride would serve as a forfeit.

Everything would be well if—

Pierre le Noir.

The name drove all other thoughts from his mind for the space of time it took him to draw a shaking breath.

It was just possible that Dracquet had the man waiting to kill Malet the first chance he could get. Malet had certainly left Dracquet in no doubt of his intentions, and as d'Anglars had said, a player in a game could have more than one reason for his presence. It would be a stroke of luck for the man to find him like this!

Malet cursed through the gag and wrenched at the cravat with growing panic. His blasted temper! He could usually keep it under control, but he had slipped disastrously—and after promising Count d'Anglars to be careful for his own safety! And now he couldn't even shout for help. He tried to twist out of the knots, but the silk held more strongly than any chain could.

He froze as he heard someone running along the path. There were at least three people pounding along toward him. His heart lurched, and he thought feverishly that if he could get his hands, tied as they were, to his coat pocket, he could reach his pistol.

He strained at the knots and then gave up, panting, as four young men came pelting into the clearing. They skidded to a halt amid the leaves and stared at him with wide eyes.

Malet's mouth twisted with annoyance even as he sank back against the tree, dizzy with sudden relief. Far from being Pierre le Noir or any of Dracquet's murderous toughs, they were obviously students, dressed in such an extreme of last year's fashion as could be achieved among the used clothing merchants at the Carreau du Temple with a limited amount of cash. They blazed with brightly patterned waistcoats and Wellington hats that looked like nothing so much as flowerpots set on their narrow ends. One of them wore a long-tailed frock coat of a pink virulent enough to smite Malet between the eyes.

This young man took in the situation at a glance, went to his knees beside Malet, and untied the gag.

"Can you get up?" asked a student wearing a shaggy beaver hat with the back part forward to disguise the fact that it was very worn.

Malet scowled up at him. "No," he said. "I can't."

"You are as big a fool as ever, Adrien!" said the young man in the pink coat. "Look at him: he's tied to the tree! Untie his feet while I take care of his hands. Your temple is bruised, sir: are you hurt?"

Malet shook his head.

"Were you robbed?" asked the beaver-hatted student as he bent over Malet's ankles. He had the handkerchief untied after a few seconds.

The pink-coated sprig had dropped to his knees beside Malet and was working at the knots.

"What happened?" demanded another, dressed in acid yellow broadcloth. "A stocky, blue-eyed old fellow told us he heard someone being attacked!"

Thank you, Vaux! Malet thought savagely. "I was waylaid by a thief!" he said aloud. "Don't bother with the knots, for God's sake! Just cut them!"

The pink sprig said, "But this is beautiful silk! It must have been expensive!" He sounded wistful. He stopped, pulled off his gloves—Malet noticed a split in the index finger—and worried at the knot.

More people arrived to jostle and stare. Malet stiffened: a man on the fringe of the crowd, his chin disfigured by the scar of a powder burn, was watching him intently. The space between them was empty. Their eyes met and locked.

The crowd seemed to fade from sight and hearing in that moment of recognition, and it was as though they were alone and waiting.

Le Noir's right hand slid into his pocket and clenched about something the size of a fist. He smiled and slowly withdrew his hand, revealing a small pistol. He took a handkerchief and wrapped it around the grip and barrel and started to level the piece just as a lady, cooing solicitously, stepped directly between them and thrust a vinaigrette under Malet's nose.

Pierre le Noir had missed his chance. Malet caught a quick glimpse of the man's expression as other people clustered around Malet to offer advice. It was full of baffled rage as he turned and slipped away.

Malet closed his eyes for a moment, trembling with reaction. The lady offered the vinaigrette again as the noise and movement of the growing crowd crashed back into his awareness.

Malet looked up at the woman, a plump, motherly sort with a round, smiling face. "Thank you," he said quietly. "You saved my life."

She capped the vinaigrette and moved away with a smile.

The knots were beginning to give a little, to Malet's relief. He felt like a lion in a zoo. It only lacked a little boy poking him in the ribs with a stick to make the impression complete.

"Poor man! What happened?"

"Attacked by a thief!"

"Here? Best summon the Police!" And one of the bystanders went running off.

"There!" said the pink student, "I think I have it! Just a few minutes more!"

A few minutes? That would be a few minutes too long! Malet suggested once more that they cut the cravat. The suggestion was discussed among the students and then dismissed. Malet took his temper in a stranglehold.

"How did he manage to overpower you?" demanded one strapping fellow in the garb of a dock worker, fixing Malet with the gaze of one who knows how to fight. His eyes lingered on Malet's shoulders and clearly speculated on his height and weight.

Malet lifted his chin and deliberately lied for the first time in over thirty years: "He had a gun," he said. There. His cheeks reddened slightly, and he looked down, ashamed.

The dock worker misread Malet's emotions. "A gun, you say!" he exclaimed. "Best not to argue with one of them! No shame to you for that!" He leaned forward. "But you are bruised: that blow to the head! He hit you while he had you at gunpoint?"

Malet closed his eyes. "That was before he pulled the gun," he said.

"You don't argue with a gun," the man said again. He broke off as more people came into the clearing, two of them wearing the uniform and the indefinably officious air of Police constables.

The men elbowed their way through the crowd until they were before Malet. "What's going on?" demanded the younger. He looked down and recognized Malet for the first time. His eyes widened, and he pushed the student in pink aside for a moment. "Chief Inspector!"

"Never mind that!" snapped Malet. "You—" this to the senior constable. "—there's a man in this park with the mark of a powder burn on his chin. I want him! Send out an all-points bulletin at once! He hasn't had a chance to go far! Find him and arrest him!"

"At once!" said the older constable and hurried off.

"But be careful!" Malet called after him. "He's armed and very dangerous!!"

"The poor gentleman was robbed at gunpoint!" said the lady with the smelling salts.

"This is no 'gentleman,' " objected the younger constable. "He's a Police Inspector!"

"The two are not mutually exclusive!" Malet hissed.

The constable met Malet's glare, paled and busied himself with clearing the crowd back.

The knots finally gave way. Malet sprang to his feet, the cravat in his hand, and tried to compose his expression to smiling benignity. "Thank you all for your help," he said through his teeth. "You can't know how truly grateful I am for your concern. I hope your afternoon is as pleasant as you have made mine!"

"That's right," said the Constable. "Move along! You will read all about it in the papers tomorrow, I am sure—"

"No they won't!" said Malet.

"No?"

"*No!*"

"Oh. Well, move along! Thank you all!"

The crowd began to disperse, some people pausing to wish Malet well and make various suggestions for his recovery from the shock of being attacked. These ranged from the offer of another whiff at the vinaigrette, which was gently declined, to the consumption of a large glass of cognac, a suggestion that Malet accepted gratefully.

The dock worker paused and said, "You probably want to put your fist through something, just now, don't you, Guv'nor?"

"You never spoke truer word!" Malet said grimly.

The man chuckled. "Eh, but you never argue with a gun!"

"A gun?" demanded the Constable.

The pink sprig pushed himself to his feet, dusted off his trousers, and started to join his friends, who were waiting on the edge of the clearing.

Malet halted him with a hand on his shoulder. "I didn't get a chance to thank you for coming to my assistance so promptly," he said, including the rest with a glance.

The young man shrugged and smiled. "You needed help," he said. "It was the only thing we could do—you might have been hurt."

"Well I wasn't, thanks in good part to you." Malet folded the cravat and gave it to the young man. "It's yours since you admired it. And here—" he gave him a gold Louis, "—I hope you and your friends will drink some champagne with my heartfelt thanks."

The young man looked at the cravat with delighted eyes, and then held out his hand. "It was my pleasure, Monsieur! And—and who should we toast?"

Malet paused and considered another lie. What did it matter?

"Alexandre Guerin," he said. "Chief Inspector, 3rd arrondissement."

"Very well, M. Guerin: the toast will be to your very good health!" the young man said.

Malet watched them leave.

"Your name is Paul Malet!" said the Constable with a grin.

Malet turned on him. "I am aware of that," he said. "I have been aware of that for a long time!"

CHAPTER THIRTY-SIX

Sometimes the Quarry Is More Formidable Than the Hunter

Larouche had spent an enjoyable half-hour following Dracquet around and throwing stones at him. His tall, shiny beaver hat made a much more satisfactory target than Monseigneur's, and the man himself, being thoroughly detested, was a better target as well.

He had come upon the man as he was speaking quickly and earnestly to a mean-looking fellow with a mark on his chin like a smear of black paint. He had seen him around Dracquet's house during the past week, and the man made him feel uneasy and vaguely sick, as though a mist of evil surrounded him.

The man had nodded and hurried off in the direction that Dracquet had come from, leaving Dracquet at Larouche's mercy.

Larouche succeeded in knocking Dracquet's hat from his head four times in a row, and then occupied himself with hitting various parts of his anatomy with stones of varying heft and sharpness. He had succeeded in driving him away after hitting him on the left side of the seat of his trousers with a particularly sharp rock.

Dracquet had hailed a cab and stepped inside, and a moment later the cab had gone off at a canter. At that moment if Dracquet, swearing and rubbing his backside, had found himself sharing the coach with Orestes in his flight from the furies, he might have discovered a kindred soul.

Larouche chuckled and made his way back into the gardens, looking for something amusing to watch. Maybe Monseigneur was still there, though he decided, in all fairness, that Monseigneur had enjoyed quite enough of his attentions for the day.

He made his way up the tree-lined Avenue de l'Observatoire, his lively eyes darting to and fro, watching the strollers, alert for any neglected food or blankets. Pickings were slim now that the weather was growing colder; he had found nothing for the past several days. Luck was with him this day: two lovers on a secluded bench, intent on each other's company, did not see him make away with their half-eaten box of chocolates.

He nibbled at a chocolate, the box under his arm, and favored those who stared at him with a smudged smile. Chocolate was delicious! He had had so little of it in his short life that this taste was like a sample of the joys of paradise.

The old woman who sold flowers at the rue de l'Ouest smiled at him, as usual, and beckoned him over to give him a carnation, which she insisted on placing in the frayed top buttonhole of his shirt. He grinned at her and offered her a chocolate.

"Not but what I should tell the cops about you, you little thief!" she said with a smile. "Eh, but I recall a time when I had boxes and boxes of these, as much as I wanted to eat!"

Larouche cocked a doubtful eye at her.

"Oh but I did!" she said. She broke off to sell a rosebud to a passing dandy. "Time was I was a beauty, and the King himself noticed me!"

"Oh?" Larouche said skeptically, "Which king?"

"Louis XVIII! He wasn't king then, of course. But I was quite the fashion for a year or so! The du Barry ruined me!" She shrugged and sniffed a rose. "It's better so," she said. "It saved me from the guillotine."

She eyed the chocolate box that Larouche offered her and finally took another. "Come here tomorrow and I will have some bread and meat for you," she said. "Chocolates are all well and good, but a boy your age needs good food."

Larouche grinned at her and ate another piece of chocolate. "This is good," he said.

She ignored the comment. "Winter's coming on," she said after a moment. "What will you do then? Have you found a place to stay?"

Larouche shrugged. He didn't like to be reminded. "I will get by," he said.

She hid a smile. "Well, if you decide you'd like something specific, I have a grandson who owns a little bistro at the rue des Morts, in Montparnasse. He's looking for a boy to wait tables and clean up for the winter, and maybe even longer, depending on how it works out. There's a bed in the stable and good pay each week. I spoke of you and he was interested. Said that if you were the honest sort of lad I said you were, there might be a place for you. Why don't you go and talk to him?"

"What sort of hell-hole is it?" Larouche demanded.

"No hell-hole," she said. "Oh, the students go there a lot and talk nonsense, just like they talked in '89! But there's no harm to them and only air between their ears! If you want to talk to him, my grandson's name is Jean-Claude Bessier. Tell him I sent you!"

Larouche grinned and opened the box again to offer her another piece of chocolate.

"Maybe I will!" he said. Suddenly the thought of winter didn't seem so terrible. He sketched a salute, like he had seen the soldiers do, and turned away. And then he froze in dismay.

Monseigneur was bearing down on them like an avenging angel, his eyes flashing, his face pale with fury.

The flower-seller crossed herself and muttered an Ave Maria. Larouche, shrinking back against the flower-stand, could only stare wide-eyed as he drew near.

Monseigneur's stride was as light and brisk as ever, but it had a sort of vehemence about it now that hadn't been there before, as though he were restraining an explosion of rage with a choke-rein. The hem of his coat, however, seemed to mirror the turbulence of his mood, for it whipped and churned as though in the force of a gale. His walking stick was clenched in his hand like a sword. Larouche saw that Monseigneur's clothing was in unaccustomed disorder. His coat was half-unbuttoned, his shirt collar was open, and his cravat, an unusually fine one of wine-colored silk, was gone.

Larouche's eyes widened and he tried to flatten himself behind a sheaf of chrysanthemums.

Monseigneur passed the flower stall without a glance, stormed across the rue de l'Est and followed the rue du Val de Grace toward the rue St. Jacques, passing through the crowds that parted before him as the Red Sea had parted before Moses.

Larouche turned to stare after him with astonishment as he swept past. The petals of the flowers quivered in the breeze of his passing.

Well! Larouche drew a deep breath and turned to the flower-seller, who was fanning herself. "Holy shit!" he said, "What set him off?"

"Something got his goat!" she said.

"Something got his whole stable!" Larouche said. "I am glad it wasn't me!" He grinned and opened the chocolate box again. "Have another," he said. "I will talk to your grandson."

CHAPTER THIRTY-SEVEN

Inspector Malet Plans a Hunt

Two hours later, Malet smiled grimly down at a sheet of paper filled with writing and handed it to Sergeant Guillart.

"There," he said. "That is a good description of the man: stocky, very broad shoulders, barrel-chested. He has white hair, very blue eyes, and he appears to be in his mid-sixties." Malet paused to finger his cravat, a beautiful new one of heavy blue Lyonnais silk, expertly knotted. He had bought it with Vaux' money.

"I want this notice forwarded to all the Police posts in Paris and the outlying communities of the Seine et Oise Departement," he said, biting each word off. "Any man of that description is to be noted and followed discreetly until he reaches his home. The address and a description of the place is to be sent to me, as well as an outline of his activities. I also want his name, if it can be obtained. But: he's not to be apprehended or..." he paused and searched for the proper word. Finding it, he added, "annoyed under any circumstances. Not yet."

He paused, and his smile became vaguely vicious. "I want this effective immediately! I want to find that man!"

"Yes, Chief Inspector," said Guillart. He scanned the description, then looked up into Malet's eyes. They were glinting with securely leashed rage. He wondered what the stocky, white-haired man had done to trigger that wrath, but he merely smiled and nodded. "It shall be done," he said. "And you asked me this morning to remind you that His Excellency will be meeting you here at 3:00 p.m."

"Thank you," said Malet. He took out his watch and checked the time. Half an hour. He rose and paced over to the pillar that lay to the left of Guillart's desk. "Well," he said. "Disseminate this bulletin, if you please, and coordinate any information that comes in. I am depending on you, with perfect confidence, as you know."

"You will be in your offices?" Guillart asked.

"The Prefect's offices," Malet corrected automatically. "Yes, I will."

"I will have one of the boys bring you some coffee, then," said Guillart, eyeing Malet's cravat. It was different from the one he recalled seeing that morning. He watched Malet turn and head toward the Prefect's offices, then frowned down at the description of the man.

Malet was intercepted by the Chamberlain, as usual, but Clerel took one look at his expression and limited himself to frigid correctness. He took himself off as soon as he had relieved Malet of his coat and hat. He gently closed the door after he left, and went back to Guillart, shaking his head.

Malet watched the door close and then sat, swearing, and buried his face in his hands. To see Lambert again after all those years! And to see him after facing a viper like Dracquet! Why? Why? Why?

He was once more confronting the paradox that had troubled him ever since he had become an officer of the Law: the good man who was nevertheless a criminal under the Law. And the opposite side of the coin was Dracquet, the evil man who was not at odds with the Law. His duty was clear as regarded Vaux. Or was it?

He raised his head and scowled out the window. Damn the man! Not only did he show up alive and healthy with a serene conscience, but he had to do so at the very moment when Malet was drawing his net tight about Dracquet! By rights Malet should concentrate his attention on pursuing the man who had been judged a criminal! After all, Dracquet had done nothing provably wrong.

Malet pushed himself to his feet, cursing, and began pacing, back and forth, back and forth across the priceless carpet. He could have Vaux back in custody within three weeks if he set his mind to it. And he would go through the heartbreak all over again. There was nothing he could do to stop it.

He turned on his heel and went to the window. The square before the cathedral was packed with strollers and beggars; a juggler was performing in a little clearing in the very center. Malet watched him for a moment and then turned away.

Good. You aren't hurt. You had me very worried for a moment... I mean you no harm...

Malet could hear Vaux' voice in his mind even as he laid out the hunt that he could direct. His mind skipped over the relentless inquiries, the unceasing surveillance, the inexorable sifting through excuses and masquerades and brought him to the moment when, facing Vaux once more as the personification of the Law, he laid his hand on the man's shoulder —

He drew up short, surprised by the picture that his mind had drawn for him, unbidden, unexpected and welcome. He had set his hand on Vaux' shoulder and said, *Go in peace.*

If only it were possible!

But was it impossible?

He had formidable discretionary powers and the ear of the Minister of Police: could he somehow use his influence to get another with the power to say it? Of course he could! The law made exceptions, and a man like Vaux, so demonstrably good, would be certain to be freed!

Malet felt a sudden chill. Or would he? There was always a risk —

"*Tchah*!" he said. He would worry about that later. There would be time to decide what to do with Vaux when Vaux was caught. He had something more important to do just at the moment. He had a viper to trap, and he would soon be meeting with Count d'Anglars to discuss setting the trap. His lordship would be interested in a few of the things Dracquet had said in the park...

What time was it? He looked at his watch. 2:55 p m. He should go to the anteroom to greet His Excellency. He pushed himself to his feet, shook out his coattails, and started for the door. The strident sound of voices just outside the room made him stop, frowning.

"I tell you, Chief Inspector, he does not wish to be disturbed!" It was Clerel's voice, uncharacteristically loud.

"What he wishes and what he gets are two different things! Now get out of my way!"

Chief Inspector Guerin's voice. Malet's mouth thinned; he set his hand on the doorknob.

Clerel's voice came again. "But I tell you, sir, he isn't to be disturbed!"

Malet flung the door open and stepped into the anteroom.

Clerel had been standing with his back to the door. He recoiled as though someone had jabbed him with a hot needle. "Chief Inspector," he said, "I do apologize for this! I tried to tell him—"

"You did nothing wrong, M. Clerel. You may go."

Guerin's eyes narrowed slightly as Malet spoke. He folded his arms with an ironic smile as Clerel bowed and moved back. "So you are here, Malet," he said.

"I assume you saw my signature in the log," said Malet with the edge of an ominous smile. "And Clerel didn't say that I was out, but that I wasn't to be disturbed."

Guerin lifted his eyebrows at Malet and pulled off his gloves. "I am afraid I will be disturbing you nevertheless," he said.

Malet's smile began to glitter. "So I have noticed. What do you want?"

The room was beginning to fill with silent, wide-eyed people. Guerin looked around and then turned back to Malet. "I'd prefer to go into your office," he said.

"We'll stay here," said Malet. "I am sure what you have to say will interest everyone here. What do you want?"

"This is ridiculous!" Guerin exclaimed. He started to go around Malet and was effectively blocked when Malet set his shoulder against the lintel with a bland smile.

"I said we're staying here. You may speak or not, as you choose, but you'd best choose quickly and stop wasting my time."

Guerin looked Malet up and down. "I want to discuss your action in commandeering one of my men and sending him off to the Bois de Boulogne without first consulting me, and your intrusion into my arrondissement a week ago."

"What is there to discuss?" Malet demanded.

"I told you to keep your nose out of my affairs!" Guerin snapped. "Your bailiwick is the 8th arrondissement, not the 3rd! Any cases pending there concern me exclusively!"

Malet locked gazes with Guerin, who folded his arms and stared back. Neither man saw Count d'Anglars enter with Sergeant Guillart and make his way quietly through the crowd.

Malet's gaze became very cold. "I believe you're familiar with the case that brought me into your arrondissement and sent your man off to the Bois de Boulogne," he said. "It certainly does concern you, but whether it does so in the way you seem to believe is a question that only time will answer."

d'Anglars, standing beside Sergeant Guillart, looked from one man to the other. He saw that Guillart was about to speak and laid his hand on the other's arm to silence him.

"I told you to keep your nose—" Guerin began.

"—Out of your affairs: yes, you have said so ad nauseam. But you have said it for the last time. As the Provisional Prefect—"

"The fact that you are keeping Lamarque's seat warm—"

"Let me remind you, Chief Inspector," Malet said with a soft intentness that made the words seem dangerous, "That while I am 'keeping Lamarque's seat warm', as you phrase it, I *am* Lamarque! And let me remind you as well that when The Prefect is in Paris, I still rank you! I am handling this in full accord with regulations and your interference does you no credit! And as for you: you will not show your face in these offices until M. Lamarque returns or I say that you may! Have I made myself sufficiently clear, or must I write it out and send it through official channels for everyone to read?"

Count d'Anglars was frowning, but he remained silent.

Guerin had come to the Prefecture expecting a quarrel, but one conducted in private. Malet's broadside had thrown him off balance, and he struck back in a way that he was accustomed to. "This is the sort of impertinence that I have come to expect from a bastard bred in a prison!" he snapped.

A wordless murmur rose from the onlookers.

Malet waited until it finally died away.

"We have reached the limit to my patience, Guerin," he said. "It is obvious that the only response that you can ever make in an argument that you are losing is a slur on my breeding. Well, I am tired of it. I suggest that you name your friends without any further delay so that we can pursue the topic in a more active fashion in the place des Vosges on a morning of your choosing. Do you understand me?"

"Good God!" muttered Clerel to Guillart. "He's finally gone and done it!"

"And about time!" Guillart returned.

Guerin hadn't spoken; the silence grew dangerous.

Count d'Anglars stepped forward through the silent onlookers. "Good afternoon, Messieurs," he said.

Malet's eyes had been locked on Guerin's with the narrow intensity of a creature of prey. d'Anglars' voice made him start, and he did not recover himself for a moment.

d'Anglars turned to Guerin. "I believe you were given an order, Chief Inspector," he said gently.

"An order! If you heard—"

"I regret that I did," said d'Anglars. "And I heard what led up to it. He is within his authority. Now go. I wish you a good day."

"Surely you can't mean to—"

"I am afraid I do," said d'Anglars. "You may go."

Guerin turned pale and then red, but he remained calm. He bowed slightly to Malet, then very low indeed to d'Anglars, turned on his heel, and left.

d'Anglars turned to the rest. "And you others have business to attend to, I am sure. See to it, if you please."

"Monseigneur, I—" Malet began.

"Not at all," said d'Anglars. "You were acting within your rights. And now let us go into your office. I believe we have much to discuss."

CHAPTER THIRTY-EIGHT

Inspector Malet En Famille

The elephant stood in the middle of the place de la Bastille with the majestically ludicrous dignity of its kind, its crenellated howdah sitting atop its back like a miniature castle, the draperies sweeping downward almost to the ground. Its harness was festooned with a riot of tassels, its feet braceleted with garlands of flowers. Large, long tusks curved to either side of its down-curled trunk. The expression was ill-tempered, and the platform, atop which it stood, looked like nothing so much as a giant blancmange.

Made of plaster, the elephant had once been white. Now, caked with the soot of thirty years of Parisian air and crumbling into ruin, it was a shade of gray seldom seen anywhere but in a set of elderly and chronically ill-laundered drawers.

Napoleon had planned to cast a monumental bronze fountain in the shape of that elephant, and the plaster one was to have been the model, but wars and other diversions intervened, and the elephant had never achieved the metamorphosis into bronze. Now it was leprous with cracks and slowly crumbling away.

The elephant wasn't crumbling away fast enough to suit Paul Malet, who had paused, as he always did, to glower at the monstrosity that, to his mind, disfigured the place de la Bastille and took away all the effect of the gatehouse that served as his headquarters. The thing was incredibly stupid, a white elephant in every sense of the term, something that belonged in a circus or a freak show, anywhere, certainly, rather than opposite his headquarters!

Malet had moved heaven and earth in an attempt to get the thing removed, to the secret amusement of the Prefect of Police and the Minister of

Police along with half the Seine et Oise Prefecture, but he had gone down in defeat: Paris had other, more showy, monuments whose upkeep was closer to the hearts of those in power. The place de la Bastille, associated as it was with revolutionary, if not regicidal, memories, was judged one of those uneasy spots best left alone. The elephant, although an acknowledged eyesore, was posing no threat to anyone and could be allowed to crumble away in peace.

Everyone else might have been amused: Malet was not. Some things are not funny, and that dreadful elephant was one of them. He had gone so far as to move his offices to the side of the gatehouse away from the monstrosity, giving to his second in command, Senior Inspector Georges Plougastel, an office that was actually larger and more luxurious than his own.

Malet clasped his hands behind his back and slowly paced around the elephant. He paused when he was once more in front of it to glare up into its eyes and swear at it before turning away to enter his headquarters.

This structure was as magnificent as the elephant was foolish. Once the gatehouse of the Bastille, it was impressive in its own right. It overlooked the calm waters of the Porte de Plaisance and faced out to the east. Four separate drum towers gathered to form the body of the gatehouse, and the main entrance, reached from the east through a portcullis set between two of the towers, was overlooked by crenellated battlements. A green sward lay before the building, but it resembled a parade-ground rather than a croquet lawn.

There was nothing soft or playful about this final remnant of the Bastille: it was a splendid architectural expression of the adjective 'mighty', and to the dirty, plaster elephant anywhere near it was, to Malet's mind, a joke in the very poorest of taste.

"M. L'INSPECTEUR, THERE is a visitor asking for you," said Constable Guizot. "Chief Inspector Paul Malet, acting as Provisional Prefect, requests the favor of an interview."

Senior Inspector Georges Plougastel nodded at the man. "Thank you, Armand," he said. "I will be down at once. Is the coffee ready?"

"Yes, M. l'Inspecteur."

"Then be a good fellow and bring some here as soon as you can, will you?" asked Plougastel as he rose and buttoned his coat.

The man bowed and withdrew.

Plougastel descended the stairs to the waiting room. Malet was standing quietly and looking around with an odd lift to his eyebrows. He looked up and smiled as Plougastel came into the room.

"You might have warned me," Plougastel complained as he came forward to clasp Malet's hand. "I thought you had forgotten us. How long has it been since you were here? Is this an inspection?"

Malet shook his head. "Only a social call, Georges," he said. "I have some things to do, and I was coming right by here. Besides, I am a little homesick."

"The elephant's still there, Paul," said Plougastel, hiding a smile. He was one of the few whom Malet addressed by his first name and he was one of only two people in Paris, with the occasional exception of the Prefect, who used Malet's first name.

"Pity," said Malet. "I was hoping you'd succeed where I failed."

Plougastel chuckled at that. "But I happen to like it," he said.

Malet sighed.

"Come upstairs," said Plougastel. "I have had some coffee brewed—"

"How did you know I was coming?" Malet asked as Plougastel took his arm and led him toward the stairs.

"You usually take a few minutes to stalk around the elephant and curse at it," Plougastel said. "I watched you. It was ample notice!"

They went to Plougastel's office, a well-appointed place, and found that coffee and biscuits had already been brought in and set up on a small table beside the fire. The men had apparently decided that M. l'Inspecteur en Chef needed something more substantial and toothsome than coffee alone. They had also brought a plate of crisp toast swimming with butter and dusted with grated cheese, some strips of crisp bacon, more toasted bread, and a pot of brandied apricot conserve.

Plougastel waved Malet to the most comfortable chair, resigned himself to the inevitable protest, insisted, set the table between himself and Malet, and sat on the other side of the fire.

"You didn't come here just to swear at the elephant, I am certain," he said as he poured coffee and warm milk into a large cup and handed it to Malet. "What's afoot? You look as splendidly healthy as ever," he added as he took a plate and heaped it with ginger biscuits, cheese toast and bacon before handing it to Malet. "Are you enjoying yourself?"

Malet took the cup and sipped at it, then set the cup down. He grinned at Plougastel and selected a slice of bacon. "More than I expected," he said.

Plougastel laughed at that. "Is the inn pleasant, then?"

"Very much so. It's on the rue d'Orsel, Georges. Very pretty, with an attractive courtyard. The building itself is well laid out, and the cooking—"

"Ah, we come to the crucial part," Plougastel murmured, sipping his coffee.

Malet shot him a disgusted look. "One must eat," he said. "And at least I am not protruding in the waistcoat, unlike some others I could name!"

Plougastel, who at forty was attempting to submit gracefully to the depredations of middle age, patted the modest bulge of his stomach and said, "Not all of us have discovered the fountain of youth, and some of us have actually learned to sit still, which burns off less energy. Besides that, it takes a larger volume of food to keep your frame stoked, as I know to my cost!"

Malet, who was in the act of reaching for another strip of bacon, began to laugh. "All right, all right," he said. "You have made your point. But Georges, the food is delicious, and the people there are very kind."

"Oh?"

"Yes," said Malet. "They made me welcome—"

"You sound surprised," Plougastel observed. "You know, it isn't such an odd thing for people to take a liking to you. They do it all the time."

Malet took a bite of cheese toast and then licked butter off his fingers. He launched into an account of the past weeks' doings, including a full confession on the identity of the Police Inspector who had been tied to the tree in the Jardin du Luxembourg.

Plougastel was very amused. "Serves Guerin right!" he said. "No wonder Emil Fougeroux was chuckling when I saw him yesterday on the way home! He must have heard the story from his man."

"Probably so. He does enjoy a good gossip." He ate two more pieces of cheese toast and then started on the apricot conserve.

"That he does." Plougastel, who had only had one piece of toast, helped himself to a slice of bacon, frowned as Malet eyed his waistcoat again, and bit defiantly into the bacon.

Malet watched him chew and said, "I will be asking for the transfer of a man to this arrondissement: one of Guerin's people, a fellow named Saint-Légère."

"Another lost lamb?" said Plougastel.

Malet shrugged. "Not quite," he said. "I have been reading his reports. He's an honest fellow with a gift for observation and an excellent sense of humor. He might need a little attention, but not much. He ran afoul of Guerin."

"Do as you see fit," Plougastel said, taking another bite. "I haven't known any of your picks to turn out badly. You should know, though: Guerin's been grumbling again."

Malet nodded. "It's this matter I am working on now."

"But I was under the impression that it's an ethics case," said Plougastel. "It's out of his hands."

"That's right," said Malet with a dark smile. "Guerin can go whistle for all of me. He tried to throw his weight around yesterday at the Prefecture, and Count d'Anglars sent him packing with a flea in his ear. But I am sure he will find an excuse to raise a stink when the Prefect comes back—which, by the way, he's planning to do in a little over two weeks—and denounce me for a misbegotten cur without breeding or manners—"

"He'd better not," said Plougastel.

"I can fight my own battles," said Malet. "I have this one nicely mapped out."

"That may be," said Plougastel, "But your men are getting tired of Guerin's insolence. There have been some rumblings."

"Good God! Stop them, then! Tell them I will be angry if there's any unpleasantness."

"As you wish." Plougastel lifted the coffee pot. "Would you like some more?"

"Please," said Malet. "You know, Georges," he said, "I can't tell you anything about this present case—the one that has put Guerin's nose out of joint—but I am expecting word from that snitch that L'Eveque used to use: Michaud. His information is crucial, and in the interest of discretion—I am being shadowed and I don't want to jeopardize the man—I have asked that he send it to you. Would you relay it immediately to me at the inn? I am always there in the evenings."

Plougastel stared. "Are you mad?" he demanded. "What would be more suspicious than to bring information to the Bastille in God's name?"

Malet smiled at Plougastel over the rim of his cup. "You're shouting," he said. "What must they be thinking downstairs? And you wrong me, I promise you. Criminals seldom think of the obvious. The thought of anyone being fool enough to send information openly to my headquarters is as unthinkable to them as it is to you. They won't be looking for it. Surely you have heard that the safest place to pick pockets is right in front of a Police precinct."

Plougastel shook his head. "I will take your word for it," he said. "The less I know of the workings of the criminal mind, the happier I will be. And don't bother to tell me I will never make Prefect, for I promise you I don't care! Tell Michaud to bring his information to me and I will carry it over personally."

Malet finished his coffee and set it down. "Very good," he said. "I don't know what I'd do without you. When you do come over, you can have one of the veal dishes they serve at the Rose d'Or."

"Agreed," Plougastel said.

"And you can meet the landlady, Madame de Clichy," Malet said in a slightly softened voice that made Plougastel look closely at him and then smile. But Malet did not see the look.

CHAPTER THIRTY-NINE

Fighting Shadows

Chief Inspector Emil Fougeroux of the 11th arrondissement was a kindly man and a courageous commander, but with an unruly streak of mischief to him. The piece of news that Constable Leygues, whose beat took in the grounds of the Jardin du Luxembourg, had brought to him early one afternoon, had been too delectable a tidbit to let pass. He had had occasion to speak with Malet several times, and he had managed each time to include a gently needling reference to trees and parks and the misfortune suffered by Chief Inspector Guerin.

Malet preserved a dignified demeanor, agreed cordially with Fougeroux on the subject of Inspector Guerin's humiliation and misfortune, and turned his attention to more crucial matters.

The sight of Dracquet's assassin in the crowd of onlookers watching him being untied from that tree had shaken him. Malet realized that he owed his life to the fact that Vaux had gagged him. Vaux had immediately sent to his rescue the most upright and innocuous-appearing group of young men he could find. If Malet had been able to shout for help, the first person to come probably would have been Pierre le Noir, who had most likely been hovering nearby hoping to ambush him. The crowd of onlookers had frustrated him, and now he was nowhere to be found.

The apparent risk to his life was enough to make Malet pause and think very carefully. The upshot of that spell of concentrated thought was an urgent request for an interview with Count d'Anglars.

"LE NOIR HAD YOU, TIED and helpless, in the sights of his pistol?" d'Anglars said, incredulous. "And you were saved because some busybody

245

of a woman stepped between you to offer her vinaigrette just as he was leveling his firearm? Good God! Why didn't you tell me this before? I will go to Our Lady of Consolation this very evening and light an entire bank of twenty centime candles!

Malet said nothing.

d'Anglars rose and paced across his salon. They were in his luxurious house fronting the place Francois Ier. He had requested that chocolate be brought in, but neither he nor Malet had so much as tasted their cups.

He rounded on Malet. "And only now do you tell me that you have been followed in earnest since the morning Dracquet came to that inn!" he exclaimed. "It surpasses everything!"

"Yes, Monseigneur," Malet said with the grim calmness of one who, facing the music, finds the tune not at all to his liking. "It didn't seem important before."

"Not impor—!" d'Anglars didn't finish the word. He shook his head. "I don't like it," he said. "I don't like it at all! You have been tailed all this time, and you saw that hired killer in the Jardin du Luxembourg!"

Malet nodded.

"And the man who tied you to the tree must have been in on it, as well! We'd better find him and bring him in!"

Malet winced. "No, Monseigneur," he said. "That particular criminal is well known to me. The incident was completely unconnected with the other. He found my pistol in my pocket and didn't use it. He'd have died rather than deal with Le Noir. I know, in fact, that he sent those lads to rescue me."

d'Anglars frowned at him. "It seems to me that there's more to that incident than meets the eye," he said. "What happened there?"

Malet schooled his face to unconcern. "An old score," he said. "I had it coming to me for a long time. It was settled, and I have matters well in hand, now. He's not the problem."

"Not the problem..." d'Anglars said. He turned and faced Malet fully and then finally shrugged. "My dear Inspector," he said, "I appreciate the crucial nature of this case, and I am aware that you have taken every precaution to safeguard the information you have gathered—"

"My notes are very comprehensive. And I have been in close communication with my lieutenants in this matter. I believe Inspector L'Eveque would be capable of stepping in as well if anything were to happen to me."

d'Anglars dismissed those considerations with an impatient motion of his hand. "Poppycock!" he said. "I personally have the power to issue a warrant for Dracquet's arrest and imprisonment. I don't like to use that power, but I'd have few scruples in this case in view of our suspicions, and you know it! That doesn't concern me: what does concern me is the question of your safety. Do you understand the magnitude of the loss this force would suffer if anything were to happen to you?"

"Bah!" said Malet. "There are others as good as me!"

"I have yet to see them!" d'Anglars snapped. He took another turn about the room and then looked consideringly at Malet. "You saw Le Noir while you were being untied from that tree, you say."

"Yes. I'd been half-expecting him, since I had told Dracquet only minutes before that I wanted nothing to do with him. I suspected that he would send le Noir after me."

"Hm. Thank God for those students, then, and the man—whoever he was—who sent them! And God bless that woman with the smelling salts!" Count d'Anglars lifted his cup of chocolate, tested the warmth of the drink, and set the cup down with a grimace. "This was too close to make me happy, M. Malet," he said. "I don't need to be warned twice. I will assign a bodyguard."

"But Monseigneur—!"

"No arguments! If you are to continue this investigation, you shall have a bodyguard accompany you. If not, then I will take you off this case and give it over to Messieurs d'Arthez and Richet."

Malet sighed and looked down at his hands. "But I have taken every precaution since then," he said.

"Indeed?" said d'Anglars. He did not sound convinced.

Malet looked up. "I have been riding cabs instead of walking. I have taken care to stay in crowded areas, and I have curtailed my evening walks, as well. No one's come near me—"

"But you're still being shadowed?"

"Not by assassins!"

"Oh?" d'Anglars said with deceptive mildness, "How can you tell?"

Malet shrugged. "You can tell," he said. He raised his eyes to d'Anglars' and said, "Please, Monseigneur. Gilles d'Arthez hasn't seen Le Noir since that day—"

"I assume our friend Dracquet has a basement and an attic in which to hide things that he wants no one to see," d'Anglars said.

Malet ignored the sarcasm. "To saddle me with a bodyguard would be like belling a cat just as he's about to tackle a nest of rats," he said. "I am closing the gap: I beg you, don't tie my hands now!"

"I don't equate protecting your life with tying your hands!" d'Anglars snapped. He added more gently, "I have already told you how valuable you are to this force as an officer. Perhaps I haven't adequately expressed your considerable value to me, personally, as a man. It would grieve me greatly to lose you."

"But if the cause is serious enough," Malet said, "an officer of the Law must be ready to give his life."

d'Anglars looked him over much as one might survey a freak at a carnival. "I concede the point," he said, "But there's a vast difference between being willing to sacrifice your life to advance a good cause and your current crack-brained determination to chase after Constant Dracquet's creatures shouting, 'Here I am: come and kill me!' "

He saw Malet's expression and fell silent. He resumed after a moment in a slightly altered voice. "Continue as you have: be cautious, take no needless risks. I will hold off assigning a bodyguard for now. But—" he frowned at Malet as he went to the bell rope, "—the next time I say that you must have a bodyguard, there will be no argument."

A NOTE WAS DELIVERED the Prefecture four days after his fight with Vaux, written on scented paper, sealed, and addressed to Malet:

Paul —

I am leaving for London in two days. Come to my house tomorrow before noon. I miss you, and I have some information for you that I believe you will find useful in your current case. I cannot be specific, but I have reason to believe that you will find it of crucial impor-

tance

Rosalie

Malet scanned the lines, then lifted the chimney from the oil lamp on his desk and held the note in the flame until it was consumed. Then he sat back, frowning, to think. He took up pen and paper after a moment and wrote:

Rosalie:

Meet me at 11:30 a.m. at the place Vauban, on horseback, instead. We can ride through the Champ de Mars. If there is no response, I shall assume that this is agreeable to you.

Paul

He folded the note, selected a wafer, heated it, and sealed the note. That done, he rose and went out into the anteroom.

Two of the office boys were sitting at an empty desk and playing at dice. They jumped to attention as they felt Malet's gaze on them, and the nearer one tried to fumble the dice into his pocket.

"Alphonse," said Malet, nodding to the boy with the hint of a grim smile.

"M-me, Chief Inspector?" the boy stammered.

"Yes. You. Take this message to the address on the front. It's urgent: see that it is given to the major-como there, and no one else. Wait to see if there is a response, and then come straight back here."

He handed the note to the boy and watched him hurry off. "Oh—Alphonse—" he said.

The boy turned. Malet tossed him a franc. "Stop and enjoy a glass of wine on the way back," he said.

The boy grinned, sketched a salute, and left at a run.

"BE CAREFUL WITH THIS fellow, Chief Inspector," said the head hostler the next day. They were standing in the inner courtyard of the Prefecture, gazing at the bay thoroughbred stallion, which had been brought over from the Police stables at Malet's direction. "I know you have had an eye to him since he was first brought in, but no one's had the chance to give him a good gallop. He needs to have the fidgets shaken out of his legs before he goes to the auction in two days."

Malet let his eyes travel down the stallion's arched neck and along his strong, sloping shoulder. The light ran in all colors along the glossy hide, almost blue in the shadows, almost golden in the highlights. "I imagine he's garnered a good deal of interest," Malet said

"The Duke of Orleans' people were looking him over," the hostler said.

"In that case," said Malet, "I would imagine that His Majesty's eldest son will win the horse." He sighed. So much for tracing the seller. It had been a shot at a venture at any rate.

The hostler handed the reins over and eyed Malet's height and build. "He's well up to your weight, but the stirrups'll need to be lengthened. Wait a minute and I will do that for you right now."

Malet thanked him and spoke softly to the stallion while the hostler adjusted the leathers. The horse was nervous; his ears had been flicking back and forth. As Malet spoke, they slowed and finally pricked forward.

"All set, Inspector," said the hostler.

Malet nodded, gathered the reins in his left hand, set his left foot in the stirrup, and then sprang into the saddle.

The stallion snorted and danced a little at the weight upon his back but stood quietly enough after a moment.

"Very good," said Malet. He nudged the horse to a walk and then a trot. The stallion moved smoothly over the cobblestones, and then eased into a rocking, collected canter.

Malet nodded, slowed the horse to a walk, and then halted. He looked over at the two gendarmes flanking the gate. "One of you step outside and see if the street is clear," he said.

The stallion jibbed at the bit and danced sideways. "Don't worry, my boy," Malet told him with a grin, "One more second and you will get all the running you want!"

The large oak doors opened inward a crack, and the younger of the gendarmes edged through. He came back after a moment. "Clear, M. l'In-specteur," he said.

"Very good," said Malet. "Open the gates and stand aside." When the gates were completely open, Malet eased the stallion to a walk that quickened to a trot and then a gallop. They swept beneath the gateway with a flick of the stallion's black tail and clattered onto the cobblestoned street.

Three tough-looking characters lounging in the shadow of the Sainte-Chappelle jumped to their feet and stared as he pounded past them, rounded the corner of the boulevard du Palais and turned onto the Quai des Orfevres. They made a half-hearted attempt to follow him, but they slowed and stopped after half a block. Malet saw them arguing among themselves; the sight made him grin.

He was at the place Dauphine; he cut directly through and then caught the northern half of the Pont Neuf and crossed the river at a tearing gallop that did not lessen until he had reached the Louvre, when he reined the stallion to a collected trot and sat back to think.

The horse shook his head and pulled lightly at the bit. Malet chuckled and said, "So you want to run again, eh? Well, then, let's run! It would be rude to keep a lady waiting!" And he turned the stallion toward the high, gilded dome of Les Invalides.

CHAPTER FORTY

A Lady Provides the Stage Setting

Rosalie Plessis flung the trailing skirt of her royal blue riding habit over her left arm and smiled up at Malet. "You always were prompt, dearest Paul," she said. "Eleven-thirty exactly!"

"I'd never dream of keeping a lady waiting." Malet swung down from the saddle and led his horse over to Rosalie. They were in the shadow of the Dome des Invalides, in the place Vauban. He took in the full elegance of her habit with its deep, plunging neckline edged with ruffles of lisle, and its wide, full sleeves, as he raised her hand to his lips.

She read his thoughts. "You approve?" she asked. "I had this from Courceline this week."

"You are completely elegant."

Her hand went to her neckline. "This isn't too décolleté, is it?" she asked. Whether by accident or design, the motion of her hand showed the tantalizing hint of soft shadows between swells of firm rosy flesh.

"Not at all," Malet replied with a knowing smile. "It suits the purpose very well." He offered his arm and then, when she had tucked her hand in it and was walking beside him, said, "Now what is this information you thought I should have?"

She gazed up at him with a direct smile. "Oh no, Paul," she said. "I know you too well. I may never see you again: I want to spend at least part of the afternoon with you. Come walk with me a ways, and I will tell you what I have."

"WHERE DID YOU FIND this diagram of Dracquet's house?" Malet demanded later. They had strolled through the Champ de Mars and were now

252

seated at ease beneath a tree. "Did you pay someone for it?"

"I drew it myself," Rosalie replied. "Dracquet had some thought of installing me there permanently as his mistress, and he showed me all around the house."

"Then you did this from memory?

"Of course," said Rosalie. "You forget my profession. I have a memory for these things—it comes from years of practicing on various stages, with sets that change from day to day." She watched Malet's expression and asked, "Can you use it?"

"I certainly can!" said Malet. He frowned at the diagram and then raised his eyes to the interlaced branches over his head. He was clothing the bare outline of the walls with the shape and height of the rooms within. He prowled through the house in his mind and stalked Dracquet through its corridors.

Rosalie, sitting beside him with her head pillowed against his shoulder, watched him and smiled to herself. "Do you find it useful?" she asked softly, as she traced the seam of his coat sleeve with a fingertip.

"Indeed I do," Malet replied. He transferred his gaze back to the diagram.

Rosalie turned a little more toward him, settled her cheek in the hollow below his shoulder, ran her fingers lightly along the breast of his waistcoat, then eased them inside to savor the satisfying swell of his chest through the fabric of his shirt. "Do you think I should request payment for them?" she asked.

Malet lowered the diagram and frowned into space. He was superimposing the outline over his memory of the house seen from the outside. The courtyard lying slightly to the side, the arched entry with a deep recess to either side of the door... "The Police pays its informers," he said as he mentally positioned a squad of gendarmes to either side of the door and stood back to see if it could be done. "They're usually quite generous... This is invaluable."

He blinked and banished the picture and looked down into her wide eyes. What he saw made him smile, but with a touch of compunction. He folded the diagram and tucked it away in his breast pocket. "Rosalie," he said.

"I had dared to hope for payment in a certain coin," she said with the breath of a chuckle at the shadow of a frown between his eyebrows as she tipped his face down toward hers for a leisurely kiss. "I am leaving Paris tomorrow, and this will be farewell."

She drew back, puzzled after a moment. "What is it, Paul?" she said after a pause.

"I can't pay you that way," Malet said.

She pushed the veil of her hat over her shoulder and stared up at him. "Why not?" she demanded. "I am in your arms at the moment, and you didn't object the other day."

"I got caught up in the past that night," he said. "And it was wonderful to remember you. I had forgotten how much you meant to me. You were a true friend, and I loved you."

"'Were,'" she repeated, speaking directly and with steady intensity. "Are you completely indifferent to me now?"

"No man could be indifferent to you," he said with the same calm intensity. "I would be less than a man if I didn't find you beautiful and desirable beyond most women. How could you think otherwise?"

The softening of the sharp, grieved edges of her expression showed that she understood.

"And beyond your beauty is your wit, your kindness— I am proud to have become your friend, and I will never lose my admiration for you. But we said our farewells years ago and went our separate ways, and I can't find my way back to you."

Rosalie closed her eyes for a moment. "She loves you, then?"

"Yes," he said. "I believe she does."

Her mouth moved into a rueful half-smile as she raised her hands to cup his face, tracing the line of his lips before drawing him gently to her for a last, quiet kiss. "If you have truly found love, I won't ask for your second-best, and I won't ask you to betray the lady. I pray she can make you happy, and I envy her from the bottom of my heart."

He took the folded diagram and silently handed it back to her.

She waved it away with a flick of her fingertips. "No, it is for you," she said. "If it makes your task easier and puts you at less risk, I am content. I can't imagine a world where I did not know that somehow, somewhere, you were part of it. You will always have a piece of my heart, and I think I still have something of yours."

"You do," he said. "You always will. I only wish—"

He did not finish the thought, but Rosalie nodded. "Sometimes I learn to value what I have had only after I have lost it," she said.

"You won't lose what you have of me," he said. He drew a long breath, and said more easily, "You sail tomorrow: can we drink champagne and toast your future?"

"And the past?" she said. "Of course."

She watched with a reminiscent smile as he got to his feet in one fluid motion and leaned down to offer a hand to her. As she watched, he paused to pick up something from the grass, wrap it in his handkerchief, and put it in his pocket.

ELISE WATCHED AS MALET took out a handkerchief—wrapped packet from the breast of his coat and handed it to her. "For me?" she said. "What is it?"

"Look and see," he said.

She opened it. "A wren's egg!" she exclaimed. "And so perfect, too! Where did you find it?"

"In a park I was in this afternoon," he said. "It had fallen out of the nest, I think, and was sheltered in the roots of the tree."

"I would never have seen it," she said, turning it over in her hand. "Your eyes must be very sharp."

"Do you like it?" he asked. "I enjoy watching birds, but I felt a little foolish saving it for you."

"Oh not at all! I love it! I will put it on the shelf here—" She turned around suddenly. "Did they have birds in that prison?"

"Gulls," said Malet. "I made a pet of one of them, once. He followed me to Marseilles when I left the prison and went into the Police. I had him for years. I named him Odysseus."

"What happened to him?" Elise asked.

"He died, finally," said Malet. "I missed him for a long time."

"But he followed you to Marseilles," Elise repeated. Her smile warmed as she gazed on him.

"Screaming for fish heads."

"Longing for your company. He didn't want to live without you."

CHAPTER FORTY-ONE

The Night of the Hunt
Part I: The Trap

Malet's spies reported that Dracquet appeared to have left Paris, as he had said. His departure, in fact, had been very well-witnessed, since the man had made himself conspicuous during it. He had gone so far as to strike his coachman when that man fouled one of the carriage's wheels on the gate.

"He called the fellow a few names that I hadn't heard since my army days," said Gilles d'Arthez, facing Malet across the table in the questioning room.

By previous arrangement, he had just been 'arrested' for loitering by the Tuileries, and he had raised such a fuss when the arresting officer tried to take him into custody that he had been placed in handcuffs and brought directly to the Prefecture to be interrogated by Malet. When the questioning was finished, he would be taken to the prison of La Force and then sprung.

d'Arthez's grimy, tired face creased in a smile. "Then he fetched him a crack across the face," he said. "It was a good roundhouse swing that drew blood! I wonder if he had any training in boxing." He shrugged after a moment and said, "There was some more commotion, then he climbed into his carriage and drove off."

"And you say the house is unoccupied now," Malet mused.

"The knocker's off the door and the windows are shuttered," said d'Arthez. "Some servants appear to be there still. I know his cook by sight, for example, and I have seen him in the past three or four days, as well as one little street-urchin who hangs around there—but there's been no sign of him or the Englishman."

"Any idea where he was heading?" Malet asked.

"The word is that he was traveling to Lyons," said d'Arthez. "I don't know anything more than that."

Malet sat back and said thoughtfully, "Richet reported that he left by the Porte de Charenton, so it would fit. And they would be going near the Bois de Vincennes, so he could easily get into another carriage and head back into the city. Hm."

He looked up at d'Arthez and smiled at the man. "Very good," he said. "I am pulling you off the case now, Gilles, and I am giving you two weeks off, as well."

"Thank you!"

"No," said Malet. "I thank you. You have done a fine job, and you have earned the rest. I will call the constables in to take you away. Make it good."

Malet sat back in his chair as d'Arthez was escorted from the room under heavy guard, swearing and spitting. He had to think. He did not for a moment believe that Dracquet had left Paris, and especially not to go to a place like Lyons.

His conviction regarding an attempted assassination of the English heiress, Victoria, was as strong as ever, but for all Dracquet's talk of power and changing governments, in the absence of any concrete evidence, Malet could do very little against the man directly. He could foil any plot at the very least, but he wanted to catch and destroy the man.

He frowned and took out his watch: 9:45 a.m., time to report to the Conciergerie. The matter of Dracquet was taking up most of his attention, but he was still acting as Prefect of Police for the Île de France, and one of his duties as M. Lamarque's substitute was to be present at the Judges' chambers for certain hearings.

He sighed and rose. It was going to be a long morning.

MALET PAUSED ON HIS way back to the Prefecture to order lunch at Le Chasseur Affamé, one of his favorite establishments near the place du Châtelet. The restaurant specialized in game dishes and was known for its beautifully spiced sauces. Malet liked the elegant decor; he was a frequent patron, and one of the reasons that the place enjoyed the success that it did.

The proprietor, M. Rothenay, welcomed him, seated him at his best table, and insisted on bringing his choicest serving of grilled squabs in olive sauce with an accompaniment of especially old, mellow burgundy wine.

"You like it?" Rothenay asked after Malet had tasted the dish.

Malet smiled at the man and said, "You have achieved a masterpiece."

Rothenay ducked his head, smiling, and then froze where he stood. "Chief Inspector," he said, "I just remembered something I think you should know."

The man's expression was odd: Malet gazed up at him as he cut a portion of breast meat, speared several olives from the sauce, and brought the forkful to his mouth. "What is it?" he asked.

"The last time you were here—it was about three days ago, if you recall—some people came to me after you left and started asking questions."

Malet chewed and swallowed. "Oh?" he said.

"Yes. Did I know who you were? Do you come here often? Do I know the way you usually take to go back to the Prefecture? How long have I known you? Do you ever come here to dine?"

Malet sipped his wine. His face was carefully expressionless. "And how did you answer them?"

"I said that anyone who didn't know you by sight was a fool," replied Rothenay. "I said that I was honored by your patronage, but as far as how often you came, how could I guess? I am the owner, not a waiter, and I don't keep a tally of my guests. I didn't like their looks!"

Malet hid a smile. "Very wise of you, in that case," he murmured. "And what else?"

"As far as how you went to the Prefecture, I said that I was one who owned a fine eating establishment and not a hired killer, so that it made no difference to me how you went back to the Prefecture, but I rather thought it was two of the three possible routes, since I didn't think you liked to swim and thereby ruled out your going by the river. I also said that I recalled once when you stopped a quarrel here, and it was at supper time, so I thought you came at least once to dine here, but I couldn't be sure."

Malet nodded. "Well done," he said. "I couldn't have told you to say it better."

"But there's more," Rothenay said. "They offered money if I would tell them the next time you came. They offered a great deal of money."

Malet frowned and cut more meat from the squab. "I see," he said. "You told them to get out and never come back, I suppose?"

"No, indeed, M. l'Inspecteur," said Rothenay. "I told you I didn't like their looks. There was one in particular who made me very nervous, a man with what looked like a smudge of oil or paint on his chin. I thought if I did become rude, they might get unpleasant, and I had a house full of customers, so I answered smoothly, and they parted from me with smiles."

"Very wise of you," said Malet once more. "And you say this was three days ago?"

"I remember it clearly, M. l'Inspecteur," said Rothenay. "You were in a temper, and I gave you my finest Riesling that I was saving for a special occasion, because I thought it might improve your mood."

"Ah?" said Malet, who tended to lapse into southern French speech patterns when he was moved. "That was very kind of you, indeed. I must thank you for your concern."

Rothenay blushed and disclaimed and then, at Malet's invitation, sat at the table, poured himself some wine, and chatted amiably while Malet finished his lunch in thoughtful silence. Rothenay suspected that M. Malet wasn't really paying attention, but he seldom had the chance to catch his breath and rest, and the Chief Inspector, though preoccupied, smiled at the appropriate moments and poured another glass of wine for him when he had finished his first.

Malet set his glass down and said, "Did those people leave you a name to contact with word of me?"

"They did," said Rothenay. Now that Malet was through, he rose and motioned to one of the waiters.

"Excellent," said Malet. He fell silent as the waiter gathered the dishes and left. When the man was out of earshot he said quietly, "I want you to get in touch with those people and tell them that I came in just now, and that I plan to dine here this evening at eight o'clock. You might mention to them that I will be returning to my house in the Marais to take care of some personal business, and I will be going there right after dining."

"But M. l'Inspecteur—!"

"Tell them this and collect the money. You may keep it with my compliments but get a good look at the people who pay you." He accepted his coat and hat from the waiter, nodded to the man, and went to the door, Rothenay beside him.

"I don't like it, M. l'Inspecteur," he said.

"Don't worry," said Malet. "You are doing me a favor."

CHAPTER FORTY-TWO

The Night of the Hunt Part II:
The Hunters and The Quarry

Malet strolled across the Seine at the Pont au Change and paused midway across to frown at the gabled slate roof of the Tribunal de Commerce. So Dracquet had sent Pierre le Noir, who had seemed like a hired killer to Rothenay, to inquire after Malet's doings the very day they had spoken in the park, had he? And he had offered to buy information regarding Malet's comings and goings and the routes he would take, had he? Interesting, indeed.

In all the shady doings that Dracquet had been tied to in one way or another—organized robbery, arson for profit, child prostitution, political assassination—cop-killing had never been part of them. But now, it appeared, things were different.

Dracquet had evaded Malet's spies; it was time for Malet to do the same with Dracquet. He had in mind something more dramatic than a supposed journey to Lyons, and it might bag a few witnesses.

It would take only a few hours to set up a trap with himself as the bait. He could recruit back-ups from several of the closer precincts, give them a sketchy idea of what was going to happen, and take it from there. Gaston Rabateau, the Chief Inspector of the 6th arrondissement, had enlisted his help from time to time and would probably be quite willing to return the favor. He could also count on assistance from Laurent Mercier of the 4th and Emile Fougeroux of the 11th. Fougeroux would be delighted to go in on any plot to catch an assassin, and so would Georges Plougastel, though Georges might be squeamish about the bait Malet proposed to use. But he could deal with Georges.

He hesitated over the question of whether he should inform M. d'Anglars of the trap but decided against it. Aside from the fact that there was nothing the Minister of Police could add to it, Malet knew that the man would be opposed to the entire affair. It would be easier to deal with his opposition if he could present a fait accompli. Success is a very powerful argument.

Malet entered the Prefecture, his mind pleasantly humming with plans, and signed in with Constable Archet, who passed him in quickly, for once. He would dispense with his sword, he thought, since he might have to run, and a sword that banged and clanked in its scabbard and tended to push itself between one's legs would be a danger. In lieu of the sword, he had a long, sharp dagger that he had bought when he was in Russia in 1812. It could easily be strapped to his waist under his coat and serve as a silent back-up weapon. His two pistols would fit comfortably in his pockets, as well, along with extra cartridges and percussion caps.

He was singing as he passed Sergeant Guillart's desk, the snatch of a dancing song he had learned in Germany as a Colonel of artillery. He had always suspected that the words weren't quite 'comme il faut', and Guillart's expression confirmed his suspicions.

"M. l'Inspecteur!" Guillart exclaimed. He, too, had soldiered in Germany.

Malet stopped and smiled down at him. "Yes?"

"Where on earth did you hear that song?"

"Germany, of course," Malet answered. He looked around, found an empty chair, and drew it up to Guillart's desk. "I have always liked it, though I haven't a clue what the words mean. Listen: give me some paper."

Guillart reached into his desk and took out several sheets. He was trying not to smile as Malet continued to whistle the tune through his teeth. "A special assignment, M. l'Inspecteur?" he asked.

"You could say that," said Malet, writing quickly. "I need to speak with Chief Inspectors Mercier, Monthermer, Rabateau and Fougeroux, and Senior Inspector Plougastel, as quickly as possible."

"Very good," said Guillart. "I will send those out by courier. I have been using Constable Vacherin for important messages."

"Excellent," said Malet. "What time is it? Two o'clock? I'd like to see them here by three-thirty. I have been asked to sit in on a conference at M. Mercier's offices right now, so I will carry that message. For the rest, Guillart, I'd be grateful if you could send these notes out as quickly as possible."

"I will see to it," said Guillart.

"Thank you." Malet headed back toward the Prefect's office. Once there, he found a pile of papers requiring his attention. Some of them appeared to be personal items; he set them aside to review later that afternoon and took care of the rest as quickly as he could. He rose and checked his watch. Ten minutes after two. Time to go to Mercier's headquarters.

EVERYTHING WAS IN PLACE by six o'clock. The various chief inspectors had departed for their headquarters after having seen to placing their men. As Malet had expected, Plougastel had raised a fuss, and been seconded, surprisingly, by Chief Inspector Fougeroux. Malet had resolved the problem by gently reminding them all of his rank.

Now things were settled: Malet would leave the Prefecture at seven forty-five, walk to Le Chasseur Affamé, arriving by eight, and eat a leisurely supper. He would walk back to his house by way of the rue de Rivoli, turn left on the rue Vieille du Temple, and follow that street of palaces past the Hotel de Rohan with its beautiful frieze of the Horses of Apollo over the stable entrance. His street, the rue Regnaud, opened abruptly to the right just past the Hotel de Rohan. The entire route encompassed winding streets bordered by high houses. It was the perfect area to plan an ambush.

He sat back in his chair and checked his watch one last time. Six fifteen. He sighed and looked at the papers on the desk. He had cleared away all the ones pertaining to business, and only the obviously private ones were left. He had time to read them before he left the Prefecture.

He riffled through them. One was a packet with Sergeant Guillart's handwriting on the cover, and another was a note from his housekeeper. He had just spoken to her that morning, and he knew that it concerned her request to purchase a spaniel puppy to keep company with Ninon, who was growing old. Malet liked animals; he had given his permission. The third was written on expensive stationery and sealed with a pink wafer. It was addressed to him in a very feminine but unfamiliar hand.

Intriguing. Malet opened it and read. An invitation from the Minister of Finance and Letitia Descaux, his mistress, requesting...

> *...the Honour of the Presence of Paul V. Malet*
> *Chief Inspector, Provisional Prefect of Police*
> *At a Dinner to Be Held*
> *On Thursday, the Tenth of October...*

Malet sighed. An invitation to a formal dinner at one of the great houses on the rue de Grenelle, and he could not accept. He did not care for Parisian high society, which had not shown itself to be much different from the criminal high society that he had met through Cheat-Death's patronage, but it would have been pleasant to speak with Letitia—TiTi, whom he had known from his days as Police Commissioner in Vautreuil. She had risen from being a prostitute to taking her place as the mistress of the Minister of Finance. Their friendship had been a longstanding and warm one, and he always enjoyed seeing her.

But it wasn't to be.

It was too late to send his regrets; he would send a letter tomorrow and apologize for his lateness in replying.

He tucked the invitation in his breast pocket.

The next item was a report concerning the officer injured at that incident in the XIIth Arrondissement. He had taken a turn for the worse and was dead. Malet sighed. He would write a letter to the widow and see what arrangements could be made to provide for the man's family.

He lifted Guillart's packet. The cover note was very brief:

> *Chief Inspector:*
>
> *Results were obtained on the all-points bulletin that you mandated far sooner than we had expected. In view of what I had perceived to be the urgency of your request, I am placing this information at your disposal for review. If you need any further information, I will be happy to send out any instructions you may deem appropriate.*

Malet's hand shook as he set the note down. So soon! He riffled through the materials and saw the name: Jacques Fanchon, and an address barely three streets from Malet's own home. And the rest of the information- He scanned it. Vaux had adopted a child, lived quietly and took an active part in community welfare. He attended mass daily, gave to the poor. Nothing had changed.

He set the papers aside. Nothing had changed. He was dealing with a very good man who was still a criminal in the eyes of the law. He had to face the heartbreak all over again unless he could find a way to obtain a pardon. If he approached the Attorney-General, or any of the judiciary —

But they had disregarded his pleas on Vaux' behalf all those years ago, why should they listen to him now? He could see the heartbreak starting all over again, and he was not sure he would be able to bear it.

There had to be something he could do! Surely, surely things had changed! There was no indication that Vaux was planning to leave Paris, and the situation with Dracquet was of greater urgency. He could draw breath and take some time to plan. If only it were not necessary!

Malet gently folded the packet and started to place it in his breast pocket. He changed his mind. He did not want this concern to hinder his action that evening. There would be time the next day when he could do some thinking. He placed the papers in the drawer of the desk and closed it with a thump.

What time was it?

He looked at his watch. He had over an hour before he had to go to Le Chasseur Affamé. He was unsettled and off-balance. He needed to collect his thoughts, to refocus. He would be risking his life this night and he could not be distracted. He would go apart and relax for a while.

He left his office and headed for the door.

Chamberlain Clerel was still at the Prefecture. He saw Malet and said, "Is the Chief Inspector leaving for the night?"

"Yes, Clerel," said Malet. "I will be going to supper at 8:00 if anyone asks. Le Chasseur Affamé, at the place du Châtelet. I am expected."

"Very good, Monsieur," said Clerel. He seemed hesitant. He added, without his usual pomposity, "You will be careful, won't you? Things do not feel quite right tonight..."

Malet nodded. "I am always careful," he said.

"Then good night, Inspector. And God keep you."

Malet went out the door. He thought he heard someone give a muffled cheer, but he saw no one on the street. A line of fiacres waited on the street, as always. He went to the nearest one and opened the double doors in the front.

"Good evening, Inspector!" the driver said. "Montmartre again this evening?"

Malet climbed into the fiacre. "If you please," he said. He would be able to breathe freely at Montmartre.

CHAPTER FORTY-THREE

Larouche Tails Monseigneur

Larouche had been bored for the past several days. He had had difficulty finding food and shelter, for the weather was turning cold, and he had spent most of his time hunting shelter and warmth among the crowded back streets of the central Parisian arrondissement, where the poor clustered.

He had lived hand to mouth, digging through scrap heaps for every bite of food he consumed and every rag of clothing on his back. He swallowed his pride and begged for alms beneath Lemaire's frieze of the Last Judgment on the pediment of the church of Sainte Marie-Madeleine near the place de la Concorde. He was small and dirty and underfed; he collected very little money.

He shivered in the cold and wondered how he could get some warm clothes to fit him. He thought he might go to the flower-seller's grandson after all. Then the weather had broken once more, and it was warm enough to leave the reeking throngs of beggars. He decided that he had earned a little fun; time to go in search of Monseigneur.

He had waylaid the man outside the Prefecture that morning and knocked his hat to the ground with a clatter. It had startled an oath from Monseigneur's lips that had made Larouche chuckle.

He had caught him at mid-afternoon, as well, when he was in the company of several other cops of obvious seniority. The attack had occasioned smiles and laughter, and though Monseigneur had smiled, too, that smile had been very grim.

Larouche had done nothing further until evening. He had snatched some food from strollers near the cathedral, who had abandoned their picnic blanket to blink at the twin towers and point at the spire. Larouche had eaten well. He had half a chicken wrapped in a napkin and tucked beneath his shirt for that evening's meal.

It was growing dark: time for Monseigneur to leave the Prefecture.

Larouche skipped across the Pont de L'Archeveché to the Quai de Montebello, and then waited in the shadow of the Conciergerie, by the Quai des Orfevres. He had been alert to any attempts to catch him, but Monseigneur didn't seem to be the type to send others to fight in his place. Although he had noticed a knot of men waiting near the end of the street...

He decided that they weren't Police after watching them. Probably enterprising pickpockets. Whoever they were, they didn't concern Larouche or Monseigneur.

Larouche was beginning to respect the man. Had he looked closely into his own heart he might have discovered a feeling of liking. Monseigneur was a haughty, proud man, but he fought his own battles and took his defeats honestly.

Larouche had a pocketful of rocks and a lively will to mischief that evening. He greeted Monseigneur's emergence from the Prefecture with a hastily smothered crow of triumph. Monseigneur paused to look up and down the street, then summoned a cab.

Aha! thought Larouche, *It's Montmartre this evening!* And no wonder: the sky was clear and bright, the air, though crisp, still held some warmth, and there was a wind. A beautiful time to look out over Paris.

He hurried to the cab and swung up to the back as it pulled away from the front of the Prefecture. He noticed that another carriage, apparently a private one, followed them.

Once at Montmartre, Larouche gave Monseigneur a good head start and then followed him up to the summit of the Butte. He felt a moment's panic when he couldn't locate the man: had he lost him? Then he relaxed and took a stone from his shirt. No time like the present, and there he was.

Monseigneur was walking slowly along beneath the evening sky. The briskness was gone from his walk and he was obviously tired and sad.

Larouche paused and lowered the stone.

Why was Monseigneur sad? He had so much to be grateful for. He was warmly clothed, he obviously ate well, and he had a place to sleep at night. Was it possible that someone's heart could ache even when it was housed in a healthy body?

Larouche knew the answer even as he formed the question. His was a wiry little body, and he had seldom been really sick, and yet the year after Père Louis' death had been the worst of his life. He had wept every night, and he had thought himself the loneliest soul in the world.

Could such a thing have happened to Monseigneur?

Larouche eyed him once more, troubled by a sudden feeling of commiseration. There was something straightforward and steely about the man, he was one who fought his own battles and would never compromise, no matter what was at stake. And, it seemed, his heart could ache, as well.

Larouche had a sudden urge to run to him and take his hand and tell him how cold it was and how difficult it was for him to keep from becoming a robber and a catamite and one of those who scouted for criminals and ran their errands. It was hard to remember what Père Louis had said about honor and virtue when it was cold, and food was scarce and there were six people to quarrel over each crumb that fell to the ground. He had the feeling that Monseigneur would understand.

But he couldn't do it. It would be a sort of surrender. He would surrender to no one.

Larouche had come to throw rocks: his target was there, and the rock was in his hand. He lifted the rock again as the man paused by the portals of St. Pierre de Montmartre and raised his head to gaze up at the stars. Now was the time to let fly, now, when he was looking upward with such weariness and longing. It would be like a blow to the face.

Larouche lowered the rock and turned away. There would be time later. He moved toward the deepening shadows at the corner of the street to wait until Monseigneur was ready to move on.

He froze. The shadows were alive with danger, and he caught a snatch of words. What were they saying? Larouche moved closer.

"...Make it count! "

"...Best shot...

"...Won't know what hit him..."

The shadows separated into four cloaked and muffled men. Their clothing was good, but they had an indefinable quality to them that spoke of those who kill for money. He saw the fellow with the gray-smudged chin holding something that glinted wickedly blue-black in the starlight. He was slowly raising it to shoulder level, steadying it —

Larouche bit off a yell as the blue glint began to level. He launched himself at Monseigneur, who was standing with his back to them and gazing out over the city and struck him squarely behind the knees. The blow folded Monseigneur over and hurled him flat to the ground as the night splintered into a roar of sound.

Larouche did not pause. He scrambled up to his hands and knees and scuttled away, then pulled himself to his feet and ran as though all the Police in Paris were after him.

Monseigneur would be all right! That would teach them to try and kill him! He belonged to Larouche!

CHAPTER FORTY-FOUR

Be Certain the Victim Is Wounded Before Giving the Coup De Grace

The blow to the back of his knees knocked Malet sprawling. The echo of the gunshot jolted him from the haze of anguish that had enveloped him, and he realized the magnitude of his slip. The trap! He had set a trap and walked away from it! He was alone, with no back-up, out in the open, and someone had just tried to kill him.

Malet lay motionless where he had fallen. He spared an instant's attention to register the feel of a lithe little body disentangling itself from his legs and pushing itself to its feet as his hand closed about his pistol. He heard swift, light footsteps fading in the distance.

Someone had just rescued him from an assassination attempt, and he had no idea who it might have been. But there was no time to puzzle over it now.

The shadows approached him, talking furtively among themselves. It would not be much longer now before the honest people of Montmartre began to stir. He drew a deep, shivering breath as though he were in pain, and then expelled it in a long sigh.

"Ah!" said one of the men.

"Finish it," said another.

They came closer and bent over him. Someone kicked him, hard, in the side. He did not move.

"I think he's dead," said a third voice.

"Turn him," said the first voice. "We'll finish him."

Rough hands took hold of his shoulder and turned him on his back.

Malet raised his pistol and fired. One of the forms crumpled to the ground as the others scattered. The second shot from his pistol winged another of them: he heard a muffled scream as he sprang to his feet.

Malet decided it was foolish to pursue them alone. He had brought his backup pistol, but he did not want to waste the shots. It would take too long to reload his other piece, and there were too many of them. He stayed where he was.

"Tell Dracquet he's made a mistake!" he called after them and went over to the man sprawled against the pavement, just before the gateway to the cemetery of Saint Pierre de Montmartre. He turned the man with his foot and frowned down at him.

The man was gasping and retching. A red foam was upon his lips. Maybe he could be saved, though Malet doubted it. It looked as though the bullet had nicked an artery.

Malet knelt beside the man and tore open his shirt. He shook his head. Hopeless. He spared a glance at the man's face. It was René Benoit. He frowned and bent to look more carefully, and as he did so, he caught a faint scraping noise behind him, as though someone were trying to approach him very quietly.

His eyes widened in the darkness and he drew a deep, soft breath, every muscle tensed...

LAROUCHE HURTLED DOWN the hill of Montmartre through twisting, steep streets, like a shot from a cannon. He knew that Monseigneur would be safe, but he also knew that the Police would be very angry, and he wanted to be far away from the dragnet that, he knew, they would throw around the district.

He descended to the place Pigalle, sat at the base of its fountain and ate the rest of the chicken that he had stolen at noon, listening with half an ear to the drunken chatter around him. Maybe he could hear something useful... You never found out about handouts if you kept your ears closed.

His thoughts kept straying to that evening's work. He had done well to keep Monseigneur from being killed. He didn't understand why the thought of that man lying dead in his blood was so disturbing. He told himself that he didn't want anyone to die, but it still didn't explain why he had been so appalled at the thought of those killers trying to murder Monseigneur. Maybe Larouche didn't hate him after all. He didn't know.

Well, Monseigneur was safe. He belonged to Larouche, as Larouche had decided at the moment he had saved his life. He was Larouche's to befriend or to pester, as the spirit moved him. At the moment he didn't know how the spirit was moving him.

He finished the last of the chicken. It was good as far as it went, but he was still hungry. He must be growing: it was getting harder and harder to fill his hungry little frame. He needed more food.

He decided to go to the tavern that the flower-seller had mentioned. A franc a week was well worth the loss of a little of his freedom. He would go there as soon as he could. But in the meantime, he was hungry.

He reviewed the various places he could go for a treat and decided that it was time he paid a visit to M. Dracquet's house. It wasn't far, and the man still owed him five francs. Dracquet might have no intention of paying Larouche, but Larouche would exact that payment one way or another, whether or not Dracquet was aware of it. Besides, Dracquet's cook, a father of four, was a particular friend.

He grinned, wiped his fingers on his trousers, and set off for Dracquet's house.

"SO IT'S YOU, YOU LITTLE scoundrel!" scolded the cook's assistant as he opened the kitchen door and let him in. "Been away for a while, haven't you? What's the matter? Get hungry?"

Larouche grinned at the man. "I didn't know you cared," he said. He got a swat on the behind for his pains. "Besides," he said, "I heard His Nibs is out of town—"

The cook's assistant looked suddenly stricken, and he hurried off toward the pantry.

Larouche rolled his eyes toward the cook.

"Don't be nosy," said the cook, who was busy stirring a pan of sauce. He set the pan aside and came forward. "M. Dracquet is still in town, and so is that English fellow, but they don't want anyone to know of it. I have no idea why, but I don't like it. They took the knocker from the door and closed the shutters, and all the curtains have been drawn, and shady visitors from England talking about some princess or other..."

The man fell silent, and he looked as nervous as his assistant. He drew a deep breath after a moment and added, "But that's not my concern, scamp, and it shouldn't be yours either. Sit down on that stool and eat this—" he set a quarter of blancmange before Larouche and put a pot of jam at his elbow. "Here's a nice sweet for you: eat it up."

Larouche didn't like blancmanges, but he did understand the theory of supply and demand. If he didn't eat this one, he knew, he would end up wishing, some time down the road, that he had. No use regretting things, so he set his curiosity about Dracquet aside and shoveled the blancmange into his mouth, drank a fair-sized glass of rich milk, and nodded from time to time as the cook talked.

It took very little to please grownups, or at least the good ones. The cook chattered on, unaware that Larouche was only paying attention with half his mind.

A sudden crash and clatter followed by the sound of angry voices cut the cook off in mid spate.

"What the devil do you mean coming to my house openly like this?" Dracquet's voice roared from the front of the house.

Larouche's eyes widened and he scurried to the kitchen door.

"Come back here!" the cook hissed. "There are some things it's best not to know!"

Larouche flashed him a look of scorn, pushed through to the sitting room door and peeked around the corner into the room. Dracquet, very red and quivering, was resplendent in a brocaded dressing gown and a tasseled smoking cap. Larouche could see a woman in the room beyond, in a state that he had heard described as 'en deshabille', but which he himself termed half-naked.

A man before him was picking himself up off the carpet with his hand to his face. "I had nowhere else to go," he objected. He flinched when Dracquet raised his hand again.

"Really! So you came here! Dolt! Get off the carpet, Declaire! You're making a mess! Why shouldn't I send you away? You botched your attempt! My best marksman! A clear shot at him and you botched it!"

"Le Noir fired at him and he crumpled," said Declaire. "René went up to finish him, and he pulled out a gun and shot. We all scattered, but not before he winged me. It was a mistake."

"I will say it was! Where's Benoit?"

"Back at the Butte," said Declaire. "He's dead."

"You left him there?" Dracquet demanded. "Good God! He will be recognized for certain! And if he saw Benoit, then he will have an inkling—"

"He said 'Tell Dracquet he made a mistake,'" said Declaire with the air of a messenger afraid of his news.

"He used my name, you say?" Dracquet demanded. "That crowns everything! You have botched it for certain—"

"But le Noir's still there," said Declaire.

Dracquet's back was turned, but his voice was easier when he spoke again. "That's something, at least," he said. "Well, you'd best get your hurts tended to. The evening's at an end for you."

Larouche drew a cautious breath. So Dracquet had tried to kill Monseigneur! That bore some thought. At least Monseigneur was safe for the moment. Larouche sighed and withdrew to the kitchen.

The cook was waiting, frowning at him. "Well?" he asked.

"Someone was killed tonight," Larouche said.

"Killed!"

"That's right," Larouche said. "It was Benoit. I think they tried to kill a cop, and they messed up. Dracquet's really pissed off."

"Watch your language!" snapped the cook, still looking shaken.

"René! Well, well! Not that he didn't have it coming to him."

"Attacked a cop," Larouche said again.

"You don't say! He was asking for trouble, then. No one in his right mind attacks a cop!"

Larouche thought of his stone-throwing ventures and said nothing. He only looked up at the cook with wide-eyed innocence. "May I have some more milk?" he asked.

CHAPTER FORTY-FIVE

Watchman, What of The Night?

Malet drew a deep, soft breath, every muscle tensed. The magnitude of his error smote him with all the force of a thirty-pound shot. They had followed him from the Prefecture, not from the restaurant. They were coming after him. They had fled only to regroup and send their wounded away. All his planning was useless: he had stepped out of his own trap, and they were between him and his friends.

He cast about for a way to get to help. Christien L'Eveque's precinct was just to the north, and he could hear sounds coming from that direction. They would expect him to try to make his way to a Police or Army post; it would be useless even to try, especially in this arrondissement, where he knew he had enemies. He considered going to the Rose d'Or, but the thought of the innocents at that inn facing a hired killer like Pierre le Noir stopped that line of thought.

Danger lay all about him, and he could not remain where he was. He was surrounded on all sides but one, and he had a sense of shadows converging upon him. The church cemetery was behind him. He whirled around, plunged into the silence of the cemetery, and flattened himself in the slight indentation formed by the lintel of the gate where it joined the wall.

He heard running feet and voices, low and swift. They paused outside the gate.

"He will have taken off east! That's where that fellow said he was heading: that's where he wants to go! You, Edouard—take Villatte with you and circle through here, then join us by the gate. I will send four others, as well. You will have to split up and rejoin us here while we check along the walls. Two of you remain here at the gate in case he tries to leave this way. We may be able to save our time and simply corner him here. But be careful: he's a tough one! Now hurry!"

The sound of grim, quiet laughter stopped the footsteps. "Fools!" said a harsh, cold voice. "You don't catch a tiger by baiting a mousetrap!"

"Do you have any suggestions?" demanded the first voice.

"Load your pieces with your heaviest shot and set up a tiger hunt," said the second voice.

Malet heard murmurs, then the second voice said, "You do what you want, le Noir. We're going after him."

"It's your funeral," said le Noir's voice.

"Then we'll be seeing you in hell," said the first voice. A moment later, le Noir's footsteps faded to the south.

Malet edged from behind the tree and gazed wide-eyed into the darkness before him. So le Noir had left them, and they were circling through the cemetery, were they, and only leaving two to guard the gate? Hm. He cast his mind over the layout and decided that the wall was too high to scale. The only way out was through the eastern gate, and it was guarded by only two people. Those two were in for a surprise.

Malet seemed to hear Cheat-Death's rasping old voice as he made his silent way back through the cemetery: *In a contest between predator and prey, it is the prey who turns to fight that is in the position of strength, for surprise is strength and it buys time. Never forget it: the weaker they think you, the stronger you really are. Always attack when they expect you to flee.*

He unbuttoned the top three buttons of his coat and reached inside his coat for his Russian dagger as he moved in among the monuments.

"WHERE DO YOU THINK he went?" asked Edouard. He was only twenty-two, and not certain he liked what was happening.

"Do I know?" demanded Villatte. "He's hard to figure out. Look, there's that hut over there—some old fellow's buried there, and they say he's got a lot of gold in the coffin with him. I'd love to get in there with a crowbar and a good, sturdy sack! Look, kid—keep watch while I take a leak!"

"Don't be all night," said Edouard. "This place gives me the creeps!" He turned and looked nervously around at the silent monuments. He could hear Villatte behind the mausoleum, fiddling with buttons, no doubt —and then he froze. He thought he heard a cry. The cry was not repeated; instead, he heard a strange, gurgling sound. "Villatte?" he said. "Villatte? Are you all right?"

He went over to the mausoleum, but Villatte wasn't there, and the side of the building looked strangely dark and wet, almost as though it had been splashed with paint —

Suddenly he knew beyond any doubt that Villatte was not all right, and he knew that he would be dead if he remained where he was. He turned, sobbing with terror, and fled west, deeper into the cemetery.

THEY WERE STANDING where Malet thought they would be, half-hidden in the shadows by the gate. He bent slightly, settled the corpse's arm more tightly about his neck, and supported it by the waist.

"Get out of the way," he said, raising the timbre of his voice. "He's hurt! That fellow in there's not human!"

It worked. The two stood aside as he came through the gate, and by the time they had recognized him and moved forward to seize him, he had his pistol ready. He spun the corpse into the path of the closest man, thrust the muzzle of his pistol up under the ribcage of the second, and pulled the trigger.

The report of the gun was muffled by the assassin's body; the man jerked and was suddenly limp. Malet shoved him aside, leveled his pistol at the other, and pulled the second trigger.

He heard shouts and pounding feet coming from the north and looked over his shoulder in their direction; his attackers were coming after him in force. It was time to leave.

He turned south just as a gunshot crashed through the stillness of the night and flung him sideways against the wall of the cemetery, gasping with the stark, fiery slash of pain across his chest. He dropped to the ground, away from a second bullet that smashed into the wall as his right hand flashed forward in a motion that was pure reflex. The Russian knife spun and glittered in the starlight for the briefest flash of time before it thudded into flesh.

He heard a shuddering gasp and saw a form collapse the ground. He slowly pushed himself to his feet and went to the man, already knowing what he would find.

Pierre le Noir was curled tightly on the ground, half turned away. He was gasping, drawing great, wheezing breaths into his lungs. One hand was clenched against the ground under his head. The other was hidden from sight.

Le Noir raised his head and watched Malet's approach over his shoulder. "Cheated!" he gasped. "Damn all-all-chances!" He fixed Malet with glazing eyes and a ghastly smile. "Twice—in my—sights. You have—the devil's—own luck!"

"I have lived too long and seen too much to believe in luck." Malet's hand was pressed to his chest. "Well, you blooded me," he said. "You can take comfort from that. Why did you come back? To kill that English princess, Victoria? Is that what made you return even when I said you were a dead man if you did?"

Le Noir's mouth twisted, and he drew a hissing breath. He lifted his hand; it disappeared briefly before him. A moment later Malet's knife clattered upon the ground. "Questioning—time at—last," He gasped. "Well, you have—earned it. I am—a goner." He raised his head again. "Here—" he said. "—turn me over—so I can—speak. Something to—say to you—"

Malet put his right hand in his coat pocket and took firm hold of his backup pistol as he turned the man. And unhesitatingly emptied his pistol into le Noir's chest as the man tried to raise his own weapon.

"You should have stayed dead," Malet said as the assassin subsided with a shudder, a thread of blood trailing from his mouth to spot the pavement beneath his head.

He bent and quickly checked le Noir's pockets. If he could find anything to tie this murder attempt to Dracquet, his danger and pain would not be wasted. He straightened after a moment, shaking his head. Nothing. And they were still after him.

He was suddenly unutterably weary. The breast of his coat, shirt and greatcoat were sodden, and the wound itself, a long gash from right shoulder to left collarbone where the bullet had caught him just as he turned, was beginning to throb. He was far from friends and safety and the night was still young.

"You knew you had to face a reckoning at my hands," he said to le Noir under his breath as he retrieved his dagger and wiped it on the skirts of the man's coat. He straightened and frowned at the blood on his hand and then looked up at the sky. "I warned you, you ignored me, and you have paid your shot just as I said you would," he said. "It only remains to see if I will be required to pay mine tonight."

He heard voices behind him; he whirled and ran down the slope of Montmartre at top speed, taking the route that Larouche had followed, praying that no one would be awaiting him at the base of the butte. If all else failed, he could go into the sewer...

CHAPTER FORTY-SIX

The Trap Sprung

L et me understand you," said Christien L'Eveque. "You were hiding in the cemetery because you didn't want to be killed by the target of your assassination attempt." He frowned over at his second. "Where did you find him, again?"

"By the wall, Sir. At the farthest western end of the cemetery."

"Who were you trying to assassinate?" L'Eveque asked. His normally happy expression had vanished, to be replaced by a formidable scowl.

"A c-cop," answered the prisoner.

"And what was this cop's name?" L'Eveque persisted with ominous gentleness.

"I don't know," the prisoner said. "He w-was tall, with a black coat—"

"What!" gasped the other officer.

L'Eveque looked decidedly grim. "You don't trouble to learn who you plan to kill, eh?" he said. "What else was there?"

"A black coat with capes. We saw him at the summit of the butte, and took a shot at him, but he killed one of us there."

"There's an officer to see you, M. l'Inspecteur," said the O.O.D., putting his head in at the door, "He says it's urgent."

L'Eveque rose and went to the door. He turned and said, "Keep him talking, Narcess." He went out and said to the O.O.D., "Where is he?" The man nodded toward L'Eveque's office. "In there," he said.

L'Eveque found Georges Plougastel warming his hands before the stove just inside the door. He seemed pale and shaken.

"What is it, Georges?" demanded L'Eveque.

"That priceless idiot Malet has vanished!" said Plougastel.

"What!"

"He set a hare-brained trap for assassins! He was to be the bait."

"Oh no!"

"Oh yes," Plougastel said grimly. "And Pierre le Noir was to be the quarry! Don't look at me like that, Christien. The man really is alive and in Paris. He—Malet—was to take supper at that restaurant that he likes at the place du Châtelet. He was to eat there at eight and then walk to his home—and he has vanished into thin air!"

"What? Wait a minute, it's ten-thirty now!"

"That's right," said Plougastel. "He didn't show at the restaurant, and they started getting nervous. I went to the Prefecture, and Clerel said he left there at seven, or a little before. Clerel said he seemed distracted."

"Paul?"

"He apparently got some bad news just before he left. One of those cops hurt during that uproar in the 5th the other night died. Clerel found the note in the Prefect's desk. It must have knocked him off his stride."

L'Eveque nodded. "Way off," he said. "But it's unlike him to drop things completely. What did he do when he left?"

"He took a cab—God alone knows where! —and I was hoping to find him here! How can such a brilliant man be such a dunce? I told him he was being foolish and so, God save the mark, did Emile Fougeroux! And we have had no word at all, no leads, nothing!"

"Good God!" said L'Eveque.

"That's not the worst of it," said Plougastel. "I had to go to the house of the Minister of Finance, interrupt a formal dinner, and tell Count d'Anglars what's happened."

L'Eveque whistled.

"The man is furious!" said Plougastel. "He told me he'd warned Malet against just such a bird-witted venture, and now it seems he's gone and ignored him. There's going to be hell to pay! By God, Christien, if he's been kidnapped—!"

"He wasn't kidnapped," L'Eveque said. "God pity his kidnappers if he had been! No, he was here, all right—"

Plougastel raised his hand to his mouth. "'Was'?" he gasped. "Is he dead, then?"

"Not dead," said L'Eveque. "Not yet."

"Damn it, man, where is he, then?" demanded Plougastel.

"I don't know," said L'Eveque. "But I think I know what happened. I have been questioning someone we brought in a half hour ago. We found him shivering and cowering in the cemetery, babbling that he didn't want to die. He just finished telling me that he was part of an assassination attempt. The target was a tall man in a black coat. A cop, he said."

"By God!"

"No, wait," said L'Eveque. "You don't understand yet! We have five bodies laid out on slabs in the morgue at the moment. One was shot at close range, two were shot point-blank. You can see powder burns around the wounds and the clothing's charred at the entry holes, too. One had a slit throat. The last one had his chest shot to pieces, but it appears that he was knifed, too. This fellow looks familiar—he's got a mark on his chin—"

"But that's Pierre le Noir!" Plougastel exclaimed.

"So it would seem," L'Eveque agreed. "And all the bodies were found near the butte."

"His work?"

"That's all it could be," said L'Eveque. "This fellow had others with him beside the five stiffs, and they're still after him. He must have fled—if only he had come to me! —I haven't a clue where he went. What if he's wounded?"

CHAPTER FORTY-SEVEN

Light and Shadows

The Quai de la Légion d'Honneur parallels the north shore of the Seine for a quarter of a mile before it ends at the Pont de la Légion. Napoleon ordered the construction of the bridge in 1802 when he founded the Légion d'Honneur, and he mandated the renaming and refurbishing of the quai, as well. The bridge is a triumph of dressed stone and carved balustrades, and the quai matches it in elegance. Unfortunately, the quai, however elegantly built it may be, was still at that time an outlet for the old sewer.

The engineers had tried: the gateway was beautifully arched, with a keystone carved in the shape of a gargoyle and a massive iron grating that looked like a portcullis from some venerable fortress, but the fact remained that it was a sewer. There was no disguising the murky, gray waters that dripped into the blue-green Seine, or the attendant smell. Or the fact that it spewed its foul waters into the river just beneath the bridge. It was enough to drive the fashionable away.

The quai served by day as a gathering place for beggars of all sorts with military backgrounds of varying degrees of veracity, as well as those women who claimed to be their wives, widows, daughters and bastards. By night it lay relatively quiet, except for one old beggar who always sat alone beneath the bridge, by the sewer outlet, and sang operatic arias for the passers-by, when he wasn't mumbling to himself and wringing his hands.

He often took shelter in the culvert, which he unlocked with a bootleg key he had obtained somehow, and he made his bed on the stone shelf that had been built into its wall.

That night the old man was warbling a solo from 'The Barber of Seville' in his reedy old voice, to the derision of a passing boatload of country folk.

He yelled an insult back at them and picked up his song where he had left off.

The aria finished, he sat with his back to the wall of the quay and stared before him, toothlessly chewing on a piece of dried bread and smoothing his hands before him in a strangely aristocratic gesture.

This had been his place for the thirty years since he had been released from the soldiers' hospital and told that he was as well as he was ever going to get, and they needed their beds for those who were really ill. He had seen many changes along this river; the only thing that had remained unchanged was the dome of Les Invalides, and now that he was getting old, he needed to keep it always before him.

He closed his eyes and hummed 'the song of the warrior-prince' from *Massinissa*.

"Do you like it?" he asked when he had finished. No one, listening, would have heard an answer; he didn't hear one, himself, but then he didn't expect to. He was talking to his ghosts, and ghosts seldom replied.

As he sat, he could see them behind his eyelids. The great armies that had marched from Paris across the face of Europe had returned as ghosts, sometimes resplendent in their trappings, sometimes tattered and bleeding. He often spoke to the pale silent ones who crossed the river above him.

He always sang for them. His voice was quavery and cracked, but his singing was the only gift an old beggar could give. The ghosts were grateful for it.

He smiled and took a deep breath. It was late, and he would be going to sleep shortly, but he should be singing. He lived to sing. And, it seemed, from the hollow, halting sound of approaching footsteps echoing along the culvert, he would have an audience shortly.

He opened his eyes and, still singing, watched the heavy iron grating swing slowly outward, propelled by a bloody hand.

The culvert was always filled with shadows and mist; the water in the sewers was warmer than that of the river, and steam rose constantly from it. As he watched, the fog swirled, became more solid, and the figure of a man emerged in a billow of mist and crumpled to its knees beside him.

The old man kept singing, but he looked the ghost over very carefully, and smiled when the specter raised its head and looked at him.

It was one of the wounded ones; the pavement was spotted with red, and the ghost's right hand was holding a reddened cloth to its breast. Wounded and exhausted, the beggar saw; the ghost had collapsed backward against the wall of the quay and was breathing in gasps. Its hair was plastered to its forehead and clung in dripping tendrils to the back of its neck.

He finished singing and smiled at the ghost again. "Good evening," he said.

The ghost drew a deep, shuddering breath and nodded. "Good evening," it said. Its breathing seemed to be steadying a little.

"You should close the grating," said the beggar. "Close it and lock it. You never know what might come out on nights like this. I will lock it for you."

He got up and did that, then returned to his seat and surveyed the ghost. "You're one of the wounded ones, I see," he said. "I am sorry for you. But you know, I have always wanted to ask: can you still feel pain even now?"

The ghost had raised its head and watched as the old man slammed the grate shut and locked it. "I think I have been like this forever," it said, pushing its damp hair from its eyes. Its exhausted gaze sharpened after a moment. "Where did you get that key?" it demanded.

"Somebody gave it to me," said the beggar. He looked the ghost over and nodded. "I wonder..." he said. "You're not in uniform. You must be from Russia."

The ghost was lifting the cloth from its chest and reaching gingerly inside with its right hand. It withdrew its hand with a hiss of pain and looked up. "I beg your pardon?" it said.

"You were in Russia," the beggar repeated. "I can tell. The worst of you come from there. You're always worn out, always bleeding, and you're never wearing overcoats. There are so many of you... What was your rank?"

The ghost's expression was an odd mixture of wistfulness and irony. "I was the Dauphin once," it said.

"Then you did survive the Terror!" said the old beggar. "But you were killed in Russia... I am so sorry for you... That's why I always sing for you. D-do you like my singing?"

The ghost frowned at him, but it pushed to its feet and stared at the grate and then across the river. "Les Invalides is over there, isn't it?" it asked, pointing.

The beggar was cut to the heart by the ghost's refusal to answer his question. He said, "Oh, they can't help you once you're dead, you know. I am always telling you folk that, but you never listen. Your comrades always go there. I suppose you will, too. Send them my love and tell them I will keep singing for them..."

"I will," said the ghost. It sounded a little grim. It paused, though, and looked down at the beggar with a slightly softened expression. "And I didn't thank you properly for everything," it said. "Your singing is beautiful. I have enjoyed it."

The old man beamed up at him. "Oh I am glad," he said. "I will sing this aria for you." He raised his voice once more.

The ghost gazed down at him for a moment. It paused to take a coin from its pocket, handed it to the old man, and then it left.

The chuckle of the river against the quay closed like a curtain behind the uneven sound of its footsteps.

WELL, WELL, WELL! A government key! How on earth had that beggar gotten his hands on it? The question occupied Malet's attention for the forty seconds it took him to pass from the quay up to the bridge and then cross the river. He could hear the man singing.

However the old man had obtained the key, it had saved his life by gaining him time. His pursuers were probably still behind him. He had hoped to lose them finally in the twisting length of the old Montmartre sewer, but he was beginning to believe this evening was one of ill omen for him.

For all that Malet was familiar with their convolutions, his passage through the sewers had been harrowing; he had encountered Clerel's dreaded coat-snatchers, who had not wanted to content themselves with merely snatching his coat. In the end he had had to fire his pistol in the stone tunnel, against his better judgment, to keep from being knifed. A ricochet had struck him along the ribs, and now he was bleeding from two wounds. That had been over an hour ago.

He had some breathing time, but it had been bought at a high price. The night was growing colder; his breath seared his lungs, and he would have to stop and rest soon. He pressed his hand against his chest. His entire right side felt wet. The wounds themselves were not severe, but each beat of his heart was costing him blood and draining his strength. He had to go to earth somewhere, and he had a trump card. Where was he?

He looked around. The dome of Les Invalides was before him and it wasn't much farther to 30-32 rue de Grenelle. He drew a deep, shaking breath and reached into the breast of his coat...

The singing stopped abruptly. He could hear the beggar saying, "No, I have seen no one but ghosts tonight. Ghosts are the only thing I ever see."

He hurried off.

THERE IT WAS, NO. 30-32 rue de Grenelle. He was almost safe now. He looked the high, wide house over, and considered. It was too shadowy in the back, and the front was a very satisfactory jumble of carriages and horses. He judged it wise to go to the front door. He took a deep breath and went up the three steps to the door, where a very superior sort of footman looked him over. "Yes?" he said. He didn't add 'Monsieur'.

Malet tried to straighten. "I must see Madame Descaux at once," he said.

The footman looked him up and down. He seemed to be taking in every detail of Malet's dishevelment. His slightly flared nostrils indicated that he had caught a fetid whiff of the sewer. "This is neither a bar nor a boxing establishment, Monsieur," he said with awful precision. "We give soup at the back door during the day. If you return then, I am certain we'll be able to accommodate you. Good evening." He started to sign to one of the throng of coachmen in the courtyard.

Malet frowned at the man. "Let me in at once!" he said. "I am an officer of the Police and this is an emergency!"

The footman was almost as tall as Malet, and impressively built. "You are drunk and filthy!" he snarled. "Be off before I call the Watch!"

Malet took his hand from the breast of his coat and offered the invitation, which was now wet with blood. "I was invited by Madame," he said.

"It's all right, Louis," said someone behind Malet.

Malet turned and saw TiTi Descaux' coachman.

The man stepped forward and opened the door. "This one's a particular friend of Madame, and he does have an invitation: I know, for I delivered it to the Prefecture just this afternoon. She'd be disturbed if he were hindered in any way. Come on in, Monsieur. The night's too cold for you to be out without a coat."

Malet drew a deep, shaking breath, and stepped out of the night. "I must ask your pardon," he said. "I'd never have intruded in such a state, but I have been followed—"

"You have been wounded," said the coachman with sudden concern. "There's blood on you. Can you walk?"

Now that there was no need for fighting or fleeing, Malet was feeling decidedly dizzy. He nodded nevertheless and took a step forward. It was a mistake; he staggered and clutched at the coachman's arm to keep from falling.

"Just barely," said the coachman, steadying him. He nodded to the footman. "Louis," he said, "tell Monseigneur that Chief Inspector Malet is here and wounded, and then send for a doctor at once! And you, Inspector—" this to Malet as he set a strong, reassuring arm about his waist, "—let me help you to warmth and a chair."

Five minutes later Malet was sitting at the large oak table in the kitchen with his head buried in his arms while the coachman issued a volley of orders to various servants, who came running with bowls of warm water, glasses of wine, a blanket, and bandages.

Malet was content to let everyone else hurry about; he was shaking with exhaustion, and his various injuries were beginning to throb with a grinding ache. All he wanted to do was sleep.

He heard a lady's voice approaching the kitchen door. The words were indistinct, covered by a hum of other voices.

Malet started to push himself to his feet as the door opened. He caught a glimpse of the hem of a gown of sherry-brown silk.

"You did well to bring him in," said TiTi, resplendent in silk and lace with topazes in her hair. "If he had been made to wait outside—!"

She hurried to him and turned him back toward the chair. "My dear M. le Commissaire!" she said. "You are wounded! Sit down!"

Deeply conscious of his dishevelment, Malet said, "I beg your pardon, Madame, for disturbing you in this fash—" He looked up and broke off. Standing behind TiTi Descaux, in full formal evening attire, were the Minister of Finance, the Minister of War, and a distance from them, his arms folded before him, his elegant features marred by a wrathful frown, Count d'Anglars, the Minister of Police.

Malet subsided with a moan and buried his face in his arms again.

CHAPTER FORTY-EIGHT

Paying the Piper Part I:
Questions and Answers

L'Eveque had taken many reports in his life, but never in the state rooms of the Luxembourg Palace, with the deponents being the Ministers of War, Finance, and Police, as well as the acting Prefect of Police, in the presence of six Chief Inspectors. But then this particular crime had many unusual aspects to it.

The attempted assassination of the acting Prefect of Police was a grave enough matter to command the interest of anyone in the government, and the broad territory over which the assassination attempt had taken place had mandated the involvement of more than one arrondissement, although L'Eveque, as the commander of the precinct in which the original attack occurred, served as the investigating officer.

The precise number of arrondissements involved had been arbitrarily set at seven, though the correct number was probably closer to four. A scrutiny of the layout of the sewer systems underlying Paris indicated that Chief Inspector Malet's path had certainly taken him underground through the 3rd, 2nd,6th, 4th and 1st arrondissements, and above ground through the 10th, but from the disposition of the various corpses found in the sewers, there was no way of ruling out the possibility that Malet had cut through the sewers under the 7th and 9th arrondissements, as well. In addition, the thieves who had attacked Chief Inspector Malet and taken his coat appeared to have come from the 9th arrondissement.

Whatever the logistics, L'Eveque knew that no one in the Police worth his salt would willingly choose to miss the chance to sit in on a questioning session that promised to be as entertaining as this one. Nor had they been disappointed.

The various Chief Inspectors—Mercier of the 4th, Picot of the 2nd, Monthermer of the 10th, and Guerin of the 3rd—had sheets of paper placed before them, along with ink and pens, but L'Eveque had yet to see any of them make any notes. Chief Inspector Guerin, very pale and silent, had not raised his eyes from the table during the entire course of the questioning.

Malet was sitting in a wing chair before them; Count d'Anglars was standing beside Malet's chair with his arm lying along the back. Nothing in the demeanor of either man gave any indication that Count d'Anglars had just privately given notice to the Provisional Prefect of Police that he was about to receive the most comprehensive and blistering tongue-lashing of his career.

"And now, gentlemen," said L'Eveque, "You have heard the witnesses. Have you any questions to add to those already posed?"

Chief Inspector Picot smoothed his forehead in a gesture left over from the years when he had had hair. "How many times were you attacked in the sewers, M. Malet?" he asked.

"Four separate times," Malet answered. He was sitting back in his chair with his eyes closed. It was very late afternoon, but he had only just been released from his guest room at TiTi's house. To L'Eveque's relieved eyes he appeared more preoccupied than weary.

"And you believe that the attacks were all at the instigation of the assassins?" Picot persisted.

Malet opened his eyes. "There are many rat packs in Paris," he said. "Most of them haunt the sewers. I don't pretend to know how they are connected. I didn't attempt to establish their affiliation before I fought them. Should I have?"

Brunon chuckled and folded his papers away. "Sensibly said, my dear Malet. For my part, I am very glad that you escaped as you did."

Malet nodded and closed his eyes again. They snapped open at the next question.

"I have a query from Chief Inspector Rabateau," said Picot, opening a slip of paper. "He inquires thus: M. Malet made his way into the sewers at Montmartre and emerged at the Pont de la Légion d'Honneur—is it possible that the Chief Inspector's path took him into the 6th arrondissement?"

Malet's expression shifted to a frown as he replied calmly enough, but with increasing vehemence. "Tell Rabateau that if the situation ever arises again, I will try to flee to his arrondissement at least for a little ways before resuming my path. Perhaps if I pole a raft down the Canal Saint-Martin, I can satisfy everyone. More than that I can't do."

The frown deepened to a scowl. "As for last night," said Malet, "I regret that my haste didn't permit me to visit all the Parisian arrondissements in descending numerical order so that everyone could participate in this raree show!"

Marshal Soult hid a smile behind his hand.

"But there's a point to the question," said Mercier. "I am still not certain where the attacks took place—was my bailiwick even involved? I can't reconcile it in my mind. Certainly, you were waylaid near M. Picot's territory, if not on it—"

"It's more likely he went through yours than mine," said Picot with a frown. "I think that was out of M. Malet's way! Do the sewers go underneath the juncture of the–"

"His attackers probably came from there, though!" snapped Mercier. "One of the corpses certainly was one of your prize criminals!"

"My prize—!" Picot began.

"Why don't I take both of you on a tour of the sewers tomorrow?" asked Malet with a thin smile. "We can retrace my route. I'd be happy to serve as your guide, and we can even—" He fell silent as d'Anglars' hand descended discreetly to his shoulder and gripped it. He flashed a sidelong glance at the Count's hand but said nothing further.

"I believe the question of venue has been settled," said L'Eveque. "If there are any lingering questions, I am certain that they can be addressed by The Prefect upon his return." He scanned his notes and then smiled at the Chief Inspectors. "Are there any further questions, gentlemen?" He paused, waiting for an answer, and then said briskly, "No? Then we shall conclude this session of questioning. With any luck, there shall be no need for another."

He turned to Soult and D'Aillard. "Accept my thanks, messeigneurs, for the evidence you have given us, and for your time and trouble in so doing,"

M. D'Aillard inclined his head and said, "We are happy to have been of use. If I, personally, can offer any more assistance, I beg that you contact me."

Soult added, "I would not have missed it for the world!"

Malet closed his eyes again.

L'Eveque hid a smile and said, "Thank you. I shall take care to ensure that you receive fair copies of your testimony. And now, messeigneurs, permit me to wish you a pleasant evening." He rose and bowed as the Minister of Finance and the Minister of War rose and left the room.

"I shall not keep you any longer," d'Anglars said to the Chief Inspectors. "It is late, M. Malet is weary and still, I fear, in some pain. No doubt you have pressing matters back at your respective headquarters. I shall make certain that you all receive copies of M. L'Eveque's report when it is completed."

The Chief Inspectors took the hint. They all left except for Guerin, who remained where he was. His face was, if possible, paler than before.

d'Anglars smiled down at Malet. "Are you feeling better now?" he asked. His voice was very gentle.

Malet looked up at him. "I am fine, M. le Comte," he said through his teeth.

"That's good," said d'Anglars. He released Malet's shoulder and went over to a chair that had just been vacated.

Guerin pushed himself slowly to his feet. Deep lines bracketed his mouth, and his voice shook slightly when he spoke. "I had no idea that this would happen," he said to Malet.

d'Anglars seemed surprised for a moment, but he said evenly, "Of course you did not. Had you known, you would have taken steps to prevent it."

Guerin turned halfway toward the Count, but he did not take his eyes off Malet. "Just so," he said. He paused and cleared his throat. "I am deeply embarrassed by—by all of this. More so than you can ever know. It should never have happened, and the fact that it did—"

He broke off, took a deep breath, and said, "Malet, I hope you will accept my apologies. We have never liked each other—indeed, we just had a regrettable quarrel—but I beg you to believe me: I have never actively wished you ill. I am very sorry." He turned and left the room.

d'Anglars watched him leave. After a moment he looked at L'Eveque and nodded to the door.

L'Eveque rose and went to shut the door. When he returned, d'Anglars asked, "How much do you have substantiating his part in those protection payments?"

"I have very little," answered L'Eveque.

Malet had been gazing thoughtfully at the door through which Guerin had left. "Those weren't his men," he said. "They weren't inept enough."

"I beg your pardon?" said L'Eveque. His smile had returned.

Malet ignored the smile. "He had some men tailing me for a while," he said. "His hired trackers were very poor. I gave one of them the fright of his life. He didn't send the killers."

d'Anglars nodded. "I shall accept that, then," he said. "We shall dispense with M. Guerin for the moment. Now it's your turn: I have judged it time to bell the cat. I am assigning you a bodyguard."

Malet transferred his frown from the door to d'Anglars' face.

"We have discussed this before in some depth," d'Anglars said. "You act-ed against my clear orders, in flagrant disregard of your own safety, in the hope of accomplishing something so insignificant when compared to the matter in hand that I find myself wondering if I have somehow managed to miss some key item in your chain of reasoning. I can't understand why you are alive at this moment. I can only thank God that you escaped the conse-quences of your own headstrong folly. Look at you: last night took its toll. You are worn out."

"It will pass," Malet said through his teeth. "I will be fine tomorrow."

"You shall be finer still with a bodyguard," said d'Anglars with the steely glint of a smile.

"I question the necessity," said Malet. "I escaped, after all."

d'Anglars' face hardened. "Don't try my patience, Chief Inspector," he said, all smiles gone from his expression. "I have too great a respect for your talents to allow myself to interfere with your way of performing the duties of your position, but when I do give a command, I expect it to be obeyed. So would you, too!

"You deliberately disregarded my orders concerning the care you were to take for your own safety and set up that trap last night—which, let me remind you, you proceeded to forget in a way that would embarrass even the most callow Junior Constable! Can you possibly be unaware that you threw this entire prefecture into an unprecedented uproar?"

Malet lowered his head, but his mouth was grim.

d'Anglars looked narrowly at him and then continued. "I am astonished that I must phrase it this way to a man of your rank and distinction, Chief Inspector, but as long as I hold the reins of the Police you will run as I command, and, by God, if you try to take the bit between your teeth it will be very much the worse for you! You would not hesitate to dismiss at once an intractable subordinate who has caused you only half the annoyance and worry that you have just caused me! I am being very kind to you, in fact. Do you understand me?"

Malet raised his eyes to d'Anglars', read the Count's expression, and lowered his eyes again. "If you command it," he sighed, "then I will obey."

"I do command it," d'Anglars said. "This must not happen again."

Malet inclined his head. "As you wish," he said.

"Will you be returning to the Rose d'Or?" L'Eveque asked. "If you are, you can cast an eye over the horse I bought for Inspector de Saint-Légère at the auction."

Malet frowned at L'Eveque. "Auction?" he repeated.

"You remember," said L'Eveque. "I attended the auction at the city stables yesterday. We tracked the buyer of that bay thoroughbred: I gave you the report: he belongs to the Duc d'Orleans now. I doubt he is in league with Constant Dracquet."

Malet sighed. "Unlikely," he agreed.

"I also bid on a horse for Charles de Saint-Légère, and he was delivered this afternoon. If you go to the Rose d'Or, you will be able to see him."

"I should," Malet said. He looked down at his hands. He added, "I forgot to tell Madame de Clichy not to expect me for supper last night..."

"She understands," said L'Eveque. "She was worried about you, of course. She sent to inquire after you, but she wasn't angry."

Malet nodded. "I'd best go back there," he said. He pushed himself to his feet—catching his breath with a hiss of pain—and checked his watch. Seven-thirty. He had been attacked almost twenty-four hours ago, and he was still tired. He was showing his age.

"You will accept the loan of my carriage to your inn," said d'Anglars. "M. L'Eveque, would you be good enough to ask my staff to have it brought round?"

L'Eveque looked from Count d'Anglars to Malet, then bowed and went to the door.

"And close the door behind you," d'Anglars directed.

Malet lowered his head and sat again.

CHAPTER FORTY-NINE

Paying the Piper Part II:
Justice and Mercy

"Now," said d'Anglars when the door had closed. "I have some questions for you to answer privately."

Malet looked up at him.

"You have been headstrong in the past," d'Anglars said. "But I have never known you to be stupid regarding your safety or anyone else's. You would have been safe if you had followed that trap as you had planned it. Although it was against my express command, it was well thought out with checks and counter-checks. It entailed some risk, but the risk was minimized. What could have happened that would so overset you as to make you forget your precautions and step outside your frame of safety?"

Malet closed his eyes. "I have already apologized, M. le Comte."

"I am not seeking an apology," d'Anglars said. "I am asking as a friend." When Malet remained silent, he went to the desk nearby, took out a packet of papers and set them before Malet. "Was it because of these?"

Malet paled and looked up at d'Anglars.

"Sergeant Guillart tells me these were brought to you just before you left for Montmartre. Since the documents are on Police stationery, I had no hesitation in reading them. They put me in mind of something in your past; I pulled your dossier and reviewed it once again."

He looked down at Malet, who was studying his interlaced fingers as though he had never seen them before.

d'Anglars' voice gentled. "Once I had done so," he said, "things became clear to me. My interest had been piqued all those years ago when a man of very high caliber and experience described his reason for declining a promotion to Prefect of Police for an entire Departement, and requesting a transfer, instead, to a slightly lower position, as 'heartbreak.' "

"Did I actually write that on an official document?" Malet asked.

"You did, indeed. And the description was apt. You were forced to investigate a close friend, and hoping, I suspect, to clear his name, you ultimately had to arrest him, testify against him and, in the cruelest twist of all, escort him to prison." He watched Malet's expression and added quietly, "I have always had an excellent imagination, my dear Malet. And in your case, your anguish was not hard to understand."

"I tried to warn him," Malet sighed. "But his conscience was clear, and I couldn't be more specific without betraying my own honor. The only wrong he did was to drop his past and try to step into a respectable life."

"And under the law that could be considered a crime," d'Anglars said. "I read the case before you came. He had spent his time, since leaving the prison, in making something of himself and assisting others. But do those virtues outweigh breaking his parole?"

Malet looked down at his hands, clasped before him. "I am not permitted to answer that, officially," he said. "And if I had tried..."

"The law deals with justice," said d'Anglars. "Not with fairness and mercy. You must do your duty and leave those with latitude to make what decisions they can."

"Yes," said Malet.

"And I surmise that this was the man who overpowered you in the Luxembourg gardens and left you tied to that tree."

"He could have killed me. I had my pistol with me and he found it."

"What?"

"He lingered because he thought I might have given myself a concussion. I fell rather heavily. He didn't want to leave me like that. When he was satisfied that I was all right, he went through my pockets, looking for a handkerchief to gag me, and found my pistol."

d'Anglars raised his eyebrows.

"I thought he was going to kill me. I suppose the blow to my head had addled me. I stopped fighting the knots and told him to get it over with."

d'Anglars shook his head.

"I thought I'd be damned if I begged for my life from anyone. He was indignant. How could I think such a thing of him? Hadn't I heard him say he meant me no harm? He put the pistol back, took out my handkerchief, and folded it into a gag."

"He spared your life," d'Anglars said. "And you a formidable threat to his liberty, if not his life. Once you were free, being a man of honor and integrity, you had no choice but to search for him."

"No choice." the words were almost inaudible.

"And then, the afternoon of that trap, you received the papers and found yourself facing the heartbreak all over again. You thought you might be able to request clemency, but things could go wrong. Geraud Clerel said you left in a very subdued mood."

Malet lowered his head again. "I thought it would all be starting again," he said, "and there was no escape. I had to go somewhere to think."

"I see," said d'Anglars. He looked at the papers and then set them aside. "I don't want a valued friend breaking his heart over something like this when it is not necessary. I have the personal authority to assess the magnitude of a crime, and to order or forbid further action. In this case, it is my judgment that this M. Fanchon is no more evil a man than you or me. Official action against him for anything in the past ends here: he can go forth with an easy heart. I take full responsibility for this decision, and I relieve you of any further involvement in this case, since your friendship with the subject presents a serious conflict of interest. As far as France is concerned, any possible case against M. Fanchon, or Vaux or Lambert, is closed, and the evidence destroyed."

He smiled at Malet's expression and put the papers in the fire. "You see?" he said. "You can set your heart at rest. There will be no more tragedy on this score, at least."

"But—"

"It is within my power," d'Anglars said. "And my mind is in no doubt. I am releasing a good man from a tragic past. Society won't suffer for this." He smiled and added, "You see, my very dear Malet, while solutions to great grief often can only be reached through labor and heartbreak and tears, sometimes they come once a wish is voiced or divined.'

Malet's voice shook. "I thank you with all my heart, Monseigneur"

"Not at all," said d'Anglars. "I only regret that I could not have stepped in sooner."

Malet pushed himself to his feet. "Thank you," he said again, with difficulty. "You have no idea how—how very grateful I am."

"Let us not discuss it anymore," said d'Anglars. "You are wounded, weary, and, I suspect, still in pain that may have had some of the spiritual to it in additional to the physical. Well, that is over now, and I am glad it is so. You can go in peace, and so can M. Fanchon. You may wish to write and tell him so, using official stationery." His voice became brisk again. "Now go to the carriage, which is waiting. I suggest you eat a good, hot meal, and go to bed as quickly as you can." He smiled and added, "Your bodyguard will report to you tomorrow. And be so good as to send M. L'Eveque in."

"HOW ODD TO SEE HIM so subdued," murmured d'Anglars after the door had closed. "Do you suppose it will last?" He paused and answered his own question. "No: it won't. He will be as maddening as ever tomorrow. I should have saved my breath."

"I think his present mood is more the result of chagrin than of illness, Monseigneur," said L'Eveque with a smile. "Only consider the defeat he just suffered: he had hoped to tie this attempt in to his case against Dracquet, but he botched his own trap through his own carelessness, as he admitted to you, and ended with nothing to show for the past evening but an impressive collection of corpses, two wounds that are probably painful and a tongue-lashing that is probably even more so."

d'Anglars chuckled. "We all suffer embarrassment," he said. "It's seldom fatal. As long as he's safe I have no cause for complaint, and I am happy with the collection of corpses, two in particular."

L'Eveque nodded. "René Benoit and Pierre le Noir," he said. "I was pleased with the contents of Benoit's pockets. Dracquet must be seething: if nothing else, he can be tied in to the attempted murder of a public official." He set his papers aside and said after a moment, "I owe a debt of gratitude to Madame Descaux for taking him in and caring for him."

"She is a delightful woman," said d'Anglars. He sat back in his chair and crossed his ankles before him. "I do wish you could have been there, my dear L'Eveque, when M. Soult and M. D'Aillard followed Madame into the kitchen, learned what had happened, and organized a search party on the spot. Poor Malet was ready to sink through the floor—he had come to a woman's house bloody, sweat-stained and smelling of the sewers, only as a last resort. Do you know, it is the first time I can remember seeing him disheveled in all our acquaintance."

L'Eveque nodded. "At least he can console himself that the assassination attempt itself was scotched, and a number of criminals arrested. I think we'll be able to put our hands on others within the next several weeks, so the evening's embarrassment wasn't in vain."

CHAPTER FIFTY

Malet Learns That It Is as Blessed
To Receive as to Give

There, Pippin. You can just see him to the east. Just coming up over the horizon: see the three stars in a row?

What am I looking for, Papa?

The row of stars. Look, Pippin: see the eye of Taurus? Look east-north-east—

J'n'comprends pas ce mot, Papa.

Say that in English, Pippin. You will never learn a language if you keep speaking your own. Now: look down from Taurus' eye and find the three bright stars in a row—

Like a belt?

Yes. Like a belt. That's Orion, the hunter. Look at him: it's the first time you have had a clear view of him. Isn't he magnificent?

Paul Malet could hear the voices in his mind, the child's voice high and clear, the older man's voice low and rough. It had been mid-October, and the sailor, Joseph Young, had called him to the ramparts of the prison to watch the stars. Orion was rising, he had said, and it was time Pippin made his acquaintance.

Papa Joseph had had a reason for all this. France was emerging from the terrible paroxysm of the Terror, all tradition, all order swept away. The child beside him had known no stability in his short life and was likely to see little more in the coming years. He had to learn to look for something to hold on to.

Malet understood that now, and he wondered once again at the chance that had brought Joseph Young to him at a time when he was lost and alone in the middle of a crowd of criminals, a little piece of spindrift blowing before the winds of his life.

He was sitting back against the luxurious upholstery of Count d'Anglars' carriage, gazing out through the window and up into the silent night sky. He was watching Orion rise higher. He was tired and stiff from his night of flight, but worse than any physical pain was the knowledge that he had spoiled his own plans and made a fool of himself before two-thirds of the upper crust of Paris. What had he gained from the past night?

Pierre le Noir...

He frowned. It was just possible that he had killed the man who might well have been chosen to murder Princess Victoria. That was something good, he thought, and well worth his pain and exhaustion.

Batten to the things that never change, Pippin, Joseph Young had said, *The stars, the moon, the sun, the sea, the earth itself...*

He closed his eyes and leaned back against the cushioned backrest of the carriage. "Oh Papa," he sighed. "Did you ever know times like this?"

The stars glittered beyond the carriage window, bright, silent and monumentally calm, in sublime contrast to the turmoil and chagrin in his heart.

He drew a deep breath and expelled it. You live and learn, and no matter how old or wise or strong you are, it's best to remember that you are never too old or wise or strong to be taken by surprise.

Someone had tried to kill him. No surprise, that: he had been expecting it. He had, after all, set the trap knowing that he would be the target for an assassination attempt. But, that to the side, he had resolved years before to give his life if necessary in the service of society, and he had not renounced that resolve.

But society had never stepped in to save his life before.

The carriage halted before the Rose d'Or. The postilion opened the door and lowered the step, and then stood aside. "Have a pleasant evening, Inspector!" he said.

Malet nodded to him and wished him the same, then drew a deep breath and turned toward the inn as the coach pulled away.

Someone had saved his life, he thought again. Who could have done it? Why had he done it? Could it have been a mistake?

He remembered the blow to the back of his knees just at the moment that the gun went off, while he had been standing wide open and exposed, gaping down at Paris like a bumpkin. That had been a deliberate knock-down, or Paul Malet had not spent his childhood in a prison learning all the dirty tricks used in a brawl!

Who had saved him, then? The body that had landed atop him and scrambled off had been small: a child? But who could it have been? Aside from his two godchildren, what child had he dealt with recently?

He frowned, remembering furious gray eyes, a mouth like a sewer, and a lithe little body twisting in his grip and swearing at him. The child who had been holding that horse. Suddenly an idea came to him: he was the stone-thrower.

His attention, inward and outward, was so captured by this thought, and he was still so wearied and humiliated by the events of the past night, that he didn't give his surroundings the sort of attention that he usually did. If he had, he might have seen a sudden shifting of shadows halfway down the street as a small, ragged child shrank back into a dark gateway and peered out at him.

Malet drew a deep breath, squared his shoulders, and went toward the kitchen door, still caught by his mood of half-awed speculation: ...The stone-thrower...?

CHAPTER FIFTY-ONE

Larouche Turns Informer

Larouche watched Monseigneur go toward the doorway of the inn. He came farther out onto the street and craned his neck as the kitchen door opened to spill golden light across the courtyard.

He pulled thoughtfully at his lower lip. So Monseigneur was alive...

LAROUCHE HAD THOUGHT he had saved Monseigneur once and for all. He had been horrified to learn, just before he left Dracquet's house, that Pierre le Noir was still unaccounted for. He had heard Dracquet say, "The finest killer in Europe! He'd better make sure of him—or I will make certain he regrets it!"

Larouche had flattened himself against the wall behind the door to the kitchen, horrified and vaguely sick. The chase was still on, then. Monseigneur was still in danger.

Larouche had left for the stable that was housing him at the moment, but though he had burrowed into fragrant, warm hay and listened to the horses in the stalls below him, he had not been able to sleep. He kept remembering the moment he had realized that Monseigneur's heart could ache, too, and he wished that he had gone to him as he had wanted to. Now he might be wounded, or even dead, and there was nothing Larouche could do to help him.

Dracquet was a murderer! Larouche had known that he was a liar and a crook, but murder was another matter entirely! To cap matters, he had tried to murder one of Larouche's particular people. Larouche would make him pay quite a reckoning for that!

But in the meantime he couldn't stop worrying about Monseigneur. In the end, he had tried to do as Père Louis had once told him: say a prayer and leave it with God. It had been very hard; he had cried himself to sleep.

He awoke the next morning with his mind made up. Dracquet must be made to pay dearly for his actions, and Larouche had an idea for a way of doing that, but first he had to find out if Monseigneur were alive...

HE HAD GONE TO THE Prefecture the next day. That would be the first place Monseigneur Inspector would go if he were unhurt or only slightly injured. He might not arrive until late in the day, Larouche knew, since cops sometimes had to talk to the Head Cop, or even the King, and he thought if someone tried to kill Monseigneur, then Malet, who was sitting in for the Head Cop, would want to know of it. But though Larouche remained there all day, he saw no sign of the man at all.

He had to know if Monseigneur was safe! He hesitated, wondering what to do, when he saw an officer of some seniority leaving the Prefecture, a pleasant-faced fellow. Larouche went up to the man and asked if an Inspector had been killed the night before, as he had heard.

The man had looked thoughtfully down at him while he motioned to a fiacre, but he had answered evenly enough. "No, son. We have had no deaths on the Force in the last day, thank God!" He had added, "And what do you know of it, my lad?"

"Nothing," Larouche had said. "I just heard some talk..."

The man had looked as though he wanted to ask a few more questions, but Larouche turned and scurried off, and the man had entered the fiacre and ridden off. Larouche, listening from a doorway, heard him command that he be taken to the place de la Bastille.

He had stepped back onto the street after the man left and stood gazing after him with his back to the Sainte Chapelle. No deaths, eh? That was good to hear, but it didn't rule out Monseigneur being badly wounded. Where would he go if he were hurt?

After some thought, Larouche went to the inn where he had first waylaid Monseigneur. He thought the man might live there. If not, he was certainly friends with the people who owned the place. He climbed a tree and watched the people come and go. He didn't see Monseigneur, but then he had not really expected to, since it was late. He planned to wait until it was dark, and then beg a handout and ask if they had anyone there who was sick.

Monseigneur's arrival in a carriage with a crested panel saved him from having to do that. He had watched Monseigneur alight. He had still seemed sad, and he was moving as though he were in pain, but his face had suddenly brightened, and he had smiled when the door to the inn had opened.

Larouche could see the dark-haired lady standing in the doorway and smiling back at him. As he watched, she went out to Monseigneur, spoke to him—he couldn't hear what she was saying—then kissed his cheek when he raised her hand to his lips. She tucked her hand into the crook of his arm, and they walked back inside the inn. She was smiling as Monseigneur turned and closed the door.

LAROUCHE DROPPED SILENTLY from his tree. So Monseigneur was safe and well. Very good. Now he could go after Dracquet.

Larouche had devoted a great deal of thought to Dracquet and Monseigneur.

There was a series of carvings on one of the churches that reminded him of the two of them. It showed Michael the Archangel and the Devil. In the first carving, St. Michael and the Devil were facing each other, towering over a tiny little figure who was, according to Père Louis, a man's soul. In the next scene they were fighting with their swords, while in the last one, St. Michael stood victorious with the soul in his arms and the Devil at his feet.

Larouche had witnessed the meeting of Monseigneur and Dracquet in the park, and that encounter had made him think of the carvings. It isn't necessary to exchange blows in order to fight. He had heard Monseigneur raise his voice and say clearly, *There is nothing you can say to induce me to go along with you in any venture, though I die for it tomorrow!*

Monseigneur had said that, and Dracquet had brought in the worst murderer in France and tried to take him at his word. Now it was time to put a weapon in Monseigneur's hand.

Dracquet had said, *I am leaving Paris tonight and I shall be away for several weeks.* And yet, he was still in Paris. He was being very hush-hush, and that, to Larouche's mind, indicated that he was about to do something that Monseigneur would probably want to stop.

Père Louis had often quoted, 'What I tell you in darkness, that speak ye in the light, and what you hear whispered, proclaim upon the rooftops.' Larouche was not sure what it meant to 'proclaim' something, but he suspected that it was similar to shouting. And he was going to proclaim a few things about Dracquet to Monseigneur that that stern, steely man would be very interested in hearing...

HE WENT BACK TO DRACQUET'S house that evening to beg a meal from the cook and spend some time gossiping with the servants.

Larouche could be quite charming when he put his mind to it. Within three hours he was filled with the cook's best pastry and some news regarding comings and goings that he thought would interest the Police very much.

"A MILOR' FROM ENGLAND, no less," said the cook. "And some important business under his hat, from what His Nibs is doing! Telling everyone he's out and keeping to the upper stories of the house, with all the windows closed! He's up to something, make no mistake!"

"A Milor'?" Larouche asked, filling his mouth with succulent lamb stew and washing it down with cider. "What's that?"

"A toff," explained the cook. "He's been here twice in as many weeks. Expensively dressed, looks like an aristocrat. English, I think—he speaks good French but with an accent like the English. Talking about some sort of princess who's coming to visit, though I have never heard her name. They're up to no good, and it makes me nervous. I have heard something about selling guns and something else about troops and some word like 'prescription', or some such! And they keep talking about 'the succession', too."

He looked suddenly tired and fearful. "I wish there was something I could do to stop it, but it would be worth my family's lives. Draccuet's a bad one to cross. I am sorry I ever took up with his household, but I didn't know..."

Larouche stuffed a piece of lamb into his mouth. "When's this Milor' coming back?" he asked as he chewed.

"I don't know," said the cook, who was chopping onions. "He doesn't tell me anything—not that I want him to! —but I was told to get a fine dinner together for Tuesday next! I have a shopping list, too, no less! The finest truffles, the best beef, wine from Grandière et Fils!"

Larouche nodded and wolfed down the rest of his stew, then consented to eat a small sugar-cake. He licked a line of milk from his upper lip afterward and treated the cook to his best smile. "Even if he's up to no good," he said, "You will do the bastard proud." He added mentally, *If Monseigneur doesn't stop him first!*

LAROUCHE WENT TO A stationer's shop the next morning, where he begged a sheet of scraped vellum, a split pen and some ink, and wrote out a note for the Police.

Père Louis had taught him his letters and basic writing skills, but he had not used them in almost a year. It took him two hours of concentrated effort, his nose two inches from the sheet, his tongue gripped firmly between his teeth, to compose a letter of only one page.

When he finished, he had a page of uneven writing, smeared where he had to lick off mistakes and rewrite them. It looked good to his eyes:

If the polise who are intressed in doins of draquett will come to his house on tusday next at seven oclok they will find a malor from angland and things that wil intress them such as he isent out of towne but is in his own home and has been for a long time and is doin things the polise wont like and want to stopp.

The servans tole me about this and sad that draqett has had a tof visiting him all sumer from angland, and he talks about a pirnces who is comin to france and what wil hapen when she gits hear. They talk about trops and a sukseshun and a perskripshun and they hope cops dont get wind of them.

Draquet is reel pist that the inspekter wassent kilt an renay benot and lenor was but he is puling in his goons for now becos the other thing is more impornt for now.

I am proclaming this to polise but I dont think the polise shuld lett draqet no thar comin, since he will becom scard and flee and wont be in town for reel and it wil all be for nothin.

I am a freind who wants nothin but the good of france and the bad of draquet. If their is antyhing els that is desared the polise can ask arond and I will anser.

A frend

He paused and added,
Ps I am glad they dint kil you

CHAPTER FIFTY-TWO

Larouche Discovers How Grownups Judge Books and Children

Whether or not Monseigneur would be interested in the note was a question that took a back seat to that of getting the note to him. Larouche discovered the hard way that grownups tend to judge books by their covers and people by their appearance. He was no one's idea of an aristocrat. He was also very young. No one wanted to speak to him.

He told the Officer of the Day that he had important information, and the man had merely cast a jaded eye over him and suggested that he think up a story that would fool someone and leave the old chestnuts to those who could give them the proper delivery.

His exchange with Larouche degenerated to a slanging-match, with Larouche having the upper hand in words of virulent foulness. The upshot was that two strapping constables had carried him bodily from the Prefecture and deposited him on the pavement outside. Once ejected from the Prefecture, he had a reaction that embarrassed him terribly: he sat before the building and cried.

Luck was with him. A plump, bright-eyed lady in a black bonnet with cherry-red ribbons, strolling along the boulevard du Palais with two little girls in tow and carrying a nicely capacious basket, caught sight of him.

"What's the matter, my lad?" she asked in a high, sweet voice.

"I need to talk to a cop about something urgent!" Larouche wailed as he wiped his nose on the back of his hand. "Those goons won't let me in!"

The lady chuckled and held out her hand. "We'll see about that," she said.

Larouche paused, doubtfully wiping his hand on the seat of his trousers, then laid his other hand in hers and followed her into the Prefecture.

He discovered then that she was the wife of one of the senior administrative officers, and something of a celebrity. She had come to drop the youngest girl off to visit with her godfather, who was an Inspector there. Her basket contained sweet pastries for the men, and there was an extra one for him, as well. She arranged for Larouche to speak with her husband before she left.

As she was preparing to leave, she took out a large, neatly wrapped package and said to the young constable who was escorting her, "Don't forget to give this to the Chief Inspector when Pauline leaves!"

The junior constable smiled and bowed. "He'd kill me if I did," he said. "Good afternoon, Madame! And thank you!"

She smiled at him and then leaned down to pat Larouche's cheek. "Speak with my husband," she said. "He will help you!" She was gone with another smile, taking the older of the two little girls with her.

Larouche was ushered to a chair, where he waited for a good five minutes before he found himself facing a plump, kindly, but stern-looking man who smiled down at him and asked his name.

He stared back up at the man and offered his note. "My name doesn't matter," he said. "This is for the big Inspector. The guy with the green eyes. He's after a certain man: well, here's some stuff for him. Just see he gets it!"

"I certainly shall," said the plump man. "And what of yourself, son? Are you hungry?"

"I already ate," said Larouche. "The lady gave me a bun." He added, "It was good!"

"They usually are," the man said with a smile. "But may I tell the Inspector you're waiting for him?"

Larouche fought down sudden panic and shook his head. What if Monseigneur knew it was he who had been throwing the stones? "It won't be necessary," he said gruffly. "He has the message, and it's all true! Just see he gets it." He paused and added, "Please."

"Would you like us to pay for a hackney back to your home?" the man asked.

Larouche bowed, as he had seen the cook do. "That won't be needful—I mean necessary," he said.

"As you wish," said the plump man as he offered his hand in the same way one man might offer it to another.

Larouche nodded and slid off his seat, then shook the man's hand, which was still proffered. "Thanks," he said.

"No," said the man. "We should thank you!"

"HE LEFT NO NAME?" MALET asked later. He was sitting at the Prefect's desk, looking down at the note with a blazing smile and then reviewing his notations beside it. Pauline Guillart was sitting on his lap and taking in the wonders of his repeating watch.

"Pauline, be careful with that!" gasped Guillart as she swung it back and forth on its chain. He met Malet's amused gaze and said, "It's a very fine watch!"

"Relax, my dear fellow," said Malet. "It's a piece of machinery. Did he leave a name?"

"Pauline, my love, give the watch back to your Uncle Malet," said Guillart. He waited until she had done so, and the watch was safely bestowed in 'Uncle Malet's' pocket and then said, "No, sir, he didn't leave a name. I didn't want to press him. He seemed a little nervous. Justine told me she found him sitting outside and crying."

Pauline wanted to cuddle; Malet settled her more comfortably against him and scanned the note. "He was probably crying from shame," he said. "With spelling and handwriting like this, I'd cry as well." He held the paper at arm's length, his smile dimming a little. "Good God! This is terrible! I don't understand children at all sometimes!"

"But you like me," Pauline said.

"I love you, Noisette," said Malet. "I just don't understand children once in a while."

"That's hardly surprising, considering that you're a bachelor," said Guillart. "I gave up trying years ago. If she's hurting you, my dear Malet, I will put her on my lap."

"No, not at all," said Malet. "I have encountered songbirds that are heavier than her."

"She also squirms, and you are wounded." Guillart pointed out.

Malet only smiled and shook his head.

"What's a bachelor?" asked Pauline, who was busy exploring Malet's waistcoat pockets and playing with his watch chain.

"Someone like your godfather," Guillart answered. He smiled to himself and added, "I think it was probably pure temper, sir. Children that age tend to throw tantrums if they don't get their way or think their dignity's been compromised. I gather he had a bit of a spat with Dominique right before Justine found him."

"Perignon?"

"Yes. The child had quite a mastery of vulgar words, from what he told me."

Malet grimaced. "That's right. Archet is out today."

"Sebastien says Archet's a piss-ant," said Pauline with a smile that would melt marble.

Malet threw Guillart a reproachful look. "Constable Archet is an officer of the Police," he said. "He's not a 'piss-ant', and you may tell your brother that with my compliments."

"Oh," said Pauline, who had found Malet's snuff-box. She opened it and took a piece of barley-sugar candy, then tugged at the watch chain again.

"This boy," Malet said, "How old did you say he is?"

"He looked between six and eight years," Guillart answered.

Malet stiffened. The stone-thrower? "Was he a street urchin?" he asked.

"What's that?" asked Pauline around the candy.

"Someone who doesn't have a mother and father to love him," Guillart answered. "Stop teasing your Uncle Malet now. Yes, he was a guttersnipe—"

"Guttersnipe..." said Pauline with a wide-eyed intentness that made Malet grin.

"It's the same as a 'snicklefritz,' " he told Pauline. He turned to Guillart. "He has quite a vocabulary," he said. "'Perscripshun': I wonder if he means proscriptions. And what on earth is a 'malor', do you suppose?" He scanned the note again and began to smile. "I think, my very dear Guillart, we're just about to nail Dracquet!"

"What do you mean?"

"I mean that my wishes have come true. Just think: a little over a week ago I was wishing for a way to get a 'mole' into Dracquet's household. And now, it seems, I have one! There was a child holding that bay horse for Dracquet, and this must be the child d'Arthez says he's seen from time to time. I am certain he's the one who saved my life two nights ago! See: he says, *ps I am glad they din't kil you*. There's too much here for it to be mere coincidence. It must be him! And he mentions a princess! It's falling into place, Guillart! It's falling into place!

'Tusday next'. Hm. That gives us almost a week."

"What do your snitches say?" asked Guillart.

Malet frowned. "He says precious little. I am beginning to wonder if I should pay Michaud another visit."

"You'd best be careful," said Guillart. "You don't want to scare him off."

Malet flung him a look such as Napoleon might have thrown at an officer of local militia who had proposed a flanking maneuver. "Is there anything else you think I should know?" he inquired.

Guillart favored him with a limpid gaze. "I can't think of anything else," he said.

"Thank you," said Malet. He began to chuckle. "Oh very well," he said after a moment. "I will send someone a little less alarming than myself. You, perhaps?"

"I'd be happy to go," said Guillart.

"Good. Do so as soon as you can—"

"Aren't we going to see the elephant?" asked Pauline. "You said you'd take me."

"Oh Lord!" said Malet.

"You don't have to," said Guillart. "There's always another day."

Malet set Pauline on her feet and shook his head. "No," he said. "I promised. Besides, my bodyguard would like to visit the Jardin des Plantes, I am certain. I have no idea why His Excellency assigned that gentle, helpless fellow to guard me: he's the one who needs a bodyguard! Gaping at the elephant will suit him better. Come along, Noisette."

He added, "Guillart, do you suppose I will have to buy him a dish of ices, too?"

CHAPTER FIFTY-THREE

Inspector Malet Commits a Theft

Malet turned and waved to his young bodyguard, sitting in the carriage from the Prefecture. "Good night," he said. "And thank you. I will see you in the morning."

He watched the carriage clatter off over the pavement and then turned toward the Rose d'Or filled with the pleasurable contemplation of the certainty of nailing Constant Dracquet and the equally enjoyable speculation on everything he would find when he had succeeded.

The note had tied Dracquet in with Benoit's and le Noir's attempt on Malet's life, but it also hinted at danger to a princess who would be coming to France. Princess Victoria, of course: and the word 'succession' had been used, as well.

Guns, troops, proscriptions—war! Dracquet had profited from war before, and he would try to do so again. Malet could arrest him for the attempted assassination—but why not keep that as a trump card in case he couldn't be caught on anything more dire?

Every pot bears the imprint of its potters' hands, however faint. Malet had learned dedication and duty at Joseph Young's knee; he owed his skill as a stalker to Cheat-Death. He was at once Cheat-Death's greatest triumph and most profound defeat.

Do as much damage as you can, boy, he had said to Malet, a lad of fifteen leaving Toulon prison. *Don't disable 'em with a pinprick when you can kill 'em with a stab to the heart! And remember: always let 'em know who it was destroyed 'em! When enough people have died screeching your name, the rest won't want to tangle with you.*

Now Malet bent to sniff one of Yvette's heavy-petaled, fragrant roses with a satisfied smile. Success was within his grasp. Now was the time to hold back, now the time to be patient. It would not do to spoil the hunt when he was so close to the kill. A simple success was not sufficient; successes could be reversed. He wanted a tour de force, and he was willing to wait for it.

This thought actually had him singing as he strolled into the stableyard of the Rose d'Or, and he hesitated only a moment before going into the stable to visit Saint-Légère's new chestnut stallion and feed some barley-sugar candies to Brutus, the big black gelding at the end of the aisle, who nickered to him whenever he passed.

He chatted pleasantly with Claude, who was busy oiling tack, and then turned to go into the inn by the kitchen entrance. Once inside, he was confronted by a table filled with pink-iced sugar cakes, obviously baked for a special occasion.

Sugar was expensive, and the prisons of France, never lavishly budgeted even in the best of times, seldom had occasion to use any of it. As a result, Malet, like many who grew up dependent on the largesse of the government, had a sweet tooth. The ranks of sugar cakes seemed numberless, and he thought that one would hardly be missed.

He came closer to the table, cast a critical eye over the sweets, and carefully selected the largest, pinkest cake, which he proceeded to eat with swiftness and economy.

"M. l'Inspecteur!" said a voice behind him. "You aren't very particular about what you eat, are you?"

Malet jumped. He turned and saw Yvette surveying him with a dishcloth in one hand and a martial glint in her eye.

Having been caught red-handed, he decided that it would be best to brazen out the situation. He chewed and said, carefully, "I certainly am particular. This one looked to be the best of the lot!"

"Shame on you! Those were for Louise Roissy's wedding! I just had enough to go around! Now look at it! I will have to bake another batch!"

"May I have one of them, too?"

Yvette, who accorded him the same exasperatedly affectionate treatment she gave her many brothers, stared into his eyes for the space of time it took to draw a deep breath, then clouted him with her dishrag. "Of all the insufferable— You are worse than any of my brothers!"

"But you will have some extra," Malet said, dodging another blow of the dishrag. "I will be saving you from having people fighting over the leftovers!" The dishrag caught him on the shoulder. "Now do stop it, Yvette, please! You will give me a concussion—and I wounded!"

She swatted him with the dishcloth once more, her face alight with laughter that pinkened her cheeks and made her blue eyes almost sapphire in the reflected warmth. "Get out of here, then, you rascal!" she exclaimed. "What a brat you must have been!"

The door thumped shut. Malet looked in the direction of the sound and suddenly smiled.

Inspector Plougastel stood in the doorway beside Elise with a piece of paper in his hand. He was staring from Malet to Yvette with the expression of one who does not know whether to laugh or hurry to the rescue. Elise was chuckling.

Malet's smile deepened. "Georges!" he said, "Come in! I see you have already met Madame de Clichy. Come meet the poor lady whom I have just robbed, all unwittingly! What can I do to make amends?"

Yvette took a closer look at the man who was approaching them. He was pleasant-looking and, fortunately, quite unalarming. She relaxed and smiled a little.

"Yvette Franchotte," said Malet, "Permit me to present to you Senior Inspector Georges-Corneille Plougastel of the 8th arrondissement. M. Plougastel is my second-in-command. Georges, Mlle. Franchotte is the second of the two landladies of this inn. I can vouch for the excellence of this establishment: you can see for yourself the charm of its two proprietresses."

Plougastel looked sharply at Malet, but he caught nothing of the brightly intent look that usually attended his friend's introductions. If anything, the man looked demure. He relaxed a little and smiled at Mlle. Franchotte before bowing over her hand. "I am very sorry to hear that you have wronged ladies of this quality, Chief Inspector, however unwittingly it may have been," he said. "Shall I plead in your behalf?"

"I will throw myself on their mercy," said Malet.

Elise, who had been watching them, looked up just in time to catch the bright, intent expression that he had missed.

But Plougastel had just straightened and was smiling at Malet. "I bring you a message that I think you will find very interesting."

"CONFIDE IN ME, CHIEF Inspector," said Elise later that evening. "What's the game?"

They were sitting in the large salon, in companionable silence, she with her embroidery, he reading *Le Journal des Debats* in front of a dancing fire. It was a mark of their growing comfort together that they often felt no need to speak.

Malet's rare smile flashed for a moment as he set down the paper. The message from Michaud had been most gratifying, bearing out, as it did, the information received from the child informant. It had also shed some light on the question of what a 'malor' was and brought Malet's mind back to Rosalie's suspicions concerning the Duke of Rochester. He had made a list of items to pursue in the case of Constant Dracquet and was now enjoying a very placid evening beside Elise.

The smile flashed and vanished, leaving him as soberly sedate as ever. "'Game'?" he asked.

"Don't play the innocent with me, M'Sieur," said Elise. "I saw that smile as you were introducing them. Who is that man?"

"I told you," said Malet, taking up the paper again. "He's my second-in-command." He eyed her annoyed expression and said, "There's no game, I promise. And as for Georges Plougastel, I consider him one of the finest men in Paris."

"Indeed?"

"Yes, indeed. Listen: he's forty years old and a widower, with three children. His wife was a lovely lady, and he made her happy while she was alive. I miss her still... She made me promise, as she was dying, to look after Georges. He's the soul of honor, a true gentleman—"

"He certainly appears so, but I don't fancy you as a matchmaker."

"I am not playing matchmaker!" Malet objected. "He came here—strictly in the line of business! —and happened to meet Yvette. I can hope, can't I? That's all I am doing."

"You shouldn't play with peoples' hearts," said Elise. "You could hurt someone!"

"Where's the harm in a casual introduction, for heaven's sake?" Malet asked. "How could anyone possibly be hurt by that? She could be very happy with him. It could be a good thing for both of them."

"Yvette was...hurt very badly once," said Elise.

"Raped, probably," Malet said, shaking out the paper and folding it again.

"What?" Elise demanded.

"I beg your pardon. I speak too bluntly at times, but it's obvious to me. She is terrified of men who carry weapons. That's why I never wear my sword around her, and I never let her see my pistols. I am certain she was at least cruelly abused, and probably she was raped. I think I know when it happened, too."

His expression was sad for a moment. It cleared, and he looked up at Elise again. "Don't worry, Madame de Clichy," he said. "I was born and raised in a prison, true: but I learned not to condemn victims simply because someone committed a crime against them. Yvette is a lady, no matter who raised a hand to her. I only wish I could have been there to stop it."

"Then you understand my concern. How would you like it if M. Plougastel took it into his head to start presenting you to eligible ladies—surely he, having experienced a happy marriage, would think that it would be perfect for you, and attempt a match!"

Malet's mouth tipped. "I don't think he could," he said.

"There are plenty of ladies to steal your heart," Elise said.

"Maybe I don't have a heart to steal," Malet said.

Elise looked intently at him and then smiled and reached over to take his hand. "Oh no, my dear friend," she said. "I don't believe that at all."

He looked down at their hands with a reserved smile. "Then perhaps my heart is no longer mine to give," he said. "And so all matchmaking is useless."

CHAPTER fifty-fOUR

The Provisional Prefect
Has Dealings with A Fiend

Larouche grinned and waved at the cook and went out the door. He walked jauntily along, whistling through his teeth. It was a splendid day, he had just eaten a good lunch, courtesy of Dracquet's cook, his whistling was going very well, and he had a loose tooth, just to the right of his two front teeth, that had reached that very satisfying stage where it can be manipulated with the tip of the tongue, to the disgust of passers-by. In addition to all these felicities, he had the added joy of knowing that he was about to put another nail in Dracquet's coffin by writing a third note to the police.

He had felt a twinge of guilt at one point, and it had been enough to make him consider calling a halt to his vendetta. No more. Dracquet, seeing him today, had ordered him from the premises in very rude terms.

'Misbegotten vagabond'!

The cook had sneaked him back in through the servants' entrance and fed him some delicious potato and leek soup as well as the remains of the past night's dessert.

The cook had given Larouche all the news, including that he had given his notice.

"There's too much afoot, and I don't like it," he had said. "I just got an offer from one of the rich folk in the faubourg St. Germain. He's eaten here, and he wants me to be under-chef. I have agreed to take the situation."

He had smiled at Larouche's troubled expression, rumpled his hair, and added, "It's not the end of the world, scamp. I will be at No. 12, rue De Varenne. You will just have to come and visit me, that's all."

Larouche had left, saddened. His mood hadn't lasted for long. He had stowed away on a luxurious carriage heading southeast. Through some skillful changes, he had managed to arrive in the 4th arrondissement in front of the classical temple that was the Bourse. North of it, part of the rabbit-warren of arcaded walkways, was the Passage des Panoramas. Now Larouche was knocking at the door of the stationer on that street.

"I will sweep your sidewalk for a sheet of paper and a pen and ink," he said to the man who opened the door.

The man laughed at him. "Our paper's expensive," he said.

Larouche shrugged. "Give me a used sheet."

"And so are our pens."

Larouche grinned up at him and wiggled his tooth with his tongue. "Then loan me one," he said.

"Done and done," said the man. "Here's the broom. And here—" he held up a washed sheet of parchment, "—is your payment when you're done. And in God's name, boy, stop fiddling with that tooth while you're here. You will scare away the customers!"

Larouche nodded and started sweeping.

TEN MINUTES LATER HE was sitting down at a desk in the back of the shop with his tongue sticking out of the corner of his mouth, the pen in his fist, and the sheet of parchment before him.

> *I have riten a masage befor. Draquett is haveing tofs com frome angland this tusday but he has changed the date to wen —*

He stopped. That didn't look right. There should be a 'D' there. He licked the word off and tried again:

> *wedenday —*

That looked bad, too. Père Louis had showed him how to write the word once. Why couldn't he remember it? He crossed it out and wrote again:

wendesday becos of winds. They are guttesicke and canot come til
then thogh the princes wil be their soon. Her name is victoria.

The tofs are named hamilton and courtenay, and cherwill—

Larouche was pleased with that information. He had had to go into
Dracquet's study and root through his papers. Dracquet had come in unexpectedly, and Larouche had dived into a cabinet and hidden for over an
hour. It had given him a chance to listen to the man as he gave orders to two
others concerning the affair of the mysterious 'toffs'.

The orders had been frighteningly explicit: travel by private coach to
Calais where His Majesty's private yacht lay at anchor. Once at Calais,
the man was to deliver a message to two seamen employed aboard the
yacht. The boat was due to sail in two weeks' time to Southampton, where
Princess Victoria and her mother, the Duchess of Kent, would board her
for the princess' journey to France.

The yacht would sail from Southampton to Le Havre, and during that
time the princess, who was known to be an adventurous soul, would be
killed in a mishap brought about by the criminal ineptitude of its crew.
An ill-secured boom, a frayed halyard, a yard coming loose from its
mast—whatever could be managed by the two assassins who had been
planted by Dracquet. Payment arrangements were covered in the letter.

The messenger was to meet three Englishmen at Calais and escort them
Paris, where they would be meeting with Dracquet on Wednesday rather
than Tuesday, since they didn't travel well.

Larouche had known that if he were found, Dracquet would have no
hesitation about ordering that he be put in a sack and pitched into the
Seine with a stone tied around his neck. Larouche valued his life, but he
lived with danger and death every day; he had emerged from the cabinet after Dracquet and the two men had left and went through the papers once
again. He had wanted to make sure the Englishmen's names were spelled
correctly.

The smell of scorching paper made him look toward the fire in the
grate. Three crumpled sheets of paper lay on the apron just before the fire.
The nearness of the flames was making them turn brown.

Larouche's hands were callused and tough. He had carefully scooted the crumpled pages toward him, opened them and scanned them. He couldn't make out some of the words written there, but the pages were drafts of instructions to the two assassins on the yacht.

Monseigneur would be very interested in them. Larouche folded them away inside the front of his shirt and then coolly took three other blank sheets of paper from Dracquet's store, crumpled them, and tossed them in the fire. If Dracquet wanted the sight of burnt paper to reassure him that no one had seen his scribbling, then Larouche would gladly give it to him.

— and ther is a milor named the duc of rochester stayin with dra-quet now.

Hes got perscripshuns listed and wepans to and they meen buysines about the pirnces. The duc wants to bee king.

I heerd they plan to sett the staje for a war and a murder wen I was in a closit an they dint no. Draquett is reel pist that lenor was kilt becos he was supost to be the mann who wil kill pirnces victoria an now thay got to make other plans.

I got masages riten by draquett thaht he was tryin to burn. They is with this an their ant a dull word in their. I took them from the far and they are jus a little chard.

Larouche thrust his tongue out the corner of his mouth and bit it.

The cook says —

He stopped. The less said about the cook the better. He spat on the paper and wiped away the words with his sleeve. The ink smeared and ran, and he had to blow on the paper to dry it.

Draquett still sas hes out of town but isnt so dont be fooled. Ther will be guns to and goons to figt if enything gos rong. So bring lots of cops and be redy to figt.

He considered, frowning, and then added:

The cook is not impercated.

I am a fiend

That written, he corked the bottle of ink, folded the still wet paper, and wrote 'Paris Perfecture' on the front. He thanked the shop-owner very politely, since you never knew when you might need a favor, and went out the door.

Monseigneur would be glad to get this.

CHAPTER Fifty-FIVE

Enter The British

What does he *mean*, the cook isn't imprecated?" Malet demanded. He was holding the note at arm's length and scowling at it. "Good God! It's wet!"

"He probably spat on it to erase something," said Guillart with a smile. "Mine do that. It makes for messy letters. And I think, my dear Inspector, he meant 'implicated'. Bear in mind that we're dealing with a little boy who hears big words and doesn't know how to spell them."

Malet took out his handkerchief, wrapped it around his fingers and lifted the letter again. He scanned it and then frowned at the back. "You will be interested to know, Guillart, that we're the 'Perfecture', and we are dealing with a fiend."

"He has all the earmarks of a little fiend," said Guillart. "A lively little lad, that one! I have enjoyed talking with him the times he's been in. He keeps saying, by the way, that this information is for 'the big Inspector with the greenish eyes.' "

Malet looked up from the note. "He seems a bright one, and he's certainly observant. And brave, if he's eavesdropped on Dracquet while hiding in a closet and then had the nerve to go through his papers and rescue these from the fire. I wonder if he knew the risk he was taking." He smoothed the crumpled pages and brushed at a burned spot. "Or how extremely valuable his assistance is to us," he added. "I wonder why he is doing this."

He stared off into space for a moment and then finally set the note aside. "Wednesday," he said. "Two days from now. I will inform His Excellency. In view of what is planned—and what we can prove—he will want to take a direct hand now. I'd best contact Lord Edwin at the British Embassy, as well. I will show him those three names: Hamilton, Cherwill and

Courtenay. It appears as though the boy went to some pains to get them right, too."

"Has Sir Robert Peel left yet?" asked Guillart.

"I am not sure," said Malet. "He was supposed to, but they were too insistent when they assured me of that, and I am not convinced... If he is in fact out of the country, I will send a dispatch to him in London. I suspect the name 'Rochester' will bring him back hotfoot."

He twitched forward a piece of paper and spoke as he wrote. "I will send this note round to His Excellency. I am taking a great deal upon myself in going to the embassy; he may wish to meet me there and participate in any discussion there may be." He took a stick of sealing wax, held it in the flame of the lamp, and quickly sealed the paper, then rang for an office boy.

"Give this to a messenger. Tell him it's urgent and must be delivered personally to His Excellency at once."

Guillart waited until the boy had left. "I will recopy all these pages for the archives," he said. "Do you want me to make you a copy, as well?'

"One that isn't wet? Need you ask? I will also need copies of his other notes. Please write them out for me while I finish this memorandum, then I am off to the British Embassy at once. Tell my bodyguard to meet me at the door."

LORD EDWIN BEAUCHAMPS, late a colonel of the Princess of Wales' Own Household Guard and a veteran of the Peninsular campaign and Waterloo, where he lost an arm, was delighted to receive Chief Inspector Malet, whom he had met when the Chief Inspector was escorting Sir Robert Peel through Paris.

There had been a brief unpleasantness with one of the clerks who had thought to amuse himself with a running commentary to his fellows on the subject of the French in general and their Police in particular while Malet awaited Lord Edwin. The young man had been appalled to hear his comments rebutted in idiomatically impressive, though provincially accented, English.

Lord Edwin had come in just then, but not too late to catch the end of the discourse, and his expression had been very grim as he escorted the Chief Inspector into his offices.

"I beg that you can find it in your heart to overlook the boorishness of the clerks here, my dear Chief Inspector," he said for the third time. They were seated in his luxuriously appointed sitting room and enjoying a glass of very fine Madeira.

Malet lifted his glass. "It's nothing, My Lord," he said. "Clerks are clerks." He sipped the Madeira and took a bite of the thin, sweet biscuit that had been brought in with it.

"They'll learn, all right," Lord Edwin said grimly.

Malet suppressed a smile. He set down the wine and took out Guillart's copy of the note. "I thought, My Lord, that you would be vitally interested in this," he said in English. "It is a tip we just received concerning some doings in which I am taking an interest. The parties involved may mean something to you."

Lord Edwin took the memorandum and the notes, scanned them quickly, and then looked up at Malet, all the color draining from his face. "Courtenay, Hamilton and Cherwill!" he said. "The Duke of Rochester! And the Heiress-Apparent-! My God! He wants to alter the succession! This is a nightmare!" He rang the bell beside his chair and directed that Sir Robert Peel be asked to wait upon them at once.

Malet smiled and sipped his wine.

PAUL MALET STROLLED past the Palais-Royal. He had dismissed his bodyguard over that young man's astonished protests, and was heading southeast toward the river, his hands clasped behind him, his head lowered.

It had been a very interesting evening. He had been right: the British had been vitally interested in the content of his informant's notes and had, in fact, been half-expecting the sort of situation they had outlined. That was the reason for Sir Robert's continued presence in Paris, a presence that Malet had suspected all along.

Count d'Anglars had arrived, looking as elegantly imperturbable as ever, and some urgent steps had been taken. A royal messenger had been sent posthaste to Calais with orders for the Police in Calais: keep *La Patriote* under constant surveillance, wait until Dracquet's message was delivered and his messenger safely away, and then place the entire crew under arrest. The messenger was to be followed discreetly until he met the three Englishmen, then allowed to leave Calais with his charges.

The 'tofs from England' appeared to be very big fish indeed, connected with His Grace of Rochester in an unsavory business that Peel had referred to as the 'Gloucester plot'. Malet, who knew a state secret when he encountered one, had not sought further information.

But also, he had been very conscious of his status as a bastard. Count d'Anglars dealt with his customary courtesy, but however kind the two Englishmen may have been to Malet, they were blue-bloods and he was not. While Lord Edwin and Sir Robert had been the soul of hospitality, Malet found himself in the awkward position of one who seeks to avoid a snub.

Once the arrangements with the Police had been made, he had excused himself and left Count d'Anglars deep in discussion with Beauchamps and Peel.

Malet was glad to be away from there. Steps were being taken to avert a catastrophe, and everyone had agreed that it would be best to wait until the night of the dinner, when Malet would arrest Dracquet and his guests. The British Embassy would support him when it came time to take the four Englishmen into custody in two days' time, and there would be no resultant international incident over the arrest of a Royal Duke. He could relax and stroll through twilight Paris, enjoying the glow of the street lamps and thinking of nothing in particular.

CHAPTER fifty-SIX

Monseigneur Meets His Own Ghost

Larouche waited patiently outside the British Embassy for Monseigneur to come out again. The night was relatively mild, and he had nothing better to do. He could not go back to Dracquet's house: it was too close to the time of the meeting. Larouche guessed accurately that Dracquet would be tightening security at the house until the meeting was over and whatever evil was being planned had been properly mapped out. It would be useless for Larouche to hope to get in there. He was his own man, or boy, and the evening's entertainment that appealed most to him was to follow Monseigneur.

He had caught the man as he came out of the Prefecture with his bodyguard and followed him to the rue St. Honoré, not wishing to annoy him, but merely to see where he went and what he did. The walk had been a leisurely one for Monseigneur.

Larouche had been waiting for the better part of an hour, but the night was mild, and he could relax and watch the strollers. The time had passed quickly.

The light in the courtyard seemed to shift slightly and he heard quiet voices speaking a language that he didn't understand. A moment later Monseigneur emerged through the gate and paused to look up and down the street. His gaze seemed to linger on the patch of shadows that hid Larouche, but he finally turned and spoke quietly to the lower-ranking man who accompanied him.

Larouche heard the other man say, "But sir-!"

Monseigneur's voice was still quiet, but the other man protested once more.

Then Larouche heard Monseigneur say, "You have heard my command

and you know my rank. Now do as you're told at once and stop wasting my time. Good night."

The other man clicked his heels, spun about, and stalked off in the other direction, past Larouche.

Larouche shrank back against the fence and watched as Monseigneur turned in the opposite direction and left. He waited until Monseigneur had gone half a block before going after him with soft footsteps.

Where were they heading tonight? The river? Larouche approved: the river was one of his favorite places.

He followed as quietly as he could, mimicking the man's strong, even walk, so different from the quick, scurrying gait of native Parisians.

They were following the rue de Rivoli, heading along beside the Tuileries gardens, now a soft blur of lamplight upon pale walkways. The vast, dark bulk of the Louvre lay before them on the right. Carriages clattered past, intent on the Comedie-Francaise, lying off to their left. Monseigneur threaded his way through the tangle with a magnificent heedlessness that Larouche, who was in considerably less danger of being run over, envied.

Monseigneur turned right at the rue du Louvre and followed it to the Pont des Arts, where he paused to look east toward the Île du Palais as it rose above the Seine like a great frigate at anchor. After gazing for a moment, he went to the middle of the bridge and leaned back against the railing with his arms folded behind him.

Larouche weighed matters, then drew his oversized cloth cap farther down over his eyes and went after him, whistling through his teeth.

Monseigneur didn't move, though Larouche knew that he was watching. The man seemed to be aware of everything that happened around him.

Well, there was no law against walking along a bridge and whistling, so Larouche walked along and whistled, his hands jammed in his pockets. When he came abreast of Monseigneur, he paused and looked the man over, aware that he was being surveyed in his turn.

"Well?" Monseigneur said. He hadn't moved.

Larouche hesitated. He could greet Monseigneur and introduce himself, and be the recipient, possibly, of a snub, or he could just stand quietly and enjoy the evening, as every citizen had the right to do.

He leaned against the railing beside Monseigneur and looked up past the double row of gilded buttons on the fine black cloth of the coat to the eyes that were fixed on him from beneath the brim of the hat. "Nice weather we have been having," he said.

Monseigneur's gaze seemed to intensify, then he nodded. "Yes," he said. "You're quite right. It's been a splendid day." His voice was softer than Larouche remembered, and he caught the touch of an accent that he hadn't noticed before, but then Monseigneur wasn't trying to shout over Larouche's curses now, either.

The man was standing quite passively, still relaxed against the railing, his head slightly lifted in the breeze that came along the river. He was showing no impatience, and he was even smiling a little.

Larouche thought it was somehow fitting that he, who had helped to provide the weapons for the fight, should be facing Monseigneur, who would be doing the fighting.

But now what to say?

Possibilities presented themselves.

You speak with an accent. Where do you come from? That would probably lead to a snub.

I am glad those assassins didn't kill you at Montmartre. No, Monseigneur might wish to bring him in for questioning.

Is my information useful to you? The same would go for that one: Monseigneur would want to question him.

Larouche paused and considered saying, *Would you like to come with me and eat some supper?* He wished he could say it, but he was afraid of what would happen if Monseigneur said he would. Where would they go from there?

None of them sounded right. It was no use. What could he say, after all, to this high-ranking cop? What could the two of them possibly have in common other than the fact that they lived in the same city?

He looked up from under the bill of the cap and said, "You got a sou you can spare, Mister?"

Monseigneur's expression altered from its calm smile. He seemed to be trying to pierce through the thick cloth cap and see the face beneath. His mouth twisted slightly, but he inclined his head, took out his billfold, opened it—and then closed it and put it back in the breast pocket of his waistcoat. He reached, instead, into his watch-pocket and took out a small leather change purse. He opened it, shook its contents into his hand, frowned down at the coins for a moment, and then selected two.

"Here," he said, offering them.

Larouche took them and nodded. "Thanks, Mister," he said.

Monseigneur returned the nod. "But, really, it is I who should thank you, son," he said softly.

Larouche put the coins in his pocket without looking at them and pushed away from the railing. "Well," he said, "So long, Mister. It's been nice talking to you."

"And to you, as well," said Monseigneur with the hint of a bow. He was using the formal mode of address such as he might use with another of his age and rank.

That made Larouche pause. He looked up at Monseigneur and saw that he had pulled off his right glove and was holding out his hand. Larouche hesitated, then shyly wiped his hand on the seat of his trousers and shook hands with Monseigneur.

He wished that he could say something else, but there was nothing else to say. Instead, he took his hat off and looked full into the man's eyes for a moment before he finally left. He headed south across the Pont des Arts toward the Institut de France.

"Please be careful, child," Monseigneur said quietly after him.

Larouche turned, but there was nothing to say, and so he merely bowed and then continued on his way. Monseigneur didn't move, but Larouche was aware of his gaze following him along the street.

He looked at the coins when he got to the Jardin du Luxembourg.

Monseigneur had given him two gold Napoleons.

PAUL MALET WATCHED the boy leave, frowning a little. He had been aware of the child following him from the British Embassy; he had stopped at the Pont des Arts partly because he wanted to see who he was and prove or disprove several theories that he had about the child's identity. He decided, seeing the boy, that he had been right: this was the mysterious young informant who had cracked the case for him.

It isn't often that one comes face to face with one's own ghost, but that child could have been him at seven, sharp-eyed, pinched with hunger, and a little furtive. It had taken courage for the boy to gather his information as he had. The gold was a sort of recognition of that courage as well as a salute from vanquished to victor, for Malet knew now that this boy was the stone-thrower. And the stone-thrower had saved his life.

He sighed and took off his hat. The child had wanted to say something: he wondered what it had been.

CHAPTER FIFTY-SEVEN

The Eve of the Hunt

Larouche's second note had been delivered on Monday. Malet acted on it immediately. Dracquet's movements were carefully watched; Malet personally reviewed all information and sent summaries on to Count d'Anglars.

The British Embassy confirmed its support of the actions of the French Police in this matter, and Sir Robert Peel asked to be kept advised of developments.

All the information received confirmed the report of the child informer. The meeting would take place on Wednesday, and the Police were ready to move in at a moment's notice.

In the midst of all this activity, to the surprise of all who were interested in the actions of the Police High Command, Count d'Anglars announced his plans for a formal dinner party on Wednesday night, and issued invitations to all the top police, army and government officials in Paris.

On Tuesday afternoon, Georges Plougastel brought over a final message from Michaud.

I have looked into the order placed by Monsieur and find that the originally projected delivery date is too soon. I will be unable to bring the goods to him until Wednesday, probably at some time early in the evening.

I understand that some assistance will be available: three men will be there to assist, if needed, but they would be best pleased if word does not get around concerning their availability, since it could lead to inquiries on the part of those not willing to pay them or avail themselves of their services.

If Monsieur is interested in the date given for delivery, he would be best advised to speak to the interested parties on Wednesday.

I am told that there will be a large number of people present with varying types of equipment, all skilled in their use. Monsieur would be wise to plan accordingly.

In addition, the matter at hand will be of extremely pressing urgency, concerning conflict as it will, so they may very well be displeased at any interruption, especially one man of foreign birth. Nevertheless, I have confirmed the date, and it will be Wednesday.

If Monsieur desires to purchase or arrange the delivery of any further goods, I must refer him to my various colleagues in Paris, with whom he is no doubt more familiar than I. I have made arrangements to return to the south, there to retire, and will be maintaining no ties with my former colleagues.

I thank Monsieur for his considerable kindness and beg leave to extend to him my deepest respect.

Joseph Michaud

MALET SET THE NOTE on the table before him and gazed unseeingly out the window onto the street. Michaud was being very circumspect, but it didn't take much imagination to understand what he was saying.

Everything was ready. If all went as it ought, Dracquet would soon be in custody, and Malet would be leaving the Rose d'Or. He would then be able to address Elise without any fear of offending or compromising her. He drew a deep breath and folded the message away.

He rose and paced across his rooms. He was restless. It always happened before he went into action, and this time was no different from the times in Spain or Russia or Germany. He had to get out of doors, to stand beneath the sky and feel the night wind against his face. His bodyguard had gone home, but what of it? Malet could take care of himself, and both Michaud and the child informer had reported that Dracquet had pulled in all his muscle. There was no fear of attack that night.

He swung his coat about his shoulders and hesitated over his hat. He shrugged. For once, he would not wear one. His sword was nearby, propped against the wall; he left it there and instead took his two pistols, made certain that they were loaded and primed, and then put them in the pockets of his coat with some extra cartridges and percussion caps.

He stepped out into the hallway. If he turned left, he would be heading toward the main stairway. A right turn brought him to the servants' stair, which took him down behind the kitchens and out by the stables. He descended the stairs and paused at the bottom to listen. He could hear Elise's chuckle, then Georges' light baritone responding.

He smiled to himself and went out the door.

The night sky opened above him, vast and still. If he stood quietly and waited he might hear, distant and clear, the music of the spheres.

The music of the spheres! He hadn't understood what that meant when he was a child. He had thought that the spheres-and by them he meant the stars-chimed as the wind blew across them, and sometimes he could hear the high, distant, sweet ringing that was less a sound than the echo of a longing in his own heart. It was still there, but the music faded if he listened too carefully.

He took a deep breath of the cool night air and stepped onto the street, where he hailed a passing fiacre and had the man drive him to the place de la Bastille. Along the way, he watched the blur of lighted windows moving past the windows of the cab.

Once at the place de la Bastille, he paid the cabby and then paused to gaze at the silhouette of his headquarters before following the boulevard Bourdon along the quiet, shining waters of the Port de Plaisance toward the Quai Henri IV.

He began to sing, exuberant snatches of tunes that suited the lift in his steps. What a magnificent night! What a splendid sky above him, still bright with the last traces of sunset! How beautiful the city was now, glowing with street lamps and the soft shine of lamplight through lace-curtained windows!

Passers-by smiled and greeted him, and he returned their salutations with a smile. All was well with him: the night was beautiful, those he loved were happy, he was in splendid health, and tomorrow held the prospect of an excellent hunt.

He was at the Pont de Sully now, with the Île St. Louis before him, the windows of its tall houses glowing in the night. He crossed to the island and strolled along the tree-lined Quai d'Anjou, looking up at the night sky through the lace-like tracery of branches. Now he was at the Quai de Bourbon, approaching the Pont Durosse, his favorite of the old stone Seine bridges.

The bridge linked the Quai de Bourbon with the right bank. He could stand there and survey the Hotel de Ville with its high, gabled roof, and, closer, enjoy the almost Romanesque outline of the church of St. Gervais. He could see the spire of the cathedral of Notre Dame and, beyond it, the broad-shouldered bulk of its towers. Now, silhouetted against the eastern sky and catching the last glow of sunset, they seemed to sparkle.

He leaned back against the railing with a happy sigh and looked up at the sky. Pegasus was galloping across the southwestern sky. Malet remembered the dreams he had had as a child, of swinging astride that great white back, seizing a handful of that billowing mane, and soaring with him across the stars.

Across from Pegasus, in the northeast, was Taurus the bull. Hercules was setting in the west, and Polaris shone to the north, clear and constant. They had been his companions, guards and comforters from the time he was a child. He smiled up at them and then let his eyes sweep across the glitter of the Milky Way. How distant they were, how serene and pure, the guardians of the sky, looking down on the tiny constellation that was Paris, making the concerns of her citizens seem so small and insignificant in comparison!

It was wonderfully restful to lean back and gaze up at them. But, Malet thought regretfully, he was not Hercules or Orion, and he did not ride Pegasus. He was one of the Guardians of Paris, and he had important work to do.

He surveyed the earthbound rat that was Constant Dracquet and began to smile again. Dracquet would be finished for good and all within the next twenty-four hours. He would menace no one ever again. He would never again be able to hire killers to snuff out the lives of those who opposed him. Never again would that impostor roam at liberty, usurping the name and house of Victor-Marie Dracquet, who had been Paul Malet's best friend before he was shot by a sniper while they were riding on patrol on an icy November day in Russia twenty-one years before.

He might, perhaps, have troubled himself a little over the question of how to arrest a member of the British royal family without causing an international uproar, but he didn't think of it. Every division of society has its own royalty, and while a man might fit into more than one division, his rank seldom does. Jacques Cheat-Death's 'Dauphin' viewed all criminals as a group regardless of their breeding. He did not believe in coddling crooks.

He turned his thoughts from criminals. All was well with the Prefecture for the time being, and all was most well with the 8th arrondissement.

And how was Paul Malet?

He cocked his head, and his smile gentled. Paul Malet was very well indeed. He loved a lady who, he was now convinced, cared for him as well. He would be able to speak openly to her once he left the Rose d'Or, and he was certain that, if he offered marriage, she would accept him. The anticipation was both painful and sweet, and the flutter of his heart whenever he thought of speaking with Elise made him feel humble and just a little foolish.

He looked up at Pegasus again, then swung his gaze east. Taurus was well above the horizon now, and Orion was not far behind. Orion was his favorite constellation: The Hunter, the Guardian. Whatever else could be said against Paul Malet, he thought, one had to admit that he was a superb hunter. Tomorrow should prove a successful chase. He inclined his head to Orion and lost himself in delicious speculation concerning the next day's probable outcome.

CHAPTER FIFTY-EIGHT

Elise Finds Inspector Malet Puzzling

Welcome back, M. Guardian Angel," said Elise some hours later when Malet returned to the Rose d'Or. She was sitting beside the fire, a screen pulled up to shield her face from the worst of the heat. She had been writing a letter earlier, and the result of that endeavor sat on the mantelpiece waiting to be posted to the Bois de Boulogne. Now she was engaged, prosaically, in darning stockings. She said, "You will be happy to know that all went most well!"

"That is very good to hear, Madame Noisette," said Malet with a bow. He turned away and took his two pistols from the pockets of his coat, unbuttoned and shed his topcoat, and laid it over a chair. "But what are you talking about?" he asked over his shoulder.

"I am not a filbert! And I am talking about Yvette and M. Plougastel!" said Elise, frowning at him over the sock she was darning. "They conversed very comfortably, and I thought it proper to leave them to chat alone while I occupied myself at the other end of the salon."

"Oh? Doing what?" Malet asked with a smile as he removed the percussion caps from his pistols and then placed the firearms on the mantelpiece while he reached for his pocket handkerchief. He paused as he caught sight of the letter and read the direction written on the cover.

Elise opened her eyes at him. She was still a little annoyed at being compared to a hazelnut. "I was sketching," she said.

"An artist, no less!" Malet said. He took out his handkerchief and wiped the smudges from the barrels of his guns as he returned the wide-eyed stare with one of his own.

Elise gave it up. "Hardly," she said. "I learned, as every properly brought up girl does."

Malet set the guns down. "What did you draw?" he asked. "Or do I embarrass you by asking?"

"Just a quick sketch of Yvette. It's in that portfolio there with some other sketches of my friends. "Some are good, and some are not—"

"Your friends?" Malet asked.

"No! The sketches! There's one of you in there."

"My poor Madame de Clichy!" Malet said on a laugh. "You must have been very bored! May I see them?"

Elise shrugged and blushed. "They aren't very good, and I just draw what comes to mind." She stopped as she saw the coat and the gloves laid across the chair and noticed the absence of a hat. Her eyes raised to Malet's hair, which was a little wind-blown. "Did you go out in this wind without a hat?" she demanded.

"I certainly did!" Malet answered. "I dislike hats: I always have! Let me see the drawings."

"You might catch cold," Elise said. She watched as Malet opened her portfolio and leafed through it. "If you hate hats, why do you usually wear them?" she added as an afterthought.

"Because going out without a hat would be like going out without trousers," Malet answered as he leafed through the drawings, addressing the second part of Elise's comments first. He paused and thought for a moment. "I beg pardon for my undress," he added with a wicked grin.

"At any rate, I have a very strong constitution," he said absently a moment later, without looking up. "I'd have died of consumption long ago without it—this is an excellent likeness!" He held up a sketch of Yvette holding a vase of roses and smiling shyly. "You did that tonight?" he said. "Impressive!"

He passed some smaller sketches of Alcide and Claude and smiled at Alcide's neckcloth. "You got the folds right," he said as he touched the knot in the cravat.

"It was kind of you to show him how to tie it," Elise said.

Malet shrugged. "He's a good lad," he said. He set those portraits aside. The next sketch was of Charles de Saint-Légère. It was dated from April of 1832. Elise had lingered over the lines of his mouth and eyes.

He seemed to be smiling.

Malet looked up at her after a moment, a slight frown in his eyes.

Elise kept darning. "Do you think it a good likeness?" she asked. "I tried to capture his smile..."

"It seems good," he said calmly, and set the drawing down. He paused and then added, "He's written you faithfully. Do you miss him, then? Shall I see about recalling him?"

She turned the stocking she was darning and replied with a chuckle, "No, don't try to act the matchmaker for me, M'sieur! Let us consider, instead, who we can marry you off to!"

Malet shrugged and eyed a drawing of Yves. "At my age?" he asked. "It's a hopeless cause! Good God, look at this! I didn't know you were fond of drawing gorillas! What a lifelike grimace! I can almost hear him grunting! Why didn't you draw him beating his chest?"

"Stop it! Yves isn't a gorilla, and you are never too old to marry. There is Madame Villefranche, for example. A lovely woman, and very well bred—"

"A poor match for a bastard, then. Who'd want to marry me? Have you no dance-hall girls or whores for me? We'd suit better."

"Nonsense!" said Elise. "Any lady would be happy to marry a man like you!"

Malet's eyes raised to her face. "Do you think so?" he asked, momentarily intent. He scanned Yves' portrait once more and then shuffled it into the pile.

"I do think so," Elise replied. "I thought so from the first, and even more now! And it is obvious that you are gently bred. One only need look at you to know."

"The Duc d'Ingres resembles a pimp," Malet said, "So much for appearances. And I was disowned."

"What is wrong with you?" Elise demanded. "Talking sense to you tonight is like trying to get a bell tone from a blancmange!"

Malet only smiled. He was eyeing a page of small drawings, mostly self-portraits she had done to test her colors.

Elise sighed, exasperated. "Well, there must have been a reason for them not acknowledging you," she said as she tied a knot in the thread and then snipped it. She set the mended stocking aside and took up another, shaking her head.

Malet shrugged. "The fact that my mother killed my father probably had some bearing on the matter," he said. "And they did offer to take me fully into the family almost eight years ago. I told them to go to hell."

Elise stared at him. "Why on earth did you do that?" she demanded.

"Because they made me very angry," Malet replied. His frown was back and quite formidable. It faded after a moment, to be replaced by a warm smile, which he directed at Elise. "The de Colberts of Beaumesnil can go and hang themselves for all of me, so let us forget them! And Madame Villefranche, as well!"

"Are you saying that she should go hang herself?" Elise demanded, falling into his mood. "Shame on you! She is a charming lady!"

Malet lifted Elise's drawing of himself and looked it over with his eyebrows raised. He was depicted beside a window, half-turned away. Elise had captured the slightly wistful expression that she had noticed several times. "I have no doubt," he said. "You know very well what I meant, Madame de Clichy."

"Well then, I will introduce you," Elise said, laughing across at him.

"No: I am too old."

"Pooh! How old are you?"

"Forty-seven next February," Malet replied. He was holding his portrait at arm's length and frowning at it.

"Nonsense! Making a match for you would be an easy task! There are plenty of women who'd welcome a chance to meet you!"

Malet snorted and got to his feet, still holding the sketches. "If you're trying to make me blush," he said, "I am sorry to inform you that it won't work. I lost the ability years ago! Let us agree to leave matchmaking aside. I was serious when I told you my heart was taken. Here are your drawings. They're very good."

"Thank you," she said. "Do you find your portrait a good likeness?"

"I can't say," Malet answered over his shoulder as he paced to the door and back. "I didn't recognize myself, if that's what you mean."

"How could you not recognize yourself?" Elise demanded. The drawing had been a labor of love: she had spent a great deal of time and care over it. "I thought it was an excellent likeness!"

He shrugged apologetically from beside the door. "I only see myself in the morning when I am an unshaven and blear-eyed oaf," he said. "I wouldn't recognize a portrait of myself if one were thrust in my face."

Elise stared at him as he turned and paced back toward her, trying to reconcile his usual bright-eyed matutinal presence with the thought of an unshaven, blear-eyed oaf. It took a moment for her to realize that he was teasing her.

She threw the mended stocking at him. "You!" she said. "M'sieur Mischief! Now what has put you in such a truly silly mood?"

He deftly caught the stocking and handed it to her. "I am not in a silly mood," he said. "I am sorry. I am just-happy."

Elise smiled at him. "Then I am glad to see it," she said. "You give yourself little time for happiness, that I have seen. Sit down: would you like some brandy?"

Malet perched on the edge of a chair. "If you please," he said.

Elise set her darning aside and rose. "Then I will join you in a glass," she said. "Wait: I will bring the brandy here." She whisked out the door before he could protest.

She returned to find him pacing again, up and down the room. She looked at him, puzzled by his mood, but smiling at him in spite of herself.

"Is everything all right?" she asked as she poured the drink and then filled a small glass for herself.

Malet took the glass from her and sat to sniff and then sip at it. "It couldn't be better," he said. "Everything is fine, in fact! By this time tomorrow, I hope, all will be most well!"

"I don't like the way that sounds. Is something about to happen?"

"You could say that.". The suddenly tigerish quality of his smile made Elise pause.

"Not—not with M. Dracquet!" she said, suddenly pale. "I don't trust the man! He is too dangerous!"

"Bah!" said Malet. "Of the two of us, he's the one in the most danger at this moment."

"But you could be killed!"

"So could he." Malet's eyes were sparkling now. He drained his glass, rose, and began pacing again. "He will be killed if all goes well!"

"What!"

"Executed is a better word. Tried and sentenced. I have everything very neatly laid out against him, and I will be springing the trap tomorrow. There's no escape for him, not unless he is very, very lucky, and I don't think he will be this time."

"But will you be lucky?" Elise asked.

Malet chuckled. "I always am," he said. He saw the concern in her eyes and softened. "Don't worry," he said more gently. "This is what I do best. I will be careful."

"See that you are. I don't want you to be hurt."

Malet stopped pacing. "We can't always have what we want," he said. "You know that. Never mind: I will be directing the arrest, and I don't like leaving things to chance."

"But it might be dangerous!" Elise said.

Malet shrugged. "Dangerous?" he said. "Paris is the most dangerous city I have ever seen, swarming with cutthroat criminals from all over the world! No one is safe!"

"They are safe when they're with you, my darling," Elise said under her breath.

Malet had not heard her. He went to the window, looked out, and went back to the fireplace to retrieve his pistols, then crossed to the chair to lift his coat and swing it round his shoulders again.

Elise watched him. "Now what are you doing?" she demanded.

"It's a splendid night," said Malet. "All stars and lamplight, with a fine wind blowing... It's the perfect night to be walking, and that's what I am going to do." He pulled on his gloves, set the pistols in the pockets of his coat, and started toward the door.

Elise watched him, and then suddenly stood. "Wait!" she said. "I will come with you!"

"It might be dangerous," Malet said, mimicking her voice.

"How dangerous can it be for me if I have my gun and you for an escort?" Elise asked. "I will be doing Paris a service at any rate, just to keep an eye on you!"

"To keep an eye on me?" Malet demanded.

"Yes, you!" Elise said. "Who knows what mischief you might get into? Wait until I get my cloak and bonnet: I know a place that serves the most marvelous pastries and jellies, and they have windows all along one wall, so you can watch the people passing on the street. That should calm you down. We'll have pastries and tea, then it's home for us both. You need your sleep, especially if you're going to be dealing with criminals again tomorrow. Does that sound all right?"

Malet nodded.

"Good. Wait here, then," she said.

She went to fetch her cloak and tell Yvette where she was going.

When she came back, Malet was looking at the letter again and reading its superscription. He set it down as she came into the room and smiled at her when he saw her, a warm smile full of affection.

"Now put this on," she said, offering the hat she had taken from his room just a minute before. "I don't want you to catch cold! Are you sure you don't want to meet Madame Villefranche? She'd be perfect for you!" Malet just looked at her as he opened the door.

She went through, chuckling, and took his arm. They walked together toward the river.

CHAPTER FIFTY-NINE

Past and Future:
Morning at The Rose d'Or

Elise awoke the next morning and lay for a few minutes gazing out her window at the bright sky. She had slept later than usual that morning. Once in a while Yvette, who usually woke her, took it into her head to let her sleep late. It generally served as a commentary on the hours Elise kept, and that is what it appeared to be this time.

Elise had not returned to the Rose d'Or until well after midnight. She had been too happy to notice the way the hours passed. They had gone to the restaurant, enjoyed the tea and the pastries, and sat there gazing out at the passers-by and talking of the past. She had told him of her disastrous marriage and her flight from Spain while he listened silently and poured more tea for her.

"I knew it had all become ugly, but I was too foolish to admit it," she said. "It was a nightmare, and I kept hoping that if I ignored it, I would somehow wake up and everything would be all right. Even after I left Raoul, I tried to pretend that it hadn't been as bad as it had. I don't know what I would have done if he had come back to Paris."

"You'd have been fine. No one, knowing you, would have believed his lies."

"Some people delight in lies more than in truth. Some would have found excuse to believe the lies." She smiled at him and laid her hand lightly atop his. "But never you, dearest. One can strike you like a bell, and you will always ring true."

She smiled into his eyes and then said, "Can we go walking? You have often spoken of the beautiful view of Paris from the Butte, and I am ashamed to admit that I have never been there. I'd like to see it with you."

"I POSITIONED THE GUNS, and I remember looking back up at the hill that towered above us and thinking how high it was. All through that day, from time to time, I would turn and see it, though I had little time even for that," Malet had said later. They had been standing at the butte of Montmartre, looking down at the city. He had been a little ahead of her, motioning southwest.

"Marshal Moncey supervised the construction of the fortifications there at Montmartre. Everyone was thinking, *This is the time—this wins or loses all!*

"The attacks started at first light, though we had heard their approach all through the night, and the firing as our guard fell back step by step.

"The enemy kept coming as we lost more and more men. I commanded that we load the guns with shrapnel, and rubble—anything we could fit in the barrels—trying to mow them down—and still they kept coming. I knew we were doomed."

He had turned back toward the city. "There was a lull in the fighting," he had said. "The word was that the Emperor was going to surrender. Some of my men said that if he was going to, then so would they. I took up a rifled musket, leveled it, and said that they would have to pass me first. I thought they might try, but just then the firing stopped. I posted some sentries, then commanded that everyone else turn in and get some rest. And then I climbed that hill and looked around."

He had fallen silent for a breath, and the austere lines of his face softened in a smile. "I had never before seen anything so beautiful," he had said after a pause. "I remember thinking how lovely Paris was, even in the midst of the smoke and slaughter. It was as though I were standing at the top of Heaven with a carpet of stars spread out before my feet. I vowed to return someday, somehow, if I survived the war."

He had raised his head and was gazing out over the city. Elise, smiling at him, could almost see him as he had been then. The image blurred in her mind and she saw him as he had been that night in the inn, when he was leaving to do battle with the monsters, and she had known that Paris would be safe.

There are moments that come unbidden to each of us, moments when we see and understand completely. Elise had gazed upon him with the sudden feeling that one piece of a vast puzzle had just been set in its proper place. She now understood clearly who he was and all that he meant to her. She realized that she had found in him the love that made her whole and healed the pain of the past forever. She knew that he would always be there for her, her valiant comrade, her treasured friend, closer to her heart and soul than any other could ever be.

She had turned toward him, filled with the joy of that discovery. She met his eyes and suddenly knew, without knowing how, that he loved her with every fiber of his being and without any tinge of selfishness. And, being a gentleman, he would say nothing to her until he could do so without compromising her.

She had never been given to introspection: she had long before judged herself below him in worth. The difference in their birth, which so troubled him, meant nothing to her. She had had bitter experience with society's obsession with breeding, and she had long ago recognized it for the folly that it was.

She had to speak. She had stretched out her hands to him. "Oh, my dear sir!" she said.

His expression had altered. He had taken her hands in his and smiled. "You must be tired," he had said. "I was selfish to keep you out so late, especially now that it's getting cold. I was so happy in your company, and I forgot the time. They say it's a sign of age. We'd best go back now."

Elise had nodded and taken his arm, feeling embraced and held, even though an observer would have seen nothing unusual in the sight of a gentleman escorting a lady along the street. They had descended the butte, but he paused when they were standing in the middle of one of the old, twisting streets and turned to face her.

"Madame," he had said, "If all goes well, I will be leaving the Rose d'Or soon after tomorrow—"

"I will miss you terribly," she said, tucking her other hand in his arm and holding him.

"And I you," said Malet. He continued with an odd note of shyness, "But I would like to return and—and speak with you on a matter that concerns you closely. Will you permit it?"

She smiled at him with all the warmth she felt within her. "Permit it?" she repeated. "I would welcome it!, I think I know what it is that you would discuss with me, and the subject would please me very much."

"Then I am content," he said. "Come, my dear. The night is growing chilly—"

"It is warm and soft as summer to me at this moment," she said, tightening her hold on his arm. "Can't we speak on that subject here and now? The stars are so beautiful, and we're alone together."

"It wouldn't be proper," he began.

"Oh, my dear!" she said on the echo of a chuckle. "What do we care for foolish propriety when we know ourselves blameless? Why can't I speak of what is in my heart toward you—"

"Hush!" he said, at once shaken and touched by her words. "You are saying too much, while I have said nothing yet—"

"Not with your lips," she said, laying her fingertips lightly against them. "I need only look into your eyes to read your heart. And it would take only a moment to frame what is in your heart with your lips. Can't we speak now?"

"My dear,,," he said, but he was smiling. He drew off his glove and then touched her cheek and tilted her face up to his.

Her eyes closed as his mouth came down upon hers, and then she was in his arms, returning each kiss with eager delight. To know how completely she loved him, and to realize that his love matched hers, was joy beyond belief.

They drew apart for a moment to smile and embrace more warmly.

She smiled up at him. "Say it," she said.

He tried to look away.

She turned his face back to hers. "How can it be wrong to voice what is in your heart for me to see?" she asked.

He would have turned away, but her hands framed his face and kept him before her. Even then, he could not meet her eyes. "You know our friendship has been a joy to me," he said.

"Am I only your friend, then, my darling?" she asked as he raised his hands to cover hers.

He did not answer her directly; she felt a light kiss against the sensitive spot where her throat joined her jaw.

She turned full into the kiss, capturing his lips and clasping him to her with all her strength.

They drew apart, shaken by the force of their response. She looked into his eyes and saw the passion that was in her own mirrored there. She ducked her face into his shoulder, suddenly shy, and a moment later his arms settled firmly around her and held her in an embrace that had nothing of passion and everything of tenderness.

"Let me take you home now," he said against her hair. "It is late, and the night is getting cold, and I have a criminal to catch tomorrow. We can wait until I can speak with you properly."

She circled him with her arms and smiled against the knot of his cravat. "Then speak to me soon," she said, tightening her embrace. "I have so much to say in return."

He smiled down at her and then gently set her from him and took her arm again.

Her mind had been alive with its new awareness; she formed the words he would say in her imagination and framed her own response. He was right: it could wait. Waiting would make it sweeter.

When they had returned to the Rose d'Or, she had surreptitiously tucked one of her handkerchiefs into the inside pocket of his coat, just for luck. He had the next day to live through, after all...

ELISE TURNED HER HEAD on her pillow and looked over at the porcelain clock that sat on the mantel of her bedroom. Nine o'clock.

She gasped and threw back the covers. Nine o'clock! And he was going to face Dracquet that day! She all but threw herself into her clothing, pinned up her hair, and hurried downstairs.

There was no sign of him.

"Where is the Chief Inspector?" she demanded of Marie. "Did he leave already?"

Marie had her arms full of empty glasses. She set them on a table and said, "Yes, Mam'selle, he left at seven, as he usually does."

Gone, then. And she hadn't had a chance to bid him farewell and God-speed. What if he were killed?

It didn't bear thinking of. Elise resolutely turned her thoughts aside. Now that she had found him, it was impossible that she would lose him. Fate would never be so cruel to her.

She went into the salon, where she had been darning stockings the night before. She had written an important letter the night before, a letter to Saint-Légère refusing him finally and telling him that she had found an-other to love. It must be posted at once.

But it wasn't in its place on the mantelpiece.

Elise frowned. "Marie, have you seen a letter I left on the mantel?" she called.

Marie came into the room. "The one addressed to M. de Saint-Légère?" she asked. "M. l'Inspecteur took it with him. He said he would send it in the official dispatch case for you. He said it would save expenses."

Elise quietly sat to gaze unseeingly before her. *Oh Paul!* she thought.

CHAPTER SIXTY

At the Prefecture:
The Hunter Sets His Snare

Yes, I know the carriage is waiting," said Malet. "We have plenty of time yet, and I am drinking my chocolate and eating my bread as fast as I can." He smiled at his bodyguard and dipped the end of the small loaf of bread that was serving him as supper into his cup of thick, hot chocolate, held it there while the bread soaked up the chocolate, and then took a bite. "Why don't you go out and tell them that I will be out directly?" he asked after he had finished chewing.

The shy young man whom Count d'Anglars had assigned to be Malet's bodyguard cast an awed eye over the ribbons and medals that brightened the dark blue and gold splendor of Malet's full dress uniform. He ducked his head when he saw that Malet had caught him gazing wide-eyed at the medal of a Commander of the Légion d'Honneur that hung at his throat on its red ribbon.

"We have told them already, M. l'Inspecteur," he said. "They are awaiting your convenience." He paused, weighing the extent of his courage, and added, "And may I tell the Chief Inspector that His Excellency's dinner party begins promptly at half past seven o'clock?"

Malet dipped the bread again and then looked up at his bodyguard. "By all means, my dear Constable," he said cordially as he raised the chocolate-soaked bread to his lips. "Tell me anything you wish!"

The young man was not unnaturally smitten to silence. Ever since he had first been assigned to serve as bodyguard to Chief Inspector Malet, he had had the uncomfortable, half-foolish feeling that he was about as effective a bodyguard for Malet as a rabbit might be for a tiger. He suspected, in fact, that Malet was more active guarding him than the other way around. He sat back in his chair with a sigh and began to twiddle his thumbs.

Malet eyed the busy thumbs and then nodded toward the corner of his desk. "Since your hands are so idle, son," he said, "You can occupy them by recopying these orders for tomorrow's distribution. One copy for each arrondissement—and see that you write them in your fairest hand."

"Yes, Monsieur," said the young man, and bent his head over the papers.

Malet hid a smile as he watched for a moment and then returned his attention to the chocolate and the bread. The chocolate was thick, rich and sweet, the bread was very fresh, with a heady smell of yeast to it. The dying sun lay in red stripes across the carpet; its warmth revived the rich scent of wool and beeswax.

Everything was set; it only remained to savor each moment as it came. He watched his bodyguard dip his pen in the ink and set it to the paper before him. He could hear the nib scratching lightly across the paper as he closed his eyes. All was in readiness; he could watch the night unfold.

The bread was finished; Malet tilted the last of the chocolate down his throat, set the cup down, and rose. "Now we're ready," he said as he took up his gold-braided, cocked hat and set it on his head.

The bodyguard came over with his evening cloak. Malet let the young man help him don the garment, his mind flashing over a thousand considerations. "The carriage is ready, is it not?" he asked.

The bodyguard stared at him, but he was learning. "Yes, Chief Inspector," he said. "I made inquiries."

"Excellent," said Malet. He took his pistols from the inside pocket of his cloak, cast an attentive eye over them, and then replaced them.

He led the way out of his office and to the boulevard du Palais entrance of the Prefecture, where the official carriage of the Prefect of Police awaited him. He cast a critically approving eye over the arms of France painted on the side panels, then surveyed the team of horses, who stood quietly in harness.

"We'll be driving to His Excellency's house at the place Francois Ier this evening, Gerard," said Malet. "You know the address."

'Gerard', who happened to be a full Inspector with the 6th arrondissement, gathered the reins and said with the proper degree of woodenness,

"Yes, Chief Inspector."

"Then let us leave at once," said Malet as he pulled on his gleaming white gloves. "We are disgracefully late."

"Yes, Chief Inspector," said 'Gerard'. He waited until Malet and his bodyguard were within the carriage, and the postilions were properly placed before whipping up the horses.

Inside the carriage, the bodyguard said, "Sir-?"

Malet, who was engaged in watching the grimy facade of the Hôtel Dieu hospital passing by on the right, said, "Hm?"

"I told you we were late! Didn't you hear me? I-I am sorry I didn't say it louder—"

"Oh, I am not hard of hearing," said Malet. "The time of my arrival at M. d'Anglars' dinner party is immaterial. There are other, more important matters afoot."

"Sir?"

"Never mind," said Malet. "You will understand shortly. Whatever happens, you are to continue to His Excellency's house and report to him. Do you understand me?"

The bodyguard nodded.

"Good," said Malet with a smile. "You will do." The clatter of the horses' hooves altered slightly as they crossed the Pont Notre Dame and turned left on the Quai des Gesvres. The carriage picked up speed.

They were approaching the place du Châtelet. Malet rapped smartly on the ceiling of the carriage. After a second, there was an answering knock from the roof.

"Very good," Malet said softly as he gathered himself and rose.

"I beg your pardon?" said the bodyguard.

Malet smiled at the young man and said, "Tell His Excellency that everything is going well."

"Sir?"

"I told you before: you will understand in two seconds," Malet said. He opened the carriage door and looked out.

"M. l'Inspecteur!" gasped the bodyguard as he leaned across Malet to slam the door shut. A sturdy shove to the breastbone forced him back against the upholstered seat.

"You worry too much," said Malet over his shoulder. He frowned out the open door and tensed, his hands braced against the frame of the carriage door. They had crossed the place du Châtelet, where the old prison had once stood, and were following the rue Saint Denis north toward the sharp left turn onto the rue de Rivoli. The juncture, usually congested at best, was crowded with carriages hurrying toward the Comedie-Francaise.

"I am leaving you," said Malet. "You will continue on to His Excellency's house and do the Force proud. I understand that there will be dancing, and M. le Comte has no doubt assigned you a charming lady for a dinner partner."

"But what—?"

"You will hear all about it tomorrow," Malet said.

"But you can't—"

"I certainly can," said Malet with a smile. "I am pulling rank right now. Don't worry: no one will blame you, even if I break my neck. Now good evening and have a good time!"

The carriage had been bowling along at a smart trot as Malet spoke; he stepped out the doorway just as they passed a tangle of dark carriages. The bodyguard threw himself forward as the door banged shut.

"Stop!" he shouted. He opened the door and peered down at the cobblestones that seemed to spin away beneath the wheels of the carriage. The sight made him desperately dizzy. He pulled the door shut and collapsed against the seat. He heard the coachman crack the whip over the horses' heads; their speed increased. He sank back against the seat with a groan.

LAROUCHE WATCHED THE carriage pull away from the Prefecture. He had no intention of being anywhere near Dracquet's house that night, but he had wanted to see Monseigneur set out for the kill. It had been worth the wait, he decided as the coach drew away.

He approved of the disguise; anyone shadowing Monseigneur would think that the man really was going to a party. Everything would be fine. He could go back to the stable where he was staying at the moment and sleep safe in the knowledge that Dracquet's days were numbered.

CHAPTER SIXTY-ONE

Rosalie Plessis' Diagram
Proves to Be of Some Use

Malet leveled his field-glasses at Dracquet's mansion. "The house is dark, and I have seen no movement for the past hour," he said. "We're ready to go in." The night was warm; he had doffed his gold-braided bicorne and evening cloak, but he still wore a Chief Inspector's full-dress uniform. The moon glinted upon the medals at his chest and flashed from the gold embroidery at his scarlet collar and cuffs.

He lowered the field glasses and checked his watch. "Eight-fifteen," he said. "They have had plenty of time to get their business well underway."

He turned to the National Guard Colonel standing beside him. "Your men have your orders: stop anyone who tries to pass your lines. Please take your position now."

"Very good, Inspector," answered the colonel, an old friend from Malet's army days. He snapped a jaunty salute and left.

Malet's smile was perfunctory. "As for you, Chief Constable: your men are clear on their orders?"

The Chief Constable standing to the other side of the Colonel said, "Yes, Inspector."

"Excellent," said Malet. He turned to the two Englishmen behind him. "Lord Edwin, Sir Robert—I have personally seen to the placement of your contingent. You and your men know the schedule and have seen the diagram of the house. I will do my best to ensure that his grace of Rochester isn't injured by my men. Now we are going in."

MALET RAISED THE HILT of his sword and rapped on the door. He could see the outline of the knocker gouged into the paint; the fixture had been removed. He moved farther into the shadows and nodded to the men who stood flattened to the walls on either side of the door. He waited until they had their pistols ready, and then rapped again.

Heavy footsteps approached the door. "What is it?" demanded a voice inside.

Malet smiled grimly. Dracquet was going to regret not having a peephole cut into the door. He said, "Delivery. Open up: I haven't got all night, and the wine'll spoil!"

There was silence for a moment while Malet eyed the door and debated the wisdom of trying to force it. His reflections were cut off as the doorknob rattled and the door swung inward to show a strapping fellow armed with a cudgel. He stood well inside the brightly lit room and squinted out into the shadows.

"We're expecting no deliveries," he growled. "We have already got our wine!"

"Then why did you send a note ordering two cases of my best sauterne?" Malet demanded. "Look at it! It's been jolted all through these streets and someone's going to pay for it here and now or I will speak to your master!"

"Get lost!" snapped the other as he stepped forward through the door. "No one wants-" his words were cut off as Malet seized his arm and, with a quick twist, sent the man staggering to the pavement.

The man started to rise; the cold point of Malet's sword at his throat stopped him. The two gendarmes leveled their pistols.

"One peep from you," Malet said grimly, "and I will ventilate your windpipe! Do you understand me?"

The man nodded. Malet withdrew his sword and signed for him to be handcuffed and led away.

No one in sight; he motioned for the squad of Sergents de Ville to follow him and stepped softly inside the house.

He glanced quickly around to get his bearings, remembering Rosalie's diagram. Dracquet and his guests were probably dining upstairs. He nodded to the men. "You: split up and go to the subordinate stairs on either side of the house." He saw that done, and then climbed the main staircase at the center of the house with his usual unhurried grace.

He paused to look right and left when he reached the top. He could hear faint sounds coming from the kitchen. The servants and bodyguards had probably been taken without any undue commotion, though from the clinking and conversation Malet could hear from the dining room, Dracquet was very confident of being undisturbed.

He could smell food ahead of him: beef in some sort of wine sauce, truffles, and a hint of garlic. He heard the clink of crystal and a rattle of silverware.

"To Princess Victoria!" cried a voice in poorly accented French.

The toast was repeated to a chiming of glasses, then another voice cried, "To the war!"

Dracquet's voice cried, "And God save the future King!"

Malet's smile thinned. Confident, indeed! But their overconfidence was his strength. His eyes narrowed as he moved softly down the hallway, his hand stilling the motion of his sword.

The voices were coming from behind a door just ahead of him. He set his hand on the knob, cracked the door, and looked inside. It was an elegant room with silk-covered walls, and fragile, gilded furniture from the reign of an earlier king. It appeared to serve as a sort of anteroom to the dining salon. Malet could see a pair of pocket doors dividing the two rooms.

The doors were slightly apart at the moment. Beyond them Malet could glimpse a table laden with silver platters and lit by branches of candles.

The talk was confident and treasonous, and well-oiled by the liberal application of wine. Malet stood and listened for a moment, then reached into his breast pocket and brought out his notebook and pencil. They were using some interesting phrases: the courts would be fascinated.

He quietly took notes for some minutes until he suddenly realized how much time had passed. He replaced the notebook and pencil, took out his pocket watch, and frowned at its enameled face. Eight minutes: what was keeping the rest of them? It appeared that he would have to find out. He turned and went back to the hallway.

The Chief Constable was waiting silently at the top of the stairs. "The goons in the kitchen are trussed and gagged, Chief Inspector," he whispered. "It took longer than we expected: there were more of them than we were told, but they won't give any trouble now."

"Excellent," said Malet. "You and your half of the squad will follow me into that room and stand behind the closest sliding door. Someone must go to the servants' stairs and tell the rest of the squad to stay where they are until I call for them. When I go into the room, I want you to send someone downstairs to bring in the back-up."

Someone in the dining salon cried, "Down with Louis-Philippe!" Malet and the Chief Constable exchanged suddenly grim glances.

"Go now," said Malet.

"Yes, Monsieur."

Malet nodded and went back into the anteroom, followed by the squad of gendarmes with their drawn swords in their hands. Lord Edwin came in with them.

Malet spared a nod for the man, but he kept his eyes fixed on the door opposite him. He could see the knob of the back door begin to turn.

Malet's eyes narrowed as Dracquet's voice raised.

"War!" cried Dracquet. "The most profitable business in the world!"

Half the gendarmes had spent some time in the armies or had lost loved ones. Malet saw some angry looks. He frowned and set his finger to his lips.

"War!" Dracquet's voice said again over the clink of glasses. "Let's drink to it! The finest money-making venture known to man! Think of it: the little ones can sweat and bleed and speak of high causes and noble sentiments, and it will be us who sit in comfort and watch our empires rise! What could be easier? Only one death—one plain little girl—and in the uproar that follows we, the masterminds, reap the profits!"

Another voice spoke in English. From the cadence of the words, the brandy had taken its toll. "In a little less than two weeks your king's yacht will sail to Southampton. My niece and my dear sister-in-law will embark, to their personal disaster..."

Lord Edwin started.

The English voice continued, "-You, Dracquet, will have a king as your friend, and all of us will be wealthier than we ever dreamed!"

Lord Edwin seized Malet's arm. "This is appalling!" he hissed in Malet's ear. "I am going in to face that viper at once!"

"Stay where you are!" Malet commanded.

Dracquet said, "Then let us drink to ourselves: the undisputed masters of Europe when the smoke from this war—"

"I insist!" said Beauchamps, starting toward the door.

Malet gripped him by the shoulders and hauled him back. "You will do nothing of the kind!" he hissed. "You will ruin everything if you rush in now! Be patient!"

Lord Edwin traded glares with Malet but finally nodded.

Malet took out his pistol and frowned down at it. One of the gendarmes, angrily shifting his feet, bungled his footing and struck a chair with his scabbard. The sound seemed as loud as a pistol shot.

"What was that!" gasped one of the men in English.

"Where was it coming from?" demanded another.

Malet shook his head at the gendarmes, tucked the pistol in his belt, behind his back, and moved toward the doors.

"It was coming from the hallway," said Dracquet.

"We are discovered!" said Rochester's voice.

"Don't be foolish, Your Grace," said Dracquet. "I am certain it is nothing of the kind. Drink your wine while I ring for Gaston."

"No!" said Rochester. "My bodyguard—"

Malet stepped through the door with a smile. He scanned the party assembled at the table and turned unerringly toward a tall, fair man with the protuberant blue eyes and the florid good looks of the house of Hanover. "I am afraid the man is indisposed at the moment, Your Grace," he said in English with the hint of a superbly contemptuous bow. "But perhaps I can be of some assistance."

CHAPTER SIXTY-TWO

Dracquet at Bay

The room was perfectly silent. Malet's words had driven all color from the Duke of Rochester's face. No one had seen the back door open to admit a squad of Sergents de Ville with a prisoner in their grip.

Dracquet's eyes flickered with momentary consternation before he slowly lowered his glass of wine. "I beg Your Grace to overlook the boorishness of this man," he said. "I shall send him about his business."

He turned to Malet and his voice was calm and contemptuous. "How dare you intrude in my house like this? Have the Police gone into housebreaking?" Each word was incisive and curt. He paused and added with an elegant sneer, "Or am I to take this as a sample of the manners you learned in that prison?"

Malet advanced to the table, his left hand behind his back. "Guy Matherne, alias Dragonard, alias Dracquard, alias Dracquet," he said as he took a folded document from his pocket with his right hand and laid it on the table, "I am placing you under arrest in the name of the king." He tapped the red seal on the document. "Here is the warrant, signed by His Majesty, himself. And your companions will be answering to King William of England. Will you come peacefully?"

Dracquet was thinking furiously, his eyes fixed on Malet. His hands lay on the tabletop. He started to shift in his seat. "This is absurd! On what charge do you arrest me?"

"You have been implicated in the attempted murder of a public official," said Malet with a smile. "Although," he added gently, "I could probably make a case for treason and sedition based on what I have just heard in the past few minutes."

Dracquet rose to his feet. "Preposterous!" he exclaimed. He lifted a little bell on the table and rang it.

"I believe your men are tied up at the moment," Malet said, bringing his left hand from behind his back. His pistol was leveled and steady.

Dracquet set the bell down and shoved his plate aside with a lightning-quick motion. His hand emerged holding a small pistol.

"Put down your gun," Malet said with a cold smile. "Even if you hit me, you know I will kill you before I die. Put it down. And your guests had best keep their hands where I can see them."

Dracquet lowered his weapon.

"Now sit down slowly and place your hands on the table."

Dracquet kept his eyes fixed on Malet's, but he obeyed.

Lord Edwin came through the pocket doors at that moment, followed by Sir Robert Peel. Both men looked straight at the Duke of Rochester.

"Good evening, Your Grace," said Peel.

The muzzle of Malet's gun lowered a fraction of an inch.

Dracquet hurled his pistol in Malet's face, whirled and flung open the doors of the cabinet behind him, revealing a narrow passageway set into the walls of the house. He dove into the passageway as the second squad of gendarmes burst into the room with their pistols ready.

"Handcuffs on all of them!" Malet snapped over his shoulder as he rushed to the passageway. The roar of a pistol behind him split the silence, but he had no time to stop. He could hear footsteps moving swiftly away from him. There was no room to fight; the passageway had been designed purely for flight. Malet hurried after the footsteps, moving sideways. He could feel coarse brick on one side and smooth wall on the other; the escape route, then, was probably relatively new, most likely an addition made at Dracquet's direction. From what he remembered of the house, they were going toward the servants' stairs. This probably opened on the landing —

He heard a door open and softly close just ahead of him as he framed this thought. The sound was followed by the snick of a lock and then the thump of a triumphant fist against the door.

Malet reached the door a moment later. His hand closed about the knob and turned. Nothing. He was locked in the passageway.

MALET BEGAN TO SMILE. So Dracquet thought he had him caged, did he? That remained to be seen.

He felt his way along the wall until he reached the outline of the door. A splinter of light had forced its way through the edges of the door. It was enough to permit Malet to get a good look at the lock. It was a double lock, but Dracquet had only set the spring bolt. It was easily broken and even more easily forced. Ten seconds' work with his penknife sprang the bolt, and the door opened quietly outward.

Malet smiled as he silently pushed the door nearly closed—his men might be following him, after all—and stepped softly onto the landing of the servants' stair. No, Dracquet hadn't troubled to read that expensive dossier he had assembled. If he had, he would have jammed a chair up against the door instead of wasting his time with the lock.

It only remained to find the man, but that shouldn't be hard. After a split second of concentrated thought, Malet ran up to the next floor and went down the hallway toward the front of the house, where the library was.

The frantic, partially hushed rattle of paper coming from a room down the hall proved him correct. He abandoned all caution and sprinted toward the sound. He set his hand on the doorknob and turned, but the heavy mahogany panel remained unmoved.

Malet swore and shook the handle. No time to pick the lock now. He set the left barrel of his pistol against the lock and pulled the left trigger.

The door shuddered.

Malet could hear feet on the stairs two floors below. "This way!" he shouted.

The sounds in the next room became louder, more urgent.

Malet cocked the right hammer of his pistol, set the barrel against the lock, and fired again. The door boomed inward and crashed against the wall to show the interior of a study, whose book-lined walls glowed with the ruddy light of a leaping fire.

Dracquet was crouched before the fire, setting piles of paper on the flames. He looked up and smiled as Malet came in. "You were long in coming," he said as he riffled through another pile of papers and set them, too, on the flames, and then rose.

The edges of the piles were beginning to blacken.

Malet stepped forward.

Dracquet lifted a poker. "No closer," he said. "I prefer transportation to execution. We'll just let these burn."

"No we won't," Malet said, moving closer.

Dracquet raised the poker like a sword. "I heard two shots," he said, casting a quick, sideways glance at the papers. "You carry a two-barreled pistol by all reports. You haven't had time to reload, so your pistol is useless. And I have a theory they didn't teach you swordplay in prison."

"They didn't," Malet said as he stepped forward. His sword was in its sheath.

Dracquet's smile intensified as he closed with Malet, the heavy brass poker raised over his head for the killing stroke.

Malet took another step forward. "Drop it," he said. His eyes never left Dracquet's face.

Dracquet's fingers tensed on the grip of the poker. "Stand back!" he snarled as the poker reached the zenith of its arc and swung downward.

Malet stepped under the swing and blocked Dracquet's arm with his left wrist as his right fist connected with the point of the man's chin in a powerful overhand that snapped Dracquet's head violently sideways. The poker flew from Dracquet's hand, glanced from Malet's gold bullion epaulet and clattered to the hearth. A left hook to the stomach a split second later laid Dracquet flat on the floor and gasping for breath.

Malet took advantage of the respite to drop a Chinese rug over the fire.

"I did learn swordplay in Marseilles when I went into the Police, however," he said as he lifted the rug, surveyed the smoldering papers, and slid them from the flames to the hearth apron with the discarded poker. "No, don't move or I will deck you again with the best will in the world! 'One plain little girl', indeed! And the next time you try to burn evidence—though you won't live so long, I promise you! —I suggest you crumple the papers first. Stacks don't burn well, and there's enough here, from what I can see, to earn you an appointment with the guillotine."

CHAPTER SIXTY-THREE

Ravelings from The Spider's Web

Dracquet, his co-conspirators and his household staff, were taken in irons to the Palais de Justice, where they were questioned at some length and then consigned to the prison of the Conciergerie.

The case against the conspirators was very clear: Princess Victoria would set sail for France aboard Louis-Philippe's private yacht and would die under very suspicious circumstances. The Englishmen, under the direction of the Duke of Rochester, had arranged for inflammatory information to be sent throughout England showing that the mishap had been caused by connivance between the House of Orleans and the Duke of Cumberland. One of the documents that Dracquet had tried to throw in the fire had detailed four possible avenues of disseminating this material and listed the 'proof' that could be produced to incriminate Cumberland and Louis-Philippe.

The French aspect of the conspiracy dealt with various munitions manufacturers and the avenues through which Dracquet would secure their cooperation. Suppliers, schedules—all had been set forth in theory under a war date of December 29, 1834. Various threads tying in with Bonapartist interests had been included, as well.

The gunshot that Malet had head as he left the dining room had been The Duke of Rochester's suicide. His body, packed in ice, had been coffined and was being returned to England. The French authorities had replaced his name in the official reports with the notation 'R_____'. Word had come from above that the sooner Rochester's involvement was forgotten the better.

"Will Princess Victoria come to Paris now?" Malet asked.

d'Anglars hesitated before he answered. "I believe not," he said. "The death of one so close to the throne will send the entire house of Hanover into mourning, and it would be most improper for Her Highness to travel at all."

"They are allowing him to quit with honor," Malet said. "While Dracquet and the others will be guillotined."

The disapproval in his voice made d'Anglars look up from a frowning study of his hands. "You know, as do I, that death extinguishes pursuit under the law, at least in this world." He added softly, "You are a very just man: admit that justice is being done in its own fashion, if not in this world, then in the next."

But Malet did not address the appeal. He said, "I am sorry to hear that the Princess won't be visiting. She would have loved Paris at Christmastide."

d'Anglars smiled, but he merely said, "I have had some part in reviewing the other documents retrieved from Dracquet's house. The murder of de Grandpré is covered there, and several assassinations that had puzzled the Police from several outlying prefectures. Smuggling, extortion—the man kept very precise records. Very foolish of him, I think."

"And Guerin: any news of his involvement?" asked Malet.

d'Anglars looked thoughtful. "So far, no. Nothing pertaining to him personally has been found."

Malet nodded.

"Shall I inform you if anything is discovered?"

Malet drew a deep breath and then released it. "No," he said. "I will learn along with everyone else if anything comes to light. I am content with that. I don't wish to gloat over anyone's downfall, least of all his. He was a fine officer. I hope he isn't implicated."

"So be it," said d'Anglars. He looked Malet over and added, "As for you, my dear sir, you are obviously exhausted. You have given very generous credit to your child informer and the honest young inspector who first brought this matter to your attention, but I do not for a moment forget that it was your unfailing diligence and intuition that made this triumph possible. I suggest that you clear your desk at the Prefecture, and then take a well-earned rest."

MALET WAS ONLY TOO happy to obey Count d'Anglars. He took time to 'spring' Dracquet's cook, whom the stone-thrower had cleared of any involvement, and then went to his home in the Marais, where he bathed and changed his clothing. He went back to the Prefecture to take care of one or two items before going to the Rose d'Or.

The coup had taken its toll. Over thirty-six hours had passed since Malet had slept. He ached, and what he needed, he knew, was a leisurely cup of coffee well-laced with brandy, and then a good night's sleep. There would be time for that shortly.

Although d'Anglars had offered the use of his carriage, Malet decided to walk to the Prefecture. He had a lot to consider.

Sergeant Guillart was awaiting him at the door of the Prefecture. "Congratulations," he said. "You're a hero."

Malet shook his head. "I acted on tips given by an honest man and a courageous little boy," he said. "You should congratulate them, not me." He paused and added, "And if that little boy ever comes by, find out his name, would you? And where he lives. I... would like to know."

Guillart snorted, but he made no other comment. "Are you going back to the Rose d'Or?" he asked.

"As soon as I go over a few things, yes," Malet said.

Guillart opened the top drawer of his desk and took out a letter. "Then would you oblige me by carrying this to Madame de Clichy?" he asked.

Malet looked at the handwriting on the cover and recognized it as Inspector de Saint-Légère's. He took it almost gently and gazed at the inscription on the front, noticing the faintly foreign look of the handwriting.

Guillart eyed Malet's expression and said, "Are you all right, Inspector?"

"I am fine. I will be the better for a good rest—as would you, my dear Guillart. Go home. And send my love to your good lady—and the children." He frowned at the letter. "Guillart," he said softly, "Did that letter to the Bois de Boulogne go out with the dispatches as I had requested the day I arrested Dracquet?"

"It did," Guillart answered. "I saw to it myself. It went out in the first packet of messages." Malet nodded.

"She sent to inquire urgently after you several times," Guillart said.

"I see," said Malet, but he did not appear to be truly listening.

Guillart smiled and gathered his papers. "It's been a long month," he said. "We have all of us have earned a rest."

"That we have," Malet said. He was still frowning at Saint-Légère's letter.

CHARLES DE SAINT-LÉGÈRE! For all that Malet had been bringing his letters to the Rose d'Or, he had all but forgotten about the man. Now all his virtues rose up in Malet's memory, vivid and strong. Young, well-bred, at ease wherever he went! The words repeated themselves in Malet's mind during his ride to the Rose d'Or with the letter burning in his breast pocket. He had formed such a sincere respect for the man, it was hard to think of him as a rival. But there he was.

The man was young and open-hearted. Malet was older, and wiser far beyond his years, with the control born of years of strife. He could make Saint-Légère look like a fool if he wished. Or, since he was the Provisional Prefect, he could arrange the man's exile to a far prefecture. Why, the Prefect of Puy de Dome, headquartered in Clermont, to the south, owed him a considerable favor, and he would be more than happy to repay it by burying an obscure Junior Inspector. Nothing could be easier.

Malet's heart rebelled even as he toyed with the thought. He remembered how Saint-Légère had stood before him and detailed his constructive demotion at Guerin's hands for his refusal to accept a bribe. To do such a thing to anyone would be a trick worthy of Constant Dracquet.

And there was, as well, the possibility that Elise loved Charles de Saint-Légère. He had seen the letter she had written him sitting openly on the mantel. What had been in the letter? In hurting the man, Malet might well hurt the lady, and that was unthinkable. But did she love him?

He thought back to their embrace along that twisting street near the Butte. With the memory of her alive and passionate in his arms, her lips against his, the words she had spoken, he could have no doubt of her feelings for him. Could he?

None at all. Malet released his breath in a long sigh and sat back.

None at all, unless —

Suddenly his certainty crumbled. Out of sight, out of mind—wasn't that the old adage? What if she really loved Saint-Légère? What if she had only forgotten her feelings for the man? It was far—fetched, but it was a possibility, and it had to be faced. Malet could not win her by a trick.

What should he do then?

He put his hand up to the letter. The possibility of throwing it out the window occurred to him, but he dismissed the thought. Even if the act itself were not despicable, Saint-Légère would be writing again. Was Malet to intercept each letter?

There was, after all, only one thing to do.

ELISE WAS SITTING QUIETLY in the salon as he came in. She looked up and saw him, and her entire face seemed suddenly to glow. She abandoned all pretense of decorum and hurried forward to take his hands, laughing and crying at once while Yvette looked on with a wide, relieved smile.

"Inspector!" she said, "I was so worried! You are all right, then? No one would tell me anything about you! Tell me you aren't hurt!" She took his face between her hands and scanned him before she kissed his cheek.

"They were under orders," he said. "I am sorry. I didn't think you would worry—"

"Not worry!" she repeated, holding him at arm's length. "Darling! How could you say that? Let me look at you! Why, you are exhausted! Are you hurt?"

"Not at all," he answered with a smile. "To all intents and purposes Dracquet is gone. He will insult you no more."

"And menace you no more," Elise said. She collected herself and released him. "You need sleep," she said. "Look at you: you are obviously worn out! Come sit down. Have you eaten?"

"I don't remember," Malet said. He seemed somehow detached, as though he were speaking to her from a distance and observing her reaction.

"I will get you some food," said Yvette.

"Thank you, Yvette," said Elise. "Sit down, sir, and stop looking at me like that. You really are tired, I see. Tell me how it went."

Malet slowly reached into the breast of his coat and took out the letter. "This came for you," he said as he offered it to her.

She took it, looked at it, and set it aside. "What is the matter with you?" she demanded. "I ask if you are hurt and you say no and give me letters, and then stare at me! Answer me! Are you hurt at all?"

He drew a slow breath and smiled, but the smile still had that distant quality that had troubled her. "No, Madame," he said. "I wasn't wounded. Read the letter." His hand rose to lightly touch her cheek.

Elise looked at the letter as she covered his hand with her own and turned her face slightly to drop a kiss on his palm. The letter was from Saint-Légère.

"Aren't you going to open it?" he asked.

She frowned at him and would have spoken, but Yvette came back at that moment with a bowl of stew and some fresh bread.

"There!" said Yvette. "Eat it all now. Alcide is bringing some wine for you, as well."

Malet nodded and tucked into the stew.

Elise opened the letter and read it. It was a response to the letter she had written the night she had gone to Montmartre with Malet. The answer was what she had expected. Saint-Légère had always been, and would always be, a perfect gentleman. She folded the letter again with a smile and looked up to find Malet watching her.

He looked down at his stew the moment she met his gaze, and finished it easily enough, but when he had finished, he rose, checked his watch and said, "I must return to the Prefecture, just for a moment. I have remembered something I must do before morning, and it is a matter of some urgency."

CHAPTER SIXTY-FOUR

Calling the Traveler Home

Malet looked up at the Prefecture, drew a deep breath, and crossed the inner courtyard to the door. The Officer of the Day was Camille Vacherin, a younger constable with a smiling face and the graceful, easy manners of an aristocrat.

Vacherin raised his head as Malet entered the double doors. His expression's habitual warmth broadened into a smile as he recognized Malet, but he dipped his pen into the pot of ink before him and said formally, "Good evening, Chief Inspector. May I see your card?"

Malet took the card from his waistcoat pocket, waited while it was duly examined, and then signed the logbook. He pocketed the card and then doffed his hat.

"It's late, Monsieur," said Constable Vacherin. "If you haven't dined yet, there's coffee here. May I fetch you a cup?"

Malet shook his head. "No," he said. "I won't have time to drink it. I have a message to write up; it must go out with the evening's dispatches to the Bois de Boulogne."

"Just as well you came, then," said Vacherin. "The courier came early. I will ask him to wait for you."

Malet thanked him and went back to the Prefect's offices. He accepted the Chamberlain's escort with a smile, declined another offer of coffee and directed Clerel to close the door behind him.

He looked around the room and then went to the Prefect's desk and sat. A gold—tipped pen of carved agate lay before the crystal inkstand. The drawers were well stocked with heavy paper bearing the crest of the French Police, and a lump of sealing wax.

He set the wax in the desk—top crucible, lit the lamp beneath it, and then centered a sheet of paper on the desk. He examined the point of the pen, flicked at a speck of dried ink, and then uncapped the inkwell and dipped the pen in the ink.

And then he paused, thinking once more of Elise. She had been so warm and vibrant in his arms that night. And yet she had written to Saint-Légère. It was possible that, faced with Saint-Légère, she might choose against him, and she would be lost to him forever.

In Paul Malet's world, a gentleman renounced a lady's friendship when she married. He risked jeopardizing the happiness of her marriage if he did not. He had no conscious thought of renunciation or sacrifice. He only knew that he would willingly do all that lay within his power to make her happy, even though the price might be his own happiness.

The ink had dried on the pen; he reached into the breast of his waistcoat and took out his handkerchief to wipe the tip of the pen. A square of daintily embroidered lawn and lace fell out. Elise's handkerchief, which he had found in his coat pocket at some point during the past night. He had forgotten.

He smoothed the delicate fabric over the blotter and gazed down at it. It smelled of verbena, Elise's perfume. He raised it to his lips with a smile, and in his mind his lips were touching hers.

He had grown to love her so quietly, so gently, and he had been too concerned with chasing criminals and observing the proprieties to plead his love for her. And yet, he thought with an oddly humble sense of wonder, she had come to love him in spite of everything. For, after all, it was she who had spoken first.

He folded the handkerchief, his fingertips gently smoothing the petal of an embroidered rose as though he were touching her cheek, as he had done just that night.

He dipped the pen once more, drew the sheet of paper forward, and wrote:

Paris

17 October, 1834

Bois de Boulogne Constabulary

Mathieu Ronsard, Commandant

M. Ronsard,

Circumstances in Paris require that Inspector Charles de Saint-Légère's return to his own arrondissement no later than Tuesday, 22 October, 1834.

Kindly make the necessary arrangements at once.

Paul V. Malet

Provisional Prefect of Police

He carefully blotted the note, scanned it, then folded it into a neat packet. He lifted the crucible, poured the wax along the seam, waited for it to cool slightly, and then set the seal of the Prefect in the wax. It was done. He would see what happened. In all fairness to Elise, he had to offer her a choice.

He looked down at the handkerchief and smiled again, a softened, tender smile. He thought he knew what the choice would be.

His sword-belt lay across the chair beside the desk where he had left it when he went to speak with the Minister of Police that afternoon. He rose, donned his coat, and buckled the belt over it. His gloves lay on the corner of the desk; he pulled them on and smoothed the cuffs. He took up his hat and the dispatch and went out of his office, pausing to check his watch and then open the back case and smile at the small watercolor portrait of Elise that he had taken from her portfolio and carefully set inside.

Constable Vacherin was approaching him; he paused with a smile. "Is it ready, Chief Inspector?" he asked. "I was coming to get it."

"Thank you, Vacherin," said Malet. "I was going out at any rate. Yes, here it is. Thank the courier for me, if you please; it was good of him to wait."

"I certainly shall," said Vacherin, accepting the message from Malet.

"And you: will you be returning to your lodgings at that inn now?"

Malet's mouth tipped oddly, but his voice was very level as he answered. "No, I think not. Not just yet. Did you read of that killing by the Pont de l'Alma? It's a thoroughly nasty business, and I have a theory... I want to look the place over by night. If anyone should inquire, tell him that I am out—and send this note to the Rose d'Or if you please. I don't want them to worry when I don't return."

Constable Vacherin nodded and escorted Malet to the door. "You will be careful, then, sir," he said.

"Always," Malet replied. He passed through the doors, closed them behind him, and paused to look down along the boulevard du Palais.

The vast bulk of the Conciergerie lay directly before him with its sharply gabled roof and conical towers. The immense structure seemed strangely dark, even though the street lamps had just been lit. Malet looked away toward the river. The relatively warm day had led to a slight fog at nightfall; Malet could see wisps of mist rising from the river below the Pont St. Michel.

He raised his head and stepped forward into the darkness and the mist.

CHAPTER SIXTY-FIVE

The Bastard and His Lady

Elise de Clichy frowned at the embroidery frame before her. Malet's message had unsettled her; it was useless to pretend that she would accomplish anything this evening. The message in itself had not been disturbing, but its undercurrents had been palpable. She took the note from her pocket and reread it:

The Prefecture

17 October, 1834

Elise de Clichy

Proprietress

The Rose d'Or

3rd arrondissement

Madame:

The pressures of my position make it necessary that I remain on duty for an indefinite time. I beg that you will not trouble yourself awaiting my return.

Believe me, etc. Paul V. Malet

Provisional Prefect

It made no sense, not after all that had passed between them over the past month. Surely, surely he could have worded such a message differently! But this short missive seemed so distant, so cold—were it not for his even, elegant handwriting, she might have thought that another had written it.

She set the embroidery frame aside and frowned at the note again, then crumpled it and tossed it into the grate.

Distance! Coolness! And this from the man who had held her at Montmartre and all but asked for her hand! She rose, shook out her skirts, and took the candlestick. She was tired, and her bed was waiting.

She would sort this matter out during the night, since she was certain she would be unable to sleep.

She mounted the stairs and went into her bedroom. The room was spare but comfortable, with light yellow wallpaper decorated with a medallion design. Lace curtains covered the window beneath a puffed white muslin valance. A Persian carpet woven in a geometric pattern of warm reds and blues covered the floor, and a smaller rug of gray and red sat before the hearth. Her bed was narrow and deep, curtained with white and covered by a whitework spread that had been part of her trousseau at the time of her disastrous first marriage. Yellow Chinese vases covered with pink peonies, imported by her father from Shanghai, sat on the mantelpiece.

She unpinned her hair and brushed it about her shoulders, then raised her hands to the pearl buttons that fronted her bodice. Her nightgown and lace nightcap lay across the bed. Someone—probably Marie—had turned down the covers.

She considered. A posset would help her sleep. Best go downstairs and mix one for herself and hope that it would help her forget her worry.

She refastened her bodice, tied her hair back with a rose-colored ribbon, and started to the door.

A knock upon the door made her jump.

"Yes?" she called.

"It's Alcide, Madame. Chief Inspector Malet is here—"

"The Chief Inspector?"

"Yes, Madame. He asks to speak with you if you haven't retired yet."

Elise opened the door and stared at Alcide. "It's late," she said. "Where is he?"

"In the large salon," Alcide replied. "He looks exhausted." He hesitated and then said, "D-do you want me to tell him you have gone to bed?"

"No," she said. "I will be right down."

He was waiting before the fireplace. Except that it was dark outside, things were just as they had been when she had first met him. This time, though, he seemed exhausted and drained, and he was gnawing his lower lip. Marie-Francoise had done that, too. On her it had been charming. On Malet it was touching, and she found herself thinking of the lonely little boy that he had been, growing up in that terrible prison, starved for love and struggling to rise above the filth around him.

And then she remembered the note.

He had heard her. He looked up as she came toward him. His eyes seemed almost black in the candlelight, and his mouth was tight, as though he were in pain.

"I received that very abrupt message you sent me from the Prefecture," she said. "You told me you wouldn't be back tonight."

"I apologize for the abruptness," he said. "I have been pushing myself too hard and it has affected my manners. I did have an emergency to tend to, and I was on my way to it, but I decided that it must wait until I settle matters here with you."

"'Settle matters'?" she repeated, hurt by his tone. "I am not in any hurry, Chief Inspector. It can wait until you are rested."

"No," he said. "It must be tended to at once. That is why I am here. I won't require those rooms any more since I will be returning to my own home tonight. There is a matter of outstanding rent owed. I believe I still owe you three weeks' rent. Are we agreed on that?"

She looked straight at him. "We are agreed," she said.

He nodded and sat at her escritoire. He took a sheet of her stationery and wrote briefly, then took another sheet and filled that. He blotted both sheets and handed them to her.

"This is a draft on my bank," he said, tapping the shorter note with the end of the pen. "M. de L'Aulnes of the Banque de France will honor it at once. The other is a receipt. If you will sign it, I can submit it with my Procès-Verbal and be reimbursed for my costs here."

Elise looked down at the papers. "I see," she said. She raised troubled eyes to his face. "M'Sieur," she said.

He spoke over her. "My belongings are packed," he said. "I will send my servant for them tomorrow. Our association in this venture will be concluded once you sign the receipt for me."

She scanned the document and then looked up at him. "Do you want me to do this?" she asked.

"Yes," he said.

There was nothing more to say. She took the pen and dipped it in the ink, then paused. "I will miss you, Inspector, when all this is—is concluded," she said.

His tired, somber expression warmed. "Yes," he sighed, leaning back in his chair and closing his eyes. "You made it very clear. Sign it, please."

She gazed down at him for a long moment, puzzled.

"Sign it quickly," he said. His eyes were still closed.

Her pen scratched across the paper. She set it aside. "Here," she said, and offered the receipt.

He opened his eyes with an effort. "Done?" he asked.

"All done," she replied.

"Then I am no longer in the terrible situation of being a guest under your roof," he said, rising. "Now—"

She lifted her chin. "'Now—'?"

He took both her hands in his and drew her to him. "Now," he said. "There is nothing in the world to prevent me from telling you that I love you as I have wanted to all these past weeks."

Elise slipped her hands from his clasp only to move into his arms and raise her face silently to his.

"Now do you understand?" he asked when they moved apart.

"I understand that you are my own darling idiot who worries too much about unimportant things," she returned a little tartly, for he had frightened her for a moment. But she raised her hand to touch his cheek.

He caught her hand and pressed it to his lips. "But I was bred and born in scandal and I didn't want it to touch you. I have loved you almost from the first moment we met, and I couldn't speak until now, not while I was a paying guest sleeping under your roof. My God, it was hard! But I know how terribly gossip can hurt a lady like you, and I wanted to spare you that pain."

She chuckled and stretched up to kiss his cheek before subsiding against him once more. "Then why, dearest, why did you act so oddly tonight?" she demanded, running experimental fingertips along his lapel, smoothing the faint line of the scar on his chin, delicately testing her new rights and privileges.

He drew a shaken breath and said, "I wanted you to have a choice, so I summoned Saint-Légère home."

Her fingertips stilled against his lips. She pulled away a little and frowned up at him.

He didn't meet her eyes. "I saw the letter you had written to him that night we went to the Butte. I was afraid you might feel something for him, still, but I wanted you to be happy, so I-I sent it in the official dispatch case for you. And you were smiling when you got his letter tonight... I love you so much. I have never felt this way for anyone before. And I thought if you did care for him— I thought you should have a choice, even if it meant you might not choose me, so I called him home just now, before I came here."

"That was when you sent that abrupt message!" Elise exclaimed. "But you didn't mean to come back when you sent it!"

"No," he admitted. "But then I realized what I had just done. I thought I might have lost you. I couldn't bear it. Madame— Elise, I can't live without you. Will you marry me?"

Delighted warmth filled her like wine, and she clasped her hands behind his head and drew him to her again.

"My noble idiot!" she said through her laughter. "I gave you my answer at Montmartre almost a week ago. You only needed to ask the question. That letter you sent to Saint-Légère for me told him I couldn't marry him because I loved another. Tonight's letter was his response accepting that and assuring me of his continuing friendship."

She looked up into his eyes and her laughter gentled at his expression. "Oh my love!" she said. "How could I look at another once I had seen you? My life was nothing but empty bustle before you came, meaningless pursuit of busyness less as a means to accomplish anything than as a way to keep myself from thinking. And then you came to the Rose d'Or, and it was as though I were seeing things through new eyes and learning of a new sort of life, one with purpose and nobility. I couldn't help loving you. Now that I have found you, I will never let you go. Now stop all this nonsense and kiss me again!"

A NOTE FROM THE AUTHOR

Thank you for reading *The Orphan's Tale, Book I, Assassination*. If you liked it, would you consider leaving a review?

For more information on *The Orphan's Tale* and my other books, you can visit my website, www.dianawilderauthor.com[1].

If you wish to sign up for my newsletter, you can do so on my website. I never share email addresses, and you can always unsubscribe by clicking the link at the bottom of the page.

---

1.   https://d.docs.live.net/0688944f20a40d8e/Publishing/Createspace%20and%20Kindle/
www.dianawilderauthor.com

Preview of Vengeance,
Book II of The Orphan's Tale

Some weeks have passed since the murder plot against Princess Victoria was thwarted. While the Heiress of England is safe now, there are other kinds of evil afoot, and winter will be coming. Enjoy some chapters from *Vengeance*, the second volume in The Orphan's Tale.

The Death of a Cop

The north wind north sent a choking cloud of black smoke rolling down the barricaded street from the flaming building in the center of the block. Chief Inspector Guerin dipped his handkerchief in the bucket of water beside him, wrung it out and then held it over his nose and mouth. "It worked," he said over the whine of an occasional bullet. His eyes, red-rimmed and streaming tears, narrowed. "They'll be smoked out. It's either that or have their powder explode under them."

A splintering crash made the young officer beside him recoil. The soldiers shifted and craned their necks.

"The windows have blown out," said Guerin. "It'll be an inferno soon. We can pick them off as they come out."

The young officer shivered.

Guerin smiled grimly. "This is police work for you, Caillier," he said. "Take a good look and count the cost while you can still change your mind." He fell silent. Police work had its share of splendor for him as well, once, but those days were long gone, and he was honest enough with himself to admit that his own greed had been to blame.

A soldier had come up behind them and was waiting.

Guerin turned. "Are your squadrons in place?"

"Yes, Chief Inspector."

A burst of firing made Guerin frown toward the center of the street. The gunshots died down again. Almost too late, but not quite.

"Very good," he said, handing a twist of paper to the soldier. "Send a messenger to the Prefecture with this note. It is urgent and must be given to Chief Inspector Malet, personally. Leave at once but tell your Captain that I want his men to follow me to the back of the shop in five minutes, exactly."

He watched the fellow leave, thinking that five minutes would be plenty of time to accomplish what he hoped while minimizing the danger to the others. He turned to the young officer beside him. "It's time for you to leave, Caillier. Give me your spare weapon and go back with the soldiers."

Caillier obeyed and watched as Guerin checked the barrel.

"Go now," said Guerin. When Caillier hesitated, he repeated the command.

Caillier stood his ground, though he paled as the rattle of gunshots sounded again. "But sir, I can't leave you here alone! You'll need a back-up!"

Guerin snorted. "I gave you an order. I'll walk with you as far as that little alleyway, then farewell."

The words stiffened Caillier's backbone a little. At the alleyway Guerin said, "My seconds will be coming up shortly with the rest of the *Sergents de Ville*. Tell them to follow me."

"But sir, if you wait—"

"There is no time!" Guerin snapped. He paused and added, almost unwillingly, "If you stay on the Force, boy, be the best you can. Find an honorable man to copy and never look back! Now go. God bless you."

He did not wait to see if the young man obeyed him. He edged down the alleyway and then paused to take a deep breath of the relatively smoke-free air.

Who would have thought that he would welcome a pack of insurgents as a godsend? But they were just that, jolting him from what had threatened to become a stupor of despair and presenting him with a solution to the dilemma that he had been facing for two weeks.

He edged along the alley wall, paused at the back street that it opened on, and listened. Voices. The shooters inside that little shop were talking urgently, speaking of killing as though it were a sport and not a crime.

He and Malet had more in common than he had first been willing to admit. He wished that he could have been more cordial to the man. They might even have become friends. And he might not have become what he was now.

He tucked Caillier's pistol into his belt and took out his own, a small two-shot English piece that fit easily into his hand.

Five minutes to right almost three years of wrong. He could not hesitate. His family's honor and security depended on it, and it was a better solution than the flight to America that he had contemplated.

He spared a thought for his wife and their children. Mathilde would have to learn to live on a widow's pension. Maybe she would see her way clear to pawning some of that jewelry that she had insisted on amassing over the years. And maybe now she would admit to that noble lover of hers.

He wondered if the man would linger once he saw that she needed money. It was an interesting thought.

He edged along the back wall of the building. Mathilde, free of a marriage that she had grown to hate, would have her lover, and the children would be provided for with no breath of scandal attached to them. It was more than he could have hoped for, and the price of their future was worth any pain he might feel.

He checked his watch one last time: two minutes.

He was at the door now. He took his pistol in both hands, faced the door squarely, and kicked it in.

"Police!" he shouted above sudden curses. "Surrender in the name of—"

The first bullet, smashing into the right side of his chest, hurled him back against the lintel. He still gripped his pistol in both hands. He pulled the left trigger. Two men pushed past him as another bullet shattered his right thigh. "—the king-!" he gasped.

He squeezed off a second shot as he fell. A third bullet crashed into his left side as he reached for Caillier's pistol. He managed to fire once more before the gun slipped from his nerveless fingers. His mouth filled with the taste of blood, and his breath came in gasps.

One minute.

More men rushed past him into a hail of bullets.

He closed his eyes. The smoke blotted out all sight, and the sounds were far away now.

"Annihilation to the oppressors of the masses!"

He felt something slam into his wounded side, but he was blind and fading out of space and time, and it was all unimportant now.

Someone lifted him from the ground. He felt rough cloth against his cheek. A uniform? Caillier? He smiled, drew his last breath, expelled it, and was gone.

THE SHROUDING SMOKE was beginning to clear, though its heavy, acrid scent filled the air. The miasma still blurred movements within it, but sounds were no longer as muffled and indistinct. Now that the firing had ceased, the sound of a bucket brigade underscored the slightly ominous hush. The wet cobblestones of the street flashed in the afternoon light.

All was quiet, but with hushed voices and wide, frightened eyes that gazed anywhere but at the row of motionless forms stretched out side by side before the gutted ruin of a store. A knot of Police and National Guard stood a little to one side, peering southeast toward the Île du Palais. The young officer with them, Junior Inspector Caillier, was hollow-eyed and shaking, but rigidly calm.

The sergeant of the Guard shook his head. That such a thing should have happened in Montmartre! Insurgents opening fire! The Chief Inspector of the Arrondissement killed!

The clatter of iron-shod hooves upon stone and the rumble of wheels intruded upon the sergeant's thoughts. The splash of the bucket brigade faltered and then stopped, wooden buckets thumping to the ground as their owners straightened and gazed toward the approaching sound.

The young officer tried to square his shoulders.

A carriage painted with the arms of Paris and drawn by four great, black horses, rounded the corner of the rue des Basques at a canter. The bystanders drew aside as the coachman pulled his team to a halt. The horses smelled the blood and smoke; one of the wheel horses jibbed and started sideways with upflung head.

The carriage door opened and Constable Caillier watched as Chief Inspector Paul Malet, acting Prefect of Police, stepped down. The Chief Inspector paused to cast a quick glance around at the wreckage in the street; his nose wrinkled slightly as he caught the smell of the smoke, but his calm expression did not change.

Caillier moved forward to meet him as Malet caught his eye. "They're over here, Chief Inspector," he said.

"Very good," said Malet. His voice was quiet and touched with the hint of an accent. He paused as the younger man joined him. His eyes lingered on the bloodied breast of his coat, then moved toward the line of bodies. "Where are Messieurs Chagnon and Guibault?" he asked. "I expected them to be here."

"They—said they were taking M. Guerin's body to Saint-Pierre to be laid out," answered Caillier. "They left me in charge. I was with Inspector Guerin as he died." He added, "I w-was holding him at the last."

Malet's expression softened. "Is this your first engagement of this sort?"

"Yes, sir."

Malet's brows drew together as he looked Caillier over. "And they left you in charge here." He nodded to a nearby constable. "If you would, please locate the Senior Inspectors and tell them to wait upon me in M. Guerin's offices. You may say that I that wish to confer with them on a question of procedure once I have finished my inspection."

He paused and then directed a warm smile at Caillier that made the young man relax and take a slow breath. "You are performing well in a difficult situation," he said as he took out a pocket notebook and a gold pencil. "Tell me what happened."

Larouche at the Île du Palais

The whispers flowed down the Butte of Montmartre, growing in number and urgency. *An attack! An attack with an army! They brought cannon!* The whispers continued to grow, sweeping along the streets, into the parks and gardens of autumnal Paris.

"I saw them!" someone cried. "Flames spewing from that café, smoke all over the streets! The Chief Inspector of the Arrondissement killed!"

"Where was this?"

The voice was light and high. A child's voice. People turned to stare. Their eyes met a slight person with wide gray eyes, spiky hair and an air of lordliness that sat oddly with his small, disheveled self. The boy opened his eyes at the speaker.

"Montmartre," the man said. "The street just beyond St. Andre du Mont."

"The Chief Inspector?" the boy said. "Was that Guerin?"

"He was the only Chief Inspector in Montmartre!"

The boy nodded.

"They have the bodies lined up!" another said. "I saw them!"

The boy turned away. They would be shouting about the deaths and the fire for the rest of the afternoon. He could remember the fighting of the summer, and he had seen enough dead bodies for the moment.

A wind stirred the trees. He looked down along the main path of the garden. Autumn was underway, and he could feel the increasing cold. He shoved his hands into his threadbare pockets and moved briskly along the rue de Sully to the place Bertrand du Guesclin.

The flower seller was there, surrounded by chrysanthemums and late roses. She smiled when she saw him. "Is it cold enough for you, Larouche?" she asked.

Larouche shrugged. "This is nothing," he said.

"It will get worse," the old woman said.

"I know." Larouche bent to touch a purple chrysanthemum. "You...mentioned your grandson? Would he want to maybe hire me like you said?"

The flower seller beamed. "He spoke to me early yesterday as he was leaving for Poissy. 'Send him to me,' he said. He used those words. 'Send him to me when I return. I've room for him, yes and a welcome, too!' So you just go to him. I'll tell you when he's back."

Larouche smiled up at her. "I'll go," he said.

She returned the smile. "See that you do, Larouche. I want you to be warm when winter comes."

PAUL MALET, CHIEF INSPECTOR of Police and, for the moment, acting Prefect of Police for the city of Paris and its Departement, paused to gaze across the square toward the cathedral's broad-shouldered bulk. The truncated towers, the rows of figures above the doors, some of them missing their heads. The Revolution had not left it unscathed, but it was now swept, clean, glowing with color and sound.

He lowered his eyes to the people clustering in the place du Parvis, the gathering place for the pilgrimages that had begun in Paris in past years. The stones had borne the footsteps of the seers and saints, the soldiers and the sinners, the victims and the protectors.

Which was he?

He had been reviewing the accounts of the past months, preparing for his accounting to the Prefect in two days. M. Lamarque was a man of great particularity, and his absence had seen a number of unprecedented developments, from commanding the Prefecture itself, to averting an international incident and, possibly, a war.

He leaned back against the wall of the Prefecture and closed his eyes. By God he was exhausted! The news bursting in upon a peaceful autumn day, the destruction of that neighborhood, the rows of bodies, and that valiant young man, the blood of his commander still wet on the breast of his uniform, abandoned to deal with the aftermath of murder and insurrection.

He seemed to feel the heat of the fire again, hear the shouting and almost taste the acrid tang of fear.

Tired and heartsick, Malet thought. The day had sounded an unwelcome echo of the past summer's unrest when workers protested against a law that restricted their ability to form unions. Rioting broke out, a police officer was killed, and some of the police had retaliated by bursting into a building thought to house the killers and gunning down all the inhabitants.

Time passed, peace had returned and Malet, concerned with protecting those in his charge, had drawn a cautious breath and welcomed the peace. It had been a busy time, his running the Police of Paris in the Prefect's absence. Busy and somehow gratifying. A disaster was averted, France was safe, and he could sit back, draw a long breath, and smile.

And now this had happened.

He raised his head to the skies over the city. Rags of clouds tumbled westward before the wind. He could see the stars through them, their quiet glitter overlaid by a sense of serenity that he needed to touch and take into his own heart.

The muted thunder of the bells announced Vespers. He pushed away from the wall, drew a long breath, and moved into the river of worshippers, passing a ragged little boy who looked up at him with wide gray eyes and shrank back into the shadows before joining the throng behind him.

About the Author

Diana Wilder was born in Philadelphia and grew up all around the United States courtesy of the United States Navy. Perhaps because of the Irish in her, she liked to weave stories for her own enjoyment about the people she met and the places she saw during her travels. She graduated from the University of North Carolina with a degree in ancient and medieval history and experience in journalism.

Her love of storytelling developed into a love of writing. She wrote her first novella, based on Kamehameha's Hawaii, in middle school. She started writing novels in graduate school and has produced four novels set in New Kingdom Egypt: *The City of Refuge, Mourningtide, Pharaoh's Son* and *A Killing Among the Dead*, all part of *The Memphis Cycle*. Another volume, set after Mourningtide and prior to Pharaoh's Son, will be published under the name Kadesh.

The heartbreak and gallantry of the American Civil war has always caught her imagination, and she served as a Docent in the Civil War Library and Museum in Philadelphia for some years. *The Safeguard* arose from her research into the Georgia theater of the war.

You can read sample chapters of all these books, published and projected, can be read on her website, www.dianawilderauthor.com.

Don't miss out!

Visit the website below and you can sign up to receive emails whenever D M Wilder publishes a new book. There's no charge and no obligation.

https://books2read.com/r/B-A-VJWG-GZYI

BOOKS 2 READ

Connecting independent readers to independent writers.

About the Author

Diana Wilder was born in Philadelphia and grew up all around the United States courtesy of the United States Navy. Perhaps because of the Irish in her, she liked to weave stories for her own enjoyment about the people she met and the places she saw during her travels. She graduated from the University of North Carolina with a degree in ancient and medieval history and experience in journalism.

Her love of storytelling developed into a love of writing. She wrote her first novella, based on Kamehameha's Hawaii, in middle school. She started writing novels in graduate school and has produced four novels set in New Kingdom Egypt: The City of Refuge, Mourningtide, Pharaoh's Son and A Killing Among the Dead, all part of The Memphis Cycle. Another volume, set after Mourningtide and prior to Pharaoh's Son, will be published under the name Kadesh.

The heartbreak and gallantry of the American Civil war has always caught her imagination, and she served as a Docent in the Civil War Library and Museum in Philadelphia for some years. The Safeguard arose from her research into the Georgia theater of the war.

You can read sample chapters of all these books, published and projected, can be read on her website, www.dianawilderauthor.com.

Read more at www.dianawilderauthor.com.